P9-DJU-803

Eternal
Flame

Eternal Flame

CYNTHIA EDEN

ℬ
BRAVA

KENSINGTON PUBLISHING CORP.
www.kensingtonbooks.com

Henderson County Public Library

BRAVA BOOKS are published by

Kensington Publishing Corp.
119 West 40th Street
New York, NY 10018

Copyright © 2010 Cindy Roussos

All rights reserved. No part of this book may be reproduced in any form or by any means without the prior written consent of the Publisher, excepting brief quotes used in reviews.

All Kensington titles, imprints and distributed lines are available at special quantity discounts for bulk purchases for sales promotion, premiums, fund-raising, educational or institutional use.

Special book excerpts or customized printings can also be created to fit specific needs. For details, write or phone the office of the Kensington Special Sales Manager: Kensington Publishing Corp., 119 West 40th Street, New York, NY 10018. Attn. Special Sales Department. Phone: 1-800-221-2647.

Brava and the B logo are Reg. U.S. Pat. & TM Off.

ISBN-13: 978-0-7582-4213-6
ISBN-10: 0-7582-4213-1

First Kensington Trade Paperback Printing: December 2010

10 9 8 7 6 5 4 3 2 1

Printed in the United States of America

Henderson County Public Library

Chapter 1

It was a damn sorry night to die, but then, Zane Wynter didn't plan on dying. Killing, yeah, that was a possibility, but not dying.

Fire exploded in the night. A white-hot mountain of flames burned right through the roof of the old three-story antebellum house on Francis Street and shot toward the sky, its greedy claws a bright orange in the darkness.

"*Sonofabitch.*" The breath of the flames scorched Zane's skin. This was supposed to have been an easy collar. Go in, knock out the demon waiting inside, claim his bounty. A simple night's work for a Night Watch hunter. After the collar, he'd planned to get a beer and maybe a fuck.

He took off his jacket and tossed it onto the ground. No sense getting ash on it.

A scream burst from inside the house. He stilled at the sound because that—that was a woman's scream. And his prey was male.

Victim inside. Not just the killer he wanted, but maybe an innocent trapped in that inferno, too.

Shit. It really was a piss-poor night. He took a breath, squared his shoulders, and knew that he had to go into that damn house. Sometimes, it just sucked to be him.

Zane raced forward even as the windows of the antebellum exploded, sending glass raining down on him. One kick and he knocked down the front door. Smoke rose, a thick gray fog. The flames crackled, and the house fell around him.

"*Jacobson!*" He yelled the bastard's name. Henry Jacobson. A demon who'd been hunting and killing for the vampires in Baton Rouge. A vamp's bitch. Seriously, what was worse? "Jacobson, where are you?" The smoke stung his nose and made his eyes water as he thundered through the rooms, searching through the smoke and flames.

Another scream. He ran for the stairs, a long, curving staircase that ended in fire and fury. Someone was on the steps. He saw a shadow in the smoke, someone hunched over, holding tight to the railing.

Too small to be his prey.

Victim. Had Jacobson been getting ready for another kill?

Zane took the stairs three at a time. Chunks of the ceiling fell, hitting close to him, and the heat scorched his skin. He coughed, choking on the smoke that thickened the air.

Zane reached out and grabbed—

"*Help me!*" Desperate blue eyes met his. Wide and dark. So dark. They reflected the flames and her fear.

The woman—small, curvy, shaking—threw her body against his and held on with all her strength. "K-kill . . . m-me . . . he was . . . g-gonna . . ." She broke off, coughing, choking, just like him.

The roof groaned above them, a long, low rumble that couldn't be a good sign. He glanced up and saw the cracks and rolling fire in what was left of the ceiling. *Fuck.*

"H-help . . . m-me . . ." She shuddered again, her body rubbing against his.

The devil could take Jacobson. Zane grabbed the woman, lifting her high into his arms. He held her close against his chest and ran back down the stairs. The flames were everywhere. The fire was so damn hot that for an instant, he thought about death.

Nah, not fucking tonight.

He concentrated, calling up the power that lurked inside

of him, the darkness that was never far away, and those flames didn't touch him. Couldn't.

The woman's lips pressed against the base of his throat. Soft lips. A delicate touch in hell.

For an instant, one reckless instant, his concentration wavered and those flames surged forward.

Cursing, he dove for the door. They flew into the night, and he turned his body, protecting hers, as they slammed onto the porch. Sirens wailed. The cavalry was coming. Always a bit late in this town.

Her fingers fluttered on his face. "Are you"—a cough—"okay?" A light voice, Southern and soft. Husky. She'd raised her body up, and now she peered at his face with worry in those big, bedroom eyes.

He didn't answer at first. Just stared at her. The woman was something else. Her skin was a pale ivory, but her high cheekbones and her straight, sharp nose were currently stained with soot. Her lips—*damn*—were full, sexy. The kind of lips a man fantasized about. A lot. And she had a thick, tumbling mass of black hair. Hair that made her skin look even paler.

"You saved me." She shook her head, sending those long locks swaying. "Th-thank you."

A crash shook the house. "Baby, I haven't saved our asses yet," he said. Then Zane grabbed her and hauled her to her feet. This was no place for a pit stop. They shot down the curving porch steps, running fast from those flames.

Jacobson.

He pushed her behind the gate at the edge of the drive. He coughed again, hard and long, clearing the smoke from his lungs. A fire truck roared up the street, finally getting close now. He held her arms, staring into those fuck-me eyes. "Was someone else inside? Did you see—"

"I-I think he wanted . . . to kill . . . me." Whispered. Her gaze fell to his throat. "H-he tried to bite me. . . ."

And he noticed *her* throat then. The red marks. The *teeth* marks. As far as he knew, Jacobson wasn't a vamp, not yet anyway. Zane didn't see the tell-tale bloodsucker puncture wounds on the woman's neck. *No vamp bite.* But *something* was going on with the guy. Maybe Jacobson had been stealing some vamp blood, and he'd started to become addicted.

Vamp's bitch.

"What happened?"

The fire truck slammed to a halt in front of the house.

She shook her head as her gaze slowly rose to once again meet his. "I-I don't know. . . . I shoved him back, we fought . . . then-then everything just exploded." Her voice dropped when she said, "He's still up there."

Firefighters ran past them, pulling hoses with them. Zane's jaw clenched as he turned away from her. He should go—

"How . . . how can I thank you?"

Now that voice was pure sex. His head turned back to hers, real slowly.

She licked her lips, a fast swipe of a small pink tongue. "I would have died without you." She pressed closer to him. "You came into that fire." She shook her head. "I've never seen anything—you were like an angel."

Oh, the sexy woman was so confused. "Not quite, baby." More like the devil. His gaze lingered on those full lips. *Definitely not an angel.*

"Hey!" A hard masculine bark.

Sighing, Zane glanced over his shoulder and saw one of the firefighters lumbering toward him. "Is anyone still inside?" the guy demanded.

"Up-upstairs . . ." the woman whispered, and they all looked at the flames.

The house seemed to collapse. Groans and shrieks filled the air, and the rest of the roof tumbled down, smashing right through the upper floors.

Firefighters scrambled back.

"Not fucking alive now," the firefighter muttered as he turned away. "Dammit!"

If the man inside was human, no, he'd definitely be dead.

But the firefighters weren't just dealing with a human. *If only.* And they'd need Zane if they were going to get that fire settled down. Lucky for them, he had a way with flames.

Like most demons, he could control the elements, and fire was *his* bitch.

But first . . .

There was the little matter of a *thank-you.*

Zane wrapped an arm around the woman's waist. He tipped back her chin with his left hand. Her lips parted in surprise and she said, "What—"

He kissed her. Caught her with her mouth open and drove his tongue inside that sweet heat. And, oh, but she was *sweet.* His tongue tasted her, stroked her, and he held her tightly against his body, loving the feel of those soft curves crushed against him. A moan rose in her throat, and her hands tightened around his shoulders.

His little victim didn't push him away. No, she tried to pull him closer.

My kind of woman.

And if those flames weren't waiting, he'd show her just how she could *truly* thank him. No time now. But maybe later.

One last lick. One last stroke of his tongue. Then Zane forced his head to lift. Her eyes were closed, and her expression a bit dazed. Her lips were red now, heated from his mouth.

He released her and stepped back.

Her eyelashes lifted, and she blinked. Once. Twice.

"Told you I wasn't an angel, baby." He let a grin curve his lips. "But if you want to show me how much you *appreciate my help* just stick around a while."

Her jaw dropped. He almost laughed. Almost . . . but his cock was shoving hard against his jeans, and the firefighters were losing their battle with the flames. They needed him.

So he turned away from her and didn't look back.

"Miss? Miss, are you okay?"

Jana Carter hunched her shoulders at the voice. More vehicles had arrived. Cops. An ambulance. She glanced to the right and found a fresh-faced EMT staring at her.

"Were you burned?" he asked her quietly, compassion flowing with the words.

She let her lips tremble. "N-no." Her "hero" had disappeared. Had tall, dark, and dangerous really gone back inside the house? To save a killer?

Stupid move. *His funeral.*

Two cops began to approach her. Time to leave. Jana pressed her lips together and realized she still tasted the man on her mouth. *Zane Wynter.* Bounty hunter extraordinaire. Yes, she knew who he was. Zane's mistake was not knowing her identity. He should have been better prepared.

Weren't the Night Watch hunters always supposed to be prepared? Like freaking Boy Scouts? Night Watch . . . the multistate bounty hunting agency had a reputation for always getting the job done. Whether the agents were chasing the worst human criminals out there—or stalking the *Other* who'd crossed the line, they brought down their prey.

Most humans didn't know about the *Other* in the world. They didn't know about the vampires, the demons, the shifters, and the hundreds of other monsters out there on the streets. They didn't know because they were blind.

Jana wasn't blind. She knew the real score in this world. And she knew that her "hero" hadn't been an average hunter, either. No, a man hadn't hauled her out of the flames. A demon had.

Angel, my ass. She'd almost choked when she told him that one.

"Miss, I need you to get in the ambulance. I want to check you out."

Ah, now that sounded promising. The ride in the ambulance would let her get away from the cops. Because those boys in blue were already eyeing her with too much curiosity and she really didn't want to get into an explanation of just why she'd been in the house on Francis Street.

Jana's knees buckled. The EMT grabbed her, and she let

her lashes sag. "So . . . weak." Though she'd rarely been weak in her life. Appearances could be so deceptive, but the EMT didn't realize that.

"It's okay!" He scooped her up and yelled for help. Seconds later, he was loading her into the back of the ambulance. The doors slammed shut behind them, and the cops were left out in the cold.

Well, with the cold—and with the flames.

The ambulance's siren screamed on and when the vehicle lurched forward, Jana smiled.

Too easy.

Or maybe she was just too good because Jana had just taken out her prey, destroyed the evidence, and even been given a getaway car. A chauffeured ride away from the scene of her attack.

Not bad for a night's work.

Poor Zane. The guy obviously thought he was the big, tough demon badass. He'd be realizing soon enough that there was a new sheriff in town.

"I didn't get the demon." Zane rubbed the back of his neck, felt every ache and pain in his body, and met the stare of his boss, Jason Pak, head-on. "When I got to the house on Francis Street, the place was a damn inferno." The flames had spread so quickly that the firefighters thought accelerants must have been used to soak the place.

Everything just exploded. The woman's voice whispered through his head. Yeah, the house had exploded all right. With a little help.

He exhaled and dropped his hand. "The bastard had a victim with him. He was still hunting." Not just hunting, but *acting* like a vamp. Trying to bite prey. No longer slicing them with claws and knives, but biting, vamp style. What the hell? "She was lucky to get out alive."

Pak's leather chair creaked as the owner of Night Watch leaned forward and flattened his palms on the desk. "Was she?"

Zane's shoulders straightened a bit. "I pulled her out of the flames." That good deed had to be worth something, right? No matter what most folks thought, he didn't spend his whole life telling the world to screw off.

"Where is she?" Pak's fingers drummed on the desktop. There was a skeletal staff in the Night Watch office then. Most of the bounty hunters were out on cases. Dragging in prey.

Pity. This time, Zane wouldn't have any prey to bring in.

"The EMTs took her to the hospital," he told Pak. "She'd sucked in a lot of smoke, and that jerk-off Jacobson *bit* her."

"Any other injuries?" Pak's dark gaze was steady.

"Uh, no. None that I saw." He hadn't smelled blood on her, but the smoke had been clogging his nose. He didn't *think* the woman had been hurt. But she'd trembled against him.

Desire? Fear? Or pain?

"What did she look like?"

Zane blinked at that. "Ah . . . pretty. About five-foot-four, curvy, black hair, blue eyes—"

"Could have changed her appearance," Pak murmured and his fingers stopped tapping.

And Zane got a *really* bad feeling in his gut. "Uh, excuse me?"

Pak's black brows shot up. "Did I ever tell you I thought you handled yourself damn well when all that shit went down with Dee?"

Dee. Dee Daniels was another bounty hunter in the office. She'd watched his ass, he'd watched hers, for years. He'd trusted the woman with his life more times than he could count. Then she'd become a vampire.

"I do my job," Zane said quietly. Just like he'd done his job when Dee changed. He'd protected her and made sure the assholes after her were taken down. "No matter what happens, *I do my job.*"

Pak rose and walked around the edge of the desk. A ghost

of a smile curved his thin lips. "Good. You know the job has to come first."

What the hell? The job always came first for him. Zane sucked in a sharp breath. "Jacobson's body wasn't recovered on the scene. The fire department was still there when I left, digging through the rubble, but—"

"But you don't think they'll find a body? Or what's left of one?"

"Jacobson was a demon." Demons and fire always mixed. "The guy was low level, but he should have been strong enough to knock the flames back, at least for a few moments." A few moments would have been all the guy needed for an escape.

"You want to keep searching for him."

Hell, yeah. "He's *my* collar."

Pak didn't blink. That dark stare just weighed him.

"Uh, boss?" Pak didn't usually get all quiet and focused like this unless he was out in the swamps, talking to the gators. The guy was a charmer, a being born with the ability to speak to animals. On the weekends, Pak would spend hours with the twelve- to fourteen-foot gators that loved to snap and feast in those muddy waters.

"I'm going to give Jude the Jacobson case," Pak said.

"The hell you—"

"Jude can go back to Francis Street. If Jacobson got away, he'll catch the guy's scent."

Jude Donovan was good at catching scents. But then, Jude was a white tiger shifter, so he'd fucking *better* be good at sniffing.

Zane locked his muscles. "Jude's good at tracking, but so am I, and you *know* I don't stop on a case until I've got my prey." Especially not if the prey was a demon. He always brought the demons down. Or put them down, depending on the case.

"Jude's got Jacobson," Pak said, staring up at him.

Fuck. Every muscle in Zane's body tightened and his hands clenched.

"Because I need you on something more important," Pak told him.

"What?"

Pak shook his head. "You can take the fire, Jude can't. That means he can't take *her.*"

Her.

"I don't think an accelerant was used on Francis Street," Pak said, "Just like no accelerant was used three nights ago at the fire on Biltmore that took out two vampires, or at the *three* fires in New Orleans that occurred over the last few months. . . . Fires all aimed at supernaturals."

Okay, Pak sure had Zane's attention. Someone was targeting supernaturals?

"They were aimed at the *Other,* but it looks like humans were caught in the crossfire. Two human scientists died."

Hell.

" 'Course, the arson investigators *think* an accelerant was used because those fires burned so fast and so hot." Pak reached behind him and scooped a manila file off the top of the desk. "A woman was spotted at the crime scenes. Average height. About one-hundred-thirty pounds."

Zane's gut clenched.

"Witnesses saw a blonde, with curly hair, running from the other fires."

Blonde. *Maybe she changed her appearance.* Now he knew what Pak meant. "The woman tonight was a *victim.*"

Pak stared back at him, that dark stare unblinking. "You sure about that?"

Too much doubt was in Pak's voice, and Zane realized that no, he wasn't sure. In this world, you couldn't be sure of anything or anyone. Damn. He might have been played. Jaw clenched, Zane demanded, "Just what am I dealing with here?"

"If I'm right, the woman you're looking for is a human with a very special gift. A gift of fire."

Shit. *An Ignitor.* A human who could create fire from nothing, who could let it burn fiery hot and so very fast. A human who could destroy too much.

"You've had experience dealing with Ignitors," Pak said.

Zane's head jerked in agreement. Not the *best* experience.

"I want you to find this one. Find her, and bring her in." The briefest of hesitations. "If the woman from tonight isn't the one we need, clear her, and move on. But I expect to have the Ignitor who *is* making these fires contained within the next forty-eight hours."

Well, it would be easy enough to find the dark-haired beauty with the bedroom eyes. The EMTs had taken her in. She'd still be at the hospital now.

Unless she ran. Unless she wasn't the victim. Unless she screwed me.

Zane forced his hands to unclench. "Sometimes Ignitors can be hard to contain." He paused, because the question had to be asked. "Is this a kill mission?" With Ignitors, there wasn't always a choice. If the fire raged too hot . . .

Kill or be killed.

"We want her alive," Pak said. Then the cagey bastard added, "For now."

How long did it take to bandage a bite mark? Jeez, it wasn't like the demon had even broken the skin. After two hours— two freaking hours—Jana managed to slip away from the nurses and the docs in their garish green uniforms. She snuck out of the hospital's exit, making sure she stayed in the shad- ows, and she hurried down the street as quickly as she could.

It took her about two minutes to realize that she was being trailed. Bad, bad mistake. She should have realized that fact in about thirty seconds.

Must be slipping.

Jana rolled her shoulders, trying to keep her body loose. In this town, she knew she had to be ready for anything. Sure, the majority of women would probably worry about mug- gers waiting in the night. She knew she was more likely to be attacked by a hungry vamp or a pissed-off demon.

No, Jacobson's dead. No way did he get out.

She hoped.

Okay. There were two ways to play this. She could attack with guns blazing or . . .

Jana stepped out of the shadows. "I-I . . . is someone there?" She let her voice tremble. Playing weak came so naturally to her. She looked weak. Small. Fragile. All the better to lie.

No one answered her. Her eyes narrowed. Time to hit the main street and get off this quiet lane. She could hail a cab and be back at her place in half an hour.

The wind blew against her face, a cold, icy wind, and for an instant, she caught the smell of . . . ash.

Her body stiffened. Oh, hell, no. That job was finished. She inched back, her gaze darting around the area. She couldn't risk being taken down.

Jana started heading for the main street. A cab would come along, it had to. And if it didn't . . .

A hand snaked out and grabbed her wrist. She screamed because that was what she *should* do.

"Relax, baby. It's just me." Zane gave her a shark's smile, one with lots of sharp, white teeth. "Your knight in shining armor."

Only he didn't look particularly knightlike then. The guy was a big, strong menace in the darkness. She knew just how dangerous he was.

"Were you following me?" she whispered and stepped closer to him. Damn, but the guy had some broad shoulders. And a wide, muscled chest.

He was handsome, in a rough, wild kind of way. Dark hair and brows, long, slightly twisted nose, lips a little thin, jaw perfectly square and strong. His eyes were dark shadows now, but she knew his piercing gaze was green. She'd seen his picture long before she met him at the fire. She always studied pictures of her targets. After all, a woman had to make sure she was going after the right mark.

"Following you?" His voice was deep, rumbling, and a shiver worked over her body. From the cold because she didn't do so well with the cold, and *not* because she found that rumble sexy.

She glanced back over her shoulder. "I thought I heard . . ." Jana shook her head and forced her own smile as she looked back at him. "Nothing."

But she knew he was watching her. Weighing her. Trying to see past her skin.

"Let me take you home," he said.

If you want to show me how much you appreciate my help just stick around a while.

Her chin rose. Was sex on the demon's mind? Or was it something more?

"What's your name?" he asked.

"Jana." The name was safe enough. "Jana Carter." She paused and shivered again. Damn.

"I'm Zane Wynter."

Right. Zane Wynter, super hunter. Demon badass. Check. "You *did* follow me, didn't you?"

"No, baby, I just got here. I saw you walking. . . ." He shrugged. "I was checking up on you. I wanted to see if you were okay."

Oh. Sweet. Also . . . *lie.*

She put her hands on his chest. "I'm okay." Good thing she knew how to play the game.

"No, bitch, you're not."

Hell, she *knew* that voice. Jana's head whipped around, and she locked eyes on Henry Jacobson. Crap—the jerk *had* made it out of the fire.

Well, mostly, anyway. He stepped under a flickering streetlight, and she saw that deep, red blisters covered the right half of his face. Blisters that stretched and twisted down his neck. His shirt had melted, merging with the skin on his chest and the stench of burned flesh filled her nose.

Knew I smelled ash.

She gasped dramatically and shoved her body against Zane's. The big hero would save her, right?

"Jacobson." Fury vibrated in Zane's voice.

Jacobson, no, Henry—'cause, yeah, he'd asked her to call him by his first name when he'd picked her up at that low-class bar—snarled. His eyes were pitch black, the perfect black of a demon's true gaze. Most demons used the magic of glamour to hide their real eye color so the humans wouldn't run screaming all the time. Henry wasn't trying to pretend right then, not trying to lull her like he'd done before.

The man wanted blood—hers. Too bad for him . . . she was rather fond of living.

"Give me the bitch," Henry growled. "And just walk the fuck away."

Oh, um, no, that wouldn't work so much as a plan.

Zane grabbed her hands, held tight, then shoved her *at* Jacobson. She staggered to a quick halt a few feet in front of Zane.

What the hell? Zane was supposed to be the damn good guy.

She blinked and shook her head. *Not part of the plan.*

"You want her?" Zane drawled. "Then come and get her."

What? *Asshole.* Was he using her as some kind of freaking bait? She was *not* good bait.

Jacobson launched right at her, running hard and fast with his hands out, with death in his eyes, and she knew if he touched her, he'd rip her apart.

Dammit. She didn't plan on dying. Not then, and certainly not by some low-budget demon jerk's hand.

Jana yanked out the scalpel she'd stolen from the hospital and screamed as Jacobson's foul stench choked her.

Not. Dying. Tonight.

Chapter 2

The woman—Jana—sliced Jacobson right across his injured arm. A hard, deep slice that had the demon howling . . . and Zane swearing.

Not an Ignitor. Pak was wrong—this woman couldn't stir fire. Shit, if she could, she'd be burning Jacobson to ash, not screaming and stabbing with—what was that?—a scalpel.

Innocent.

And he had one rule. Just one. On his watch, no innocent woman would ever be hurt while he was there.

So when Jacobson knocked the scalpel out of her hands, and Jana stumbled back, Zane lunged forward and did what he'd been dying to do all night.

He got ready to kick some demon ass.

Zane caught Jacobson's hand, squeezed hard and heard the demon's breath whoosh out when the bones crunched. "Get behind me," Zane ordered, and Jana rushed, nearly tripping as she hurried to obey.

A human. Small and defenseless. And Jacobson had been ready to kill her.

"Not your fight," Jacobson gritted out.

"Asshole, I've been looking for this fight for days." He grinned. "And if you hadn't been hiding like the coward you are, I would've already kicked the shit out of you."

Fear widened Jacobson's black eyes as he struggled to break free of Zane's hold. "I just want *her*."

"You're not getting her." Playtime was over. He'd run his test on Jana. Seen what he needed to see. *Not my target.* Time to end the game.

Then the prick head-butted him. Well, tried to. Zane jerked back, punching out hard at the same time, and Jacobson fell to the ground.

Footsteps thudded behind him. *Jana . . . running away.* "Wait!" His head swung toward her.

And that asshole demon charged him, grabbing Zane around the waist, and they both went down hard, slamming into the pavement.

Jana kept running. The thud of her footsteps echoed in Zane's ears.

"Don't worry about the bitch," Jacobson grunted, and oh, damn, but the guy's face was wrecked. "The others will get her."

What? Others?

"You think you're so bad . . . hunting your own kind." Jacobson plowed a fist into Zane's face, and Zane took the punch because he wanted the bastard to keep talking. "Fucking traitor, want to be human, *can't—*"

This time, Zane caught the fist that came at his face. And because the demon had pissed him off, Zane broke two of the guy's fingers.

Jacobson howled. Zane squeezed tighter. "Who are the others?" he demanded. He couldn't see Jana anymore. That woman sure moved fast for a human.

"L-let . . . g-go . . ."

Zane smiled. "No." It was his turn to head-butt. He smashed his forehead into Jacobson's nose.

The demon crawled away, gagging as blood flew from his broken nose.

"Something you should know," Zane murmured as he rose to his feet, brushing off his hands. Jacobson was still on the ground, moaning. "I like to fight dirty." Then he drove his booted foot into Jacobson's side. Paused. Then did it again. The demon curled into a ball. "Next time, leave the humans alone."

"Bastard!"

True. But flattery wouldn't stop him. *Where was Jana?* Zane risked one moment to let his gaze rake the darkness.

That was when he heard her scream.

"You're a naughty girl, Jana." The angry whisper blew against her ear.

Damn the supernaturals in the city. They were *everywhere*, and it sure seemed like they were all gunning for her. Why was she becoming Ms. Popular?

"Let me go," she said loudly, really hoping that Zane had caught her scream. And, come on, what had been up with him shoving *her* at the crazy demon? Hadn't the guy ever heard of protecting the weak? Hadn't she looked weak enough for him?

"You're a hard woman to track." The jerk didn't let her go. He just shoved her up against some smelly alley wall. She couldn't see his face. Since she was human, she didn't get bonus vision in the dark. Just a body that could break too easily. And had, too many times.

"Wh-what do you want?" *Come on, Zane, haul ass.* She didn't need to see in order to know the identity of the man who'd snuck up on her and now held her in his too cold and too tight grip. She hadn't planned to meet him tonight. *Hadn't been ready.* But she'd known that he was watching. He was one of those pricks who liked to watch while the world went to hell around him.

"I want to make sure you understand the rules of the game." Great. He'd pushed her hair to the side and now his breath was on her neck. She *really* didn't want this guy's mouth on her neck. She didn't want him anywhere near her.

If Zane's not coming, then I can take care of him. I can do it.

As long as Zane wasn't there to see. . . .

Her breath came out on a long, slow rush. "I understand the rules." *He* didn't.

"Then why the hell did you go after *my* man?" His claws pressed into her chest. Right above her heart.

Jana stilled, barely daring to breathe because she'd just caught the glint of fangs in the dark. When a vamp's fangs were that close to your throat—*hell.* And those claws *hurt.* He hadn't shoved them too deep, not yet, but if he wanted, the guy could cut her heart out in less than two seconds' time.

I hate vampires.

"How was I supposed to know he was yours?" She started talking, fast, but kept her voice quiet now. "He's a demon, I thought—"

A growl. "You thought wrong. You're not supposed to attack the demons."

Wasn't she? Sometimes, the jobs all ran together.

"I let you live after you took my men—"

Right, those two evil, sadistic, murdering bastards had been *his* men.

"I tracked you, could have fucking drained you dry, but I let you live."

The vamp smelled like a graveyard. Jana tried real hard not to inhale too deeply.

"You're alive because I want you to hunt," he snarled, "and you hunt who *I* say. I'm the one in charge, bitch."

"*Jana!*" Oh, finally, Zane's voice. Talk about taking his sweet time.

"He's the prey. The first you'll take down for me." The freak licked her neck. Licked her. "And I want him to *suffer.*"

What? *Zane?* He wanted her to attack Zane?

"Show me just what you can do, bitch. Kill him, or die."

She nodded weakly. Because, really, what choice did she have?

He released her, finally moving those claws away from her heart. The wounds he'd made ached, throbbing dully. Her head sagged forward. She inched toward the light. Toward Zane. He was running fast, racing to get to her.

"*Kill him.*"

She glanced back at the vampire hiding in the shadows. Jana took two more steps away from him, turning so that she had the best view of his hulking body, and then she smiled.

"I'm not still in this town just so I can be your bitch," she whispered and let the frightened act vanish. The vampire froze, and she knew he'd gotten a good look at her face. Her eyes. "I stayed to take *you* out." He'd been her target all along, but she'd missed him that first night. Then *he'd* gotten the jump on her. Sometimes, a woman had to wait and find her perfect killing time.

Now.

And here she'd thought it would be hard to lure the vampire to her. All she'd had to do was light the right fire under his little demon minion, and she'd gotten his personal attention.

"*No!*" He lunged at her.

But she wasn't in the mood to get her heart torn out right then.

Zane raced into the alley, his legs pumping, adrenaline powering his blood.

And he smelled flames.

Then he saw the fire sputtering near the dumpster. He waved his hand, and the flames quieted.

"Jana?"

She wasn't there. He crept forward and stared down at the charred remains on the ground. *Fuck.* The stench stung his nose.

"*Jana!*" But she was gone, and a hot fury began to burn in his gut because Zane realized that he'd been played. For the second time, he'd been taken in by a pretty, lying face. A face that hid a real monster behind the cloak of innocence.

He snatched out his phone. Dialed Pak. One ring and his

boss picked up. "We're gonna need a cleanup crew on Range-line." Dammit. *Played.* "And you were right." He paused a moment, watching the smoke drift in the air. "The woman's not a victim." *An Ignitor's back in town.*

The demon was strapped to the table, his legs and arms se-cured, and the blood had dried on his face.

"I thought I told you that Jude would be taking over the Jacobson case."

Zane shrugged at Pak's words. "The bastard came after me. What did you want me to do? Let him walk away?"

"Not you, asshole!" Jacobson tried to lunge up, but the straps held tight. "I was after *her!*"

Zane pulled over a chair and got real close to the demon. Close enough to touch, to hurt. "Who is she?"

Jacobson would be transferred out soon enough. Pak had plans for the guy, but first . . .

"Where did you meet the woman?" he pressed. *Jana.* Was that even her real name? Jude was running a search on her. Maybe the shifter would turn up some intel on the name, but in the meantime—

Zane was in the mood to get answers from the demon, and he would have those answers, one way or another.

"Fuck you!" Jacobson spat at him.

Zane blinked. "Wrong. Answer." He drove his fist into Ja-cobson's face. Payback could be a bitch.

"Ah . . . Zane?" Pak's voice was completely flat.

Jacobson spit out a tooth. "You think . . . you're so much fucking better than the rest . . . of us. . . ."

Zane's shoulders tensed.

Jacobson laughed. A ragged, rough sound. "But you're worse. . . . Under the skin . . . *you're worse!*"

Zane smiled at him. "You really don't want to see just how much worse I can be."

Pak's arm came down on his shoulder. "Zane . . ." A slight warning there.

Zane didn't glance back at him. "This demon knows about your Ignitor, Pak." A woman he'd literally had right in his hands—twice—and he'd let her slip away.

Because he was looking straight at Jacobson, he caught the demon's flinch. Ah . . . "Where did you meet her, Jacobson?"

Jacobson's lips firmed.

"*Where?*" Pak demanded.

"Some damn bar! Bitch came up to me." His lips twisted, showing his bloodstained teeth. "She was all over me."

Every muscle in Zane's body locked.

"She wanted to leave, so I took her to my place. Then she tried to burn me!"

Tried? Succeeded. Those blisters would take a *long* time to heal, even with a demon's enhanced recovery system.

"In the last two weeks, you've picked up three women from bars in the area," Pak said, the words so calm he could have been talking about the weather. His hand lifted from Zane's shoulder, and Pak came to stand at his side. "We found the body of your first victim. You took her to the vamps, didn't you? You let them drain her dry."

Jacobson stared up at him, his eyes burning with black rage.

Pak crossed his arms over his chest. "We haven't found the second woman yet."

The bastard laughed again. Laughed. "You won't. There was nothing left of her. Not when the vamps finished."

Put him down. Zane knew Jacobson wasn't one of the demons that would be turned loose one day. You didn't let a rabid dog back out to hunt.

"Then you came upon a new lady. . . ." Pak's voice pitched lower. "One who was 'all over you.'"

"She was, she—"

"Did this woman ask you anything?" Pak cut across his roaring words. "Did she say—"

"The whore just burned me!"

"But you got to live," Zane snapped. "Her last victim wasn't so lucky." He grabbed the knife from the sheath on his leg and put the blade right at Jacobson's throat. "You're not gonna be lucky much longer."

"Zane . . ." Pak's whisper.

Jacobson started to smile.

"Don't slice too fast," Pak continued. "You want him to feel the pain."

Jacobson's black eyes widened. "No!"

So Jacobson was another one who loved to torture prey, but couldn't stand pain himself. "Who'd she kill in the alley?" *The others will get her.* Jacobson *knew* the guy who'd burned, no doubt.

Zane let the blade cut through skin.

"Vincent!" Yelled. "Shit! I-it was Vincent Gunner! He was with me. There were two humans there, but he—he told 'em to stay back, that we could handle her."

"But you couldn't, could you?" *Vincent Gunner.* He knew the name. A powerful vampire on Night Watch's kill list. Gunner had been a cruel asshole who enjoyed slowly bleeding humans dry—women. Only women.

Had he picked the wrong prey? Or was something more going on here?

"Hey, Wynter!"

Zane's head lifted at Jude Donovan's call. The shifter stood just inside the doorway of their holding area. Jude clutched some papers in his hand and lifted them toward Zane. "I found your girl."

Zane glanced back at the demon. The knife still bit into Jacobson's flesh.

"I'll finish him," Pak said.

And Zane knew he would. Knew Pak would get every drop of information, and then he'd eliminate the demon's threat.

Zane stepped back.

"I need some help!" Jacobson told the charmer. "Get me a doctor, get me—"

"You're a demon," Pak said. "You'll heal from just about anything."

"I want out, man. I need—"

"Some folks are waiting on you, Henry."

The demon jerked on the table, straining against the straps. "A jail's not gonna hold me! Nothing can, nothin—"

"I didn't say you'd be going to jail." Still no emotion in Pak's voice. "I just said that folks were waiting on you."

Jacobson's case had been a government deal. Because, yeah, the government knew about the supernaturals out there. They liked to pretend they didn't, better for the public image that way. But they knew, and they had their own "extermination" list.

Jacobson was at the top. Some men and women in black would be coming for him soon and, after they picked him up, Jacobson wouldn't be returning to Baton Rouge again.

Zane caught Jacobson's whimper just as he reached Jude's side. The demon seemed to finally understand. *This is the end for you, Jacobson.*

Jude held up the pages, and the first thing Zane saw was . . . her.

No, not Jana. Not exactly. Different hair. Blond. Different eyes. Brown, not blue. Same mouth. Same nose.

Pak had told him a blonde was seen at the other scenes. *So she'd dyed her hair.* And he'd found a black-haired lady at Francis Street. "Who is she?" he demanded.

They left holding, walking back to the Night Watch's main offices. "She's got some aliases," Jude told him. "Katherine Tanner, Judy Bright, Melissa Jones. But from what I can tell, her real name's Jana Carter—"

Jana. Wait, she'd given him her real name?

"She was put in a juvenile facility when she was thirteen. She stayed there for five years." Jude's bright gaze met his. "Apparently, the woman liked to start fires."

Fuck.

"Police want her for a series of fires in New Orleans," Jude said.

Zane took the pages and scanned the info. His prey was thirty-one, five-feet-four inches tall, and one hundred-and-thirty-three pounds.

"Her stepfather died in the fire that landed her in the juvie facility," Jude continued. "I guess she started young."

Looked that way.

A killer? He'd stared right into her eyes and hadn't seen what she really was. He was slipping. Or maybe she was just real good at lying.

"From what I can tell, she's been selling out her services to the, ah . . ."

Zane glanced up at him, eyes narrowed.

"Highest bidder for the last few years. If you've got a supernatural you want taken down, she's your girl. Vamps, charmers, low-level demons . . . she's a real equal-opportunity killer."

How can I ever thank you?

Such a sweet, lying mouth. He stared down at the picture again. At her. He'd really thought she might be innocent.

He kept making the same dumb-ass mistakes.

"You gonna be okay on this one?" Jude asked quietly.

The office buzzed around them. Phones rang. Voices called out. The fax machine beeped.

Zane tucked her picture into his back pocket.

Jude frowned. "Look, I know the last Ignitor case you worked with was—"

"I handled her, didn't I?" Zane fired back, breaking through the words.

Jude's head moved in the faintest of nods.

Handled her. Such cool words for the death he'd given the other woman. "I can do my job. I can do what needs to be done." The same spiel he'd given Pak, but he meant the words. Nothing, no one would stop him.

"Good." Pak spoke from behind him, and Zane tensed. "Because Jacobson gave me a location. He says the woman found him in a dive called Dusk. It's a new club that opened on St. Antony and—"

"I know the place," Zane said, exhaling. Word traveled fast in this town. "It's a den." A demon's den. The place for his brethren to go in and take their drugs of choice. Darkness rode many of his kind, and the drugs, oh, they tempted.

"Oh, shit, man, I can take this one," Jude offered. "I know you—"

"Can take on a den any day of the week." Damn, but he regretted the drunken night he'd made the mistake of spilling his past to the tiger shifter. That guy never forgot anything.

"Then go get her," Pak said, "bring her in. No matter what it takes, *bring her in.*"

Time to take another killer off the streets.

"You shouldn't go in there." The husky, *very female* voice stopped Zane cold just as he prepared to climb the steps leading up to Dusk.

The voice was laced with a soft drawl, edged with a breath of sex, and it crawled over his body like a caress.

A demon shoved past him, heading inside Dusk, and when the door opened, the beat of the music blasted Zane's ears and the scent of drugs burned his nostrils.

"Of course, you don't have to listen to me," she murmured. *Jana.* He turned his head a few inches to the right and saw her slide from the darkness. "It can be your funeral."

She looked vulnerable. Small, delicate. Almost helpless as she stood in the shadows with her arms crossed over her chest. Watching him with such big eyes.

But her words . . . "Ah . . . did you just threaten me?" He moved away from the door. Turned his back on the den and began to stalk her.

She crept once more toward the shadows and he followed her. His heart rate kicked up. *She's making it too easy.*

"You won't believe this," she told him, "but I'm not the threat tonight. Well, not the one you need to be worried about."

She was close enough to grab now.

A soft sigh slipped past her lips as her hands dropped to

her sides. "You shouldn't have come here. You should've just taken the demon in and called it a day."

A shocked laugh broke from his lips, one without a drop of humor. "Lady, you *killed* someone in that alley."

She flinched. "The vampire would have killed me. I didn't have a choice." Her right hand lifted and rubbed against her chest. Thanks to his demon-enhanced senses, he saw the blood on her shirt, and he caught the coppery scent on the wind. "What did you want me to do?" she asked, and heat blasted through her words. "Just stand there and let him cut my heart out?"

A muscle jerked in his jaw.

"Or maybe I should have waited for you," she muttered, those sexy eyes narrowing, "like he wanted. I should have waited, and then I should have made sure you were the one who didn't walk out of that alley."

His hands flew out and he caught her, pulling her close and lifting her right off her toes. "Don't make the mistake of thinking I'm easy to kill."

Her chin inched up. "And you don't need to make the mistake of thinking you're immortal. Everyone can die. *Everyone.*"

"You'd know, wouldn't you, baby? You kill for the highest bidder."

She didn't blink. Those eyes stayed locked on him, still blue. The fire hadn't lit within her yet. If it had, her eyes would have been blood-red.

"Do you know what I did to the last Ignitor who came at me with fire in her eyes?" he demanded. Her mouth was temptingly close. He'd kissed that mouth before. Tasted her. Wanted more. *Fool.*

A guy's dick could get him into some serious trouble.

"Dumb ass," she said, and his eyes narrowed. "I'm not charging up. I'm trying to *warn* you."

"About what?"

"My . . . services." The right side of her mouth kicked up

into a hard smile, and damn if a dimple didn't wink at him. *Deceptive package.* "Who do you think the number-one target is in this town? Who do you think the demons want taken out? The vamps?"

Shit.

"That's right. *You.* The vamp in that alley wanted you taken out, and he sure wasn't the only one to want a fried demon handed to him." Her gaze darted behind him to Dusk. "The demons sure don't like that you've been hunting your own kind."

Fuck 'em. "I don't hunt them all." What? Was he defending himself? To her? "Just the ones who cross the line." His fingers were digging too hard into her arms.

He took a breath and let her slide back to the ground, let her feet touch down, but he didn't free her. Wouldn't. He had plans for Jana Carter.

"What line?" she asked him, shaking her head. "The one *you* made up? The one that says some folks are bad, some are good, and smart, all-powerful you gets to punish the ones you *think* screwed up?"

He glared at her. Like she could judge him.

"Maybe I *should* let them rip you apart." Her tongue flashed out to lick her bottom lip.

He couldn't help it. His stare dipped and followed that fast lick. His body tightened. *Damn.* He took a breath and swore he tasted her. "If you'd been smart, you would've left town. After you killed the vamp, you should have run."

"Maybe." A shrug. "But you came into the fire for me."

Because he'd thought she needed him. Thought she was a human who'd needed rescuing. The truth was that the woman could have gotten out of that house without the flames even touching one inch of her perfect skin.

"No one's ever tried to save me before," she added. "I thought you were . . . sweet."

He growled.

"So I wanted to even the score." Another shrug that sent her dark hair settling over her shoulders. "I knew you'd come looking for me. I figured it was only fair to give you a warning."

Fair? The woman who torched for a living wanted to talk fair? Zane could only shake his head. "Thanks, baby, but believe me, I don't need *your* help."

Her gaze slid away from his once more. Back to the club. He caught the whisper of fast-moving feet and the scent of booze and death. Battle-ready tension had his heart slamming into his chest.

"You sure about that?" she asked and that same half-smile lifted her lips, making her dimple flash. "Okay. Have it your way, then, stud. Take 'em all."

He spun around, his eyes zeroing in on the entrance to Dusk. Sure-damn-enough, the demons were snaking out the front door. At least ten of them so far, and their black eyes—filled with fury and hate—were all locked on him.

Jana's hand pressed into his back, a warm, sold weight. "Have fun with the fan club," she said and then her shoes thudded as she ran away.

Two seconds later, the demons closed in on him.

Chapter 3

Jana ran for fifteen seconds. Then ten more. Then, ah, hell, she spun back around.

She couldn't see Zane anymore. Her big, bad demon was in the middle of a pile of bodies. She heard the thud of flesh, the snarls from the attack, and she knew he was probably on the bottom of that pile.

"Bet you're wishing you'd taken my help now," she whispered and clenched her hands into fists as her body began to charge. The air around her warmed. "Don't worry, demon. I pay my debts." He'd come for her, so she'd be there for him.

Then . . . *even*. No more debt. Free and clear.

A demon flew through the air and slammed into the concrete. He didn't get back up.

A faint sheen of red fell over her vision, like a mist. Jana marched forward with slow, determined steps. Her breath seemed too loud, too raspy. Her heart felt too slow, and the heat covered her like a blanket.

"Get away from him!" she called out.

Another body flew from the mound. One guy, a demon with a long, twisting scar on his right cheek, just turned tail and ran.

These wouldn't be the strong demons. Not attacking en masse like this. The weak ones hunted in packs. Especially when they were going after a big kill.

A knife glinted. *"Get away from him!"* she screamed the words again and, this time, her voice cut through their fury.

Three demons turned to look at her.

So did Zane. He wasn't on the bottom of the pack. He was still standing. Swinging, knocking back demons and *grinning* like some kind of madman.

More demons were running out of Dusk. Like freaking sharks, they could smell blood in the air.

Soon enough, they'd be smelling fire.

A smile lifted her lips. The rush of heat had her whole body tensing, her nerves jumping.

Nothing like it.

A line of fire sprang at her feet, then the flames raced for the demons. Their yells and curses filled the air as they faced the new threat.

The flames flickered, twisted. *Ah . . . fighting power with power.*

Whenever possible, she avoided the demons. After all, they knew how to play with the elements, and she didn't like to waste energy pitting her power against theirs. But . . .

These guys were no match for her.

She fed the flames, and they burned hotter. Two more demons ran away. The door of Dusk slammed shut.

More yells. More grunts. Zane caught the wrist of the demon with the knife. Zane wrenched down hard, and Jana wondered if he'd broken the man's wrist. Looked like he had.

The knife clattered to the ground. She let her flames close in tighter.

"Pull it back!" Zane's bark.

The flames were dancing close to him.

The fire licked a demon. He screamed when the flames lit his clothes and he fell, rolling on the ground to battle the fire.

"Jana!"

The flames were at Zane's feet. His gaze met hers over the fire. No fear was in that stare—and it was a completely black stare. With the flames all around him and the bloodlust fuel-

2209726

ing him, the glamour was finally gone. No more sexy green eyes. Just demon darkness.

She was looking right at the demon he tried to hide. Tried, failed. She'd seen the demon from the first moment.

She exhaled, and the flames began to flicker.

Zane ran through the fire.

What? "Zane!"

But the flames didn't burn him. Didn't even seem to have actually touched him. Then he was in front of her, grabbing her arm, hauling her close, and the heat of the fire pulsed beneath her skin. When his eyes widened, she knew he felt her heat. Warm to the touch, just like a sunburn, but one she'd gotten from the inside out.

Burn, baby. Burn.

His eyes were black. She knew the red glow of the charge would still fuel her stare. No lying, no hiding for either of them. Two monsters in the dark.

She swallowed, but didn't back down.

"I thought you were running away," he said.

She'd thought so, too. "You were outnumbered." And more demons could be coming for him at any minute. They could talk later. "Look, we need to get out of here."

"Yeah, we do." Then his hands moved, fast, and something clicked around her wrist. Wait—*clicked?*

Oh, damn. No, no, he just hadn't—

"We need to get out of here, baby." Another click.

Her gaze dropped to her hand. A shining, silver handcuff circled her wrist. Another cuff circled his, locking them together.

"And don't think about burning through it," Zane warned. "That metal's made out of a titanium mix, and it's got a polymer coating that'll block you. It's something special that was designed just for someone like . . . you."

Her teeth snapped together. "I saved you," she gritted out, seriously pissed. Is this the way he thanked people?

But the guy was already moving. Spinning and lunging down

the street and jerking her with him. It was either go with him or be dragged behind him.

Asshole.

Yeah, yeah, *this* was why she didn't help people. Because when you did something nice, folks had a tendency to bite the hand that helped them.

Or handcuff it.

"Get in," he ordered. They were beside a car. A flashy red sports car. He had the driver's door open, and his gaze swept behind her, probably checking to make sure the demons weren't getting ready for a second round. They weren't. They were busy licking their wounds. "Slide over to the other seat."

So easier said than done. She climbed inside the car. The gearshift rammed into her knees, her ass shot into the air, but she—finally!—made it to the passenger seat.

He jumped in behind her and shut the door. The engine purred, and they shot away from the curb.

"You can't do this," she said and that was *not* fear tightening her gut. She wasn't afraid. Nothing scared her, not anymore. She hadn't been afraid since the day she'd learned how to fight her own monsters. "I didn't do anything to you. You can't—"

"You've got a bounty on your head, baby. A bounty I'm collecting."

The guy didn't even look at her as he threw that out.

Her eyes slit. "I'm betting the bounty on you was worth a hell of a lot more." And she hadn't taken it. Because she was the crazy one, obviously.

"Oh, and just what am I going for these days?" Not worry in that deep voice. Not even a hint of concern.

Jana sucked in a deep breath. Then another. Then she tried counting to ten. No, that didn't work. She was still pissed. "Let me go," she told him quietly. "If you don't, it will be the worst mistake you ever make." Probably the last, too.

Now he did glance at her, and his smile was icy. "No, trust me, it won't be—"

Then a semi plowed into the side of his flashy little car. The world spun, glass crunched, and Jana screamed.

"Just cut off his damn hand."

The words drifted through Zane's mind, easing past the fog, just as he felt something sharp press against his wrist. *Cut off his damn hand.*

Oh, the hell, *no*. His eyelids flew up, and his eyes locked on the dumb punk who had a knife in his fist, a knife that was pressed against Zane's flesh. "Don't even think about it," Zane growled.

The guy flinched, and his head flew up, revealing wide, bloodshot eyes.

"Do it, Ron!" The scream of someone who was gonna pay—the other idiot, the one who was holding Zane down on the hard pavement. No, the one who *thought* he was holding him down. Zane lunged up and sent the guy flying.

The man with the knife, *Ron,* scrambled back. "No, shit, we just want *her.*"

Her. Jana. Zane's gaze cut to the left. She was beside him on the pavement. Since they were still bound by the cuffs, his move had jerked her up. But her eyes hadn't opened, and she swayed, looking like a broken doll. She was pale, so pale. Her hair concealed half of her face, and her head tipped forward.

"Take off the cuffs, man," their would-be knifer said. "Just take 'em off and *walk away.*"

Zane blinked. "She's my bounty." Was this prick really trying to steal her from him?

A soft *snick* reached his ears. The other idiot was back. Only this time, he had a gun. One that was cocked and ready. His red hair stuck out from his head in thick patches, and his eyes, small and dark, were locked on Zane. "What she *is,*" the guy said, "is a nightmare you don't want."

A soft moan spilled past the nightmare's lips.

"Aw, shit, man, she's waking up," Ron muttered.

"Hit her." A fast order from the gunman.

Ron pulled his fist back and got ready to take that punch. *The fuck no.*

Zane let the beast out. One thought, just one . . . and he had the asshole with the knife flying back through the air and thudding into the redhead with the gun.

The gun fired, the bullet went wide, and Zane scooped up Jana. He held her cradled against his chest, barely feeling her weight.

They were still in the road. A deserted road at three a.m., and his car was a wreck near the broken light post.

A trap. Two in one night?

But, no, this trap hadn't been for him this time. For her.

"Jesus, he's one of them!" the redhead yelled and that gun came up again. Zane pulled his power close, got ready to—

A line of fire flew at the gunman. He swore and stumbled back, dropping the gun.

"Run," Jana whispered in his ear, and he realized the woman was awake—had *been* awake that whole time. *So good at playing weak.* Had she just been planning to lie there and let the jerks cut off his hand? Probably. That would have made it easier for her to get away.

"Run," she said again, her voice stronger, her breath blowing lightly against his ear. "They'll have backup soon. . . . Too many of them. They'll take us. . . ."

"I'd like to see them fucking try." He tightened his hold on her as he stared at the wreckage of his car. His baby. Aw, hell. They would *pay.*

"They . . . have drugs."

What?

"Not bullets in those guns. *Run.*"

Zane heard the *snick* of the gun's trigger too late. He lunged to the side. A steel fist slammed into his upper arm, and Zane's hold on Jana weakened.

"Dammit!" His head whipped back.

That bastard still held the gun—and he was getting ready to fire again.

Zane gathered his power and prepared to blast the asshole once again—but his knees gave way.

"No!" Jana hit the ground first, thudding hard against the pavement. He sagged behind her. But the woman moved fast. She jumped to her feet, wrenching him with the cuffs, and her flames raced for the two men.

An engine roared in the distance. Tires squealed.

"They're coming." No fear in her voice . . . but her voice—it sure sounded far away. Weird, when she was standing so close.

A thick heat began to spread through his blood even as a wave of nausea had Zane sucking in a deep breath.

"Get. Up." She was yanking at him. Trying to pull him to his feet. "If you don't move, they'll get us both." Her eyes were glinting in the night. "*Get up.*"

He looked at his left arm. Blood trickled from the hole in his shirt. *Not bullets in those guns.*

Drugs.

The beast inside began to claw and scream.

"Come on!" Her nails bit into his chest. "Don't just stand there and let them take us!"

And he was standing. He'd made it back to his feet. The fire around them rose higher. Higher.

"Run with me," she whispered.

With his body already feeling leaden, but his heart beating too fast, he did. Zane knew there wasn't much time, not long at all depending on the drug they'd given him.

He could feel the darkness calling to him. The slide had already begun.

"Got to slow the other cars down . . ."

He saw her eyes narrow for an instant. Then an explosion rocked the night. A roar echoed and rolled down the street.

Zane managed to turn his head and, *oh, hell* . . . his car was in pieces, burning pieces, and the big rig was covered in flames, too.

But the flames were blocking the road, and two black SUVs were trapped behind the fire.

"Move that ass, Wynter!"

Her voice cut through the drone in his head, and he moved. One foot in front of the other. *Move. Move.*

Voices shouted behind them. Doors slammed. *Hold it together. Get out of there. Hold it—*

"Get on!" she yelled, pulling at the cuff.

He blinked. Jana was straddling a motorcycle. A motorcycle that she already had throttling. He climbed on behind her.

"You're gonna have to stretch your arm," she told him. "Stretch your right arm and wrap the left one around me so I can hold the handlebars."

He stretched. His thighs pressed tight to her as he sealed his body to hers. His left arm throbbed, but he held her as close as he could.

A hot tension began to slip through his blood. A dull ache blossomed behind his eyes. And that darkness beckoned. *So tempting.*

"Hold on." She gunned the bike. They bolted forward, streaking fast as another steel fist hit his back.

Sonofabitch. They'd shot him. *Again.* He hunched his body and tried to protect her as best he could. A chill shook him, a long, hard shudder, and his breath blew against her hair.

"Zane?" He heard her shout over the roar of the engine. "Are you okay?"

No, no, he wasn't. His eyes squeezed shut. The drugs were slipping through his body, dragging him slowly down into hell. A hell he'd promised never to visit again. He wasn't okay, and before he was done with her, before the *thing* inside was done, Jana wouldn't be, either.

"What the hell happened? This was supposed to be a simple retrieval mission!"

Ron stared at his feet, refusing to meet his boss's stare. Mostly because he knew the boss didn't like it when folks looked too long at her face, and his eyes did have a tendency to wander. "She . . . ah . . . the demon had handcuffed himself to her. We couldn't get them apart—" He'd waited too long to cut off the bastard's hand. He swallowed. "But Ben shot him. The bastard took two tranq shots." And those shots could take down an elephant. The demon would be out soon, and he'd drag the woman down with him.

Those cuffs.

They'd be easy prey once the drugs kicked in.

"You dumb sonofabitch."

The icy growl had his gaze flying up.

"You drugged a *demon*," she snapped. "They don't react the same way humans do to the tranq. Hell, they never react the same way to *anything*."

Because they were freaks. He licked his lips. The boss held a too-tight grip on her gun. "It'll just knock him out. He'll be a dead weight slowing her down." Then his job would be easy. Kill the demon. Take the woman.

The boss lifted her gun and aimed it right at his chest. "It won't knock him out. It hasn't knocked out *any* demon we've tried it on."

How was he supposed to know that? "Wh-what will it do?"

"It will either make him high. It will boost up his power and give him a rush he's never had. Or . . ."

He gulped. Her finger was tightening around that trigger. Only, her gun was loaded with real bullets.

"Or it will make the bastard psychotic. He'll turn on the woman and kill her long before we can get to him." She stepped closer, her pale blond hair floating around her face. "And if that happens, guess who else will be dying?"

The promise was there, glittering in her dark gaze. His eyes began to dart to her scarred cheek. . . .

"Now let's get the hell out of here!" she shouted. There were sirens wailing, coming close now. No way could anyone miss the flames. The cops would swarm any minute.

They couldn't be on the scene then. Everyone scrambled inside the two SUVs. The boss shoved him inside with her.

"Get to Jana Carter's safe house," she ordered the driver. "If she's running, she's going to try and disappear."

The guy threw the SUV into reverse, and the vehicle spun back. He shifted gears and drove the SUV down the street, easing right past the line of approaching cop cars.

Jana had to get them off the road. Had to get them someplace safe before the assholes back there came hunting again.

"Are you with me?" she shouted as the engine growled.

Zane's body was pressed close to hers, and he seemed . . . heavier.

"Zane?"

His lips were next to her ear. No helmet, not for either of them. If they crashed, even his demon blood wouldn't save him.

Nothing would save her.

Her fingers tightened around the handlebars. "Zane?" Shouted louder.

"H-hurt . . . you . . ."

She tensed, but kept her eyes on the road. *Can't go back to my place.* Ten-to-one odds said they already knew where she lived.

Can't go to a hotel. Not like she could check in with the demon handcuffed to her. Explaining that to the desk clerk would be—

"If . . . h-hurt you . . ."

Oh, that just didn't sound good. What the hell was happening to the guy back there? That left hand of his was holding way too tight to her waist.

"B-burn me . . ."

Hell.

They needed a safe place to crash and they needed it *now.*

The instant Baton Rouge Police Captain Antonio "Tony" Young saw the flaming remains of the red Corvette, his gut clenched, and he knew hell had come calling.

Antonio jumped out of his car and rushed forward, grabbing one of the uniforms already on the scene. "Where's the driver?" Because he *knew* that car.

The young cop spun to look at him, and gulped when he saw Antonio's face. "D-don't know, s-sir . . ."

Those flames were burning so high. Antonio couldn't see the front seat of the car. The 'Vette was smashed to hell and back, and all that fire . . .

"We found 'em this way. Abandoned rig and the sports car—"

A rig that had smashed right into the driver's side door.

It takes a lot to kill a demon.

He released the cop and yanked out his phone. He punched in Zane's number. Waited, waited . . .

Customer not available. The automated message clicked on, and he nearly shattered his phone.

Dammit. Antonio paced away, feeling the heat from the fire singe his skin. If Zane wasn't answering, there was only one person he could contact.

He called Pak. Nothing happened at Night Watch without that charmer's approval. Nothing. So it was past three a.m., Pak was probably at home, sleeping, but . . .

"What do you want, captain?" Pak's smooth voice asked with no hint of sleep slurring the words.

Antonio cast a fast glance back at the wreckage, hunched his shoulders, and paced around the fire truck. "What kind of case is Zane Wynter working on right now?"

Silence.

Come on! "Pak, don't screw with me right now. I've got a crew of humans out here on Montgomery Lane, and I need to know what we're stepping into." Because he knew the real deal about the world. He knew that all the nightmares people had—those nightmares were *nothing* when compared to reality.

Once upon a time, he'd thought the worst things on the streets were the human killers who sliced and diced their prey. Then he'd met the vampires. They drained their prey, tortured them, made them beg for death, and then wouldn't let them die.

Humans weren't the worst predators on the streets. Not even close. If only.

"There's an Ignitor in town," Pak finally said.

His gaze darted to the flaming vehicles. "No shit." He exhaled. "Have you talked to Wynter in the last thirty minutes?"

"No."

"Then we may have a problem." May? Who was he kidding? "I'm staring at Zane's car right now, and the flames burning it are bright enough to light the whole damn block."

The cabin looked deserted. Jana shoved down the kickstand and steadied the bike. It *looked* deserted. Hopefully, it actually was. She'd scouted out this area before, just in case she needed a place to crash.

And I do. I really, really do.

The wooden cabin was buried in the swamp. A long, ramshackle pier ran from the side of the cabin and skated out over that murky, green water.

"Okay, demon, we've got to move." She tried to roll her shoulders, but his weight was too heavy. "Zane? Come on, Zane, *move!*"

She felt him flinch. Then he eased back and slid off the motorcycle. She followed him, her thighs still trembling a bit. It had been far too long since she'd gone for a wild ride on a cycle.

"The motorcycle should be safe behind these bushes," she said. "We can go inside"—it looked like no one had been there in months, a very good thing—"and then figure out what the hell we're going to do next."

He just stared down at her. Dawn had finally come, lighting up the darkness, and she could see a faint rim of green around the outer edge of his irises, but the black coloring—

that demon black—was darkening. The lines on his face were tight and hard.

Jana licked her lips. "Zane?" She tugged her cuffed hand. The metal bit into her wrist.

Alone with a drugged demon. Hello, dream date.

As she stared up at him, the green in his eyes disappeared, and only the black was left. Just that deep, soulless black.

B-burn me . . .

She turned away from him. Not like she could *get* away from him, though, not with that freaking fireproof, *Other*-proof metal chaining them together. But when she started moving, he did, too. That was something, right?

It's okay. He's one of the good guys. He worked for Night Watch. He brought down the paranormals who hurt humans. He hunted them, he brought them in, or he took them out.

One of the good guys. Right, that's what she had to remember. She risked a fast glance back at him. It was just that he didn't look particularly *good* right then.

He looked like he wanted to eat her.

Jana grabbed the doorknob. Twisted. Locked, of course. Because who would leave a cabin unlocked for any squatter—*like me*—to come by and enter? Oh, well. She lifted her foot and kicked the door.

That hurt.

Swearing, she limped back. Zane's left arm wrapped around her and pulled her to the side.

Okay, he felt *warm,* and she sure needed some warmth right then. After a charge, all of the heat left her body too fast. And it was cold out there in the swamp. The cold cut of air knifed right to the bone.

Not saying a word, Zane lifted his foot and kicked the door. The lock snapped, the door flew open, and—

And he pushed her inside.

Darkness. Dust. That musty, closed-in smell that a place got after being sealed up for too long.

She exhaled and tried not let her nose twitch. "I need to take a look at your wounds." Not that it would do much good. The drugs would be in his system now. "I need—"

"*You.*" Guttural. That rough word was the only warning she had. His hands caught her arms and he spun her around, pressing her back against the wooden wall of the cabin. He crowded her in and locked his hard, hot body against hers.

The demon was aroused. His cock pushed against the front of his jeans. No mistaking that thick swell. Especially not when his lower body was crushed to hers.

Her hand pushed against him. "Zane, you're hurt. You've got to—"

He jerked her cuffed hand up with his, forcing it above her head. Then his left hand caught hers and lifted it high. He pinned her to the wall. Her eyes had adjusted a bit to the interior of the cabin, and she could see him better now. The stark planes and angles of his face. His eyes . . .

So dark.

One of the good guys. He came into a burning building to save me, he's not—

His mouth crashed onto hers. He caught her gasp, and his tongue drove into her mouth.

The kiss was too rough. His lips were too hard. Too demanding. He didn't ask, didn't seduce, he just *took.*

His hips thrust against hers, that thick cock sliding against her, letting Jana know exactly what her demon wanted. *Me.*

Her heart slammed into her chest. Her nipples were tight, too sensitive.

And damn but that demon could work his tongue.

No! This shouldn't be happening, she knew it. *Drugged.* Hell. The guy probably didn't even know what he was doing. *Or who I am.*

She tore her mouth away from his, panting. She needed to—

His mouth went to her throat. Licking, sucking, honing in on the spot that always made her knees go weak. Oh, hell, *right there.*

She choked back a moan. He was warming her with his lips and his lust. Warming her, just when she'd started to grow cold from the after-effects of the charge.

Part of her wanted to hold him tight. Wanted to dig her nails into his back and hold on for the wild ride that she knew would come. But . . .

But the man had taken two tranqs, and she knew what the drugs could do—demons could be so weak.

Her eyes squeezed shut. "Zane . . . this isn't *you*." Yeah, they'd kissed before, but that had been different. A skilled play of tongue and lips. Seduction. A tease.

This was desperate. Wild. Rough.

And, dammit, she *liked* it. Because the charge from the fire had burned off. The need that it left behind—always left behind—had her gut tightening. Adrenaline had filled her blood as she used her power, and without that rush, she was lost, shaken, *needing*.

He freed her left wrist. His hand snaked between them and found her breast. Zane fondled her through her bra, and her nipple pebbled even more for him. Her sex creamed, and she couldn't help it—she arched her hips against him.

He wrenched open the top of her shirt, sending buttons flying. Then his hand slipped inside. Hot flesh, callused fingertips touched her. He yanked her bra out of the way and strummed her nipple.

Her teeth clenched. *Not right. He was drugged.* This wasn't . . . *Jeez, that felt good.* But . . . "Zane!" The word burst from her.

His hand was sliding down her stomach, heading for the snap of her jeans.

Heat rolled off his body. Delicious, wonderful heat. But his eyes were blank. His touch too fierce, and—

Jana twisted and managed to break away from him. She took two stumbling steps, then the handcuffs yanked her back.

Fuck.

His left hand rose and curled around her throat. Her pulse

raced against his fingers. *Demons and drugs* ... everyone knew that was one screwed-up combination. So what, the tranqs had been some kind of sexual stimulant for him? Just great.

She turned her head and met his stare. "You're drugged, Zane. You don't know what the hell you're doing." *But it sure felt good.*

He blinked. Once. Twice. Real slow, and he almost looked like a robot she'd seen on a sci-fi show once, trying to process information.

His gaze dropped to her shirt front, to the gaping neckline and the black bra that was all too visible. "I know exactly what I'm doing." His voice came out deeper, rougher than ever before. Rough, but no emotion. Too flat. Not *his* voice.

"Wh-what?" *If* ... *hurt* ... *you* ... The guy had been trying to warn her before. Such a damn good-guy thing to do.

"I'm fucking you."

Chapter 4

Need ate at his gut. A white-hot, burning need that fired Zane's body from the inside out. He could smell her. *Jana.* Her scent was all around him, the rich scent of her sex tormenting him.

Take.

His vision had narrowed to her. He could barely hear what she was saying because his heart drummed too loudly in his ears, the blood flowing too fast and hard.

Take.

She trembled in his grasp. Trembled. Small and weak. Ready for him. Her mouth . . . red and swollen. He'd kiss her. He'd touch her. He'd fuck her. He'd do anything he wanted.

"I don't want to hurt you," she said, her eyes big and wide. "I know you said . . . but I *don't* want to."

Hurt him? Nothing could hurt him. No one.

"I don't want to, but I will. And you'll probably even thank me for this tomorrow." Her chin tilted back. "Take your hand off me or—"

He laughed at her. Laughed, picked her up, and tossed her onto the old bed in the corner. Dust billowed in the air.

"I warned you," she said, then bit her lip as fire crackled in the air. A hot, thick circle of orange flame.

He waved his hand and the fire vanished.

"Wh—" She shook her head, sending that black mane flying over her shoulders. Her eyes narrowed, and the fire flared again.

With barely a thought, he put out the fire. The power of the demon burned wild and free in him, pulsing, just beneath the skin.

His knees hit the mattress, and then he covered her body. "That the best you got?" Wouldn't be good enough. Nothing would.

A thick, choking darkness pressed against him, and she was the only damn light he could see. Her . . . and her flames. Already flickering again.

His face hovered over hers. "You can't hurt me." His temples throbbed. And her smell . . . *fucking driving me crazy.* There was nothing like the scent of a woman's arousal. And Jana was aroused. He smelled her cream, and he had felt the tight buds of her nipples. "Nothing can hurt me."

"Really? Sorry to do this but . . ." Then her knee drove into his groin. A vicious, fast drive that sent pain radiating through his body. "But our first time together *isn't* going to be while you're flying on tranqs."

Fuck. His hand locked around her hip. The light around her face began to fade, even as the flames flew higher, burned brighter. His fingers clamped onto her flesh.

Burn, let the fucking fire burn, can't touch me, can't hurt me.

"Zane?" A breath of sound, a gasp, lost.

Her gaze caught his. There was fear in her eyes. Fear lurking in that river of blue.

Afraid . . . of me.

Monster.

He had her on the bed. His body shoved hard against hers. What the hell was he doing?

His back teeth clenched, and he fought through the waves of lust, through the darkness tangling his mind and the need that stole his breath.

"Something's wrong with you . . . your eyes. . . ."

He squeezed his eyes shut and fought to pull back the beast. But he was slipping off the leash. *Slipping.*

Her breath whispered over his face.

"It's okay," he lied, and he forced his hand off her hip. *Her scent.* "I'm in control now." His fingers gripped the old, dirty covers. Ripped them. His lashes lifted, slowly. Her eyes were on him and she instantly trapped his gaze.

Bed. Jana. Sweet flesh. Hot fire.

"It's okay," he said again, growling the words and hoping like hell that he could stay in control. *Focus.*

What was happening to him? His body was so tight. Ready to explode. And he wanted her more than he wanted breath. Wanted her, open and ready, with the heat blazing around them. No, *from them.*

His head was going to explode. A hard, fierce pounding thundered at both temples, and a flicker of light danced in the air.

"Jana, it's going to be all . . . right."

Her breath sighed out.

He could hold on to his control. He could keep the devil inside. He could—

Jana shouted his name, and Zane blacked out.

"Zane? *Zane!*"

He'd crashed on top of her. His eyes had flickered in those last few moments, shooting back and forth from green to black, and she'd thought, really thought for a moment there, that he was coming back. Him, Zane, not the demon inside him.

Then his eyes had flashed pitch black.

And he'd slammed into her. No, *onto* her.

She tried to suck in a deep breath. Tried and failed. Oh, the guy weighed a ton. *Of course.* And he had her smashed into the lumpy mattress. "Uh, Zane?" She tried tapping his shoulder.

Nothing.

His head was nestled in the crook of her neck. He breathed softly now, the light puffs of air sending a shiver over her each time they touched her sensitive flesh.

Alive, just passed out.

She shifted a bit as she tried to maneuver from underneath him, but the guy was pure muscle. Thick muscle.

Her breath rasped out, and she stared up at the ceiling. "Great. Just great."

Trapped beneath a demon. Talk about one hell of an ending to her already screwed-up night.

Antonio stared at the fax he'd just received. The woman in the grainy photo didn't look particularly dangerous. Delicate features, wide eyes. Sexy mouth.

But if he'd learned anything in this business . . . well, it was that the surface lied.

"Put out an APB for Jana Carter," he told Officer Penton. The fresh-faced kid stood next to him, watching with narrowed eyes and nervous hands. "This woman is wanted in connection with a series of arsons in New Orleans," *and probably a few in Baton Rouge.* "We've got intel to suggest that she's in the area."

"Yes, sir."

"Tell the cops out there to be careful. This one is *extremely* dangerous."

"She's armed?"

Didn't have to be armed to be dangerous. "Yes," he lied. He seemed to spend most of his days lying. "She's not to be approached. If she's spotted, I want to be contacted ASAP." He held Penton's stare, driving the point home. "*No one is to approach or try to apprehend her without me.*" Because if the cops went up against someone like her—

He'd be cleaning up the ashes.

Penton nodded quickly and hurried off to spread the news. Antonio looked down at his watch. Almost noon. It had sure taken Pak a long time to play ball and send that fax. The guy must have been holding out, hoping for word from Zane. Word that hadn't come.

Where was the demon? Was he alive? No bodies had been found in the Corvette, but that didn't mean Zane was still breathing. Not with an Ignitor out there. If she'd been letting her fire free, the poor bastard could be surrounded by the flames.

Zane awoke to find himself surrounded. Soft, silken flesh cradled him. A sweet, feminine scent flooded his nostrils. When he opened his eyes, he found himself staring at Jana's sleeping face.

What the hell?

Her eyes were closed, and her lashes cast dark shadows on her cheeks. Her skin looked even paler today, and he noticed a small, dark mole near the corner of her left eye. Her hair spread on the old pillow behind her, a tangled darkness.

Carefully, slowly, he eased up. Her body was wrapped around his, not under it. One of her arms was around him, while one of his held her waist. Her leg was between his, and her head tilted close to his.

And her shirt was open, revealing black lace and the upper curves of her round breasts. A line of red scratches marred her smooth flesh.

He sucked in a sharp breath and wondered what was going on. Had he done that? Had he hurt—

"Are you with me?" she asked, her voice a husky whisper.

Hell, yeah. He cleared his throat. How had they gotten in bed? Just what had they done? Her jeans were still on, so were his, so . . . no sex.

That was a good thing, right? His temples ached like a bitch, and he swallowed, tasting copper on his tongue.

Jana's lashes lifted, nice and slow, revealing those sexy eyes. Sleepy and dark blue. "Do you even know who I am?"

He licked dry lips. "Trust me, baby, you're pretty unforgettable."

Her gaze searched his. "Then what's my name?"

He let his brows rise as he studied her. "You mean the name you seem to be using again this time? It's Jana. Jana Carter."

She exhaled.

"Now, *Jana*, why don't you tell me just what happened." *And why we're in bed together.* Sure, he'd thought about fucking her, but then he'd found out about her little tendency to burn on contact.

"What do you remember?"

"A big rig slamming into us." *My car.* Someone would pay. "Some assholes shooting. . . ." He frowned, struggling to recall and shove past the thick fog in his mind. "I got hit."

"You were hit *twice*." She eased her arm away from him and tried to slide her leg from between his thighs.

A bright, hard, painful memory flashed through his mind.

"Ah, remember that, do you?" She stilled, and her lips quirked just a bit. Not enough to make her dimple flash.

Images flew through his mind. *Jana—her mouth red and open. Pinned against the wall. Her arms over her head. Her breath panting out.*

Her shirt open, gaping, his hands on her flesh. Tight nipples. Pebble hard. He'd want to taste her.

Fire. Surrounding him.

Jana . . . on the bed.

"*I don't want to hurt you.*" The memory of her words filled his mind.

He jumped from the bed, moving fast, only to have her yell as she tumbled after him.

The cuffs.

He froze, staring at her wrist. Still bound. He took a breath and tasted her. "What did I do?"

She blinked and seemed to *see* him. "Ah. Guess you are back now." Jana pushed herself up, stretching a bit, and the few remaining buttons on her top strained with the movement. He leaned forward, trying to give her more room to move. Where were the cuff keys? His left hand dove into his pockets. Nothing. Figured.

Jana just sat there, staring up at him, with no expression on her pretty face.

How was she so calm? *"What did I do to you?"* He remembered need. A white-hot lust that had thundered through his body and driven all sanity from his mind. *Take.* The hunger had been too much. He'd wanted her. Planned to have her, then—He swallowed. "Did I hurt you?" *No, please, shit, he didn't want to—*

She laughed at that. A light, quick chuckle, and she swung her legs over the side of the bed. "I'm not easy to hurt."

Lie. She was human. Human with some strong psychic powers, but human nonetheless. "I shouldn't have—I don't know why I—"

Jana rolled her eyes. "You were drugged, dude. You took two hits of the tranq. You got handsy, and then you collapsed, that's all."

All? His back teeth were clenched so hard his jaw ached. "I don't . . . do particularly well with drugs."

"What demon does?"

So she knew.

But she wouldn't realize just how dangerous he could be when the drugs were in his system. She didn't understand just how lucky she was to still be breathing.

He stiffened his shoulders. "I'm sorry." The words were stark. "I shouldn't have touched you." He sucked in a quick breath and just caught more of her scent.

Her head cocked toward him.

"Whatever I did to you"—he held her stare, because the shame was his—"I'm sorry."

Her face softened, just for a moment, and he heard her mutter something that sounded like, "Being a good guy again . . .", but then she rose and turned her back on him.

His lips pressed together.

"You stopped." She glanced back over her shoulder. "Yeah, the drug had you wired for a bit, but you pulled back. You got your control." A little shrug. "But then you passed out before you could get off the bed."

The drumming of his heart echoed in his ears. "You're telling the truth?"

Now she did smile. A big, wide grin that, oh, hell, flashed the dimple in her cheek. "Would I lie?"

Yes. "What about the marks on your chest?"

She glanced down at herself, and the smile faded. "These aren't from you. They're courtesy of the vampire who caught me in the alley."

The one she'd torched. The bastard *had* attacked her.

"I've seen other demons on the drug." Her voice pulled his eyes back to her face. A flicker of sadness appeared in her gaze. "Even with one dose, they don't know what the hell is going on." A considering pause as her stare measured him. "You must be pretty strong."

He wasn't going to touch that one.

But she, apparently, was. Jana faced him fully, one brow up. "What are you on the power scale? An eight? Maybe pushing nine?"

The demon power scale. A scale that ran from one to ten. One being the low end, the demons who barely had any power above a human's latent psychic talents. And ten being the demons who could bring hell to earth.

"I'm strong enough," was all he said.

"Hmmm." She lifted her wrist, raising the cuffs and his hand. "Then get these things off, demon. Get them off, and we can just walk away from all this."

If only. "A witch I know put an enchantment on 'em." Standard protocol for Night Watch containment gear and weaponry. A little bonus Pak had always insisted on throwing in. "I can't break them." She deserved the full truth. "And even if I could, I couldn't let you walk away."

Her lips parted. Soft lips. So soft.

"You're damn well kidding me," she snapped.

"No, baby, I'm not." He straightened his shoulders. The hunt hadn't gone down at all like he planned, but he was sticking to the rules. He'd been an ass, and he'd regret last night for years to come—*drugs or no drugs, I shouldn't have scared her.* But he had a job to do. "There's a bounty on you. You've got to pay for what you did."

Her lips formed an outraged "O."

"I'm taking you in."

"*Someone save me from good guys.*" She punched her index finger into his chest. Hard. "I could have *killed* you while you slept."

Why hadn't she?

"Let me go," she told him, dropping her voice, but keeping her eyes up. "Walk away from me. Trust me, it will be the best move you've ever made in your life."

"You're my bounty." And there were dead bodies she had to answer for.

She shook her head. "You're a fool. You're gonna get caught in the crossfire. You'll die. Or you'll just wish for death."

Like he hadn't done that before. He'd died when he was sixteen, and the demon inside had taken over. He'd been fighting the devil ever since. "Promises, promises, baby."

For just an instant, one instant, her eyes seemed to flare red.

Zane stiffened, but then the blue flooded back into her gaze.

She licked her lips, and her eyes darted around the cabin. Darted, then paused somewhere just over his shoulder. "This sucks."

Yeah.

"Come on." Then she started marching away from him, heading toward a shut door.

"What are you—"

"It's been over nine hours, demon. I've got to use the bathroom." She grabbed the door and slipped inside. "Now be a good Southern gentleman, and don't even *think* about looking at me."

Southern gentleman? Since when?

The cuffs were a damn inconvenience, but they'd be free soon, both of them. He'd take her to Night Watch, turn her in, and be rid of his Ignitor.

Case closed.

No more temptation. No more fire. No more Jana.

"Damn demon," she muttered.

"Jana, I'm—"

"Save it!"

Sorry. He bit the word back, but the guilt burned in him. He *was* sorry. For what he'd done to her last night . . . and for what he would be doing, soon.

The demon was really going to turn her in. Jana followed Zane outside the cabin. He stopped, and glanced around the area, obviously searching for the motorcycle.

Would he remember where they'd stashed it?

Nope. That glinting stare turned back on her, and he lifted one dark brow. What? Did the guy really expect her help? He was turning her in!

She smiled back at him and just waited.

"Jana . . ."

Her body hurt. Ached. That car crash hadn't been an easy hit, and she was sure she sported a ton of bruises beneath her clothes. She needed a hot bath—for the aches and to wash away the blood. She needed some food. And she needed a bed that didn't smell like crap.

Instead, she'd get—what? Jail? A fast trip to some human slammer? How long would she stay there?

"I hate being locked up," she muttered. She'd already spent too many years being caged. Her gaze drifted around the swamp. Open. Free. *This* was what she wanted. Why couldn't everyone just leave her alone and let her have it?

"Then maybe you shouldn't kill people."

His words had her stiffening. "You don't know a damn thing about me."

Faint lines bracketed his mouth. "Don't I?"

"What? You typed my name in some computer at Night

Watch and all of a sudden you *think* you know about me? You think you know—"

"I know you started your first fire when you were thirteen. A fire that killed your father."

"*Step*father." There was a difference. An important one.

He crept closer. Not that those cuffs let him stray too far. "Why? Why the hell do you do it? You don't have to hurt people. You don't have to use the fire at all. You could've been normal—"

Was he crazy? "Demon, I'm as far from normal as you are." Did he think she'd chosen to be like this? Did he know how many nights she'd cried and begged God to just let her be normal? Jana sucked in a long breath. "And I don't know what you've heard about Ignitors. . . ." Because it wasn't like her kind were thick on the ground. "But when the flames start that first time, there's no *controlling* the fire." Not when the flames burn so fast, and you scream and beg for it to stop.

Only for the fire to flare hotter.

It had taken her years to learn control, and those lessons had been painful.

"You've killed people with your fire." A muscle flexed in his jaw.

"Oh, and you're Mr. Innocent?" Doubtful. She'd never met an innocent demon. "I bet you've just gone your whole life, and you haven't ever hurt anyone, right? You've never—"

"The last person I killed was an Ignitor."

Didn't expect that. Jana swallowed and studied him, letting her eyes sweep over his face. The curl of his lip seemed cruel. His eyes too sharp and hard.

He stared at her and said, "I broke her neck. She never even knew I was coming for her, not until it was too late."

Well, damn. Goose bumps rose on her arms. Not from the cold. Not this time. "Why?"

"Because she was working with a band of vampires. She was torturing my friends, and I wasn't going to stand by and watch them die."

So she'd died instead.

His hand lifted. Dammit, Jana flinched. But he was just brushing back her hair. His knuckles grazed her cheek. "Now it's your turn."

Her breath caught.

"Why do you do it? Make me understand. Give me something here. Why'd you start the fires?"

Screams that wouldn't stop. "Because I could." That's all she'd say. Was that a fair exchange of information? No. But then, she hadn't forced him to answer her question.

And she wouldn't answer his.

Jana spun away and marched for the thick line of brush, dragging him with her. "The motorcycle's over here."

Because even the idea of being turned over to the folks at Night Watch didn't seem so bad right then. But ripping her soul open and baring her past to the demon? *Yeah, rain check, please.*

She didn't bare her soul for anyone. Her secrets were hers, and she planned to take them to the grave.

They stopped for gas at some rundown station. The bike vibrated beneath her legs and exhaust drifted around them until Zane killed the engine.

He was driving this time. The big, bad demon in control.

Jana heard a gasp when she got off the motorcycle, and she turned her head to see an older lady with stone-gray hair and narrowed eyes staring at her. No, not at her exactly, but rather at the cuffs.

Fabulous. Between the cuffs and her gaping shirt, Jana knew she was the image of wholesomeness. Oh, well. She flashed the lady a smile. "He's a little kinky." *So am I.*

Zane swore.

The lady's jaw dropped. Then she slammed her door and drove away with a squeal of tires.

Her smile spread a bit. A growl reached her ears. She glanced at Zane and found him frowning at her. "What?"

He jerked the gas nozzle out of the tank and shoved it back into place on the pump.

"Come on." She sidled closer and ignored the stench of gasoline. She always had to be careful at places like this. One wrong thought . . . *boom!* "Are you trying to say that you don't have a kinky side? Because I'm not buying that." She put her hand on his chest. Let her fingers rest just over his heart. A nice, fast beat. "I saw you last night, remember? I know just how wild and rough you are inside. You wanted sex, fast and hot."

His nostrils flared and his heartbeat kicked up even more. Interesting.

She tipped her head back. "Have you had a few fantasies? While we were on the road, and I was wrapped around you, while we're chained together, have you thought about—"

"What kind of game are you playing?" he demanded and she heard the arousal in his voice. She could see it in the taut lines of his face. If she looked down—she'd peeked when they'd hopped off the bike—she knew he'd still be hard for her.

What kind of game was she playing? The only kind she liked. The dangerous kind. But she was running out of options.

"Get on the bike, Jana."

She didn't move. "You know"—she let her lashes lower, veiling her eyes, and she dropped her hand—"I could burn this whole place in about two seconds."

He wrapped an arm around her waist and lifted her up. No strain there. Such a strong demon. Zane had already healed from the injuries he'd gotten in the wreck and from the tranq shots.

He eased her onto the motorcycle and kept his left hand around her a bit too long. "You could, but you won't."

She blinked. "And how do you know that?"

"Because you scoped the place when we pulled up. You saw the two kids pumping up the tires on their bikes, and the old man behind the register inside." He paused. "You saw them, and I saw *your* face."

Dammit. He'd seen *too* much.

"You're not blowing anything up here." He eased in front of her and started the cycle quickly. He knew how to hot-wire, too. Figured.

The cycle roared. "Hold tight," he ordered, like she had much of a choice. "Just another twenty minutes and we'll be back in the city."

Yeah, they'd had to drive for a while because she'd hauled butt and gotten them as far away as she could last night. Only to be dragged back now.

She closed her eyes, waiting for him to shoot the cycle forward.

Nothing happened.

Jana opened one eye and found Zane gazing at her over his shoulder. "What?"

His brows were low. "If you were really a cold-hearted killer, it wouldn't matter about the kids."

Just figuring that out? Give the man a cookie. "I'm saving all my fire for you, lover."

He laughed. Flashed her those too-white teeth and laughed.

Then the motorcycle surged forward.

Jana held on tight. The guy's muscles were like stone beneath her hands and her hair whipped behind her. No helmet. She might as well be begging for death.

Once he dumped her at Night Watch and those powers that be decided what to do with her, well, she just might actually beg.

No.

Begging didn't do any good. She'd begged before. When she'd first been locked up. Begged to see her mom. Begged for help.

She'd gotten nothing.

Then when those bastards out there on her trail had learned about her power, she'd begged to be left alone.

What had Zane said? *Normal.* Yeah, she'd wanted to be normal. She'd begged for that, too.

Begging got a girl nowhere, fast. Fighting, shoving, letting the fire rage—that was the only way to make a difference.

When she got to Night Watch, she'd do whatever was necessary to stay alive. And if she had to let out the flames, then the place would burn.

And if innocent people were inside?

She pressed her face against Zane's back and wondered just how far into the darkness she was willing to go.

The motorcycle took another curve, nice and slow. Zane hadn't driven fast. He'd been careful the whole time. After one accident, maybe he was worried about a repeat. She sure was.

They eased from the curve, heading down the long road, and sirens screamed at them.

What? Jana's head whipped around just in time to see a patrol car fly out of its nice, sneaky hiding place on the side of the road. Blue lights flashed, and the siren wailed louder.

Go. Faster. Faster.

She always had the same response to cop cars. Mostly because those cars were usually chasing her. Just like this one.

The motorcycle began to slow down. "No!" she shouted.

But Zane was stopping. He pulled the motorcycle over to the side of the road and shoved down the kickstand.

Her nails bit into his side. "What are you doing?"

He turned his head and met her gaze. "We aren't wearing helmets. The guy's got to stop us."

She gulped. Right. Helmets. A normal stop. *And such a Boy Scout thing for the demon to say.*

Zane climbed off the bike. The handcuffs glinted in the light.

"And what are you going to tell him about these?" she asked. She wanted those things to be ash at her feet. Unfortunately, her fire didn't work on them. She'd tried burning them last night. No luck.

"I've got my bounty I.D." He shook his head. "The cops can check me out."

"Can he get us keys—"

"Step away from the woman!" The barked order carried easily to them.

Here we go. Jana looked at the cop. A young guy, with light blond hair, a handsome, if soft face, and a perfectly pressed uniform.

The cop also had his gun up and aimed at Zane.

She straightened on the motorcycle.

"Easy." Zane lifted both his hands, which, unfortunately, made her hand lift, too.

"The guy's crazy!" No harm in trying a little maneuvering, right? Jana jumped off the bike and focused her desperate gaze on the cop. "Help me." Her voice trembled. "He's—"

"What the hell are you doing?" Zane snarled at her. Then, louder he said, "Officer, my name's Zane Wynter. I'm a bounty hunter with the Night Watch Agency. This woman's a wanted—"

"Undo the cuffs." The cop had stalked closer. His clipped words cut right through the air. "Undo the cuffs and let her go."

Jana blinked. Ah, yeah, that had been easy. She could look desperate and pitiful when she wanted but—

Too easy.

Tension knotted her gut. That gun was aimed straight at Zane's chest.

Zane started to lower his arms. "I've got my I.D. in my back pocket, just let me—"

"*Take off the damn cuffs!*" Spit flew from the cop's mouth.

"Ease up," Zane said, and his hands froze. "I don't have the key on me."

The gun barrel jerked a bit. No, it didn't jerk. The guy was re-aiming. Setting up his shot so that when he fired—

Oh, hell. "Zane!"

The cop fired.

Chapter 5

The bullet hit the middle of the handcuffs. It couldn't break the *Other* proof metal, so the bullet ricocheted and blazed a path of fire down the side of Zane's right thigh. *Fuck.*

Zane fell to the ground, dragging Jana down with him. He rolled, fast, putting his body on top of hers. *Shield her. Keep her safe.*

"*Sonofabitch!*" Not his scream, though it sure could have been.

He glanced up to see the cop charging him. "I just want her!" the guy yelled.

Why the hell was everyone after his bounty?

"He told me not to hurt you," the cop threw out, the words directed at Jana as he strode forward and raised that gun. "But with him, *deadly* force is fine."

The hell it was.

Jana trembled beneath him and her skin warmed. She was charging up, getting ready to unleash her fire on this jerk coming at her.

"*We're not armed!*" he shouted at the cop. "Stand down!" What the hell was the guy thinking? And who was this "he" the cop was talking about? "I told you, I'm a hunter with Night Watch, you need to—"

The cop smiled and aimed that gun right at Zane's head.

His finger was already squeezing that trigger. Oh, screw this. Zane focused and sent a wave of power slamming into the cop. The trigger-happy jackass screamed and flew through the air. The gun fell from his hand just as he slammed into the front windshield of the patrol car.

The cop didn't get up.

Zane did. His fingers curled around Jana's, and he pulled her up with him.

"Is he . . . dead?" she asked.

"No." The guy would be starting to twitch a bit soon. Zane had knocked him out, not killed him. "Come on." They weren't going to stand around and wait for another bullet to come flying at them.

And if I killed a cop . . .

The paperwork would be a bitch.

They climbed onto the motorcycle. She wrapped her arm around him tightly. Blood dripped from his thigh. As they surged forward, he demanded, "Baby, why does everyone want a piece of you?"

Hell, he needed to get in touch with police Captain Antonio Young. Tony would have his back. He always did. Tony knew the score, and how to keep the peace.

Most days.

"I don't know." Her whisper came softly to his ears and only his enhanced hearing let him catch the words. But it didn't take enhanced senses to know she was lying.

Fifteen more minutes until they were at Night Watch. Fifteen more minutes and he'd be there. . . .

But a cop had just tried to kill him. A cop who hadn't cared about his position as a bounty hunter with Night Watch.

He glanced in the side mirror. No sign of the patrol car following them. The road branched up ahead. One side would take him back to the city. The other would lead him down a longer, curving path that wound back to the swamp.

His hesitation lasted for only a few seconds. Then he headed toward the swamp.

"Zane?" Her hold on him tightened. The lady must have

studied the area pretty well before coming to set up shop in the city. Figured. "Where are we going?"

He heard the faint hope in her words. Did she think he was going to let her go? Just walk away?

Let her.

His fingers clenched around the handlebars. "Got to make a phone call," he growled back. His cell had burned in the flames, so he'd have to find another phone.

He'd planned to just drive back in to Night Watch, but now, no, now he was gonna check in first. Just to make sure there weren't any more surprises waiting for him.

Surprises like a cop who'd been ready to blow his head off and steal his bounty.

Her hands were shaking. Jana balled her fingers into fists and stared at the faded walls of the gas station. Zane had stopped at the first phone booth he'd seen, one at a closed station that seemed to be falling into the swamp.

The windows of the booth were busted out. The phone book had long been snatched, but the phone, lucky for Zane—*unlucky for me*—still worked.

Now he was calling his boss. Probably arranging her pickup. And that was fine. She'd be better off once she was away from Zane.

But he'd covered her body with his. When that cop had been bearing down on them with that gun, Zane had protected her.

Freaking good-guy routine. Why'd he have to do that? Why'd he have to keep acting like she mattered?

A killer. That's all she was to him. She needed to remember that. Hell, he probably would have jumped in front of any bounty that had been threatened. No matter what the crime, you had to protect the cash cow, right?

"Something's wrong with this case," Zane's hard voice broke through her thoughts, and she knew he'd made contact with Night Watch. She glanced at him and saw that his brows were drawn low, and his jaw flexed with anger.

"Yeah, yeah, I've got her." His gaze slashed up to meet hers. *Hot.* She swallowed. That green gaze seemed to burn with intensity.

And she did like the fire.

Jana licked her lips. His gaze dropped and lingered on her mouth.

"*She's* not the problem."

Uh, okay. Now her eyes narrowed.

"I've got her under control," he said.

Oh, did he?

"It's the assholes after her that I'm having trouble with. Shit, yeah, I know what happened to my 'Vette—I was there."

Jana almost winced. Okay. Sure, *she'd* been the one to torch his car, but there hadn't been a lot of choice there. The car had already been smashed, anyway. Not like the thing had been in mint condition before her flames got to it.

"Some jokers came up and rammed us. Get this, they weren't firing bullets. They used some kind of drugs instead."

She really wished she had shifter hearing right then. She would have loved to hear what the person on the other end of the line said because Zane's eyes flashed black for just the briefest of moments.

"*No.* I'm fine." The green poured back and he stared at her. "Under control now."

Was he talking about her again? Or himself? Jana pulled restlessly at the cuff. Her wrist was aching. She wanted that damn thing off. Wanted to be on the motorcycle, riding fast and free.

"A cop stopped us about fifteen minutes ago. He tried to shoot me. No, no, I'm not fucking kidding you. I identified myself, and he still took aim. He wanted Jana."

Ah, so now she was "Jana" and not just his "bounty"? "That's something," she muttered.

"I took care of him." His gaze sliced around the area. Probably searching to make sure the cop hadn't found them. "But you need to talk to Antonio. Find out what's going on." A pause. "Right."

Was the guy gonna talk all day? She exhaled and rubbed the back of her neck. A hot bath would be heaven. She had so many scrapes and bruises on her body. Hell, forget the bath, she'd even settle for a shower.

Maybe even a shower *with* Zane. Because one last wild ride, before her freedom was ripped away, oh, that was tempting.

She bet the man would look phenomenal wet, those muscles glistening . . .

"Do I want you to send out a retrieval team?"

His words had her heart racing and the gaze she'd accidentally dropped to his chest flew back up to his face. She couldn't help it, Jana shook her head once. *No.* Better the demon you knew, right?

And if she knew those assholes after her, they'd trail any retrieval team. Zane would never make it back to Night Watch. Neither would she.

The handcuffs were keeping them together and, though Zane didn't realize it, those cuffs were the only thing that had kept him alive so far.

His eyes tightened just a bit at the corners. "No, I'll bring her in. We'll be there within the hour."

Then the call was over. He hung up the phone with a soft click of sound.

"You want to tell me why that cop was after you?" He stepped closer to her, his body brushing against hers.

"You're in over your head," was what she told him. "Haven't you realized, things aren't what they seem?"

"Things are never what they seem." He let the glamour vanish from his eyes so that she could see him as he really was. All that darkness. The back of his left hand brushed her cheek. "Did you really start those fires in New Orleans? Did you kill those two humans?"

Ah, the humans. Humans equaled innocents, right? She stood on her tiptoes and let her mouth come close to his. She wanted his lips. Wanted his tongue.

So she'd take them.

Jana pressed her mouth against his. Her tongue snaked inside the crease of his lips, pushed inside to slide against his.

A rumble built in his throat. And then his hands were on her, the cuffs pulling her hand back as he curled his fingers around her waist. His hips rocked against her, and the long, hard heat of his arousal was more than obvious.

Take the pleasure. Enjoy the rush. Deal with the hell that comes later.

Oh, so tempting.

She opened her mouth wider, loving the thrust of his tongue. Wishing his cock was driving into her sex the same way.

His mouth hardened on hers as the need burned between them. Her legs shifted restlessly against him as the lust pumped through her. Her panties were getting wet. He wasn't the man she should want. He wasn't safe. But . . .

He was strong. Sexy.

And she'd touched his wild side once.

Zane's mouth tore from hers, and Jana could have howled in frustration. "Did you do it?" The words were so deep that she almost couldn't understand him.

Jana swiped her tongue over her lips and tasted him.

Zane's cheeks were flushed. *"Did you do it?"*

Then she realized what he was asking. The building in New Orleans. The humans. The fire. She smiled at him and, still on her toes, she came in close and licked his upper lip.

His body tensed. Rock hard.

The two of them together—it would have been a fantastic ride. Her lashes lifted, and she gazed up into his eyes. "Yes, I burned them." She let her smile widen. "I burned that pit to the ground, and I didn't care that they were inside." She'd actually made certain they *were* inside.

Sometimes, she was a stickler for details like that.

Because she knew Zane was going to turn her in, she went for broke. She whispered the secret she'd kept. "I could hear them screaming. The fire killed them, not the smoke." They hadn't died easily.

Pain for pain. The bastards had deserved to suffer. But would Zane believe her if she told him that? No one had ever believed her before.

Not her mother.

Not the doctors.

Not her lovers.

Why should he be any different? Hell, his job was to take her down. He'd read her bio. Seen everything she'd done.

Maybe that's why she wanted him. He knew everything. Knew the hell she'd brought, and he still touched her. Still kissed her with passion and lust, like she was any other woman.

But then, he wasn't just any other man.

"No regrets?" he asked her, voice gruff.

She eased away from him. "Not a one."

His fingers touched her mouth. "When you lie . . . the right side of your mouth kicks up."

What?

"It almost looks like you're smiling, but it's a lie, too, right?"

Jana turned away from him. She'd have to watch herself with Zane. But she wouldn't be with him much longer. "Why'd you say it would take an hour to get back to Night Watch?" She stared at the swamp. Those trees were so twisted and hunched. And the water such a dark green.

"Because we don't want to risk running into our cop friend again. We're taking the long way home, baby." His hand pressed against her back, urging her toward the motorcycle.

He climbed on first. She followed, moving to hold him tight. She was getting pretty tired of following him, but her leash didn't give her much choice.

"Did they deserve it?" he asked, not starting the engine. "Did they deserve to have the flesh burned from them by the flames?"

She pressed her cheek against his back. Sometimes, she just felt tired. "Yes."

Since he couldn't see her face, he wouldn't know if she was lying . . . or telling the truth.

Antonio pulled to a stop at the scene just as the ambulance arrived. The patrol car was parked on the side of the road, its light still flashing. The cop—a rookie named Peter Harris— was propped up beside the car. Blood trickled down his face, and his head sagged back.

Antonio jumped out of his car and ran to Harris. "What the hell happened here?" When he'd gotten a report of the 10-108, officer needing assistance, his gut had cramped. Then he'd heard the radio call: *Wynter and the woman had been on the scene.*

Harris tried to stand, but he slid back down to the ground with a groan. The car's front windshield was smashed, and glass shards lay scattered all over the road and the nearby grass.

But there was no sign of Zane. Or of the woman.

"Saw the woman . . . APB . . ." Harris sucked in a sharp breath when the EMT began to check his head wound. "She was . . . riding on a motorcycle with some guy—the bastard attacked me." His gray eyes stared up at Tony. "Threw me ten feet . . . but I-I swear I never saw him . . . move."

Antonio didn't let his expression waver. "Describe the bastard, officer."

"B-big guy . . ." The EMTs were loading Harris onto a stretcher. "About six-foot-two, maybe three." His lashes lowered and he blinked a few times. "Two-two hundred pounds." His head sagged a bit.

"What color was his hair? His eyes?" Antonio pressed

Harris didn't answer. The EMTs tried to take the injured cop to the ambulance. Antonio stepped right in their path. "Harris isn't going anywhere yet." Not until he could figure out what was happening.

"Harris!" He injected a note of steely command into his voice. The cop's eyelids jerked open. "Describe the man, *now.*"

"B-black hair. Caucasian . . . early th-thirties."

Okay, that description only fit thousands of men in the area.

"Heard her call . . . his name." The cop blinked, then met Antonio's gaze. "Z-Zane . . . she said Zane."

What the hell are you doing, man? "I gave strict orders that the woman wasn't to be approached. I was to be notified before any apprehension effort." Cold, clipped.

Harris licked his lips. "They were . . . on a motorcycle. . . ."

"He's got a concussion, Captain," one of the EMTS said, breaking through Harris's words. "We need to get him checked at the hospital."

In a minute. Antonio didn't move.

"I just stopped them . . . because they didn't have on . . . helmets. I stopped . . . them." A hard swallow. "And he attacked."

But that didn't make any sense.

"*Sir* . . ." The EMT's face was flushed a dark red. "He needs to be in a hospital."

Clenching his teeth, Antonio moved to the side.

"You never said"—Harris's voice had grown weaker— "she had a . . . partner."

Because he hadn't known that Zane was working with the woman, and he sure hadn't expected the hunter to attack a cop.

What are you doing, Zane? What the hell are you doing?

Antonio turned away and marched back to his car.

Threw me ten feet . . . but I-I swear I never saw him . . . move. Harris's words echoed in his mind. The cop didn't understand. Zane hadn't actually moved. He was such a strong demon, he didn't need to move. With just a stray thought, Zane could have thrown the cop. With a wave of his hand, he could have killed the guy.

But he hadn't. Zane had let the cop live, and he'd protected the woman.

"Sir!" Another uniform hurried toward him. This time, the officer was female. The uniforms were swarming the scene like bees now. "Do you want to launch a search in the area for the woman?"

Antonio let his stare drift down the road. No sign of a motorcycle now.

"And what about the man?" she pressed. "Do we need to put out an APB for him—"

"Forget the man. Just concentrate on her." *Jana Carter.*

"But a cop was assaulted, one of our own." Her red brows snapped low. "We need to—"

"You need to do whatever the hell I say." He sounded like a prick, but she'd have to deal with it. "I'll take care of the man. You focus on *her.*"

Before he threw his friend to the wolves—or the cops—he needed to find out exactly what was happening with Zane. If he found out that the demon had crossed the line, well—

Then I'll be the first one in line to take him down.

Zane eased the motorcycle to a stop near the curb. The Night Watch building waited, just a few blocks away. He could easily see the stark lines and the old bricks of the hunting office.

He braced the kickstand and killed the motor. This was it. Time to turn in his bounty.

Zane looked over his shoulder. Jana's face was as smooth and blank as marble. No heat in those dark blue eyes. No fiery emotion on her face. Just . . . blank. Empty.

He didn't like that. The woman was many things, but "blank" wasn't one of 'em.

"Come on," he said, rising. "It's time to get you inside." But, dammit, something felt *wrong.*

I burned that pit to the ground and I didn't care that they were inside. Hard words, but when she'd said them, Jana's voice had trembled.

He stared down at her hand and frowned when he saw the dark skin around the handcuff. "Fuck." He reached for her wrist, lifting it lightly. A circle of dark bruises had already formed on her flesh.

"Don't worry about it," she said, and her voice was as cold as her face. "I bruise easily. A human trait. We just aren't built strong enough."

His fingers feathered over her skin, and Zane heard the soft rasp of her breath. "I didn't mean to hurt you." He'd thought she would be deposited at Night Watch less than an hour after he'd cuffed her. He'd never planned on all . . . this.

Her gaze held his.

The woman was beautiful. No, *sexy*. He could still taste her, and he wanted more.

But . . . *killer*. If the file was right, he was staring at a cold, calculating killer. One who torched for money. An assassin.

Until now, she hadn't struck him as cold. With her face locked in that icy mask, with her eyes so blank—yeah, frigid came to mind.

Before, though, she'd been a different woman. Wild. Passionate. Never cold. And when she'd talked about New Orleans . . .

His fingers curled around her right wrist. "Tell me about New Orleans. Tell me what really happened."

Night Watch waited just over her shoulder. The place could keep waiting.

Her smile was sad. "Why? Are you going to save me, demon? Are you going to help me? Turn your back on everything you know and protect me?"

That last line caught him. "Just what do you need protecting from?" Not what, who.

She didn't blink, but the right side of her mouth kicked up, just a bit. "No one. I'm the badass Ignitor, remember? The world needs to fear me."

She was, but she was also right about something else: Humans were weak. So easily broken. Killed.

She tugged away from him, shifting her body to face the Night Watch building. "Let's get this over with. If we stand around out here, we might as well paint bull's-eyes on our backs."

"*I can help you.*" The words were torn from him. It didn't

have to be this way. She didn't have to keep charging up, didn't have to keep killing. There was more to her. He knew it.

Jana tossed him a quick look over her shoulder. "No, you can't." The cold glass had shattered in her eyes. He could see her pain and sadness now.

Then she looked away, and he felt like she'd slugged him. "Jana . . ."

The doors to Night Watch burst open. Three hunters ran out and headed for them. Jude led the other two men, his blond hair shining in the sun as he charged for Jana and Zane.

"Guess that's the welcome party." Her attention focused on the hunters. Her silky black hair dipped down her back. "We don't want to keep them waiting."

She stepped forward, tugging him with her. His eyes focused on Jude. This was what he wanted. What he had to do. *Turn her in.* They'd take her inside Night Watch and—

The explosion shook the street. The blast threw the three hunters to the ground as the windows of Night Watch exploded and fire blazed from the windows. Car alarms screeched down the street, and smoke billowed into the air.

And Jana just stood there, staring at the burning building. The building that housed his co-workers. His friends.

She'd gone back too easy.

"Fuck!" He spun Jana around. "What the hell did you—"

Horror was reflected in her wide eyes. Shock. Her eyes—they were blue. Not the red of an Ignitor charging up.

Still blue.

She hadn't set the fire.

If not her . . .

His gaze flew to the building. People were running out, coughing, screaming.

He raced for the building.

"Zane!" Jana stumbled after him. Shit, *the cuffs.*

"We've got to stop it!" They could. Or at least they could push the flames back long enough to get the people to safety.

But, dammit, those flames were so hot that he could already feel their breath on his skin.

Pak stumbled out with ash coating his face. He had his hands around one of the female hunters, and they were both gasping. Charmers didn't have the enhanced strength of the shifters and demons. They were almost as weak as humans.

And there *were* humans inside that building. Humans who wouldn't last long—humans who were probably already dead.

Too hot.

He sent a blast of power at the flames, forcing them back. "See if you can get control of it," he told Jana. "We've got to get them out, we—"

Jude surged to his feet. His fangs were out, his claws ready to rip and slash. "What the hell? That bitch burned Night Watch!" He lunged for Jana.

Zane stepped between them. *"It wasn't her."* He shoved his left hand against Jude's chest. "Dammit, shifter, stand down. We can help!"

Jude growled at him.

"Trust me," Zane snapped right back.

Jude's eyes searched his. Then the shifter inclined his head in a grudging nod.

They all ran for the building, with Zane in the lead. They plunged right into the smoke and the screaming flames.

Survivors. They had to find the survivors and get them out. The heat scorched his skin and Zane threw his power at the fire, sending the flames sputtering back. Jude grabbed an unconscious hunter from the office on the left and threw the guy over his shoulder.

Jana coughed behind him. *Human. Weak.*

He glanced at her, his eyes watering. Her stare was red now, reflecting the flames, and he knew she was using her power to control the flames. No, to make her *own* fire in an effort to gain control of the other flames. Fighting fire with fire actually fucking worked.

They advanced slowly, painfully, through the smoke and

fire. He passed two bodies. A secretary and a hunter who wouldn't be making it out. Then they found a demon, low level, cowering in the storage room. They pushed back the fire and sent the guy running for safety.

The fire had eaten too much of the walls. Groans echoed from above them, and Zane knew the roof wouldn't last much longer.

Jude was back, coughing and panting beside him.

"Anyone else?" Zane had to shout the words.

Jude's head tilted to the right. That shifter hearing was far stronger than a demon's.

The shifter pointed. They raced for the door. Ripped it open.

Penelope Evans, a new hunter, lay slumped on the floor. Her red hair stuck to her face. Jude grabbed her and hoisted her into his arms.

"Anyone . . . else?"

A hard shake of Jude's head. "Not alive."

The ceiling groaned again, and plaster fell to the floor. Time to get out of hell. Zane waved his hands, shoving back the fire as Jude raced for the door.

"Come on," he told Jana, covering his mouth with his left hand, "let's—"

She slumped beside him. Fell into his arms.

Too much smoke.

Dammit, how dumb could he be! Ignitors could start the fires, they could shoot out those flames, but their bodies couldn't handle the smoke. That's why they worked better from a distance. Long-range assassins. See the target, send the flames, escape.

He held her tight against his chest and ran for the door, dodging the lingering flames and the falling debris. *Hold on, baby. Hold on.*

Zane burst through the broken remains of the front entrance just seconds after Jude. He rushed forward, nearly slamming into the firefighters who charged toward the building.

EMTs were there. They tried to take Jana from him. Tried to pull her from his arms. "No, dammit!" He coughed and tasted ash. "We're cuffed!" They weren't taking her any place without him. He held her tighter and hurried to the ambulance. She'd need oxygen, fast. She needed to breathe clean air. Her mouth and nose were stained with ash. He put her on the stretcher. The EMT placed a mask over her face.

"Get her a blanket!" Zane held her hand, probably too tightly but screw it. "She's freezing." Her body had begun to shake. "Jana?"

She moaned into the mask.

He was such a fucking idiot. She couldn't handle the heat. He *knew* that. *All* the *Other* knew that about Ignitors. They could bring the heat, but the smoke—hell, it was fucking poison to them. *They could control the flames, not the smoke.*

A heavy hand landed on his shoulder. He looked back and saw Pak staring at Jana.

"It wasn't her!" Zane fired. "Look, I know what you're thinking," what he'd thought, "but it wasn't her. She helped me. We saved as many as we could!" But Zane had seen the dead, and he would remember them for the rest of his life.

Hollings, the charmer who had a way with the ladies. Giles Lang, the hybrid demon who'd been trying to fit in. Stacey Keith . . . ah, hell, she'd been a year away from retirement.

All gone.

His thumb brushed over Jana's knuckles. "She didn't do it," he said again.

"Then who the hell did?" The fierce question didn't come from Pak. Jude had stalked up to the ambulance, and he watched Jana with eyes that glowed too bright. "There was no accelerant. I didn't catch so much as a whiff of scent—"

Jana's fingers tightened around Zane's. His gaze snapped back to her face. Her eyes were opening, slowly, and the twinge of red still remained.

"A fucking Ignitor."

She flinched at Jude's snarl.

Zane hunched over her. "Back off!" He took a breath. Her eyes were on him. "It's okay." His voice was still rough, but softer, for her. "You're going to be all right." She looked so vulnerable. So defenseless. Another one of her tricks? A quick deception?

No. She'd fallen in that inferno. She'd sagged in his arms, and fear had iced his heart. "Just breathe, baby."

But she was shaking her head. She shoved off the mask and started coughing.

"Jana!"

Tears leaked from her eyes. "How . . . many dead?"

His lips thinned. "At least three." The fire had been too strong.

As he watched Jana, the vulnerability slowly disappeared. She swiped away the tears from her cheeks. The fear and the horror disappeared from her face until . . . nothing remained.

Now she's pretending. The mask was back, and he didn't like it one bit.

She pushed up on the gurney and the blanket fell away. "We need to get out of here," she whispered, her voice hoarse from the smoke. "This was an attack, it was—"

"*Wynter!*"

Aw, hell. *Not* what he needed right then. His gaze flew to the left. Jude was already edging back, and Captain Antonio Young was shoving his way through the crowd to get to them. The guy's badge gleamed on his hip, and the butt of his gun poked from the holster on his side.

"Zane?" A thread of worry whispered in Jana's voice. "A cop?"

Their last encounter with a cop hadn't gone so well. But this time would be different. He realized he still had a hard grip on her hand. Zane forced himself to let her go. "It's okay, baby, he's on our side."

Then Tony was there. His glittering eyes swept over the group and lingered on Jana. "Ms. Carter?"

She nodded. The red still lingered in her gaze. Her eyes appeared bloodshot now.

"Jana Carter, you're under arrest." Tony reached for her hand and hauled Jana to her feet.

"No, man, wait!" The *other* cuff glinted between their outstretched hands.

But Tony shook his head. "You know she's going in." He jerked his thumb back at the burning building. "Seriously, what the hell were you thinking?"

Jana laughed. A hollow, mocking sound. "Guess he's not on *our* side." Her chin tilted up, just a bit. "Maybe he's just on yours, hmm, demon? Use me, then throw me to the wolves."

No, that wasn't—

Tony started reading Jana her rights.

Fuck.

Chapter 6

The door to interrogation room three closed with a soft click. Jana took a deep breath. Not like this was the first time she had found herself in one of these tiny rooms, sitting at an old, scarred table, and facing off against a cop who wanted to throw her butt in jail.

"I'm Captain Antonio Young," the cop said, as he took a step closer to her.

"We know who the hell you are, Tony," Zane muttered from her side. Because, yeah, they were still handcuffed. Still locked together. Covered in soot and ash, they'd been through fires hotter than those in hell, and they were *still* cuffed.

The cop—Tony—raised one dark brow. "You know who I am, Ms. Carter?"

Well, she did now, so Jana kept her face expressionless. Oh, she *hurt*. Every part of her body ached, and she just wanted to crawl into bed and sleep for a week.

Preferably without being handcuffed to a demon.

But at least the cops had sent some food in to her and Zane. Only because of Zane's connections. Otherwise, Jana knew she never would have gotten those stale doughnuts and that coffee with the grounds floating at the top.

Tony pulled out the chair across from them, and its legs scraped against the floor. "Which one of you wants to tell me what the hell is going on here?"

"If I knew," Zane said instantly, "I'd tell you."

Of course, he would. "Good" guys always liked to rat to cops.

"Hmmm." Tony's dark eyes dropped to the handcuffs. The metal shined on the top of the table. "Guessing those are P.P.?"

"P.P.?" Was that frog's croak hers? Great. Her life was fan-damn-tastic.

"Paranormal protected," he murmured.

So he knew. Good for him. "What are you?" she asked, straining to make her voice stronger. Damn smoke.

His gaze shifted to hers. "I told you already, I'm a police captain."

His eyes were so dark they almost looked black. The guy had a deep olive skin tone, a perfect face, and a voice like warm honey. "You an incubus?"

He blinked and, wait, did his high cheeks redden?

"He's no damn incubus," Zane said and a thread of anger roughened the words. Sure, he'd gone through the smoke, but he sounded perfectly normal. Demon strength and healing powers had their benefits. "He's human."

"We can't all be demons," the cop said quietly.

A human who knew Zane's secrets? Interesting.

Tony leaned forward. "Why'd you attack my man, Zane?" The question was fired fast.

His man? Oh, the other cop. "Because your *man* fired on us," Jana answered immediately, not waiting for Zane to respond. She wouldn't let Zane take the heat for this. Not when that cop had come out with his gun blazing.

Tony's lips tightened. "Bullshit. I gave an order—"

"Oh, you gave it all right," she shot back, her hands knotting into fists. "Deadly force was fine as long as it was directed at Zane, right? What's a dead demon when—"

But the cop wasn't looking at her. He shook his head, slowly, and a deep furrow appeared between his eyes. "He fired on you?"

Zane lifted his hand, raising the cuffs. "First he tried to . . .

ah, break us apart with a bullet. When that didn't work, well, he said I was the expendable one."

"Fuck." Not disbelief. Shock. Wait, did he believe what they were saying?

Jana glanced between them. "You ordered a hit on him, you—"

"Ease up, princess," Tony said.

What? Her eyes narrowed on him.

"I've got a rat in my unit." Tony shook his head again, and his shoulders slumped a bit. "What the hell is happening?"

The guy was playing innocent, *that* was happening. She'd never met an innocent cop. Plenty who were on the take. Plenty who knew how to look the other way, but innocent? No way.

"How'd the fire start at Night Watch?" Tony asked, and that fast, the cop's eyes were back on her.

Jana shrugged. "You tell me, *princess.*"

His eyes narrowed, just a fraction. "You're a wanted woman. How about I just go and throw you in a cage until it's time to haul you back to New Orleans?"

"*Tony,*" Zane's voice snarled, "you're not—"

She yanked on the cuffs. "You really going to throw us *both* in jail?"

Tony put his hands on the table and leaned toward her. "I know what you are."

"Bored?"

"Dammit, Jana!" Zane's hand slapped on the table, making it shudder. "Just let him—"

"You're an Ignitor." Tony pressed closer. "You like the fire, don't you? You like to see those flames dance and destroy."

She didn't speak. Beside her, Zane seemed to be all but vibrating with tension.

"Zane was going to turn you in at Night Watch, wasn't he?" The cop's dark stare held hers. She could see the faintest flecks of gold around his pupils. "That's why you're cuffed. He was forcing you to come with him."

She stared back at Tony and didn't speak. Her hands flattened on the table.

"That made you angry, didn't it? You couldn't get him to let you go, and it pissed you off. And when Ignitors get pissed"—a brief pause—"things have a way of exploding."

"She didn't do it," Zane gritted out. "Trust me on this, okay?"

"I would." Tony's gaze slanted to Zane. "But I can't be sure if your brain's talking, or your dick."

Her nails scraped over the tabletop.

"You left with her last night." Tony exhaled. "You stayed with her, *all* night. While you were cuffed, I'm sure the two of you were playing . . . nicely."

"I was fucking drugged! I was out of my head, I don't know—" Zane broke off and rolled his shoulders, as if he were shaking off the memory.

"Drugged?" Tony blinked. "*You* were—"

"You found my car, right?" Zane's lips tightened. "Some assholes hit us. Slammed into my 'Vette. They fired at us and caught me twice with some kind of drug."

"Who were the 'assholes'?"

Jana shrugged. "Why don't you go ask your cop? You know, the one who was so eager to shoot Zane and take me into custody?" She bared her teeth in a hard smile. "I'll give you ten-to-one odds that he knows exactly who *they* are."

Tony glared back at her, but after a few moments, he eased away and turned on his heel, marching for the door.

"Tony?" Zane called.

"I'm going to find Harris," he said and yanked open the door. "He's the cop who pulled you over."

The one who'd tried to kill Zane.

"Yeah, you go find that little bastard," Zane said, and she heard the underlying threat in his voice. *Find him and let me have him.*

Jana didn't take a full breath until Tony left the room. When the door clicked closed behind him, the tension eased from her shoulders. Well, some of the tension eased.

Her gaze darted to the mirrored wall on the left side. Was she still being watched?

"Tony won't let anyone view us. He won't run the risk of them finding out what you are."

Jana glanced at him.

Zane ran a tired hand down his face, streaking the ash. "What *we* are."

"You sure about that?" She didn't have enhanced senses. She'd never know if someone was there.

Zane tossed a glance at the mirror. "I'm sure."

Okay. That was something. "We've got to get out of here." Her palms were slick with sweat.

One brow climbed. "Baby, we're not going anywhere." He caught the edge of her chair and hauled her closer. "Three hunters are dead. *Dead.* The Night Watch Agency was torched, torched right before—what a damn coincidence—you were scheduled to be turned in."

She swallowed. Time to gamble. "We know it wasn't a co-incidence." She risked a quick glance at the mirror. If some-one was there, she was slitting her own throat. "*We need to get out of here.*" A heated whisper.

Zane shook his head. "You tell me what's happening. Tell me who targeted Night Watch, *my* people."

She'd already warned him to walk away. He should have listened but, apparently, the demon didn't listen well. "If you know, you're dead." They wouldn't let him live. Demons were expendable to them.

"No, baby." His fingers brushed over her cheek. "When I know, *they're* dead." Soft menace underscored the words.

The wooden chair was so hard beneath her. "Get me out of here, and I'll tell you everything."

"Tell me, and we'll work on getting out." His fingers curled under her chin and tilted her head back. "Was it those men in the semi?"

Those men had been humans. They wouldn't have been able to handle an explosion that big. "No . . . probably some-one else in the unit."

"The unit?"

Her smile felt sad on her lips. "You don't really think you're the only hunter out there, do you?" A hard, brittle laugh. "While you're hunting your prey, who do you think is hunting *you?*"

His brows climbed. "Those jerks were humans. Humans can't—"

"Some humans are very good at hunting." Especially if they forced someone else to do the grunt work. "Some humans don't think demons and vampires and shifters deserve to live in this world. They think monsters should be put down, by any means necessary." She'd been that means before.

"That right? And these . . . hunters . . . why do they want you?"

She had to glance at the mirror. *What if someone was watching?* "Why do you think?"

"Because you're their weapon of choice?" Disgust. "All they have to do is aim and you fire?"

She wouldn't flinch. "I've been trying to get away from them for over a year. Why do you think I burned down that compound in New Orleans? They'd been holding me there."

So many days stuck in that damn cell. Trapped.

Tony thought he'd lock her up again? Oh, hell, no. No one would lock her up.

"Bullshit. You could have burned your way out any time—"

"I have to see in order to burn." He knew that. "They kept me blindfolded or locked in a pitch-black cell." Hell wasn't always hot and bright. Sometimes it was dark . . . and so quiet. "The first time they slipped, the first time the blindfold came off . . ."

She could still hear the screams. Jana licked her lips. "Their mistake. I got out." She'd made sure she brought that building down behind her.

"But now they want you back."

"Looks like it." They were wasting time. One cop was already on their payroll. Where there was one, there were always half a dozen more. They'd be at the station soon. Maybe posing as cops. Maybe dressed like lawyers. But they'd be there to take her.

And what would happen to Zane?

"Give me a name."

Her lips parted. Footsteps thudded outside the door. *Tony was coming back.*

Zane's eyes stayed locked on her. "Tell me who's after you. *Tell me.*"

"They said—they said they were members of Project Perseus." *Perseus.* The guy from Greek mythology who'd fought the monsters.

But some monsters didn't need to die.

"Did you work with them? Did you kill for them?"

Jana took a breath. *The right side of your mouth kicks up when you lie.* "Yes."

His eyes narrowed.

"If I stay here, they *will* come for me, and they'll kill anyone in their path." No telling how many cops they already had on their payroll. "They're framing me, forcing me against the wall."

"And what—you want me to bust you out of jail? Baby, that's just—"

"A jail won't hold me." Simple. "I can burn my way out, and I will." Because she wouldn't wait on them to come and get her.

"No, you won't." He blew out a breath. "Not when there's another way."

Hope began to stir in her chest. "You'll help me?"

His jaw clenched.

"Zane?"

The interrogation room door swung open. "We've got a problem." Tony marched inside, shaking his head. "Officer Harris seems to be *missing* from the hospital. He's not answering his cell, and no one knows where the hell he is."

"We have to get out," Jana said. Didn't he see what was

happening? Another Ignitor . . . or a damn powerful demon . . . had set the fire at Night Watch. It was only a matter of time until they came for her.

A setup. The team after her must have bugged the phone lines at Night Watch. They'd known she was coming. They'd started that fire *for* her.

Why? So that the cops would haul her to the station? Of course, the cops on scene would pick her as suspect number one. With her history, there was no way they wouldn't have hauled her in for questioning.

Those bastards knew that.

Zane's fingers tapped on the tabletop. "I need to be on the streets, Tony."

"*You* can be. She can't." He exhaled. "This case is shit. We both know the woman gets off on the fire, are you sure—"

"You don't know what gets her off." Zane's voice. Cold and hard.

"You *know* better than to let the case get personal." Tony stalked around the table and grabbed Zane's arm. He hauled Zane to his feet, grabbing for the cuffs. "Let's find a way out of these damned things and you can get on the streets. You can find Harris for me—"

He never finished his sentence. Zane's fist plowed into Tony's jaw, and the cop went down. Hard.

Jana jumped to her feet. "*What are you doing?*" She'd thought the cop was his friend.

Zane pulled her forward as he rolled Tony onto his back. "I'm making sure we get out before the bastards after you get to us."

He'd attacked a cop. Not a very "good" guy thing to do.

Zane glanced back at her. "They herded you to the station. They're going to be sending someone for you. Maybe Feds, maybe someone pretending to be Feds, but they'll have paperwork, all nice and neat, saying they can take you into custody." He paused. "They'll take you, and no one will see you again."

No, he was wrong. They'd take her . . . and they'd *use* her. The price for her life would be death for others.

"Come on, we need to get the hell out of here." He frowned down at the cop. "Sorry, Tony."

Sorry? *Sorry?* "What's going to happen to him?"

"He'll get to deny helping us escape. He'll have the bruise to prove he was hit. He'll be clear. . . ." Zane hurried away from the table, pulling her with him. "And, in a few minutes, so will we."

His fingers curled around the doorknob.

She grabbed his shoulder. "This place will be crawling with cops! We won't be able to just walk out, we can't—"

"Tony sent 'em away."

"Why would he—"

"Look, baby, *trust me* on this, okay? Tony knows the deal around here. When he found out Harris was missing, he knew what was going down. Hell, why do you think he came close enough for me to hit?"

The cop had wanted them to escape? Since when did a cop want someone to break out?

"Not like it's the first time we played this game. . . ." Zane inched open the door and gave a nod. "All right, we're gonna have to move quickly. Don't fight me. Whatever I do, just go with it, okay?"

She would have gone with just about anything right then. She nodded her head in agreement and then realized he couldn't see the move. "Let's get out of here."

"On three . . ."

He began to softly whisper the count, and when he got to three, they ran into the hall, darting fast in a series of twists and turns. The place looked deserted, but she could hear voices, phones. She kept her head down and followed Zane, moving as quickly as she could.

Five more feet, and they were at a door with a red exit sign. *Go, go.* Footsteps tapped behind them.

Zane shoved open the door and yanked her across the threshold. The door shut with a clang behind them.

Jana's head was pressed against Zane's chest. She could hear the fierce pounding of his heart, racing so fast.

"Stay behind me," he murmured, and then he pulled back. They eased down two flights of stairs, going deeper into the bowels of the precinct.

Minutes later, they came out in the garage. Squad cars were scattered around, waiting.

Time to steal another ride?

"Don't even think about it," Zane said. "The second we vanish in one of those, every cop in the area will be after us."

"Then what are we going to do?" Someone would be raising the alarm any minute, she knew it, she knew—

"See that door? It leads to the alley. Come on, move that sweet ass, baby."

She hauled ass.

A hard push from Zane, and the door flew open. They stumbled outside. She looked to the left, to the right, and—

"Damn, hoss, it took you long enough," a deep voice rumbled and Jana froze. "I was starting to think I'd have to come in and haul your sorry hide out."

Zane grunted and headed for the big, blond guy—the guy from Night Watch. The shifter who'd gone into the fire with them. The guy stood next to a green pickup truck, his arms crossed over his chest.

"It's not as easy to slip out of a police station as it is to slip into one," Zane said and opened the passenger side door.

Jana jumped in as the blond hurried around the truck and opened the driver's side door. She had to ask, "How did you know we—"

"Tony called. He said you needed a ride." The shifter fired up the engine. "Lucky for you, I was in the neighborhood."

It's not the first time we've played this game. Huh. The cop really had been helping them.

Zane crowded in on the other side and she was squeezed between the two big, masculine frames. The blond hit the gas and the truck sped forward. "Got orders from Pak to take you to a safe house. He wants you to stay there until we can get this shit straightened out."

"How many dead, Jude?" Zane demanded.

Jana licked her lips.

"Five total," the guy—Jude—said. "You got the rest out."

Five people. Why had they died? To teach her a lesson? Her hands fisted and her nails bit into her palms. She'd make sure the bastards paid for this.

"They knew we were coming, Jude," Zane said and his arm rubbed against hers. Hell, his whole body rubbed against hers. That strong thigh was pressed to her leg.

"They probably tapped the line," Jana forced herself to say what she suspected.

Jude grunted. "Maybe. Pak's doing a housecleaning. There's no way that fire should have started, not with our security systems in place."

A housecleaning?

Jude turned a hard left, and the truck drove down a long, narrow road. "Lady, if you're such a badass, why'd you go running *into* the fire?"

She lifted the cuffs. "I didn't exactly have much choice."

Zane's finger touched the edge of her mouth, and she realized that the right side of her lip had hitched up.

Lie.

She swallowed.

Zane edged closer to her. His breath feathered over her ear when he said, "As soon as I get you alone, you're telling me everything. *Everything.*"

But he wouldn't want to hear her secrets, and she didn't want to tell them. Sometimes, she liked to forget who she was, and what she'd done.

"They made it personal," he said, the words dark and deadly and a shiver slipped over her. "They came after my people, and they're damn well going to pay."

She turned and met his stare. Black, not green. The demon was out to play. "I tell you, and then you let me go?"

He'd broken her out of jail. That had to mean something, didn't it?

He held her stare. His expression never changed. "Of course."

And this time, she was the one who knew: *lie.*

"Where the hell are they?"

Antonio cracked open one eye at the screeching voice. He was flat on the floor, and his jaw ached like a bitch.

He'd also spent the last five minutes pretending to be out cold. *Like Zane could really take me with one punch.* The guy thought he had a fist of steel—not so much. Especially not since Zane had a tendency to pull his punches with friends.

Antonio let a moan break from his lips, and he made a show of pushing himself off the floor. "Wh-what . . ." He shook his head. "What happened?" Did he sound weak enough? Maybe.

He squinted and allowed his gaze to drift around the room. He saw the shoes first. Two-inch black heels. Long legs. His gaze rose. A woman stood in the doorway of the interrogation room. Her dark blond hair was pulled back at her nape. Her green eyes glittered—oh, yeah, a lot of rage there.

A man was behind her, tall, balding, and peering over her shoulder.

"Who are you?" Antonio asked as he rose to his feet. He shifted his jaw. Zane hadn't pulled the punch *that* much. "What the—where the hell are the prisoners?"

The woman shook her head. "You expect me to believe this bull?"

He stumbled and his legs rammed into the thick table.

A badge was slapped onto the table. "FBI Special Agent Kelly Thomas." Her red nails tapped the badge. "I'm here to pick up your prisoner, Jana Carter." She paused a beat. "And you'd better tell me that Ms. Carter is just down the hall, getting fingerprinted."

"I . . . don't remember. . . . Something hit me. . . ."

She swore and spun around, colliding with the guy. "They're gone! Christ, we've got to call headquarters."

The guy jerked out his phone and began punching numbers.

She tossed a hard glare back at Antonio. "Captain Young, you've made a serious mistake."

"Mistake? Lady, I was assaulted!"

Her lips curled in disgust. "You think I don't know about you? You chose the wrong side."

His shoulders straightened. "And what side would that be?"

She snatched back her badge. "The side with the freaks. You want to screw with them, that's your mistake."

Screw with them?

"It's a mistake that I'll make sure you regret," she promised.

He waited until the lady and her partner stormed out, then he took out his phone. Two seconds later, he'd connected to the most powerful man in Baton Rouge. "Hey, Pak. I got a name for you. Kelly Thomas." He listened a moment and then said, "You were right, she came for the Ignitor."

The FBI agent would realize soon enough . . . he never did a damn thing that he regretted. Could she say the same thing?

They were dropped off in the swamp and left at a cabin that lurked on the edge of darkness. *Another cabin.* Only this one looked much better than their last shelter.

"*Your* place?" Zane asked Jude when he climbed out of the truck. "Does Erin know about this?" Jana followed him around the front of the truck. Who was Erin? Another hunter?

"Uh . . ." Jude blinked slowly. "Are you asking if the *assistant district attorney* knows that I just aided and abetted an escape from the Baton Rouge Police Department?"

"Yeah."

Jude tossed him a set of keys. "Sure she does. The woman knows everything I do."

Zane's fingers curled around the keys. "Thanks, man."

A wide smile, one that flashed with lots of sharp, white teeth, stretched Jude's mouth. "Now we're even, demon."

Until next time.

"A motorcycle is around back, *with* helmets. If you two need to make a quick exit . . . well, just watch your asses."

"Will do."

"Lay low, Zane. At least until we figure out who we're up against."

Jana felt Zane's stare shift to her. "Don't worry. We'll be figuring out this game very soon."

He thought she'd tell him. He wanted all the dirty little secrets, and he deserved to know.

She just . . . didn't want him to know the truth. But, really, what was a little death between two friends? Not that they were actually friends. . . .

The other hunter drove away. Dusk was coming, falling fast, and bringing a chill to the air. They went inside and, though the place was small, Jana was happy to see a *clean* bed. And food. Sweet, blessed food.

And . . . a bathroom. With a shower. Oh, heaven.

"I want to know about Project Perseus."

Of course he did.

"Tell me who the big players are. Tell me what the hell they want."

She didn't want to talk then. It had truly been a pisser of a day. Jana began to strip.

Beside her, Zane stiffened. "Ah . . . what are you doing?"

He was a bright demon. Surely he could figure this out. She kicked off her shoes. Shoved off her socks. Then her fingers went to the buckle on her jeans.

"Jana!"

The jeans hit the floor. She kept her panties on, for now. Jana slanted him a fast look. "In case you haven't noticed"—

but she was sure he had—"I'm covered in ash, grime, blood, and who the hell knows what else. I'm showering." She took a nice, slow breath. "And since you're stuck to me, you're coming in, too." Zane. Hot water. Naked flesh.

Things were about to get wild.

Just what she wanted. What she needed.

No past. No secrets. Just them.

"Do me a favor?" she whispered and raised her brows. The cuffs would be a problem for her, but there was a way around them. All he had to do was . . . "Rip my shirt off?"

Payment Receipt

Henderson County Public Library (HCPL)
270-826-3712
www.hcpl.org
Tuesday, May 28, 2013 2:11:18 PM

WALKER, MEGAN R.

Title   : Blue's big musical movie
Item barcode : 33009001576380
Material type : DVD
Reason   : Overdue Item
Charge   : $1.00

Title   : Diary of a wimpy kid : Dog days
Item barcode : 33009002391284
Material type : DVD
Reason   : Overdue Item
Charge   : $1.00

Total charges : $2.00
Paid   : $2.00

Account balance: $0.00

Renew items online, by phone, or in person.
Overdue & reserved items cannot be renewed.
Fines on videos & DVDs are $1.00 per day. Fines
on books, audio tapes, & CDs are $0.10 per day.

Chapter 7

"What?" The word broke from Zane, more a growl than anything else.

"Can't really shower with it. Can't get it off over the cuffs." She shrugged and gave him a smile that sent all of his blood rushing down south. "Rip it for me?"

He swallowed and his gaze dropped to her panties. Black panties that were little more than a scrap of silk. "We don't . . . have to do that." The fingers of his right hand uncurled. Jude, bless him, curse him, had slipped him a key. "I've got your ticket to freedom, baby."

Her eyes widened and a pleased smile blossomed on her lips. Damn. She was gorgeous when she smiled.

He lifted the cuffs. He shoved the key in, and the lock *snicked* as the cuffs sprang open.

Then they were free. The cuffs fell to the floor.

Jana stared up at him. Her legs were curvy, smooth, and he wanted to touch them. No, he wanted to spread them and drive fierce and hard inside.

He'd been chained to the woman for over twenty-four hours, and he'd been hard for her most of that time.

Focus. There were questions that needed to be asked. Answers he had to get.

But Jana was lifting the edge of her shirt, revealing her midriff, and he wasn't about to look away. He'd never pretended to be a saint, and he was horny as hell right then.

She tossed the shirt to the floor. Her bra matched the panties and the upper curves of her breasts thrust against the black material. The woman had *great* breasts. Round and firm. What color were her nipples? What would they taste like?

"You're dirty, Zane."

He blinked. Ah . . .

"You might as well shower with me." Then she turned away, her hips rolling in a tempting sway as she headed for the bathroom. As she walked, her hands lifted and she unhooked the bra. It fell in her wake. She glanced back at him. "No drugs are controlling you this time. You know what you're doing now. So do I."

At the bathroom door, she ditched her panties.

His breath hissed out, and his hands fisted.

A moment later, the water roared on. His eyes squeezed shut. She'd be sliding under that water soon, the liquid dripping down her body. Covering every inch of her pale flesh.

If he went in that bathroom, he'd take her. He'd drive into her until they both came, until the need that had been riding him finally eased.

Sex wasn't part of the plan. Sex wasn't—

Fuck it. His eyes flew open, and he bounded across the room in two seconds. He yanked off his shirt. Kicked off his shoes and socks. Lost his jeans . . .

He wrenched back the shower curtain and saw her. Wet hair. Water glistening on her face. On her body.

Pink nipples. Like ripe cherries. He'd always liked cherries.

"What took you so long?" Jana whispered as she reached for him.

Her fingers were wet and warm. Her flesh so soft. He took her mouth, driving his tongue past her lips even as the water pounded down on him.

He'd wanted to fuck her from the first moment he saw her. They'd been surrounded by fire—and he'd *wanted her.*

Zane wasn't used to denying himself pleasures. He'd tried

to hold back with her, but it just wasn't his way. Taking, that was him.

His fingers curved around her hips. She had a fantastic ass. An ass that had driven him crazy. But . . .

His tongue thrust against hers. Zane caught her gasp and he lifted her, easing her back against the tiled wall.

Her thighs parted. Smooth, pale thighs. Thighs that had hugged his hips on that motorcycle. They'd clung so well, and he'd wanted them wrapped around his waist as he thrust deep into her.

Not a safe woman to want. He *knew* that. But then, he wasn't a safe guy.

His fingers slipped between her legs, and he found the hot core of her body. He eased one finger inside her. *Tight.* Sweet hell. She'd feel so damn good around his cock. He pushed another finger inside her, and she tensed.

His lips broke from hers. "Easy."

Her eyes were wide, the pupils big, and red stained her cheeks. But she shook her head. "I don't want easy." Husky, sensual, like whispered sex.

She widened her stance, giving him better, *deeper* access. "Just because I'm human"—a light laugh—"I won't break."

Good to know.

Jana licked his neck, and then he felt the press of her teeth on his flesh. *Yes.* His cock jerked, and his fingers thrust harder into her sex.

Her breath panted out, and she arched against him. "More."

He'd give her as much as she could handle.

"*Zane!*"

He shifted before her, curling over her, and he took one tight nipple into his mouth. *She tasted incredible.* Better than cherries. Much better. He sucked her, tonguing the nipple, and her sex squeezed his fingers.

Oh, yeah, this was going to be good.

Jana's nails dug into his shoulders as he enjoyed her nipples. Sucking, licking, letting her feel the edge of *his* teeth.

Vampires weren't the only ones who liked to bite.

There were no tender touches, no soft looks between them. The heat was too intense, and this—this was no sweet, romantic union.

Sex. Need. Lust.

He lifted her high against the wall. She wrapped her silky legs around him, and his cock pushed against the eager entrance of her sex.

Fuck—condom.

Almost snarling, he jerked back.

"Zane?"

He picked her up in his arms and strode out of the bathroom. The woman didn't weigh a damn thing. He lowered her onto the bed, admired the view of the pink flesh between her legs, and he yanked open the nightstand drawer.

Come on, Jude. Don't let me—ah. A box of condoms waited inside the drawer. Zane was back to owing the guy.

He snatched one out, ripped open the package and rolled the condom over his cock. Jana watched him with those wide eyes, her lips full and red.

Want them on me.

Next time, he'd make sure he got her to use that sexy mouth on him.

But for now . . . His fingers curled around her thighs, and he spread her wider. With one hand, he guided his cock to her entrance. He stared down at her, saw the need and the driving lust in her eyes.

A match for me.

He thrust into her, a long, hard plunge. Her moan filled his ears, and her legs locked tightly around him. Harder, deeper, he drove into her. Again and again. The mattress dipped beneath them, her nails raked his back, and the hunger spiraled higher, hotter.

His hand eased between their bodies. He found her clit and stroked that tight bud. Her head tipped back, those breasts begging for his mouth, and he leaned over her and licked her nipple even as he plunged into her.

Deep.

Her sex squeezed him, so fucking tight.

In. Out. In.

"Zane . . ." The whisper of his name. Her sex grew slicker around him as her body tensed. Her climax was close.

He wanted to feel her come. *Would* feel her.

His thumb pressed against her clit even as he thrust into her once more. She came, a hard ripple of pleasure around him, and her face went blank with pleasure.

Yes. Her inner muscles squeezed his cock.

And his control broke. He shoved into her, as deep as he could go. Again and again. Her scent surrounded him. Her body was crushed beneath his, and her sex—so warm and wet and—he was fucking going out of his mind.

Good.

Hell. *Better than good.*

His balls tightened. He slammed into her once more.

Then he climaxed, shouting her name. Pleasure pounded through him, a release so intense his whole body shuddered.

Pretty damn perfect.

The heat seared him to the core.

She pretended to sleep. Jana lay in Zane's arms, her eyes closed, her breath slow and easy, and she forced her body to stay relaxed.

He'd left her only long enough to shed the condom. He'd fed her. Brought her sandwiches from the kitchen. And now he held her.

She didn't want to talk to him. Didn't want to answer all the questions she knew he had.

What was the point of talking? Lies would do them no good.

Her body still ached, a good, delicious ache. Her sex shivered every few moments with little aftershocks of pleasure that hummed through her system.

The demon was good in bed. Not really surprising.

What was surprising . . . she wanted him again. *Now.*

It was dangerous to want something—or someone—too much. She knew that. Wanting could make you weak.

She'd wanted the sex. Wanted the blast of pleasure and the rush of release that would let her forget, even for a few moments, the life that was hers.

And she'd wanted *him*. Not some nameless stranger from a bar. A man who didn't know how dangerous his lover was. *Zane.*

Because he knew what lurked inside of her.

But with the passion sated, he'd be back to business again. She wouldn't tell him the truth. Couldn't.

Her left arm was thrown out over the pillow. No more handcuffs.

Jana breathed slowly. Zane hadn't moved in the last five minutes. His breathing was light, steady. *Just like mine.*

She risked lifting her lashes, just a crack. His eyes were closed. In sleep, his face was just as hard. Just as dangerous. No softening in slumber for him.

She couldn't let herself forget what he was. *Demon.* One who'd come hunting for her. Sex wouldn't change anything for him. When the time came, he'd still turn her over to Night Watch and he wouldn't look back.

So she wouldn't look back, either.

Slowly, carefully, she eased away from him and off the bed. He shifted a bit, his hand reaching out to follow her, and she froze.

His fingers curled around her pillow, and the frown that had appeared between his brows eased away. Jana started breathing again.

She scooped up her clothes, hopped over the handcuffs on the floor, and crept for the door. No need to waste time looking for the keys to the motorcycle. She'd hotwire the ride and be out of there in no time.

But at the door, she hesitated and glanced back at Zane. His tan body was surrounded by the stark white sheets. He looked sexy, rumpled.

She swallowed. Staying with him wasn't an option. She knew that. Sex had been fun—okay a *lot* more than fun—but it couldn't ever be more than a good time.

Bad things happened to people when they got too close to her. Most of 'em couldn't stand the heat.

Good-bye, Zane. She couldn't let him turn her in, and he would. Once he'd gotten the info he wanted about Project Perseus, he'd go back to collecting his bounty. And what would she do? Live the rest of her days in a cage?

No.

Jana dressed and then slipped out of the cabin. No more looking back.

Zane waited until he heard the soft click of the door closing, then he let his eyes open. His hand smoothed over the sheets that were still warm from Jana's body.

She hadn't waited long to turn tail and run. Hot sex, slam-bam, then she'd been gone.

He'd expected her to run, but . . .

I'd hoped I was wrong.

Innocent people didn't run. He'd learned that lesson a long time ago.

Anger began to churn in his gut. The woman had thought he'd be blinded by the sex. That she'd just be able to slip right past him.

Think again.

He rose from the bed and marched to the table. Jude had left a cell phone for him. He punched in the shifter's number. Jude answered on the second ring, just as Zane heard the roar of a motorcycle's engine flare to life outside.

At least she had a helmet this time.

"She's on the move," he said, running a hand down his face.

"We put a tag on the bike. We'll be able to follow every move that she makes. Get dressed."

Follow because the motorcycle had been a lure for Jana, and she'd taken the bait. No, she was the bait, and he hadn't even realized what game Night Watch intended to play with her until he'd arrived at the cabin, and Jude had mentioned the motorcycle.

Why tell a bounty about an escape vehicle unless you *wanted* her to escape? And then, when Jude had tossed him the keys . . . one glance at the shifter's blue stare and he'd known exactly what Pak wanted them to do.

Let her run. Let her think she was safe. Then track her.

Because while Jana hadn't started the fire at Night Watch, she *was* tied to those flames. The bastards who had set the fire were after her. If Jude and Zane watched her, if they followed her, they'd find the murdering assholes they wanted. Because those assholes would come after her again.

"Where are you?" he asked Jude, as he yanked open the door.

A green pickup shuddered to a stop right in front of the cabin. Zane lowered the phone. Of course, the shifter would have stayed close.

"Come on," Jude yelled through his open window. "I've got the GPS linkup in the truck."

Zane slammed the cabin's door and hurried around the vehicle. He jumped inside, and seconds later, they were racing away from the swamp. He realized his knuckles ached because his hands were clenched so tightly.

"I didn't expect her to run so fast," Jude said as his gaze flickered to Zane.

"Neither did I." And, yeah, stupidly, he'd actually hoped she wouldn't run. He'd hoped Pak and Jude were wrong, that their plan wouldn't work. He'd wanted to open his eyes and see Jana lying next to him, and he'd wanted her to tell him about Project Perseus. Wanted all her secrets.

Fucking delusional.

"You slept with her, didn't you?"

His jaw clenched.

"Come on, hoss, you sleep with every attractive woman you meet." Jude whistled as he turned the wheel to the left. "I just didn't expect you to screw a killer."

Zane's eyes cut to Jude. "*Watch it.*" His voice was lethal and the power within him built, shoving against the bonds of his control.

Jude's gaze darted to him. "What? A friend can't tell you that you're fucking up? With her, you're crossing the line."

He *knew* that, but walking away hadn't been an option. Taking her had been the only choice.

Then *she'd* walked away. But he'd get her back.

"You know, she could be working with them." Jude's voice was softer now. The truck shot past the pine trees, blurring their limbs. "Not once have they tried to actually hurt *her*. Even the cop tried to shoot you, not her."

So Jude had already talked to Tony and gotten all those details, too. Figured. "She's scared of them." He'd seen the fear in her eyes.

"That woman? She's scared of something? You sure about that? She didn't seem like the fearful type to me."

Zane realized he could still smell her. Her scent was all over his skin. Hell, no wonder Jude realized they'd slept together. No way a shifter nose could miss the scent of sex. "She's afraid of someone." Not something.

Afraid and angry.

"There's a chance she could just turn tail and slip out of the city." Jude's fingers were tight around the wheel. "Pak said if she does, we stop her and bring her back."

"She won't leave Baton Rouge, and she's not just going to sit there and wait for them to come after her." Zane was certain of that. "She'll fight." *I can still hear their screams.*

They hit the highway. Jude glanced down at the GPS and turned right. "Yeah, that's what I figured." He paused. "But whoever we're up against, these bastards were strong enough to level Night Watch, even with the protections we had on the place."

It wasn't like this was the first time Night Watch had come under attack. But it was the first time anyone had made it past the high-tech security and the paranormal charms that protected the place.

He licked his lips—*tasted her*. Damn her. She shouldn't have left. She'd tried to distract him with sex. *Yeah, that had worked*. Then the moment she'd thought he was weak, she'd left him.

"She could be walking right into hell," Zane said. Going in alone. "She said they had her before, but that she managed to get away. . . ."

"Well, Pak couldn't find any intel on Project Perseus. So either its cover is too good or—"

Or Jana was bullshitting him.

One way to find out. "Hurry the hell up, Jude. We don't want to give our Ignitor too much of a head start."

I'm coming, baby. Are you ready?

When Jana got back to Baton Rouge, she didn't stick to the shadows. She drove the motorcycle right down the main roads, revved her engine as loud as she could, and hoped the bastards would find her.

She was in the mood for some heat.

It was after midnight, but the city wasn't sleeping. Far from it. Jana knew just where to go in order to find the trouble she sought.

Four turns later, a fast blast into the darker side of town, and she braked in front of Dusk. Demon Central. One thing about demons . . . the lower-level demons were such sellouts. Always willing to turn on a friend or, hell, anyone. It hadn't just been coincidence that the big rig had hit them after they left Dusk.

Someone had made a phone call. Someone had fed the bastards her location, even given a description of the car she and Zane had been using.

That someone was about to feel her fire.

She jumped off the motorcycle. Once she'd gotten back to the city, she'd taken twenty minutes to run by her place and change clothes. No one had jumped out to confront her. Pity. She'd been ready for them.

Now she wore black. Tight shirt. Long jeans. And boots made for kicking ass.

She strolled up to the bouncer. He glanced her way, a quick gauge to see if she was using glamour. When he realized she wasn't, he hesitated until she shoved a fifty into his hand.

Then he let her into the demons' den.

"Damn." Zane reached for door handle.

Jude grabbed his arm. "Easy, man. Easy. She just walked inside. No way has she made contact with anyone yet."

"This is the place where those demons jumped me!"

"Demons are always jumping you."

Zane didn't take his gaze off the door. "This was different. It was a trap. They'd been waiting for me. If I'd gone into that place . . ."

How many would have come at him?

"You would have ass-kicked your way out?" Jude asked dryly.

His lips thinned. "Yeah." He would have.

"So why didn't you go in?"

"She stopped me." *You shouldn't go in there.* Yet she'd just strolled in, rolling those sexy hips. "She said that there was a hit on me, that the vamps and demons had been wanting her to take me out." Only she hadn't taken the hit on him. She'd never come at him with fire in her eyes. Not once. Not even when he'd cuffed her.

For a supposedly cold-blooded killer, that didn't make a lick of sense.

"So there was a hit, she didn't take it, and the woman tried to protect you?" Jude's fingers drummed on the wheel. "Interesting."

Zane rolled his shoulders.

"So in return for her bit of community service, what did you do?" Jude asked.

"I cuffed her."

The bark of laughter came fast and hard from the shifter.

Zane didn't glance his way. His eyes were on the club. "She shouldn't be in there alone."

"Relax. Nothing's happened yet."

His back teeth clenched. "How the hell do you know that from out here?"

"Because I don't smell any smoke. Your lady hasn't started having her fun."

Jana stood in the middle of the den, her gaze darting to the dark corners and closed doors. The demons were so strung out here. Her nose ached from all the bitter scents. Demons and drugs . . . sometimes, there wasn't any other way for them to shut out the darkness.

She knew a lot about darkness.

There wasn't a bar in the place. No band, either. Why pretend? The people there wanted only one thing.

Pleasure. The sweet release the drugs would give them.

Her gaze tracked to the right. She needed to find a familiar face . . . ah.

Demon number one on her list. The demon with the scar sliding down his right cheek, one of the demons who'd come charging at her and Zane. Also one of the demons who'd been so quick to flee when he realized Zane wasn't going down.

She stalked toward him. The guy blinked at her, and narrowed his eyes. "I . . . I know you."

Jana took a breath and let the fire heat her blood. She knew her eyes would redden. "Yes, you do."

His jaw dropped, and he tried to scramble back. A low-level demon, he wouldn't be any match for her flames. Her power would easily subdue his.

"Not so fast." She gave him a slow smile. "I just want to talk." She reached for him, and he swore at the heat in her touch.

"I-I didn't . . . I didn't know they were tryin' to kill you!" The words burst from him and spittle flew from his mouth.

"I heard—heard there was money if an Ig-Ignitor was spotted. . . . Just wa-wanted some cash!"

Now, really, that had been sickeningly easy. "What's your name?"

He shook his head.

"Asshole, *what's your name?*" She knew he'd see the flames in her eyes.

"M-Morris . . ."

"Who'd you call, Morris?"

He stared up at her, his black eyes bulging. "They'll . . . kill me." Whispered.

She laughed. "And what? You think I won't?" She leaned in close. His back was slammed against the wall. No place for him to go. "I can burn this whole place down before you can blink."

Morris started to shake. "H-had a cell number . . ."

"What is it?"

Another owlish stare.

She sighed. Great. "Do you still have your cell phone?"

A few jerky nods.

"Then get the damn phone out and call the bastards again." The number would still be on his phone. She jabbed her index finger into his chest. "Tell 'em that you found their Ignitor, that she's pissed, and that she's burning a den."

"B-burning?"

"You and your boys made a few mistakes the other night. You ratted me out, and I really don't like it when folks betray me."

"Y-you said you wouldn't t-take the j-job."

Ah, so he'd heard that part somewhere, too. Wasn't he the informed demon flunky?

"The second mistake"—she waited a beat and let the charge grow—"You came after my demon."

His bushy brows bobbed. "Your—"

"Make your call." Jana felt the heat begin to rise. "Then you'd better get the hell out of here."

Because it looked like the only way to stop those assholes

on her tail was to show them that they did *not* want her. They needed to see that they couldn't control her, and if they came too close, she'd exterminate *them*.

Demons began to run out of the den.

"Oh, hell," Jude muttered.

Zane's eyes narrowed. "What's—"

"Smoke," Jude said, and an instant later, Zane caught the scent.

Fire. Zane shoved open the door and rushed out of the truck.

"Wait! Zane, dammit, *wait!*"

But he wasn't waiting. Jana was in there, the fire was raging, and he wasn't just going to sit outside and watch everything burn.

A demon slammed into him. A guy with pale cheeks and a long, twisting scar on the right side of his face. When his gaze met Zane's, the demon began to scream.

A hard hand grabbed Zane's shoulder and spun him around. The demon ran away, still screaming.

"The woman controls fire. She can handle this," Jude snapped at him, not releasing his hold. "It's not like she's some delicate flower. She's—"

"Bait?" he bit out as the smoke drifted from the open door of the den. "She's just bait so it doesn't matter what happens to her?"

"She's not—"

"You don't know what the fuck she is." And, friend or not, he let his fist swing out. Jude stumbled back, probably more in surprise than anything else because it was hard to knock a shifter on his ass. Zane whirled and ran for the den.

He shoved demons out of his way. Knocked them to the side and shouted Jana's name.

The crackle of fire answered him.

Inside, he didn't see anyone. Human or demon. Just an empty den. Had she gone out the back? Had she—

"You shouldn't be here." She appeared in the thick smoke and came toward him with eyes flashing red.

He grabbed her arm and pulled her close. "And you damn well know better than to start a fire *around* you." His hold was as strong as the cuffs had been, and he hauled her toward the door. She shouldn't be around the smoke for too long, she *knew* that. Did the woman have a death wish?

They burst outside, into the night. The other demons had fled the scene, desperate to escape from the flames.

"You shouldn't be here," Jana said again, shaking her head.

"Oh, really?" His fury broke free. "Where should I be? Still at the cabin where you left my ass? Still sleeping off the sex while you get to burn this place to ash? I don't think so, baby."

She blinked. For an instant, she almost looked . . . hurt. But then, "I was cleaning up *your* mess, demon. These assholes attacked you, remember? Were you just going to let them go?"

"No." Now that was just insulting. "I handle my own business, my way."

"Oh, really?" Her hands were on her hips. The building burned behind her. "Your way wasn't working."

"And burning the building down around them was gonna work? That's execution, that's—"

"I gave them a chance to run!"

What?

She shook her head. "You really shouldn't be here." Her shoulders slumped a bit.

"News flash." He stepped closer to her, making her tilt her head back to hold his stare. "Wherever you are, I'm gonna be there." His breath rasped out. "Did you really think I'd just let you walk away? From the moment you slipped out of bed, I knew every move you made."

She swallowed. "You . . . this is a setup?"

His gut clenched. *All or nothing.* "You're the bait, baby. The juicy, tempting bait to bring out the bastards who torched Night Watch."

Jana's lips parted. Then she smiled, a sad twist of her lips. Her dimple didn't appear. "Is that all I am?"

A police cruiser raced to the scene with its sirens wailing. An unmarked SUV flew up behind it.

A woman jumped out of the SUV, her hair flying. At the sight of the gun in her hand, Zane tensed. *Hell, here we go again.*

Tony scrambled from the back of the SUV, running up to the woman's side. Good, at least one guy with sense was with the cops.

"Look," Zane said, raising his voice so they could all hear him clearly, "we can—"

The woman fired her weapon and shot Jana in the chest.

Chapter 8

Jana fell back, and Zane lunged for her, catching her just before she hit the ground. Her eyes were open, stunned, and the red was already bleeding out from her gaze.

She shuddered in his arms, and her eyelids began to close. The heat began to lessen behind him as the flames died.

"*Fuck!*" The world seemed to explode around him. Or maybe he exploded. The beast he'd tried to keep in check roared—a loud, enraged cry of fury that burst from Zane's lips. A cry that was her name.

The scene shifted around him as the colors faded away until everything was gray. No black and white. No good or evil. Just pain and fury.

"Zane . . . don't-don't let her . . ." The barest whisper of Jana's voice. So soft. "Take . . . m-me."

"She's not dead, demon," the woman's voice rang out as she stepped closer. "Just drugged."

His hold on Jana tightened. He rose, cradling her in his arms. Her head fell back against his shoulder.

The blonde gave him a steely smile. "If you don't want the same shot, put her down and step away." Her gun aimed at him.

Zane got ready to blast the bitch.

Then Tony stepped to her side. "He's not a threat." His eyes were on Zane, but the words were directed at the woman.

"He's Zane Wynter, the man known to have been keeping close company with Ms. Carter for the last few days. And he's a person of interest in the Night Watch fire." She paused, her eyes narrowing. "He's also the man who escaped from your custody, so excuse me if I don't believe a damn word you say, Captain." Her gun was still pointed at Zane.

"He's a hunter with Night Watch! He's not a criminal!" Tony argued.

Screw this. Zane lunged down the steps with Jana tight in his arms. *Hold on, baby.* Where the hell was Jude? They needed to get out of there. There were more sirens, and that meant more cops would be coming any second.

But would those cops be backup for Tony or for the blonde?

"I told you to put her down!" the woman yelled and her gun jerked. "I said—"

Tony snatched the gun from her hand. "You're not shooting at him."

"And you're going to get your ass thrown off the police force!" She shoved past him. "*Put her down!*" She yanked a wallet out of her pocket and held it up in the air. "I'm with the FBI. I'm Special Agent Kelly Thomas."

Big fucking deal.

"I've got a sniper on you right now," she continued, voice flat. "The same sniper that took down your shifter friend."

Now that made him freeze. He turned his stare on her and met her pale, glittering green eyes.

"Jana Carter is a killer," she told him. "You don't want to fight for her."

More SUVs and cop cars swarmed the scene.

"Lady," Tony snapped, "you don't know what you're dealing with here. *Let them go.*"

"I know exactly what I'm dealing with." The wind tossed her hair. "I'm staring at a demon and an Ignitor."

Zane dropped his glamour. "No, Special Agent . . ." Jana barely seemed to be breathing in his arms. "You're staring at one very *pissed* demon." Where was the sniper? Was the claim about him bullshit?

She marched closer. Tony followed her, keeping his hold on the gun he'd taken from her. Her smile was brittle. "Jana Carter's on the extermination list."

Zane stiffened. He'd heard about the list. Heard rumors for years that the FBI was monitoring the most dangerous of the paranormals and putting them on their extermination list. But . . . Jana?

"Do you know how many people she's killed?" the special agent asked.

Jana didn't look like a killer then. She looked weak and pale. Vulnerable.

"Give her to me," Kelly said. "And you can walk away. I'll clear up the situation with Night Watch. Clear you with my supervisors, and you can go back to doing your job—a job that's just like mine." She exhaled and her gaze dropped to Jana. Her stare hardened as she said, "Tracking and killing the monsters out there."

Zane's gaze drifted to Tony. Other cops were there now, standing back, but with their weapons up. If there was a sniper waiting, would he shoot to kill? Or was the plan to drug him, like they'd already drugged Jana?

Kelly raised her hand and motioned with her fingers. Two men hurried forward. "Take her," she told them. "Load her into the SUV and make sure she's secured."

Tony stared back at Zane. Waited.

"Give her to us," Kelly said, "and you're clear. You know what she's done. You hunted her because of it. Now you've done your job. You can get your bounty, get the cops off your back, and walk away."

She made it all sound nice and easy. But . . . "You'll kill her." He caught sight of Jude's truck.

Her lips thinned. "She's on the list."

"Fuck your list." He'd made his choice. "You're not getting her." Zane let his power out. For the first time since he was sixteen years old, he willingly let the demon part of his nature take control.

A blast of power launched, rolling like a wave, and every

human around him hit the ground. They fell, bodies sagging, immediately unconscious as they slammed into the earth.

He hurried past the bodies. He rushed to Jude's truck. The shifter was there, but slumped over the steering wheel. Those bastards *had* shot him. Hell. Zane shoved Jude over and climbed inside, carefully placing Jana on the seat between him and Jude. His fingers brushed over her cheek, then his hand clenched into a fist.

His gaze swept the area, lingering a moment on the special agent. He lifted his hand and twisted the key. Then he slammed his foot down on the gas and roared out of the lot.

And no one moved to follow him. They couldn't—he'd knocked them all out.

"Holy shit." She lowered her binoculars, very glad that she'd decided to hang back once she'd heard the sirens. "Did you *see that?*"

Her partner, tall and quiet, grunted. "He knocked them out." He didn't sound impressed.

He should. "That demon just knocked out twenty humans at once." *Twenty.* Hot damn. "We've got us at least a level eight." She'd never captured a level eight. Five had been her highest demon bag.

"I thought we were killing him?"

She yanked out her phone. "The plan's just changed." Oh, it had changed all right. She had a level eight—or higher—demon in her lap, *and* she knew the guy's weakness. Too perfect.

Why, that demon would be even more useful than the Ignitor. Not that the bitch was proving to be particularly useful but . . .

But she was some fine bait.

"I want that demon." She spoke into the phone, knowing other eyes were out there, watching the demon race away with *her* prey. "Follow him. Hunt him down."

Zane Wynter was a hunter, just like she was. He hunted monsters, too. But the difference between them . . . he *was* a monster. She was just a human who had to clean up the mess the beasts made. She'd been cleaning up their messes for years. *So tired of cleaning up their shit.*

"If we can, take them both." Because her Ignitor was so useful, and she did prefer to work with humans. "If the woman starts the flames again"—because she knew a taunt when she saw one—"shoot her—shoot to kill." Sometimes, you had to cut your losses. "He'll be more valuable to us." The things she could get that demon to do. . . .

He already hunted his own kind. She knew the stories about him. So what she had in mind for him wouldn't be too different.

Killing demons. Killing vamps. Killing shifters. Killing all the sick paranormals who made the world into a nightmare.

At first, Project Perseus had tried fighting them with human weapons. Guns. Bombs. Then they'd stepped up the game—and started using chameleons. Humans with enhanced genetics, the chameleons were perfect at sneaking up on the paranormals. They could drop their heart rates, slow their breathing, and ambush even shifters. The chameleons had taken out so many monsters. So many . . .

But the real way to win the battle might just be by using one of the *Other's* own. A demon half-breed to deal death.

She smiled as she gazed through the binoculars. *Perfect.*

Carefully, she stepped over the sniper's still body. He was human, which was unfortunate, because she'd had to kill him. But, really, if he'd taken the shot, she wouldn't have learned anything.

Now, she knew everything she needed to know. *New prey.* Prey with a weakness.

"What the hell?" Jude came awake in a rush, jerking upright with his claws out and up—just the way Zane expected him to wake.

Zane grunted and kept the gas pedal pinned to the floor. "Wanna tell me how you got taken out?"

Jude exhaled hard, and his head wrenched toward Zane.

"Taken out?" The words were a little raspy. They wouldn't be that way for long. Shifters, especially rare, white tiger shifters like Jude, were fast healers. That healing ability was why the tiger had only been out ten minutes.

"I found you unconscious in the truck." Jana lay slumped between them. No telling how long she'd be out. "Way to watch my back, tiger."

"Fuck." From the corner of his eye, Zane saw Jude run a shaking hand through his hair. Then his hand dropped to his neck. "*Drugged.*"

Yeah. And if the sniper had been out there, why hadn't he taken a shot at Zane? His psychic blast wouldn't have been strong enough to carry more than a block. The sniper *could* have taken him.

"Who did it?" Jude demanded, and he finally seemed to see Jana. "Aw, hell, her, too?"

Zane's jaw clenched. After a moment, he said, "She was shot right in front of me." He hadn't expected the special agent to take that shot. If her gun had been loaded with real bullets . . .

Darkness rose around him and the truck began to tremble. "Zane?"

"A woman claiming to be from the FBI was there." He forced his hands to ease their too-tight grip on the steering wheel. He sucked in a couple of deep, slow breaths. *Control. Jana was going to be all right.* "A Special Agent Kelly Thomas. She said Jana was on their extermination list."

Jude froze. Yeah, they all knew about the list. They'd even been hired a few times to make sure the exterminations were carried out for particularly dangerous paranormals.

But . . . *Jana.*

Zane yanked the wheel to the left. "She wanted me to just hand Jana over, knowing they were gonna kill her. Agent Thomas wanted . . ." He braked hard and turned to meet Jude's bright stare. "I'm *not* turning Jana over to the Bureau."

Jude whistled. "Do you know what you're doing?"

"When is it standard procedure for the FBI to drug hunters? Huh? When? They drugged you, Jude. Attacked first, and didn't plan to ask questions later."

The tiger shifter's lips tightened. "I'm pissed as hell about that—" And his fangs were still out. Those claws still ready. "But Jana—"

"If the agent wanted Jana dead, she could have killed her." *While I just stood there. Fucking stood there.* "But she drugged her. She didn't shoot to kill." Because the agent wanted Jana for something. *To use her?* Aim and fire—everyone knew that was the way to use an Ignitor.

His gaze returned to Jana. She still barely appeared to be breathing. Her face was so pale, and dark smudges lined her eyes. "I'm not turning her over," he said again. "She didn't burn Night Watch. And before anyone plans her extermination, I want to know exactly what happened with those humans in New Orleans." He wanted to know everything. Every detail of her life. How had she become a killer?

How had he?

"You're lettin' this get personal," Jude warned.

Yeah, he was. "Get out of the truck, Jude."

The shifter blinked. "It's my truck."

Zane brushed back the dark hair that had fallen over Jana's cheek. "I need the wheels because I've got to get cover and figure out what's going on." His eyes once again met Jude's. "The FBI is gonna be looking for me now, too. I don't want them to come after you."

"Screw them." Said instantly. "The day I'm worried about some jerk-offs in suits . . ."

"What about Erin?"

At the mention of his lover's name, Jude blinked. "What about her?" A distinct edge had entered his voice.

"She's the ADA. How would she feel about you being on the run?"

"Erin trusts me." Absolute certainty.

"But she doesn't need to get pulled into this." He still wasn't even entirely sure what *this* was. "And neither do you." Zane sighed. "This is gonna get bad, *real* bad."

"All the more reason you need me." Jude's smile showed off his sharp teeth. "I know how to do bad."

"So do I." The shifter didn't really know just how powerful he was. He'd worked hard to keep Jude and the others in the dark. Sometimes, you didn't want the whole world to fear you—and sometimes, you did. "I need you to work with Tony. Find out if that special agent is legit. Use Pak's contacts at the Bureau, and then call me." He still had the replacement phone Jude had given him.

The shifter measured him with a long, hard look. "Is she worth being hunted?"

He'd never been hunted. Always predator. Never prey.

"Don't blow your life for a good fuck."

"Get out of the truck, Jude." There was no more time to waste, and he really didn't want to punch out his friend.

Growling, Jude got out of the truck. "Don't trust her, you hear me? She's dangerous. The woman could fry you—"

He laughed at that. "No, she couldn't." He was probably the only one she couldn't burn. She could let her fire rage, and it wouldn't so much as blister his skin.

Jude slammed the door. "Watch my truck, okay? Watch—"

Zane left him, racing the truck forward and speeding down the road. After he found a place to lay low, he needed to make Jana tell him the *truth*.

Don't trust her. Maybe though, just maybe, he could make her trust him. If he did, then he could get to Project Perseus— and give the assholes some serious payback.

But she'd have to trust him first. Have to think that she could rely on him for everything. Anything.

One killer, trusting another. Right. Fate would laugh her ass off at that one.

*   *   *

When she opened her eyes, Jana became aware of two things. One . . . she was in a bed. A strange, lumpy bed that smelled of stale cigarettes. Two . . . she wasn't alone.

Since the last thing she remembered was standing in front of Dusk and getting shot—that bitch was so gonna pay for that—Jana didn't move immediately. She kept her breathing nice and easy, even though her heart galloped in her chest. Slowly, she let the charge build within her body. Her gaze stayed on the peeling ceiling above her, on those faint brown water lines.

If the Bureau had taken her in for extermination, they'd find out that she wasn't that easy to kill, and if they didn't want to kill her . . .

I'm not going to be their pit bull. She was sick of being a weapon to the world.

The energy built inside her. More, more. The blast would come hot and strong and—

"Turn it off."

The words were clipped, cold, but the voice—*familiar.* Zane. She rolled onto her side and blinked in shock. He'd been beside her at Dusk. Standing right there when the agent fired. "They got you, too." But why? Zane was a hunter, not—

"They didn't get me." His chest was bare, and his dark hair was mussed, as if he'd been running his fingers through the mane.

Her breath caught. "I don't . . ."

"Did you know you were on the extermination list?"

No sense lying. "Well, Night Watch was after me, so I figured the FBI was, too. Hell, I figured the FBI was probably the one who was paying your fees." So why was she there?

"I don't want to hear any lies," he told her.

But she was good at lying.

"Why were you in Dusk?"

Jana blinked. Okay, she hadn't been expecting that question. "Why were you there?" Convenient, too convenient, and— Jana jerked up, sending the covers sliding off her body.

"You followed me." Understanding was bitter as her memory flooded totally back.

He didn't move. "Did you really think the sex would distract me so much that you could just walk away?"

She took the slap and realized that Zane had taken off her shirt *and* her pants. "Where are my clothes?"

"Is that a technique you use a lot?" Icy words. "You seduce your way out of trouble?"

Jana swallowed. "I didn't have sex with you as part of some master scheme." She jumped from the bed and started searching the motel room. The obviously cheap motel room. She'd spent her share of nights in plenty of rooms just like this one.

"Then why did you?" Nearly a growl as some heat broke through the ice.

She found her pants and turned back to face him. "Because I wanted you." For once, she'd just taken what she wanted. She'd known it wouldn't last. "I knew we didn't have any future." Future—what was that? "I wanted you, wanted pleasure—so I took both."

His green eyes glittered. "How many men have heard that line?"

She threw her pants at him.

The guy moved then—*fast*. He lunged across the room. His hands locked around her upper arms, and he yanked her close. "I didn't turn you over, Jana. The FBI wanted you. They just wanted me to walk away, but I *didn't turn you over*."

She stared up at him. "Why?"

"Because I'm a fucking idiot." His breath expelled in a rush. "Because when that woman fired on you, I was ready to rip her apart." His head lowered toward hers. "Because when you fell, I lost control."

A demon losing control? Never a good—

"Because once wasn't enough for me."

Her heart slammed into her ribs.

"I want you, I want the pleasure, and I'm damn well not done with you yet."

Not done with her? Yeah, that was classy. That was—

"You want me," Zane said.

Yeah, she'd just said as much.

"I'm fucking on fire for you."

Jana knew a few things about fire.

"If this isn't what you want, then say no, and say it fast." His hold gentled. Stroked instead of captured. "But I've spent the last five hours watching you, worrying that you wouldn't wake up—"

"I-I'm fine." It wasn't the first time she'd had that particular drug of choice fired on her. Humans woke up with no ill effects. Shifters had a bitch of a headache and demons—*don't want to go there.*

"You're not getting away from me," he said, "not until I know what's happening."

Right then . . . "I don't want to go anywhere." And when she wanted to leave, she would. The demon wouldn't stop her. No one would stop her.

He kissed her. She expected a hard kiss, a blaze of passion and anger and fire.

Instead, she got . . . *gentleness.*

Jana tensed and her hands lifted. Her nails dug into his arms. No, no, that wasn't—

His lips caressed hers. Softly. So soft, and his tongue whispered into her mouth.

She used her hold and tried to pull him closer. She didn't want soft. She didn't want slow. She wanted—

Zane's head lifted. He stared down at her, his eyes darkening. "It's not gonna be fast this time." The words sounded like a threat. He picked her up and held her easily in his arms. *Control.* He had it in spades at that moment. She could feel his strength, reined in, all around her.

Zane carried her back to the bed and lowered her onto the mattress. His hands skated down her body and caught the edge of her panties. "Not fast . . ." he rasped again, and slid her panties down her legs.

His fingers were rough, with calluses on his hands, but his touch was easy as he stroked her skin.

"You're so damn beautiful," he whispered.

Her breath caught.

"I think we need to pick up where we left off." His jaw tightened. "Before you ran out on me."

Hit. "You don't want the problems I have to knock at your door." His hands were movng up the inside of her thighs and talking was a bit hard right then. "You don't . . . ah, I'm just a bounty, remember?"

"I don't fuck my bounties."

But he was about to fuck her.

"You stopped being a bounty the minute the cuffs hit the floor." He eased her thighs apart and opened her wide to his gaze.

"What am I?" Because she needed to know. Not a freak, not a weapon, not—

"The woman I want." His fingers touched the folds of her sex. "And right now, you're mine."

He was hers. Right then, *hers.*

Zane shifted his body, and his breath blew over her exposed sex, sending a shiver through her. "Let's see just how hot you burn," he said.

Zane put his mouth on her.

Jana nearly jerked off the bed. "Zane!"

His lips feathered over her sex. Then she felt the wet lick of his tongue, a slow swipe right over the center of her need.

Her heels dug into the bed and her hands grabbed onto his shoulders. Not to push him away—oh, no—to jerk him closer.

His fingers brushed against her, then one long finger pushed inside her straining core. In, out, that finger plunged in maddeningly gentle thrusts. *Not enough.* And his mouth kept caressing, that tongue stroking, and Zane tried to drive her out of her mind.

Her nails bit into him.

"Easy, baby. I'm going to enjoy you."

No, he was going to make her crazy.

His finger pulled out of her. Her body tensed. No, she wanted—

His tongue pushed into her sex just as his thumb pressed against her clit. Jana's breath choked out and her body went bow tight.

He growled against her, the vibration shaking through her sensitive flesh and that tongue—the demon *knew* how to use his tongue.

She arched her hips against him. Wanting more, needing . . .

His mouth left her. "Open your eyes, Jana."

Her eyelashes flew open, and she found his black stare trained on her. The lamp on the nightstand threw weak light on the bed.

"You're not coming, not yet."

Oh, but she'd been close. She wet her lips. "This some kind of . . . torture?"

"No. Pleasure. Only pleasure." His gaze was heavy lidded. "You said you wanted pleasure, remember?"

She'd also said she wanted *him*. "Take off your jeans." She wanted them flesh to flesh.

He yanked his wallet out of a back pocket.

What—

And he pulled out a condom.

He'd planned his seduction. Why did that make her hesitate? So he'd known they'd sleep together again. Big deal, right? She'd wanted to sleep with him.

"Doubting, baby?" His fingers went to the buckle of his jeans.

She shook her head, refusing to admit the doubt, even to herself. Her fingers slid between them, and she took the condom from him. "My turn." Because she didn't like that fine edge of control he held.

Jana wanted to see the control shatter. No, she wanted him to shatter right before her eyes.

He unzipped his jeans with a slow hiss of sound. She

reached for his cock and found it thick, hard, and swollen with need. She stroked him once with her left hand, a long, slow pump from root to tip. Because she could play the game slowly, too.

She stared into his eyes. So dark, her demon's eyes. But fire could burn in the dark. She'd seen it happen plenty of times. "Do I get a taste?" she asked.

A muscle flexed along his jaw and he eased away, sliding back onto the bed. She rose, following him, and stretched her body so that when he lay back, she was over him, right over that cock that reached for her.

His flesh was warm beneath her hand, heated with his need and lust. When she touched the tip of his erection, a drop of moisture appeared. *My taste.* Jana leaned forward and licked that drop, tasting the wild blend of man and sex. Her tongue licked over the head of his cock, then slid just under that broad tip.

His hips jerked, just a bit.

Control.

The demon had it tonight.

She opened her mouth. Jana let her breath blow on his flesh, then she took his cock inside, parting her lips around him. She sucked his flesh, moving her head in an easy rhythm, but then going faster, taking more as his taste filled her mouth. Wanting more, wanting—

"Not yet," he rasped and she found herself on her back again, with him over her. Jana blinked, not even remembering how she'd moved. Her hands were on either side of her head, and her legs were spread open. He rolled the condom over his cock and pushed his shaft against her.

His fingers eased beneath her back, and he unsnapped her bra. When the material fell away, he took her left breast into his mouth. Sucking. Licking. Letting her feel the light score of his teeth.

She twisted beneath him as the ache between her thighs made her shudder. This wasn't her style. Fast, hard, she needed—

His cock slipped inside her. One inch. Two.

Her sex clamped around him.

"You're so slick. . . ." His head lifted. "And fucking tight." Another inch.

"*Everything*," she whispered, demanded. "I want—"

He drove balls-deep into her. Jana came at once, a hot blast of pleasure that fired through every cell in her body. She arched beneath him as a moan broke from her lips. Zane started to thrust, fast and deep—*thank you, finally!*—and the orgasm spiraled longer, wilder, hotter.

His cock stretched her, filled her sex to bursting, and the deep thrusts slid his shaft right over her clit.

Aftershocks of pleasure hummed through her body. Her eyes were open, on Zane, locked on the darkness of his stare. Brutal lines of lust etched his face, but he kept his hold easy, and he kept driving into her with those long, hard thrusts.

The second orgasm rocked through her.

"Fuck!" His control broke. He slammed into her, plunging again and again, and the scent of sex filled the air.

He froze, then a long shudder worked his body. The darkness of his eyes heated, and Zane called her name.

Jana wrapped her arms around him, held him tight, and realized she'd never felt better.

Never felt better . . . and never been in more danger. Because if the demon holding her so tenderly, kissing her shoulder so sweetly—if he found out about all the things she'd done in New Orleans, *he'd* be the one handing her over to the FBI and putting her up for extermination.

Dawn was coming. Jana lay in bed, her demon's arms around her, and watched the trickling rays of light break through the blinds. She hadn't slept after the sex. Neither had Zane. Guess he'd learned from his mistake before.

They'd lain in bed. He'd held her. It had felt . . . nice.

Weak. You're letting yourself get weak with him.

She cleared her throat and forced herself to speak. "So

what's the plan?" She glanced at him and found his gaze already on her. "You're not going on the run with me."

"You're not running."

Her breath expelled. "Well, since I'm not planning on dying, I don't see a lot of choices here." Not like she could just stay there and wait for the FBI to come and pick her up. *Not ready to die, thank you.*

His fingers feathered down her arm. "There are always choices."

Easy for him to say. He hadn't spent five years locked up in hell. She'd gotten out at eighteen, but then she'd just traded one prison for another.

"I need to know . . ." His eyes narrowed. "I need to know about the people you've killed."

"Why?" She tugged away from him and rose from the bed.

"Because you're not the cold-blooded killer you pretend to be."

Her lips pressed together. Not that he could see the tremble anyway. She had her back to him. "Wow, aren't you the sweet-talker."

"Tell me about the first fire."

Screams. Pain. Flames that burned so fast. "They say you never forget your first," she murmured. She'd tried, but had never forgotten the sound of Greg's screams . . . or the smell of his burning flesh.

"I've heard there's no control with an Ignitor's first fire."

She jerked on her panties and heaved up her jeans. "You've heard right." A bitter laugh slipped from her lips. "I didn't even know what was happening." Jana hooked her bra and tugged on her shirt. "I was so scared. My skin felt like it was on fire." Her hand dropped to her stomach and pressed hard. "My gut was churning. I thought I'd explode."

And she had.

No, *he* had.

Jana turned back to face Zane. She lifted her chin. He had sat up in bed, and the covers pooled around his waist. "I thought I was normal. Just like everybody else, and then the fire came." She shook her head, remembering the taste of fear. It tasted a lot like ash.

"An Ignitor's power hits at puberty."

The man sounded so damn clinical, but he was right. She nodded.

"And it's usually spurred on by an extreme emotional upset," he said quietly.

Give the guy a freaking cookie. So he'd done his homework on Ignitors.

I killed the last Ignitor who crossed my path.

He climbed out of bed. Naked, strong. He grabbed his pair of jeans and pulled them on, then he stalked toward her. "Were you upset, Jana? When that first fire broke free, were you angry?"

Her back teeth clenched. "Yes," she gritted out. She'd been angry and so scared. Because her mother had been gone. She'd been in that house, just her and—

"Your stepfather died in that fire."

She didn't speak.

"Did you want him to die or did the fire get out of control? It would have been so easy to burn out of control. . . ."

Jana laughed. Zane didn't get it. Was he really trying to give her a way out? "I wanted the bastard to die. I stared at him, and I thought, over and over, that *I wanted him to die.*" She swallowed. "And then flames raced across his skin and he started screaming for me to help him." *Bitch, fucking help me! Help me!*

Zane stared down at her, and his gaze seemed too intense.

"I wasn't going to let him touch me." Her voice sounded hollow. "I wasn't going to let him punch me again, and I told him—" She cleared her throat. "I told him if he tried to hit me once more, I'd kill him." So many bruises. So many broken bones. Her mother had always been there with excuses when anyone asked what happened. *She fell down the stairs. Jana's a clumsy girl. You'd think a thirteen-year-old would know how to ride a bike better, wouldn't you?*

Her fingers brushed across her jaw. It had been wired shut

for weeks after the fire. "I warned him," she said. "It was his fault," she'd told herself this over and over, "that he didn't listen."

Zane's lips parted. "Jana . . ."

Her hand flew up and hung in the air between them. "*Don't.*" Anger fired the word.

But he shook his head. "I can't—"

"I don't need your pity." She knew pity when she heard it. "I'm not some damaged kid who needs you to hold her and make everything better." Not anymore, dammit.

"I know that."

"Greg Burgess deserved what he got." Because if she hadn't killed him, he would have killed her, and she knew it. "I didn't expect the fire, and afterwards, hell, no one believed me. They thought I'd set everything up . . . staged the scene and lured him to his death." Bastards. The DA had said her jaw had been broken from the force of the blast. He'd said she was too close when she ignited the accelerants and that she'd been thrown across the room.

What accelerants? She'd burned Greg with her power.

But Greg, the bastard, had always kept plenty of booze around. And they'd been in the garage when the fire started. With the oil and gas and . . .

You're lying, girl. You set the fire. You burned that man alive. The DA's voice was so clear in her mind, even after all these years. *Did he beg you for help?*

Yes, he had.

"You were protecting yourself." Zane's voice was a low rumble and she glanced back at him. His hands were clenched into powerful fists, and the faint lines near his eyes looked deeper than before.

"I was," she said, and it was true. Greg's ghost didn't haunt her anymore. Jana took a long, deep breath, and then she let her lips curl. Because she wasn't a victim, and Zane needed to see that. She wasn't some damsel he needed to rescue.

She could rescue herself. In the fairy tales, she wasn't the trapped princess. She was the fire-breathing dragon, and she'd burn anyone who got in her way.

She had.

"I killed to protect myself then." True. "But I'm not a scared girl anymore."

Zane's head tilted a bit to the right as he studied her. "So the others you've killed? Were you protecting yourself then?"

The rush of anger broke through her control. Did she need to give him a whole damn life story? Did she have to justify every move? "You want to compare kills? Your hands have blood on them, too, Zane!"

"I never claimed they didn't."

"You might be one of the good guys, but you've crossed the line for duty, I know you—"

His laughter stopped her cold.

Jana blinked. "Am I missing a joke?" The guy had a real piss-poor sense of humor. Good in bed, lousy humor—noted.

The laughter faded, but his lips maintained that slight twist of amusement. "Ah, Jana . . ." He shook his head. "I have to know . . . What in the hell ever made you think I was one of the good guys?"

Chapter 9

A good guy? Oh, the woman had it wrong. Very, very wrong. When he'd listened to her story about her dick of a stepfather, the last thing he'd felt was *good*. If he'd known Jana back then . . . *I would have gotten rid of the bastard for you.*

Now he understood so much more about her, and Zane realized . . . he and Jana were a lot alike. Maybe too much.

So young when we first killed. So much power.

Jana shook her head and stared up at him a bit blankly, all that wild, dark hair loose around her face. "You *are* a good guy, Zane. You-you work for Night Watch. You're a hunter."

"You mean a licensed killer." He shrugged and tried to keep his voice careless. Real hard when the woman was making him care more than any other had. "They pay me to hunt, but even if they didn't, do you really think I'd be doing anything else? Some of us were born to hunt. To kill." He paused deliberately. "But you know that better than anyone else, don't you?"

That pink tongue swiped out again and his cock hardened. *Down, boy. Not now.* He hadn't meant to give in to the lust before. Wrong place, wrong time. But he'd watched her while she'd been out, he'd—dammit, *worried*—and when she'd woken, he'd wanted.

He wasn't used to not taking what he wanted. So he'd taken her.

And had one hell of a fine time. *But I still want more. With her, I always want more.*

What was he going to do about that problem?

A veil seemed to fall over her face. "How'd you get us away from the Feds?"

He shrugged. "It wasn't that hard."

"Bullshit. I-I remember being in front of Dusk." Her forehead wrinkled. "I remember—"

"Why did you go there?" he interrupted, inching closer to her. He had the feeling the woman might break and run at any moment, and that wasn't an option. She wasn't going to leave him.

She blinked.

"Why'd you go back to Dusk?" That point had been bothering him. "Did you have a contact there?"

Her eyes—such a deep blue—widened. "Guess you could say that." Her shoulders rolled. "The bastards from Perseus came after us too fast. I knew someone at Dusk must've tipped them off about us. Demons aren't exactly trustworthy."

He ignored the jibe.

"So I figured if I shook some cages—"

"You mean started some fires."

"—that I'd get somebody to talk." She frowned at him. "And I did. A demon named Morris. The bastard with the scar who turned tail and ran when the fight got hot."

Excitement had his heart pounding faster. "He gave you a contact?"

"No, I got him to *call* his contact. I told 'em if they wanted me, they could find me at the burning den."

"Fuck. The fire was your beacon?" Not real subtle, but then, she wasn't exactly a subtle kind of woman.

She smiled at him. And it was . . . a real smile. Warm. Her dimple winked, and he swallowed.

"No, Zane," she said, "the fire was for you."

"What?" She could always surprise him.

"I didn't like the way the demons ganged up on you. I wanted to send a message, and I did."

"I don't need you fighting my battles." He could handle any demon, any day of the week. But . . . she'd gone back to avenge him? That was . . . sweet, in a Jana way. Maybe some girlfriends would cook a guy dinner.

Jana cooked his enemies.

Wait—*girlfriend? What the hell am I thinking?*

Her hand lifted and slid over the stubble on his cheek. "You're welcome."

What?

Her hand dropped. "I was waiting for those bastards from Perseus to show up, but the FBI got there first." Her lips tightened. "Actually, *you* got there first." She waited a beat then said, "Bait, huh?" She didn't seem angry. Just curious.

Bait. He didn't like the sound of that.

"Guess you realized there were bigger fish than me out there, right? What, does Night Watch have a hard-on for Perseus now?"

"You could say that." And a hell of a lot more. "We lost five agents in that fire. We don't take kindly to losing our own."

Her gaze searched his. "What are you going to do? Do you really think you can take Perseus down?"

"Yeah, baby, I do. And you're gonna help me blow the bastards to hell."

He ditched the truck. Jude would want to rip him apart when he found out, but Zane had to abandon the shifter's ride. Someone would have seen it at Dusk, and there was no point in continuing to advertise their presence.

It wasn't hard to find another vehicle. It wasn't legal, either. But he'd learned long ago that you sometimes had to go outside the law in order to get a job done.

"The Feds and the cops are going to be looking for us," Jana said, turning to glance at him. They were in an older model Ford. Nothing flashy, nothing fancy. The kind of car you forgot two minutes after you saw it. He'd switched tags twice, just as a precaution.

"They're not going to find us." They had about thirty more minutes to go before they made it to New Orleans, and Zane damn sure wasn't planning to stop for highway patrol.

"The FBI will have splashed our pictures all over the news. Every cop in the area probably has our descriptions." Her voice was flat. Just stating the facts.

"Baby, every cop in the area got your description days ago. Hell, those in New Orleans had it years ago, and you're still not inside of a jail."

"I'm good at hiding."

Yeah, he'd figured that.

"And when I was working for Project Perseus, they made sure the cops stayed off my back."

The car almost swerved off the road. "You *worked* for them?" What the hell?

"It was either go after their kills or find my ass inside of the jail you just mentioned."

He glanced at her from the corner of his eye. Her attention seemed to be on the blur of pine trees.

"I didn't want to go back to jail," she said quietly.

Then why did you kill?

Her head turned toward him. "Things aren't black and white."

He frowned.

"Maybe they are for you." A mocking laugh. "Not for me. They've never been that way for me. So when Perseus told me that I'd be doing the world a favor, that I'd be taking out monsters who hurt women and children, hell, yeah, I was tempted."

Her nails scored across the seat, and the grinding noise seemed too loud in the car. "They gave me dossiers. Told me when and where to strike, and they paid me well. I'd never had much, but suddenly, I had a chance for everything. And all I had to do was light a few fires."

Zane realized he was hitting ninety, and he forced his foot to ease off the gas pedal. "The ones you went after . . . were they killers?" She'd taken out vamps in Baton Rouge. Vamps were known to be—

"Does it matter?" She paused. "Will you think better of me if I say that everyone I killed while working for Perseus was evil? That they were all murderers who needed to be put down?"

"Were they killers?" he asked again, refusing to let her rile the beast.

"Some were. At first, they all were." She blew out a breath. "But then Perseus started thinking there wasn't any such beast as a *good* supernatural. Hell, to them, the only good supernatural was a dead supernatural. Vamps, shifters—they needed to be put down. All of them."

"You're a supernatural." Was that why they were trying to put her down, too? His gaze darted to the rearview mirror.

"I'm a human first. A human with a psychic skill . . . that means I'm a tool for them. Not good enough to ever invite over for dinner, but good enough to use. They like to use enhanced humans—Ignitors, charmers—my handler told me that sometimes monsters had to kill monsters."

"Your handler?" Now they were getting someplace.

And that black SUV that had been following them for the last ten minutes was getting closer. He could see the other vehicle so well in the rearview mirror.

"My handler was a real sweetheart named Beth Parker. Human to the core, and a woman who got off on death more than anyone I've ever seen." Disgust tinged her words. "She didn't take so kindly to me wanting to leave the fold."

"Oh?"

"So I made sure I gave her one hell of a kiss good-bye."

"*What?*"

"She was with those asshole scientists who held me at the end in New Orleans. Since I didn't want to play ball with them anymore, they decided to cage me. Then when they couldn't change my mind . . . they decided I was expendable."

The SUV was getting closer. He started edging back up to ninety.

"They strapped me to a table and got ready to cut into my head. They thought the secret to the fire was in my brain. That something was wired differently. And that bitch Beth just stood there, watching, while I screamed."

His own fury rose.

"I hadn't attacked a human since my stepfather. I'd said I never would again. . . ." Her words trailed off. "But I wasn't dying on that table for them. Beth made it out of the flames, but she got the kiss of fire on her hand and face. She won't ever forget me. I made sure of it."

Well, damn. "You play hard, don't you, baby?"

"I don't play."

The odometer trembled up to ninety-five, but that SUV was still gaining.

"They don't play, either, Zane, and they sure as hell aren't going to be opening the door and offering a welcome smile to us when we get there."

But the men who'd slammed into them with the big rig had wanted her alive. And the cop had wanted her alive, too.

It was fine to kill me, but they want her breathing.

That didn't really make sense if they were just planning to kill her later on.

"Don't worry about opening the door," he said, "I can manage that just fine—"

The SUV rammed into their bumper and the Ford lurched forward. The minivan in the right lane let out a long, desperate honk.

"Zane!"

He held tight to the wheel and floored the Ford. Unfortunately, flooring it meant that it only went about ten miles per hour faster.

The SUV hit them again.

Jana jerked around and stared behind them. Her breath rasped out. "They're already found us."

He wasn't sure they'd ever lost them.

The minivan plowed into Jana's side and she screamed.

What? The minivan? He hadn't seen that one coming.

The minivan hit again. Metal groaned as the door caved in. "*Jana!*"

She didn't answer. He risked a fast glance at her. Her hair was a dark shield around her head and—

And the front of the minivan burst into flames. The vehicle swerved and plowed into the trees.

That's my girl.

But before he could speak, the SUV took aim at them once more. Another hard hit from behind made his teeth rattle. "Shit!"

"I can take care of them."

Yeah, he knew she could. But they were about to head into more traffic and if the fire got out of control . . .

Jana unsnapped her seat belt.

"What the hell are you doing?"

"Aiming."

She crawled into the backseat. Her ass brushed his shoulder. Aw, damn.

He glanced in the mirror.

Smoke rose from the hood of the other vehicle. The driver of that SUV must've gotten the message that she was sending because the brakes squealed as the SUV shuddered to a stop.

Zane got them the hell out of there. "Are you okay?"

"I'm fine." But she didn't sound fine.

He adjusted the rearview mirror and saw her slump in the backseat. "But if it's all the same to you," she said, "I'm staying back here." Her lips curved in a tired smile. "And that, lover, was our welcome wagon."

"Your police captain is collaborating with the perpetrators," Kelly Thomas charged, pointing her finger at Antonio. "Not only did the bastard let them escape his custody once, he did it *twice!*"

Harold Evans, the chief of police, lowered his bushy brows and stared at Antonio. "That true, son?" His hard Southern accent rolled on the words.

Antonio narrowed his eyes. "I wasn't the only one at that

club. *She*"—the agent who was seriously pissing him off—
"was right there. They got away from both of us, from half
the PD, from—"

"I had a shot," Kelly said, her cheeks flaming. "I could
have taken out that hunter!"

"Uh . . . hunter?" Harold asked, rubbing his grizzled jaw.
Gray stubble coated his sagging chin.

"Zane Wynter, the hunter from Night Watch," Antonio reminded him, though he knew the reminder wasn't necessary.
The slow-Southern-boy act was just that . . . an act. Men
didn't come any sharper than Harold.

"And he's teamed up with the arsonist?" Harold shook his
head. "*Why?*"

"There's no proof he's teamed up with her—" Antonio
began.

"Bullshit." Ah, the agent was eloquent. Normally, he
rather liked that in a woman. In her, not so much. "Wynter
had Jana Carter *in his arms.* All he had to do was surrender
her to me, and this nightmare would have been over."

Instead, Zane had unloaded on them all and taken the
woman who the hell knew where. Antonio sure hadn't seen
that move coming. But then, Zane had surprised him a few
times before, too.

"You took my weapon," Kelly snapped. "If you'd just
stood the fuck down, I would've had Jana Carter in custody."

The small office seemed too hot. He could feel the heavy
weight of Harold's stare.

"You knew my gun didn't have bullets in it, Captain. Just
enough drugs to put them both down." Her breath huffed
out. "You *knew* that."

Time to cut the bullshit. Everyone in that office understood the score. "And you *know* what drugs do to demons."
He shook his head. "It might not have knocked him out. It
could have set him off—it could have made him rabid and
the guy could have attacked us all!"

"He *did* attack us!" she threw out.

"Demon." Harold grunted, holding up his hands. "The hunter's a demon." He raised one brow. "What's the girl?"

"An Ignitor," Kelly bit out. "An out-of-control Ignitor who needs to be put down."

"But you weren't putting her down," the words slipped out instantly. Antonio leveled his stare on the agent. "You were just knocking her out."

"Because I don't get the pleasure of killing her."

Okay, that was *personal.* The job and personal issues didn't mix. The special agent should've recognized that fact long ago.

Papers rustled as Harold opened the files on his desk. "You used drugs on her because your boss, Anthony Miller, gave orders that Ms. Carter was to be brought in alive, and deadly force was to be avoided *at all costs.*"

"He's not my boss."

"Fine. He's the senior agent."

"And his ass is in Miami right now. He doesn't even understand what's happening here. He doesn't—"

"I know Miller." Harold folded his hands on top of the desk. "He understands everything."

Her hands fisted at her sides. Her right hand seemed a little too close to her holster. "Wynter might have been a good hunter once, but he's obviously turned, because of *her.* She has that effect on men. The woman seduces, gets men to trust her, then she betrays them." Her breath rushed out as she stalked toward Antonio. "Your friend is in over his head. Even a demon can't control her fire."

His brows rose. "Now that would depend on just how strong the demon is."

Her eyes couldn't narrow much more. "We requested Wynter because he'd handled Ignitors before. He killed the last rogue, I—*we*—thought he could handle her, too."

The picture suddenly became clearer. "You contracted with Night Watch, and you were *hoping* the demon would kill your Ignitor, weren't you? You didn't want him to apprehend her, you wanted him to execute her." He stalked closer to her.

"Your hands would've been clean then, right? You would have done your job and gotten your wish. Jana Carter would be dead."

Her smug smile was his answer.

Hell. "Zane Wynter doesn't kill for sport."

She laughed at that. "He's a demon. Of course, he does."

He was aware of old Harold stiffening and the temperature in the room dropped a good ten degrees. But the special agent didn't seem to notice that change. "You think all demons are evil?" he asked her, just to be sure he understood.

"They're demons, aren't they?"

"Uh . . . you know it's biological, right? It's not like they're the devil's minions, they're just—"

"Supposed to be descended from the Fallen. Right. Whatever. They're not human. I've stared into their eyes. Their *real* eyes, and I know they're evil. Just as evil as *she* is."

Antonio could only shake his head. "You don't have a lot of faith in people, do you?"

She didn't answer.

Right.

"What did Jana do to piss you off so much?"

"You mean, other than go on a burning and killing spree for her entire life?"

"Yeah, other than that." He felt Harold's eyes on him.

"She—"

"I've heard enough." Harold's bearlike growl filled the room as he shoved to his feet. "Special Agent, you need to go check in with your boss."

"He's not—"

"Check in with your *senior officer*." His right hand held a fountain pen in its white-knuckled grip. "Maybe he's got word on your would-be prisoners."

"Fine." She jerked her thumb toward Antonio. "What about him?"

"Don't you worry about Antonio. I'll handle my man."

"See that you do." One hard nod, then she whirled on her heel, and stormed for the door. Of course, the woman didn't open the door and softly shut it behind her. No, she slammed the damn thing hard enough to make the framed commendations on Harold's wall shake.

"I don't believe I much like Special Agent Thomas," Harold said, and Antonio glanced at him just in time to see the chief of police drop the glamour from his eyes.

Demon black eyes stared back at him. Antonio had always carried his suspicions about the chief, but . . .

"We're not all fucking monsters. The special agent and those dicks at the FBI with their extermination list—they need to realize that."

Antonio exhaled. "Am I suspended?"

"Hell, no." That pen stabbed toward him. "What you are is on your way to New Orleans. I got a report that Wynter was headed that way with the woman."

"But I don't have jurisdiction—"

"Screw jurisdiction. I'm not letting Agent Thomas get her hands on Wynter first. He's a hunter, but he's also one of mine."

"Yes, sir."

"Get your ass down there. Find Wynter and *find that girl.*"

"Carter? What do you—"

"It's come to my attention that she may know certain . . . pertinent facts . . . about a group the FBI has been trying to infiltrate for years. A group that is quite dangerous." He paused. "To folks like me."

"Sir?"

"If Jana Carter has got the info I need, I do not, *do not,* want her winding up in Special Agent Thomas's hands first. I want her, understand?"

"I think I do."

"Good, then, son, because if you want that promotion that you been chomping at the bit for, bring 'em both back. *Alive.*"

Unfortunately, that last part might not be so easy. Especially since he was a cop who happened to be one-hundred-percent human . . . stepping into a world that wasn't.

Good thing he knew exactly where to go for some para-normal backup.

"Why are we going into a hospital?" Zane asked, shaking his head. "We need to get to Perseus before—"

"This *is* the way to get to Perseus." Jana stared at the swirling ambulance lights. Our Sisters of Mercy Hospital was booming tonight. She and Zane had gotten into New Orleans earlier, then laid low until the sun dropped.

As soon as the night fell, they'd been ready to hunt, and the hunt, well, it began *here.*

"There's a nurse inside. Her name's Nancy Gilbert." Low on the Perseus totem pole, but she was still a way to make contact. "She reports to the group on any . . . unusual patients that check in." Like a twenty-year-old girl who'd escaped a four-alarm fire without any burns.

Stupid. I'd just stared up at the nurse and said, "I did it." After so many folks not believing her, she'd sure never expected the nurse with the cold gray eyes to believe her.

Or to pump her full of drugs and have her taken from the hospital.

"We need to get you in there, and we need you to fake an injury." Her gaze darted over him. "Or maybe we should give you a real one."

He held up his hands. "Thanks, baby, but I'm fine with a fake injury." His eyes narrowed. "Will this woman recognize you?"

"No." The last time she'd seen Nurse Nancy, Jana had been sporting short, streaked blond hair, darkly tanned flesh, and she'd been five years younger.

Now that she'd gone back to her dark hair and her skin hadn't seen the sunlight in months, she doubted Nancy would recognize her. Nancy had only been with her a few hours that fateful night, anyway.

Not that Jana had ever forgotten her. You didn't forget the woman who changed your life. *Payback.*

"So how do we get from point A to point fucking Perseus?" Zane demanded.

She grabbed his hand. *Now or never.* "Leave that to me." If he wanted to walk into hell, she'd take him and maybe, just maybe they could bring down the devil together.

Then I'll be free.

If only.

Running hadn't worked—they'd just come after her. They'd keep coming, until the Perseus group was stopped. Zane was strong; she knew he was high on the demon scale. Would he be strong enough to stop the bastards? *I hope so.*

She and Zane hurried forward, and as soon as Jana caught sight of two EMTs returning to their ambulance, she let out a high, desperate scream. "Help me!" She shoved against Zane, sending him stumbling. "My brother—he's—" She whispered to him, "Hit the ground."

Zane collapsed.

"He's having a seizure again! Oh, God, he's been having them almost constantly, and I don't have his meds, I don't—"

The EMTs—a man and a woman—rushed over to them. Jana held onto Zane's hand, clinging tightly and, because she was one fine actress, she let the tears track down her cheeks as the EMTs loaded Zane onto a stretcher and rushed him inside the hospital.

"What kind of medication is your brother taking?" one of the EMTs demanded.

"Uh . . . uh . . . rufinaide."

The EMT blinked and squinted at her.

What? That was a seizure medication, wasn't it? Just then, Zane moaned and his head sagged against the stretcher.

"It's over," she whispered, letting her own head drop forward. From the corner of her eye, she saw a familiar figure bustling over to them. Nurse Nancy always liked to take a look at every new arrival. After all, that was her job.

Jana had been back a few times over the years, back to take a look at the nurse. *You screwed me over, Nancy.*

When paranormals were sick or injured, usually it was

harder for them to mask exactly who—what—they were. Nancy counted on that. She preyed on their weakness. Everyone at Perseus did.

The EMT said, "We need to get him stable and—"

"What's going on here?" the nurse asked.

Jana squeezed Zane's hand. Hard.

His eyes fluttered open, and in that instant, she caught his demon-black stare.

Nurse Nancy sucked in a sharp breath.

A blink from Zane and his eyes were back to green. "Wh-what happened?" His head turned slowly, and he focused on Jana. "Did I . . . *Shit, the hospital.*"

He shoved up, but the EMTs grabbed his arms and tried to hold him down.

"Easy, sir, you've had a seizure. You need—"

"Fuck what I need." He broke their hold in an instant and surged to his feet. He wavered for a moment, and his body shuddered.

Okay, so the guy was a pretty good actor, too. She'd need to remember that.

He caught her arm and hauled her close. "You know better than to bring me here," he muttered. "You know . . ."

Nurse Nancy stepped in front of them. "I'd like to talk with you a moment, sir."

He shook his head and, keeping his hold on Jana, skirted around the nurse.

"We can't let him leave!" the male EMT called out. "He might have another—"

"I know why your medicine isn't working," Nurse Nancy said calmly.

Of course, she knew. Meds never worked the way they were supposed to work on demons.

Zane froze. Then he tossed a hard glare back over his shoulder. "Oh, you do?"

"Umm . . ." The nurse didn't wear one of those annoying white uniforms. She wore dark blue scrubs, and a stethoscope dangled around her scrawny neck. "Come with me into the back. Let me check you out thoroughly, and I can explain everything."

Right. *Step into my web.* Nancy was a pretty woman, with gray-streaked black hair and the faintest of lines around her eyes. She didn't look like the devil. Really, she didn't.

Zane glanced back at Jana. "What should I do?" he asked softly.

She stared into his eyes. "We need help. Let's see what she has to say."

He gave a curt nod. Together, they turned to follow Nancy. But the nurse held up one hand, stopping her. "I'd like to speak to him privately."

Not going to happen. "I'm his sister. I go where he goes."

Nancy's lips tightened.

"She goes," Zane snapped.

"Fine. Follow me."

And they marched right past the EMTs. Poor EMTS, they were still blinking and trying to figure out what was going on.

"In here." Nancy pointed to a small examining room. "Just sit down. I'll be . . . right back."

They went inside. Nancy closed the door behind them and sealed them inside.

Zane frowned.

"She's gone to make the call." Ah, but she'd watched this routine a few times. Not that Nancy knew that. "She's letting her contact know that she has a potential in the area."

"A potential? Is that what I am?" He yanked his phone out of his front pocket and tapped fast on the screen. He put the phone to his ear and a few seconds later said, "Pak. Yeah, I'm in New Orleans." A brief hesitation, then he said, "I need you to run a check on a nurse Nancy Gilbert at Our Sisters of Mercy Hospital. She's about five-foot-four, forty-five to fifty years old and—"

His gaze flew toward the door. He shoved the phone back into his pocket.

Nancy opened the door about three seconds later. She had

a bright, friendly smile on her face. "Sorry, I just needed to assure the EMTs that you were in capable hands." She laughed, a light tinkle of sound. "You'd think I'd never treated a patient before!"

Jana inched closer to Zane's side. "Why aren't the meds working?" She really didn't want to bullshit through the chit-chat. Might as well get to the main show.

The door clicked closed. Nancy's smile dimmed. "First . . . I'm going to need some background information on my patient."

Zane narrowed his eyes.

"Your parents . . . what are their names?"

"Why does that matter?"

"Because I need to see if you have a family history of—"

"Fuck, she doesn't know." Zane charged forward. "Let's get out of here."

Nancy put a hand on his chest. "You're a demon."

Zane stiffened.

Nancy's gaze darted to Jana. "The question I have . . . are you a full-blood or a hybrid?" She blinked and seemed to realize they might not know what she meant. "Ah . . . a hybrid would be a mix, a—"

Zane backed away from her touch, and Jana saw the muscle flex in his jaw. "I know the damn term. Yeah, my mother was human but that bastard who fathered me wasn't."

Oh, nice touch. Perseus would be all over a hybrid. They'd want to recruit him, not kill him. They did love that human blood. And the powers that be over there would really get off on a demon killing other demons.

"Demons don't always respond the way they're supposed to when they are given human medications," Nancy said, her voice quiet and calm.

"I'm *not* a demon."

"Hybrid," she murmured and her gaze darted to Jana. "And you . . . ?"

"I'm human. I'm his half-sister." Said fast because she knew Nancy would be able to rustle up a demon who could check her out. A demon could look right through the veil of glamour and see another of his kind. If one took a good look at her . . . no sense pushing that.

"I see."

Jana knew exactly what the nurse meant. Nancy wasn't interested in her.

"I have some friends." Nancy turned her attention back to Zane. "They work with people like you. They can help you."

"Bullshit. No one can help me. I've been trying for years, fighting this thing inside—"

Nancy's eyes narrowed. "Does it tempt you, this beast inside?"

He didn't speak.

"Does it call to you . . . taunt you with the power that it has?"

Jana didn't roll her eyes, but it was a near thing.

"I know I can do any damn thing I want," Zane's voice rumbled, so dark, and Jana's gaze darted to him. "If I let my control go, there's no stopping me."

Now that sounded so real. Maybe too real. Her tongue snaked over her bottom lip.

"Have you ever let go?" Nancy's eyes were fixed on him.

A grim nod. "Once."

Nancy leaned forward. "What happened?" Eagerness glittered in her gaze. Hungry vulture.

Zane straightened his shoulders. "I killed the bastard who claimed to be my father. I sent the demon back to hell."

Well, damn. The man really was one class-A actor, and a pretty good writer, too, because that was just the kind of story Perseus would eat up.

Demon killer . . . destroying even your father because of what he was.

Nancy smiled. "Good for you," she said. "Sometimes, there are some folks that just need to be put down."

Sometimes. But those folks weren't always demons. Humans could be just as evil.

Nancy's gaze darted to Jana.

Jana swiped her hand over her cheeks, wiping away the tear drops that she still let fall. "It's been so hard," she whispered.

Nancy gave her an understanding smile, one oozing fake sympathy. "I'm sure it has. But everything will be changing for you now." She turned toward the door.

"Where are you going?" Zane asked, taking a step forward.

"I need to call a friend. He can come and get you. He'll make sure you're safe for the night."

Safe and snug inside Perseus. Just what Zane wanted. Hmmm . . . maybe they *would* be opening those doors wide open . . . making them welcoming for him. The guy had just played Nancy perfectly.

"I'm afraid you won't be coming with him," Nancy said, that stare once more landing on Jana's face. "You understand, don't you? Your brother needs to be around others who understand him."

Yeah, this wasn't part of the plan. Jana blinked and lifted her chin. "I understand him just fine."

What? Was that pity filling Nancy's eyes? The last thing she wanted was for that witch to pity her. "Your brother is special," Nancy said. "My friends can help him, but if you come—you'll just be in the way. They don't have a place for someone like you."

Because Nancy thought she was simply another human, one without special skills. If she'd been a paranormal, Nancy would be getting ready to send her off—either to use her or to kill her. But a straight human got a pass out of there.

Only she didn't want that pass this time. She wanted to stay by Zane's side. The guy might need her. No, he *would* need her.

"I'm going—"

"Home," Zane said, interrupting her. He turned his head

and his eyes met hers. "Go home and wait for me. I want—
I want to see what these people have to say. If they can help
me . . ."

Now he was kicking her to the curb, too.

But, wait, wasn't that supposed to be what she'd wanted?
She'd been trying to get away from him since the beginning,
but now . . . Now she didn't want to let him out of her sight.
She didn't trust Nancy. Didn't trust anyone in Perseus. What
if Zane wasn't strong enough to bring them down?

"I'm coming with you." Her fingers caught his and held
tight. "We're a team, remember?" He'd been watching her
back. She'd watch his.

He glanced down at their fingers. Then slowly, carefully,
he pulled away from her. "Not this time."

Shit. The demon was cutting her loose.

This had *not* been part of the plan. They really should
have talked more before storming into the hospital. Maybe
agreed to, oh, she didn't know—*not desert each other.*

Nancy opened the door, and the woman had a near-smirk
on her face. "Your brother will be fine. Trust me, he's in good
hands."

The hell he was. But the demon was the one calling the
shots and if he wanted to go solo, if he wanted to risk his
sexy neck, then who was she to make the idiot see reason?

She rose onto her toes and brushed her lips against his
cheek. "Watch yourself," she whispered. Then she pulled
away. Her steps were slow as she made her way to the door.
"You'll . . . take care of him?" she asked Nancy, casting one
last look back at Zane.

"You have my word," the nurse assured her. Right. The
woman's word? That wasn't worth the breath it took to speak.

Jana slipped into the white-tiled hallway. Her shoes squeaked
on the floor. She could see her image staring back up at her
from that gleaming tile.

Run . . . make a break for it. The demon had told her to
go. She could wash her hands of him and break free now.
Maybe he'd succeed and take down Perseus. Then she'd just

have the FBI jerks on her trail, but she could shake them, no problem. Especially now that she knew they had such a hard-on for her. She'd be hyper-aware of them, and they would *not* catch her again.

Yeah, she could run now. Run, and never look back. Maybe she'd even head to Mexico. Get some sun.

It was the smart thing to do.

He told me to leave.

The exit doors waited for her. A few more steps, and they swished open silently, giving her easy access to the night.

Run.

She wasn't perfect. Far from it and, in that instant, she was tempted. After all, she'd run plenty of times in her life.

An EMT bumped into her, his shoulder clipping her arm.

Running was easy.

She took three steps back. The doors slid closed before her. The demon had saved her twice now. She'd always thought it was important to pay your debts.

Besides . . . she really owed the folks at Perseus an ass-kicking.

Don't worry, Zane. I've got your back.

Chapter 10

They blindfolded him and, because Zane was playing the game, he let them do it.

Nancy crawled into the car with him and sat to his right. He could smell her—the antiseptic scent of the hospital, stale cigarettes, and vanilla body lotion.

A man drove him. The same guy who had smiled apologetically and said he'd need to blindfold him. The guy barely looked older than eighteen, and he had sun-streaked blond hair, a little too long, and blue eyes.

The car snaked through the city. Turning left, right. At first, Zane tried to keep track of the turns, but the kid was fast. The car's engine growled as he sped through New Orleans, taking them deeper into the heart of the Big Easy.

"When did you know what you were?" the kid asked, and the kid, he was a demon. Zane had caught a glimpse of his eyes, too. *Before he blindfolded me.*

"When I was sixteen." Zane figured keeping as close as he could to the real truth about his past was the easiest way to go. Less chance of screwing things up that way. That was why he'd given Florence Nightingale the real deal about his past.

"I always knew," the kid said. The car slowed, then stopped. Probably at a red light. "My dad never let me forget, not even for a moment, that I was *different*. He loved telling me how I was *just like her.*"

Behind the blindfold, Zane blinked. "Your mom was a demon?"

"Ummm . . ." The car picked up speed again. "She seduced my dad, then dropped me off and cut out of town. She left us both." Bitterness. Pain.

Zane eased out a slow breath. "Maybe you were better off without her."

The kid didn't speak and Zane didn't know what the hell else he was supposed to say.

"Why did you kill your father?" Nancy asked and the question fired right at his gut.

Can't forget about her. "Because he deserved it."

"*When* did you kill him?"

The truth. "When I was sixteen years old."

The silence in the car grew thicker then. Darker. He could feel the tension, so thick it bore down on him like a lead weight until not-so-sweet Nancy said, "Good for you."

The car braked again, but it wasn't a slow stop. The demon up front killed the engine. "Welcome home," the guy said.

Home? Not likely. More like welcome to hell.

If she wasn't so good at hotwiring cars, Jana would have been shit out of luck. But if her correctional time had done anything for her, well, it had introduced her to a new group of friends.

Some of those friends had come from homes that were too much like her own. Homes where the mothers or fathers liked to use fists every night on their kids. Or they liked to touch . . . when and where they shouldn't.

Once she'd gotten out of juvie, she'd made sure she helped her friends. Nothing lethal. They'd just wanted to send some messages. They hadn't believed that she could start the fire with her mind. No, they'd just thought she was one world-class pyro, and they'd wanted her to use her skills to keep their monsters away.

Monsters. Sometimes, you just couldn't escape them.

So she'd done her part. She'd watched out for them. When Lillie McGill—her "roommate" from juvie—had gotten out and headed home, Jana had tailed her. The first time Lillie's father had come at Lillie with his fists, Jana used the fire to write STOP on the wall next to him.

She hadn't killed him. Hadn't even touched him with her flames. Her fiery message had been enough to send the guy scrambling to church and to rehab.

No, she hadn't needed to let the flames lick his skin. Besides, back then, she'd been too scared to kill again.

Not that the fear had lasted long. Not once Perseus got ahold of her.

Lillie's father found Jesus, though he didn't realize the devil had been the one to send the message. He'd never touched his girl again, and Lillie had made sure that Jana had a first-class education on boosting cars.

Fair trade. Sure seemed like that now.

Jana kept the PT Cruiser in sight as it weaved through the streets. Since she'd been gone, Perseus had changed their location. They did that as part of their protection strategy. They changed locations every few months. Tricky bastards.

She kept a few cars between her and the other car. Not so many that she would lose sight of the Cruiser, and not too few because she didn't want the folks in the Cruiser to see her.

They swept past the St. Louis cemetery and the white tombstones rose up past the wrought-iron fence, ghostly markers to map the trail to Perseus.

Her fingers tightened on the wheel as a shiver skated down her spine. She'd never been too fond of the cemeteries in New Orleans. Because she knew, unlike most of the tourists, that some of the dead could really come out and take a bite out of their unsuspecting prey. And with all those folks out there working their summoning spells—spells they thought were simply harmless games they'd read about in books—well, she knew better. *Nothing harmless about them.* She'd seen her share of walking nightmares.

More miles passed. They shot through a neighborhood. Looked so normal. Things always *looked* normal.

Then the houses began to disappear. The storm a few years ago had destroyed a lot here, and folks hadn't rebuilt. Not that she blamed them, not one damn bit.

Where are we going? The car ate up more road. Some factories dotted the street now. Warehouses.

Finally, *finally*, the Cruiser pulled into the lot near a warehouse. Above the wooden doors, two white masks had been painted onto the red wood. One smiling, animated face; the other crying, with a tear drop sliding down the white cheek. Mardi Gras masks.

She drove past the building and made sure not to let her car slow for even a second. In her rearview mirror, she saw the driver climb out of the vehicle. Looked like a young guy. Perseus did like to recruit them young.

The guy glanced up and he stared after her car.

She didn't accelerate. Didn't zoom out of there with a squeal of tires. Jana just kept her speed nice and easy. She took a left at the corner, aware that her heart was slamming into her ribs. She'd find a place to stash the car, then she'd go back for Zane.

She knew where he was now. Knew exactly where Perseus was.

She smiled.

Guess who is coming home? Time to raise a little hell.

They took his blindfold off the minute the heavy metal doors swung shut behind him. Zane blinked, and his eyes adjusted almost immediately to the darkness. Handy little demon side effect. The darkness never hindered his vision.

Monsters surrounded him. Dragons with fire shooting from their mouths. Horned bulls the size of buses. An angry Poseidon sprang forth from the sea, with his trident up and ready to attack.

"It's a float graveyard," the kid said, shrugging. "Once the parades are over, you got to find some place to store 'em."

Zane glanced over at Nancy. Her hands were twisted in front of her. "I'm going to be leaving you soon."

He'd make a point of seeing her again.

"Davey can take you in the back. He'll introduce you to the folks who can help you." Her breath heaved out on a sigh. "This is going to be good for you." Her face and voice seemed so sincere. "This will be a whole new world."

"I'm counting on it."

She offered him a trembling smile, then her head inclined toward the kid. "Okay, Davey. You take him back there, then you can come and drive me to the hospital."

Now that was odd. "Why don't you come with us?"

Fear flashed in her eyes, just for a moment. "I-I need some air."

Right. There was plenty of air to breathe right there.

She turned away.

Davey waited with his brows up. "You ready?"

Hell, yes. Zane rolled his shoulders. He marched behind Davey, weaving through the floats. Dark, massive shadows hung in the air.

He heard the metal door open behind him, a loud screech of sound. Nancy—going to get her air? Davey stopped and turned back to face him. The guy pointed to another door on the left, a wooden one this time. "This is it."

Fucking finally.

"Glad you're here, man." Davey flashed a tired, lopsided smile. "You're . . . you're like me. Good to know I'm not the only one."

The only demon? Not even close.

"My old man said I was evil." Davey's chin lifted. "I'm not. *We're* not. We couldn't help the way we were born."

No, they couldn't.

"We're gonna change the world," Davey said with a quick nod. "Make it so much better."

Was that really what Perseus was telling its recruits? Because how did killing good people at Night Watch make the world *better*?

Davey pushed open the door, and Zane got ready to kick ass.

Getting inside the warehouse was easy. Too easy. Jana found a broken window on the left-hand side of the building and slipped right inside.

Then she hesitated because *really* that should have been harder. Especially if this was the new base camp for Perseus. It should have been . . .

"I was wondering how long it would take you to show up."

Lights flashed on, a blinding explosion of illumination that lit up the warehouse. At the same instant, Nurse Nancy jumped from behind some boxes and grabbed Jana's arm.

Jana charged up, ready to burn—

The nurse slammed a needle into her arm. "Didn't really think I'd forget you, did you, Jana?" The smile on her face chilled Jana's blood.

Jana wrenched back, but she could already feel the drug sliding through her veins. "How did—"

"I never forget a face." Footsteps pounded as others jumped from the shadows. "And certainly not yours. Guess you could say it's burned into my memory."

She'd burn her all right. Jana stumbled and slid to her knees. *Charge, come on, charge.* She shoved the darkness back and demanded, "Where's . . ."

"Your brother?" A laugh. Nancy had the syringe gripped tightly in her hand. "Or rather, the hunter Zane?"

Played.

"Don't worry. We've got him just where we want him to be."

Trap.

"No!" *Charge.* She felt the heat build in her body. *Build . . .*

And fire shot across the warehouse, seeming to burst from the giant green dragon's mouth and lunge toward Poseidon.

Come on, come on. She didn't have much left in her, but she wasn't going down without a fight. The fire snaked forward and raced toward the two assholes in black who were lifting their guns toward her. Oh, no, they should know better, they should—

Water burst from the sprinklers overhead. Heavy, gushing waves of water that banked her fire even as she tried to stir it again.

"We planned for your arrival," Nancy murmured.

Another guy in black—freaking guards, she'd never forgotten them—ran toward her through the smoke. Her body slumped as the drug spread through her blood. *Can't be happening.*

Shit, sometimes it just didn't pay to try and do the right thing. Next time, she was running and looking out just for number one.

Next time.

Jana sucked in a deep breath of air. *One more charge.* The asshole was closing in on her with his gun clutched in his fist.

The guy slammed the butt of his weapon against the side of her head. Right before her cheek hit the cement, she felt the fire escape, and she heard him scream.

When he heard the scream, Zane leapt to his feet. Good old Davey had dumped him in some kind of holding room—looked for all the world like an interrogation room at the Baton Rouge PD, complete with what Zane knew to be a two-way mirror—and he'd been biting back his rage and trying to keep his control.

Then he heard the scream. Zane ran for the door. He grabbed the handle and jerked—locked. Right, like that was gonna stop him. He jerked again, using some of the enhanced strength he usually kept carefully banked. The lock shattered and the door flew toward him.

He raced in the direction of that fading scream. His nose twitched. What the hell? Was that—

Smoke.

Jana. Had she come after him?

Davey jumped in front of him. "Wow! Man, wait, what are you doin'?"

He shoved past Davey. "Someone screamed."

Davey grabbed his jacket. "The guards will handle it."

"There weren't any fucking guards there when we came in." If there had been, he would have noticed them, he would have—

Davey laughed. "Sure there were, man. They're chameleons, though. You don't see them unless they want to be seen. You're gonna find lots of strange folks here."

Chameleons. Human chameleons. He'd heard about them. They could blend in with almost any background, could lower their heartbeats and respiration so much that they were often undetected, even by nearby shifters. Unless the atmosphere got damn hot, you couldn't make a chameleon come out and play if he didn't want to.

Unless it got hot . . .

He shook off Davey and rushed for that last door.

"What are you doing?" Davey yelled. "Stay here, they're watching—"

Oh, yeah, he just bet they were. He was at the door. This time, Zane didn't bother with the lock, he just kicked out and the wood shattered.

So much for his cover.

He burst into the cavernous room. Water poured from the ceiling, pooling on the floor and mixing with the smoke. Through the downpour, he saw them. Nurse Nancy, grinning, holding a syringe, and three, no, four assholes in black, all standing in a circle around—around—

One of the assholes lunged forward and grabbed something. No, someone. He hefted Jana up in front of him and put his gun to her sagging head. "Take another step, demon, just one more . . ." The guy's bulging eyes locked on Zane. The right side of his face was red and blistering. Jana had let him feel her fire before the bastard took her out. "And I'll make sure she never opens her eyes again."

He stilled and stared at the man. Long and hard. Marking him. Because he'd already seen the blood trickling down the side of Jana's face.

"Good." The chameleon smiled, the grin pulling at the burnt skin of his face. "Nice to know you realize who's in charge."

The fuck he did.

The sprinklers turned off abruptly and only small drops of water fell onto Zane's head.

"You need to come back with me," said a quiet voice from behind him. Zane glanced over his shoulder. Davey was there, gazing at him with demon black eyes. "*Now.*"

"Don't worry," the chameleon with a death wish said, "we'll be bringing the fire bitch, too." His wet hair stuck to his head.

"We wouldn't think of leaving dear Jana behind," Nancy added. "Not when she went to so much trouble to come and join our little party."

Jana. "You knew who we were. The minute we walked into the hospital, you knew."

She just stared back at him as drops of water slid down her face.

"Why the hell did you bring me here? So you can try to kill me?" He lifted his chin. "Come try and take your best shot." If he could distract the chameleons, maybe he would have a chance of getting Jana free.

But no one took his bait, and Nancy, well, she blinked and looked confused. "Why would we want to kill you?" She walked toward him. Her eyes were all wide and fakely earnest. "We want you to join us."

And she was bat-shit crazy.

"If you don't help us, then we'll make sure that your lover"—her eyes cut to Jana—"begs for death."

Wasn't she Miss Sweet Sunshine.

"Come with me," Davey said again, with steel in his voice. "Come willingly or we'll drug you, too."

He spun around at that. "The hell you will."

"I will." Davey lifted a gun. Now where had the kid gotten that? He'd been unarmed before.

Zane wondered if he could move fast enough. He couldn't blast the guy. Usually a demon's power wouldn't work on another demon, so he wouldn't be able to take Davey out psychically but—

"Don't try it," Davey advised. "This drug's a new mix. The last demon we shot didn't survive even an hour before the darkness took him."

Zane weighed him. Davey didn't look quite so clueless and young anymore.

"We want you alive, Wynter," Davey said. "But if you fight us"—his lips pulled down—"then you'll both die."

Aw, the guy sounded like he'd regret that. *But he'd still kill us.*

Davey held out his hand. "Give me your phone."

His phone had a tracker in it from Night Watch. They would have followed him after his last call. They'd already know about this place. Zane pulled out his phone and tossed it to the kid. Davey caught it and instantly smashed the phone in his grip. "Now head to the back. We'll be going out the southside exit. There's another car waiting for us."

What?

Davey lifted one brow. "You didn't think this was really headquarters, did you? We're barely above sea level here. Those rooms you saw, that's all we got here, but the loading area in the back makes for a perfect getaway so no one sees us leave." The barrel of the gun lowered. "Guess you could say this place is our testing grounds."

Bastard. *Smart.*

"Now let's get the hell out of here." Davey glanced at the chameleons. "And, shit, Nancy, do something about that one's face."

"We lost him," Pak said, his voice carrying easily over the phone to Antonio. "His signal just went dead."

Hell. Antonio glanced over at Jude. The tiger shifter had both hands locked on the wheel. "Give me his last location."

"A warehouse on Bienville, number 8-1-2." A pause. "I don't like this, Tony."

Join the club.

"If those assholes who torched my building have him . . ."

"Then they've picked the wrong demon to screw with," Jude said, his shifter hearing easily picking up Pak's words. "Because no one messes with Zane and gets away with it. The bastard is more lethal than they can imagine."

"Tell Jude to watch his ass," Pak said in Antonio's ear. "These bastards seem to have a hard-on for hunters and the last thing I want them to get is a tiger's pelt."

Jude's knuckles whitened. "Not gonna happen."

"You're the contact man on this, Tony," Pak told him. "They trust humans, so if anyone can get past their guards, it'll be you."

Great. No pressure.

"The FBI left town right after you," Pak continued, "so watch out for them. You'll have company soon."

Jude's borrowed car hurtled forward. "We'll make sure everyone feels welcome."

Doubt that.

"I did some research that I thought you might find interesting."

The soft, sly tone in Pak's voice immediately had Antonio stiffening.

"Seems that Special Agent Kelly Thomas has a personal grudge against Jana Carter."

"Yeah, tell me something I don't know."

"Okay." A brief pause. "She's got that grudge because Jana killed her brother. Seems he was one of the scientists working at Perseus when Jana burned the lab in New Orleans."

Oh, hell. "Was he undercover?" Because if Jana had killed an FBI agent, the woman was more screwed than he'd thought.

"That I don't know."

Of course. Things couldn't be that easy.

"Dee's checking that angle now. Once we know something, you'll know."

Dee? Dee Daniels was back working with Night Watch? If she was back in business, they could sure use her backup. Nothing like having an all-powerful vampire on your side when things got bad.

"I want this group taken down." Intensity fueled Pak's words. "We hunt the ones who are evil, who've crossed the line. We don't destroy the innocent."

Antonio exhaled. They just had to *hurry* and get to New Orleans. "Don't worry, we'll get them."

"Just don't let them get you."

Zane held Jana during the van ride. He didn't give the asshole chameleon a choice. When he was close enough, Zane just grabbed her and held her tight.

The chameleon sneered at him, the right side of his face blistering even more.

Davey joined them in the back of the van. Three armed chameleons, the nurse, and Davey all sat in the back. What a fun group.

Jana's breath rustled against Zane's throat. She was alive. That was the only reason the chameleons were still living then.

His gaze tracked back to the burned chameleon. He stared at him, feeling the burn of his rage, and for the first time, Zane let his power surge straight into the mind of a human.

The chameleon's face—except for that fiery cheek—went stark white. His eyes bulged even more and his breath wheezed out.

"*Don't.*" The warning came from Davey. "Don't even think about killing him."

Because he could. It would be so easy. With a stray thought, he could kill the chameleon. He was strong enough. The idiots didn't understand just who they had in their midst.

"Don't want him to die," Zane murmured. *Not yet.* "I just want him to suffer." And he looked deeper into the man's mind. *Jeremy,* that was his name.

A high-level demon could easily manage mind control over a human. Zane had never enjoyed the sport because he'd watched what his father had done with that particular power. Watched his mother be abused and tortured from the inside out.

He'd never thought he'd force his way inside a human's mind, but . . .

But the bastard had been ready to pull that trigger. He'd *wanted* to pull it. Jeremy's thoughts were right there for him to see and feel. Clear as day. The chameleon hated Jana. He'd wanted to put that bullet in her brain more than he'd wanted his next breath.

"You don't like her because you're afraid of the fire," Zane whispered to the bastard. "But you don't understand. That little kiss she gave you on the cheek is nothing compared to what I can do." *What I'm going to do.* He blasted the last thought into Jeremy's head.

Blood trickled from Jeremy's nose.

"Get out of his head," Davey ordered, grabbing Zane's hand. "Get out or I'm taking her away from you."

Try.

The van braked. The door at the front squeaked open. Zane held his grip on Jeremy's mind, just a little bit longer. "He doesn't like you, kid," he said to Davey. "He thinks demons are too high up on the food chain. At the first chance, he'll stab you in the back or slit your throat." It was true. Maybe Davey wasn't strong enough to get inside the chameleon's mind or maybe he'd just stayed out because they were both supposed to be on the same twisted side, but the chameleon planned to come gunning for Davey.

For every demon he could find.

"Bastards . . . killed my f-family. . . ." More blood leaked from Jeremy's nose. "D-deserve to . . ."

"*Jeremy.*" Nancy jabbed a needle into his arm. Ah, Nancy

and her needles. He'd have to watch out for her. Jeremy shuddered, then slumped to the side.

The connection ended in an instant.

Davey shoved open the back doors of the van. "Let's take the party inside."

Moving carefully, keeping a tight hold on Jana, Zane climbed from the van. One glance and he knew they were outside the city. *The swamp.* The smell hit him even as the insects chirped, their calls filling the air. The thick, twisting trees of the swamp surrounded them. Two big, metal buildings stretched across the terrain, half hidden by trees and the fog.

"This way." Davey turned and didn't even glance back to see if Zane followed.

But with the goon squad behind him, all brandishing their weapons, it wasn't like he had much of a choice. Well, he did, actually. He just wasn't taking over this game until he saw all the players up close and real personal. Who waited in those buildings?

"We'll send someone back for Jeremy." Ah, so Nancy didn't care about leaving her pit bull behind. Figured.

Zane tightened his hold on Jana and headed for the first building.

"You're giving yourself away, you know." Davey still wasn't looking back, and his voice was whisper soft. Just for Zane's ears. "When you show you care about something, someone, it can make you weak."

"I'm not weak."

Davey stopped in front of the building. Two guards were there, with guns holstered at their hips. Zane noticed the video cameras then. Set up for surveillance all around the perimeter.

"This used to be an army training area. For training Uncle Sam didn't want the world to know about." Davey tossed him a cold smile. "Perseus . . . inherited the facility when the U.S. government forgot about it."

Bullshit.

They went inside the facility and headed down a long, winding hallway. More cameras. Motion sensors. Figured. Big Brother was definitely watching. After a while, they stopped in front of a shining black door.

"You're gonna be given a chance in here." Davey's shoulders were tense as he stared at Zane. "I'd advise you not to blow it." Then he knocked softly on the door.

A feminine voice told them to "Come in," and Zane stepped into the spider's web.

A blond spider. A pretty spider with dark brown eyes, an elfin face, and a broad smile. A spider who also happened to have raised, red scars on the back of her right hand and the side of her face.

I burned the bitch.

So he'd found his prey. "I guess you're Beth Parker."

"I am." Her head inclined toward him. "And you're a hard man to catch, Zane Wynter." She walked around the desk. Her gaze dipped, just for a moment, to Jana's still body. "But I knew with the right bait, we'd be able to lure you in."

The right bait was standing in front of him. "Let me guess . . . you and your team just got back from Baton Rouge."

She smiled. "And we just missed you . . . thanks to those idiots with the FBI."

"You missed me at Night Watch, too." Every muscle in his body was tight, but his voice was easy and soft. "But I think you got a few of my friends."

Beth shrugged. "Unfortunate collateral damage."

What. The. Fuck.

"Jana was our target, and we had to make certain she wouldn't find any sympathetic authorities in your area."

"You killed five people." And what was up with that subtle emphasis she'd put on *"was our target"*?

Beth stared at him. Didn't blink. Davey shut the door behind them. "There was ample time for escape. The supernaturals should have moved faster." She shrugged again, as if to say: *Not my fucking fault they didn't get out.*

"You know, we could have killed you at the Mardi Gras

warehouse." Her teeth were white and a little sharp for a human's. Her smile was just cold. "But we let you live. Do you wonder why?" Her gaze darted to Jana. She sighed a bit, roughly. "Why don't you put her down on the couch? There's no sense holding—"

Jana stirred against him, then her body tensed. He glanced down and saw her lashes flutter open. Confusion and a haze of pain cloaked the blue depths. "Zane?"

"It's okay, baby."

"No," Beth said clearly, "it's really not."

Jana's eyes widened in understanding, and she jerked against him, tumbling from his arms. She staggered and managed to land on her feet, but she kept a death grip on his arm. "*You.*"

"Hi, Jana." Beth's smile dimmed a bit. "Glad you finally came home."

He felt the fury vibrate through Jana's body, and he expected fire to erupt in a blaze across the room.

Nothing happened.

"The drug slows the charge," Beth said, as if reading his mind. "She won't be able to fire up for some time."

"I don't need to fire up—" Jana lurched forward. "I can still kick your ass!"

Davey grabbed her, catching both of Jana's arms, and pinning them behind her back.

Zane lunged, ready to rip that kid apart.

"Easy." Beth held up her hands. "There's no need for this to turn violent, not when I want to help you both."

Help them?

Jana stopped fighting against Davey. Her eyes were trained on Beth.

Beth's gaze was on Zane. "You're something special, aren't you?" she murmured. "I didn't see it at first. Didn't realize . . . not until I saw you at Dusk."

Oh, hell, she knew what he could do.

"What are you on the power scale?" she asked. "Nine, a ten?"

Zane didn't answer, but he decided it was time he let his power out. Time to rip into Beth's head and tear Perseus apart.

"Won't work." The faintest of lines appeared around those doll eyes of hers. She tapped her temple with her index finger. "I've got a spell in place to keep you out. Once I knew how strong you were, I figured I'd better call out the big guns."

"Zane?" Jana's soft voice. Lost. Confused.

But he knew she wasn't lost. The woman was just biding her time as she planned her next move. Damn, he loved that about her. She was a fighter. In a few more seconds, he knew she'd be going after Beth.

Provided he didn't beat her to the punch.

"It's rare that a hybrid demon has your strength." Beth studied him like he was some kind of bug. No, an experiment. To her, that's probably all he was. "You know that makes you a valuable commodity." Her head tilted back. The better to watch him. "And to think, I originally thought Jana was the prize. I didn't realize what I'd found in you."

"Oh? Is that why you gave your goons the all clear to kill me when they slammed their semi into us that night?"

The woman didn't blink. "Back then I thought you were expendable."

Great. Expendable.

"Here at Perseus, we put humans first. Jana's a human, so she was the priority."

There it was again. Only the emphasis wasn't so subtle on the "*was the priority.*"

Beth sauntered toward him. The woman actually put one of her fire-engine-red nails on his chest. "You have all of a demon's strengths, but inside, where it matters, you're human." She stared up at him. "You've killed demons before. You killed your own father."

He was aware of Jana stiffening in Davey's hold.

"You kill them, you hunt them." Beth let her hand fall

away. "Because you hate them, don't you? You want to wipe the bastards off the earth."

Well, wasn't she a warm Christmas card greeting. "I *am* a demon."

"Your mother was human. That wasn't some bullshit cover story that you fed Nancy. It was the truth."

So she'd done her homework on him. Was he supposed to be impressed?

"Zane?" A different note had entered Jana's voice. One he hadn't heard before, but he could still identify it. *Worry.*

"Your father killed her," Beth said. "He showed you just what those freak demons are at their core. But you showed him just how strong humans can be. Because it was your human side that fought back."

Her smile was too satisfied as she continued. "It's your human side that let you walk through the door. We want that human side. We want you."

He laughed then. He couldn't help it. "You actually think I'm gonna work for Perseus? Lady, you're out of your mind."

"Uh, yeah, Zane, she is," Jana said.

Beth's eyes narrowed. "I don't think you understand. You're a wanted man right now. The FBI is after you, and the Baton Rouge PD thinks you were involved in the arson at Night Watch. They think you've been working with your lover, Jana Carter, a known criminal, to set a series of fires in Baton Rouge *and* New Orleans."

She paused and glanced over at Jana. "Just so you know, there was another fire in New Orleans tonight. Witnesses *will* say they saw you at the bar right before it burned. You and Wynter."

"It's their M.O., Zane." Jana's lips tightened. "They make their recruits become the hunted. Make them run out of options."

"No." Beth said this instantly. "I'm not trying to make you run out of options—"

"Bullshit, Beth!" Jana fired back. "You took every one of

my options away. You set me up for fires, and you turned me into a wanted woman!"

Beth inhaled a deep breath. "You set the first three fires." One blond brow rose. "You're not innocent, Jana. Don't pretend to be for your new lover." Then Beth made a mistake. She sauntered too close to Jana.

Oh, he saw it coming even before Jana shoved back against Davey with her upper body and slammed both feet into Beth's stomach.

The blonde doubled over, gagging. Davey swore and hauled Jana back.

"Get her out!" Beth lifted her head. Her eyes glittered with fury. "Put her in containment." Her gaze darted to Zane. "Put them *both* in there. Let them calm the hell down."

"I'm plenty calm!" Jana shouted. "Calm enough to kick your ass even without the fire, calm enough to—"

"The last time I had you on my table, you were begging to live." Beth's scarred hand was over her stomach, and her eyes were icy cold. "You'll be begging again soon enough."

Jana's chin notched up. "And you'll be burning."

Beth's lips trembled, a small move, and he knew that she understood Jana's words were a promise.

"Can you still feel the fire on you, Beth?"

"Get her out!"

"Can you?"

"*Out!*"

They were thrown in a meat locker. Well, that's what it felt like to Zane anyway. A small, tight, metal room, with the temperature set to chill.

"Bastards," Jana snarled even before Davey swung the door shut. A four-inch-thick steel door. She glanced over her shoulder at Zane. "Can you get us out of here?"

He let his powers push out, let them ease against the door and he immediately felt the containment field. "They've had a witch here."

"Of course they have." She shoved her hair out of her

eyes. Her hand shook. "Probably the same witch who's protecting Beth from you. Did she set up a field around the
room?"

He nodded. "I can't get out." Flat. Well, technically, he
could get out, but not without his psychic blast hurting her,
maybe killing her, because in order to overcome the spell,
he'd have to let his power surge through at full level.

He walked closer to Jana and skimmed his hand carefully
down her bruised cheek. The bruise would be there for days.
Humans. It took them so long to heal.

She flinched at his touch.

His gaze held hers. "Why did you follow me?"

She swallowed.

"You could have run."

The blue of her eyes seemed so deep and dark. "And left
you alone?" Her shoulders dropped a bit. "No. I couldn't do
that." She brought her body close to his. "You know they
have cameras on us. They've got this room wired for sound
and video."

He couldn't see the cameras but he believed her.

"They're watching us. Waiting for us to make a mistake."
Her voice dropped lower. "They like to use your weakness
against you."

Davey already thought he knew Zane's weakness.

"I came back," she said, her voice clear and loud. "Because Perseus ruined my life."

True. But . . . her eyes said something different. *I wasn't
leaving you alone.*

"Are you really a hybrid?" she asked him.

His back teeth clenched. "Yes."

Jana nodded. "And a level ten?"

That he wouldn't answer. Not with those cameras on
them.

She leaned up on her toes and pulled his head down toward her. Her lips feathered over his lips as she breathed,
"Come in . . ."

Wrong time, wrong damn place, but at those words, a hot

surge of need fired his blood. Her body was close, pressing so softly against his, and her rich scent was all around him.

But she'd been hurt. Drugged. And he fucking wasn't planning on performing for an audience.

"Come in," she whispered again. "I need you to see . . . *me.*"

It took a moment for the real meaning of her words to sink in, but then he understood. She wasn't talking about sex. Not talking about pleasure.

She knew how strong level-ten demons were, and she was giving him permission to go inside her mind. *Come in.* Giving him permission to learn her every secret, her every thought.

I need you to see . . . me.

Jana eased back and stared up at him.

Come in.

His power wouldn't work against the spell locking them in the room, but there was nothing locking him out of her. So Zane took a breath, stared into her eyes, and went *in.*

Straight into the fire.

Chapter 11

The fire was all around him, burning so hot and fast. Screams echoed. Screams that came from him—no . . . her.

The fire he saw, the twisting orange and gold flames—it was in Jana's mind. Her memories.

Paint peeled off the walls, boiling and dripping even as she screamed for the fire to stop. Screamed and choked on smoke. Screamed for help that didn't come.

And the flames wouldn't stop.

Zane sucked in a deep breath and fought through the memories. Jana's first fire. He could see the charred body of her stepfather. Hell.

Another scene flashed in his mind's eye. *Jana hunched over a wooden table as tears trickled down her cheeks. "I-I didn't mean for it to happen!"*

A balding man in a suit loomed over her. "So you admit you started the fire!"

"I didn't mean to—"

"You started the fire. He died."

Her eyes squeezed closed. "I want my mom."

"Too damn bad because she sure as hell doesn't want you. She knows you're a killer, and she never wants to see you again."

Jana's fingers trailed up Zane's chest. He knew she was

right in front of him, but the images of the past were all he could see then.

Jana walked forward, one foot in front of the other. The juvie facility was behind her, the hard gray walls looming like thick fog in the light. Her clothes were clean, her steps slow. She stared at the cab that waited for her.

"Where to, Miss?" the driver called out.

She didn't speak, but Zane heard her thoughts so clearly, heard her—I don't have anywhere to go.

The images whirled through his mind. Jana, a few years older, with dark red hair now. She was in a diner, and a guy was yelling at the waitress. No one said anything when he started cursing at her. But when the waitress ended her shift, Jana followed the woman.

Jana watched through an open window, and she saw the waitress and her two kids . . . and the man who'd come to the diner, drunk, to make trouble for her. The woman's husband.

Only the guy wasn't just yelling now. He was hitting the wife and the kids.

Anger fueled Jana's blood. Hot, thick fury and the charge she'd swore never to feel again coursed through her.

"The charge can come from anger, from rage. . . . It's so easy to stir the power. You just need the right stimulant." Her voice echoed in his ears as her fingers trailed down his chest.

When the wife ran out of her house, holding the kids, bleeding, she found Jana in her yard. "I can make sure he never hurts you again," Jana said.

The woman stared back at her with terrified eyes and a broken jaw. Then she nodded. She didn't question Jana, didn't say so much as a word. But then, maybe she couldn't speak. Her jaw had doubled in size and the skin had already started to darken.

"Take the kids away," Jana ordered. "They don't need to see . . ."

Then she walked into the house. The man came at her, swinging hamlike fists.

She trapped him in fire. Fire that she stirred, and he screamed and said she was a monster.

"If you ever go near her or the kids again, I'll burn the flesh right off your body. You won't even know I'm there watching you until you smell the smoke. Smoke that will be coming from inside of you."

"You should have killed him," Zane said, the memory of his mother fighting with Jana's images.

"He killed himself a week later. The drunk bastard drove straight off a bridge."

And he could see it. Because Jana had seen it.

More images tumbled through his mind. More fires, more threats. Not death, though. Her fires hadn't killed anyone until . . .

A vampire grabbed her in a dark alley. She screamed, but no one came running to help her. The vampire shoved her against the side of a building, and he opened his mouth wide. "Ready to die, bitch?"

The fire charged through her once more. "Don't! You don't want to—"

His teeth drove into her neck.

Jana let the fire free.

"I found out later that the folks from Perseus had seen everything that night. They'd had the vamp under surveillance. In another few minutes, they were going to move in and save me." Her finger pressed against his chest. "But I saved myself first, and they saw what I could do. I was taken to the hospital right after that attack. Jesus, *a vampire*—I didn't even realize those guys existed until that night. I thought I was the only freak out there."

But she wasn't a freak. Beautiful. Sexy. Dangerous.

"I told good old Nurse Nancy too much, but it wouldn't have mattered, really. Perseus already had me in their sights."

The image in his mind changed. He saw . . .

Jana, sitting in a small chair. Beth sat on the other side of a dark, wooden desk. "You didn't know about the monsters, did you?" Beth asked quietly.

Jana shook her head.

"They're evil, Jana. They're strong and they're evil and someone has to save all the innocent people in their path." A pause. "You've saved people before, haven't you? You've let your flames burn, and you've saved lives."

Jana didn't speak.

"We need someone like you, Jana. Someone who is strong enough to fight back against them. Someone strong enough to kill them."

She flinched at that. "I haven't—"

"You killed the vampire." Beth's lips pursed. "Vampires burn so easily."

"Look, I don't know what's going on here, I don't know what's happening—" An edge of hysteria entered her voice.

Beth rose and walked to Jana's side. Her eyes were glass hard. "Let me sum things up for you. Monsters are real. They're evil, and if we don't stop them, they will destroy everything good in this world."

"She showed me then. Took me on stakeouts with Perseus guards to see the monsters she wanted me to target. She wanted to point me and aim me and let my fire burn a path through every supernatural she wanted eliminated." Her breath shuddered out. "When I didn't play ball, she just reorganized her game. She made me the bait, and the paranormals started coming after me. I had two choices then. Fight back or let them kill me."

"Whore, you think I'm gonna let you burn me?" A demon walked from the mouth of a dark alley. His black gaze locked on Jana. "I heard about you. An Ignitor who thinks she can hunt the demons here. Think-fuckin'-again. We're huntin' you!" Three more demons sprang from the shadows, and they attacked her.

And the fire had burned.

"I think she wanted to test my fire. To see if it was strong enough to use against demons." Flat. She shrugged. "Since demons can conjure the flames, too, maybe she had to know just what her guinea pig could do."

What could she do? One hell of a lot. She'd burned her way through the demons.

"I've never gone up against a demon stronger than a level seven before." She gazed up at him. Waiting. "But I suspect a level seven or higher could easily beat back my flames."

Easily.

"Perseus told me the demons I'd taken out were killers. They showed me the photos of their victims. They told me I had a damn gift." Her lips twisted. "I'd always thought God cursed me, and here these people were telling me I had a gift."

More fires flashed through his mind. But Jana wasn't killing. Burning. Warning. But not killing. Demons ran. Shifters fled. No, she hadn't killed. She didn't kill . . . unless she caught the paranormals preying on humans.

A vampire caged a girl up against a tree. The girl—hell, she looked like she was about twelve. Her head was twisted, her neck bared, and the vamp's teeth were buried deep in her throat.

"Let her go!"

But he didn't stop drinking. Didn't stop slurping down the girl's blood with deep, greedy gulps.

So Jana let her fire burn. It raced toward him. She controlled it perfectly. The flames caught his legs but didn't touch the girl. The vampire whirled back, screaming, and lunged for her. The fire surged up, consuming him as the girl cried and stared at Jana in horror.

"She didn't understand that I was trying to help her. To her, I was just another monster."

As her voice filled his head, he realized then that Jana hadn't spoken, not out loud anyway, from the moment she'd first whispered, "*Come in . . .*"

He was in her mind, her words floating through his head, and she was guiding him. Showing him the things she wanted him to see. Telling him about her past. Baring her soul. A soul that wasn't perfect. Tarnished, just like his. But one that wasn't evil.

"They sent me after a shifter about a year ago. Told me he'd been cutting the throats of co-eds in the area." Again, her voice was only in his head. Soft, flowing. Jana.

"But I never went for a straight kill on my targets. I watched first, and he—he wasn't doing anything wrong. I followed him for a solid month, and I never saw him even raise his voice to anyone."

An image flashed before him. *A man, thin, tall, with bright blond hair. He walked down the road with the streetlights flickering over him.*

"He was a wolf shifter. They told me all wolf shifters were psychotic. That he had to be put down to stop the killings." Her breath rasped out. Her scent surrounded them.

The man stopped at the mouth of an alley. A woman screamed. He ran inside. Two men had a woman pinned between them. They were ripping her shirt while she screamed and begged for them to stop.

"He shifted and saved her. Those men will wear his marks for the rest of their days, but the girl didn't get so much as a scratch from him."

Not a killer's M.O.

"When Perseus found out I hadn't eliminated him, well, they weren't pleased with me."

Jana and the wolf faced off. Another dark night, this one with a full moon. Perseus agents were in the background, easing close with guns ready.

"They set us up to meet. A recipe for death."

The wolf stared at her, his muscles locked. Saliva dripped from his fangs.

"I was supposed to burn him."

The wolf threw his head back and howled. A long, sad wail of mourning. Then he walked to her and lowered his muzzle.

"He wasn't attacking me. He wasn't attacking anyone. So I stood back, and I let him go . . . and he wasn't the last."

But Perseus hadn't liked that.

"Just because you're a monster, it doesn't mean you're evil.

I broke into Beth's office. I found out that she'd been doctoring the files. That wolf—his girlfriend had been killed by a *human* serial killer. The killer slashed her throat, and she bled out before the shifter could get to her. Yeah, the shifter *had* killed, but he killed the bastard who murdered his girlfriend. Not anyone else. All those other girls . . . a human murdered them all."

But Perseus had still put the shifter on their hit list.

"Guess the powers that be at Perseus didn't like that I started questioning their orders. . . ."

Jana lay bound to a hard metal table. Two men in white lab coats loomed over her.

"But I was tired of being their pit bull."

"You should have just done your job, Jana. Killed the freaks and done your damn job." Beth's voice. She stepped forward, her arms crossed over her chest. "We don't tolerate failure here."

"Bite me." The words came, slow and sluggish because they'd drugged her.

Beth's lips tightened. "The wolf is going to die. It's a matter of time. He's going to die and so are you."

Then the two men reached for her, scalpels in their hands.

"They liked pain." She swallowed. "I wasn't the . . . only one they worked on. While I was with them, I saw—I saw the supernaturals they brought in. Those doctors cut them open. Hell, they did it while they were *alive*. They cut them, and they tortured them just to see how much pain they could take. We were all just experiments to them."

And he saw the blood-soaked images. One after the other.

"They made a mistake with me. They needed to keep me conscious while they cut into my head, and they didn't drug me heavily enough."

The damn scalpels glinted. Each bastard had one gripped in a white-gloved hand. "Today we slice into that brain. Let's see if she's wired to burn."

Jana's eyes had gone to the men. Marked them. Even as Beth's high heels tapped across the tiled floor, Jana let the power swell. The heat spread through her as the charge grew, burning hotter, hotter as it swelled with her rage.

The fire erupted.

He jerked back, almost feeling the flames on his skin. But, no, that hadn't been real. The room was cold. Ice cold. Jana stood before him. Just her. No flames.

"They've improved on their drugs since my last . . . stay." Again, he heard her thoughts because he was still in her mind. "They're keeping the room cold to further lock down my power. Unless I can charge up, I'm going to be powerless, and they *know* that."

She stepped forward. Closing the space he'd created when he stumbled back. "I need to get warm." Whispered in his mind. The fingertips she pressed to his cheek seemed so cold. Not like Jana's hot touch. *"Help me."* When she exhaled, he saw a faint puff of white near her lips. *Too cold.*

He wanted to help her. After what he'd seen . . . fuck, life wasn't black and white, he *knew* that. Jana wasn't the heartless assassin he'd originally pictured. But he'd already known that, even without slipping into her past.

His gift. He didn't just pick up on thoughts when he went into someone's mind. He *saw* the person's life. Hell, that was one of the many reasons he never went inside a human's head.

Sometimes, you didn't want to see the dark deeds that should stay hidden.

Jana's past wasn't pretty, but then, neither was his.

"Sex can charge me." The words echoed in his mind though her lips never moved. "When the lust burns inside, it'll push back the fog from the drugs and help me to fight the cold." Her gaze held his. *"Don't let me be weak when they come back for me."*

Zane swallowed.

"Please." Her whisper broke the air and broke him.

His mouth pressed against hers even as his hands reached for her. He pulled her close, so close, crushing her against him. There'd be no time for finesse. No gentle loving. The assholes out there could come in at any moment, and he'd be damned if he left her weak.

The moment their lips touched, the lust flared between them. The need, the desire that was always so close when she was around him erupted. Her lips were soft, silken, and her tongue moved eagerly to meet his.

Her nipples stabbed against his chest and a low murmur rolled in her throat. She might want him to touch her so that her power would come back, but she also just wanted him. That was damn good, because he sure wanted her.

Zane lifted his head and his power poured out. It surged around them, and a gray fog swirled in the air. The fog thickened, tightening, making a wall around their bodies, and blocking the preying eyes. There was no way he'd let those bastards see him with Jana.

Her lips lifted in the briefest of smiles. "I knew you were strong," she whispered and took his mouth again. Lips, tongue, *need*.

His heart thudded in his chest. The assholes watching the cameras would freak out when they saw the fog. They wouldn't have much time.

Enough time . . .

His hands pushed between them. He found the snap of her jeans. Jerked the button, eased down the zipper.

"Zane . . ."

He shoved the jeans down. His fingers pushed under the elastic edge of her panties and found plump, sweet flesh. Her nails sank into his arms as she held on tight.

"Burn for me," he whispered as he let his mouth feather over her throat. "Burn." His fingers stroked her sex. His thumb pushed down on her clit and the scent of her arousal teased his nostrils.

He wanted her legs spread wide. Wanted to lick his way across that pink flesh. But . . .

No time.

His cock shoved against the front of his jeans. Hard, swollen, and probably getting an imprint of a zipper on the flesh.

Take her, take—

His fingers plunged inside of her. Two fingers, knuckle deep. Jana rose onto her toes, even as her eyes widened with a surge of pleasure.

She wasn't burning yet, but she would be, soon.

Footsteps pounded in the hallway. *Fuck.*

Not enough . . . not enough.

He bit her on the neck, a rough score with his teeth. Not too hard. A marking because demons liked to mark their prey, too.

His fingers withdrew, then drove deep. Again, again. He worked a third finger into her. She was slick and eager now, her flesh yielding so sweetly to him.

"Zane . . . *hurry . . . no time . . .*" Her hands went to his waist. Fumbled with the snap of his jeans.

More footsteps, closer, *closer . . .*

"I need you in me," she said, her eyes wide, hungry, lost. "Zane, I need—"

His thumb pushed over the center of her need. His fingers claimed her flesh again, and her whole body stiffened. Jana stared at him with wide eyes.

And came.

He kissed her, thrusting his tongue into her mouth even as his fingers continued to thrust into her silken warmth. Thrusting and drawing out the orgasm that squeezed his fingers.

Voices rose in the hall. The door began to squeak.

He kept his mouth on hers. His lips were softer now, easier. The lust still rode him, a hunger so deep that he ached. *Want inside. Want her legs around me. Want her sex squeezing me.*

He shuddered against her.

"*Jana!*" Beth's angry voice.

Fucking company.

He eased away. Jana stared up at him. A frown pulled her brows low. Her cheeks were flushed. Her lips parted.

Zane bent and pulled up her jeans. Her hands reached out, tangling with his. "Why did you—"

He shook his head.

The door burst open.

With a wave of his hand, the fog slipped away, and he found himself staring at Beth and six armed guards. Zane moved forward, putting his body between them and Jana.

"What the hell have you done?" Beth demanded.

Not nearly as much as he would have liked. But Beth didn't know that. The Perseus agent didn't know a damn thing.

"Get him out of here," she barked and a light puff of air appeared before her mouth. Was it really that cold? Once he'd started touching Jana, he hadn't even noticed.

The guards marched toward him. Zane lifted his hands, more than ready to blast them back.

"We've got a friend of yours waiting to meet you," Beth said and he didn't like the calculation in her eyes.

"Doubtful. I don't think any of my *friends* would be here."

"Ummm." Her gaze tried to flicker to Jana, but he didn't move. They weren't getting to her yet. Every second that passed was a second she got stronger. *Don't worry, baby, you won't be weak.*

"I'm sure you've realized that we must have used one very powerful witch to keep you locked in this room." A delicate pause, and Beth didn't strike him as the delicate type. "Not that we *wanted* to lock you up, but until you can see reason, we have no choice."

Oh, yeah, right. They were doing a bang-up job of convincing him that Perseus was a bright, shiny, happy corporation—of killers.

"Everyone always has choice," he threw back. Like his choice right now was to let these idiots feel his power or . . .

Or wait. Because every damn snake had a head and if he wanted to destroy Perseus, he had to take the head. Cut the thing off. If he just blew his way through the flunkies, he'd be wasting his time. But it would feel *real* good.

"*You* have a choice now," Beth said. "You can go with the guards and get reacquainted with your friend, or you can leave the facility."

Leave? Sure, they'd just let him walk out. Did he look stupid?

"I notice you aren't giving me any choices." Jana's quiet voice carried easily, and then she stepped to his side. A swift glance showed she was all buttoned up. Her clothes were back in place and no trace of passion or lust showed on her face.

Meanwhile his cock was still up and aching—and even the guns pointing at him weren't slowing him down.

Jana shivered, a quick movement that shook her body. A movement that Beth caught because her lips began to twist—but she stopped herself before smiling fully. Instead, the agent said, "Oh, Jana, I'm sorry, is it too cold in here for you?"

Another delicate shiver. "Cold? No . . . I'm just fine." Her shoulders straightened.

"Go with the guards, Zane," Beth urged him. "Let us reassure you about Perseus without Jana's . . . ah, bias . . . coming in the way."

Bias? Is that what it was?

"And Jana . . ." Now Beth's eyes locked on her. "Your status has recently changed. You are no longer a person of interest for Perseus. If you leave tonight, you won't be followed again. You'll be free."

What? They'd gone to all the trouble of tracking her, they'd locked them in this ice box, and now they were just going to let them both walk?

Bullshit.

"You don't come after us," Beth continued, "and we'll forget you exist."

Baring her teeth, Jana said, "Don't know if I can make that promise."

"Well . . ." Beth's head inclined toward her. "Perhaps you and I can make a deal."

Now what the hell was that about?

"I doubt that, lady." Jana's arms crossed over her chest.

"Mr. Wynter?" Beth motioned to the guards. "I really must insist you leave with my men now."

He let a smile curve his lips. "You know, I think the guys with the guns really wreck this lie of a friendly conversation." But he walked forward. He'd come to Perseus for a reason, and he wasn't leaving until he'd finished his mission. Zane tossed a quick glance back at Jana. *You okay?* He let the question drift on the psychic link they'd made.

She gave the briefest of nods.

"Of course, she's okay," Beth said. "I think you'll soon realize that Jana is a lot stronger than she looks."

Well, shit, *Beth was psychic.*

"I've already realized it," he said, striding for the door and guarding his thoughts now. "I think you're the one in for the surprise."

When Zane left, the door shut behind him with a hollow clang of sound. Jana didn't move. She kept her eyes on the woman she really wanted to rip apart, the only woman in the room with her.

Beth Parker. The agent who'd lured her in. The agent who'd stood there and watched while she was tortured. The agent who'd turned Jana into a wanted woman.

You took away my life.

"What the hell kind of game are you playing now?" Jana asked. She knew Beth was psychic. They both were—that had been part of Beth's Perseus recruitment spiel. *Come . . . be with others who are just like you. You don't have to be alone anymore.*

Blah-fucking-blah.

"I'm not playing a game." Beth's heels tapped on the tile as she crossed toward her. "I'm trying to show Mr. Wynter that Perseus isn't as evil as you think."

Jana laughed at that. "That's right. You're *worse* than I think."

Beth shook her head. "Things were going so well. I was pleased with your progress." She sighed. "Then that shifter screwed things up for you."

"You mean things got screwed when you wanted me to kill an innocent man?" The lady was good at twisting details.

Beth's eyes narrowed. "He wasn't innocent. He'd killed a human."

"A human who murdered his girlfriend and half a dozen other girls. Call me crazy, but I think that's justifiable."

"You don't understand." Her jaw clenched and Beth gritted out, "Once the wolves start killing, they can't stop. He'd crossed a line. He was psychotic. He'd attack again and again—"

"Then why didn't he kill the girl in the alley? Huh? Why didn't he kill me?"

Click. Click. The heels were moving again. "If we don't stop the paranormals out there, they *will* take over our world. Humans will be damn servants. Prey. We'll be the food they hunt at night, and we'll have *nothing*."

She'd heard that spiel before, too. At one time, she'd believed it. "They're not all bad, Beth."

"They're sure as shit not all good, Jana."

"No one's all good." *Not me. Not you.*

Beth inclined her head. The red on her cheek looked even angrier in the hard light. "I know." A touch of sadness coated the words, but then she lifted her chin. "I've been authorized to offer you a deal."

"Bullshit." Were they really back to this? Jana uncrossed her arms and let her hands slip to her sides. "You've been authorized to kill me. You think I don't see right through this act? I knew the minute you took Zane out of here that you'd be coming at me." She kept her mind blank, not wanting Beth to pick up on her plans.

But Beth's brows rose. "Killing you was never the plan for me. You're a human. I don't kill humans."

Liar, liar. Beth might not *like* killing humans, but she executed the ones that got in her way, and she didn't hesitate. "Oh, right, your preferred method of attack with humans is to wreck their lives. Make 'em into wanted criminals and—"

"I was simply trying to bring you back home." Again she spoke with that wistfulness that could have been sadness. "I liked you, Jana. In so many ways, you reminded me of"—a light laugh—"me."

"Well call me a freaking mirror." Fury spiked in her blood.

Beth's gaze raked her. "There are two ways this can work."

Jana stared at her and pictured darkness. A wall of perfect black in her mind.

"You're not strong enough to take Perseus down. You don't even have a clue of just how powerful we are. You can try." Beth shrugged. "But you'll fail."

"You know what? This polite bullshit is wearing thin. Zane's not here, so you don't have to pretend you're anything other than a cold-blooded killer—"

"Option two is that I take that fire away from you."

Jana's mouth went dry.

"Ah . . . I've got your attention, don't I? You know we can't just let you loose out there, Jana. If you're not on our side, you're too dangerous . . . as you are." Beth exhaled heavily. "But with a few modifications, you wouldn't be a threat anymore. You'd just be a regular human. Like all the others we protect."

Still spouting that protection bull, but . . . "You can stop the fire?" She had to ask.

A slow nod. Beth's blond hair brushed against her fire-stained cheek. "You can be normal, Jana. It will only take a few moments. Just a few. Then you can walk out of here and have the life you've always wanted."

The temptation was so strong. "You've been hunting me all this time . . ."

"Because you're too dangerous with the fire." Her jaw hardened, stretching those scars. "Without it, you're no threat."

"But if I keep my fire . . . ?"

Beth didn't speak. But then, Jana already knew the answer. *Keep it and die.* Because she wasn't just going to have the chance to walk away with her power.

"Don't you want to be normal?" Beth inched closer. "Don't you want to know what it's like to have a family? Real friends? To not be the freak who's always standing on the outside?" Beth's hand lifted. The hand marked with the raised and red flesh reached toward Jana. "I can give it to you. I can give your life back to you."

"And what do you get?" Because she wasn't a fool. No way would Perseus toss her this shiny, tasty apple without having one big worm crawling around inside of it.

"We get you off our asses."

If only it were that simple.

"It *is* that simple, Jana. Just take what we're offering, and walk away."

Davey waited for him in the hallway. When he saw the guards lead Zane out, his lips tightened. "I got him, okay, guys? Go take a break."

The guards didn't move. Davey straightened away from the wall. "*I've got him.*"

They shuffled back.

"Beth wants me to take you to meet the witch," Davey told him, thrusting back his shoulders. "She thinks Jana's screwed with your mind. Convinced you that we're evil."

No, when they'd blown up Night Watch—*that* had convinced him.

"But maybe . . . maybe if you can hear that we aren't monsters, if you hear that from someone you trust, you'll believe us. You'll realize that Perseus isn't some sick nightmare that needs to be put down." A deep breath. "We're a group that you can join. You can help us, we can help you, and in the end, we'd make this world one hell of a lot better."

Zane stared back at him. *Someone that you trust.* At those words, he'd gotten a real bad feeling in his gut. There was only one witch that he truly trusted in the world. She'd disappeared from Baton Rouge a few months back, right after Dee Daniels, another Night Watch agent, had almost been killed. "Take me to the fucking witch." *Now.*

Davey turned away and led him down the hall. Past the locked, metal doors. Past more guards.

Zane's heartbeat thundered in his ears. There was no way, no damn way, that they were talking about the same witch. They couldn't be. They—

Davey opened a door. The room inside was dim. A long, skinny table, a few chairs, and a woman waited inside. The woman spun toward them, her hair—so blond it was almost white—flying around her face. Oh, hell.

"Zane? she breathed his name.

He stared at the witch he'd known for five years. His ex-lover, a woman he'd trusted with his darkest secrets: Catalina Delaney.

"Go ahead, Catalina," Davey said, walking closer to her. "Tell your friend the truth about Perseus. Tell him that Jana Carter lied to him. Tell him what we're *really* like."

He stared into her moss-green eyes—eyes the color of the swamp she'd been raised in—and waited for the truth. Because Catalina had never lied to him before.

"They're not evil, Zane," she whispered. "They want to save the world. Not destroy it."

No, she'd never lied to him before.

So why was she starting now?

Chapter 12

"We aren't the only humans with psychic powers." Beth licked her lips. "There are others out there, so many others."

Really? Where had they been all her life? While Jana was feeling like a freak, *where* had they been?

"Some powers aren't strong. Some people can just see the briefest glimpses of the future. So many have weak talents."

She just stared at Beth. Being weak wasn't really an issue for her when it came to power.

"Others are stronger with more . . . unusual gifts."

'Cause what? Creating fire was common?

Beth's gaze pinned her. "Recently, we found an individual with a power we'd never imagined."

"Good damn deal for you." She was charged enough. She didn't even feel the cold anymore, though Beth had started to shiver. Time to blast her way out of this room. Time to blast Perseus apart. There were other paranormals imprisoned here. She'd bet on it. She could free them, get to safety, and—

"This woman we found . . . she can touch you and take away your power."

Jana's breath caught in her throat.

Beth smiled. "I thought you might be curious about her. You see, if she touches you, all that wonderful fire will go away, and you'll be normal again. You won't be a threat to Perseus."

She wouldn't be a threat to anyone.

"We'll leave you alone," Beth promised. "And you can just walk away. You'll be able to live a normal life."

Jana's breath shot out on a long, hard exhale.

Beth held her gaze. "Do you want that, Jana? Would you like to be normal? To be just like everyone else? All you have to do—"

The door opened behind Beth and a young girl walked inside. The girl appeared to be maybe nineteen or twenty. She wore thick glasses, and she had long, straight brown hair that hid half of her face.

"All you have to do," Beth said again, "is just let her touch you."

"You're lying, Catalina," Zane said. He shook his head. "Did you really think I wouldn't be able to tell when you lied to me?"

She smiled then, a wide, full smile. "No, Zane. I was *sure* you'd know." Then she lifted up her hands and said, "Now, please, help me get the hell out of here!"

A dozen guards exploded into the room behind her.

Davey yelled, "What the fu—"

Zane shook his head. So much for the lying front. His power erupted and hit them all.

Jana's hands tightened into fists. "Don't take another step."

The girl stilled.

"What happens when she takes the fire away?" Oh, so tempting. "Where does it go?"

Beth blinked. "Nowhere. It won't hurt anyone."

Bull. "You take it, *where does it go?*" Because this crap wasn't making sense. Perseus had been desperate to get her back. So desperate they'd tracked her across Louisiana. If they'd just wanted her out of the picture, she would have been dead.

They didn't want her dead. They wanted her alive. *Because they couldn't take the fire from a dead woman?*

The girl wasn't speaking. Her dark eyes looked so big behind the glasses, and her skin was stark white.

An alarm sounded then. A high-pitched, whining alarm. Beth flinched and swore. "Dumb bitch. She should've just done her damn part."

What?

Footsteps pounded outside. Sounded like guards were racing toward them.

Beth's face hardened. Her hand lifted, and she stabbed a finger in the air toward Jana. "The demon is going to die. If he won't help us, then we'll rip him apart."

Shit. So much for playing nice. Now the mask was gone and she was back to seeing the real Beth.

"But first . . ." Beth said, pausing as the guards spilled into the room. "First we're taking that fire from you. We're taking it, and we're going to make sure you're nothing but a corpse when we leave this room."

Now, *this* was the Beth she knew and hated. "Bring it, bitch." Jana let the charge shoot through her. "If you think you're strong enough, come on." A line of fire split the floor between them. *Charge more. Charge.* "Let's see if you still like my fire."

"Shoot her!" Beth screamed at the guards. "Not the head or the heart, but shoot her! Take her down!"

The bullets flew through the air as the flames blazed higher.

Zane scooped up Catalina and held her tight. He ran out of the room and into the narrow hallway. That screaming alarm pierced his ears. A constant, high-pitched wail that threatened to burst his ear drums. He blasted his power out in waves, knocking back every guard he saw as he shoved his energy at them.

Jana. He needed to get to her. He didn't know how long her charge would last and—

"Zane?" Catalina's breathy voice. He glanced down. Her eyes were fluttering open. Witches were so incredibly strong. He'd figured that she would wake up fast.

He put his back against the nearest wall and eased Catalina to her feet. "What the hell are you doing here?" The last time he'd seen her, they'd both been in a shit-forsaken vampire hell. The vamps had surrounded Catalina with fire. *Burn, witch.* He'd gotten to her in time, saved her from the touch of fire, but she'd still left. Still left because . . .

"*I'm not the one for you.*" Her words echoed through his mind. Catalina had scryed to see the future, and what she'd seen had made her run.

He hadn't heard from her in months. Had she been here the whole time? Trapped by Perseus?

"It's not like I wanted to be here." Her breath shuddered out, and she yanked up the sleeve of her shirt. There, on her upper arm, he saw two thin white lines. Scars. No, hell, *no.* Binding marks. He'd only seen them once before in his life, but he knew what they were—*marks to bind a witch's power.*

"I don't have a coven to protect me." Her gaze was steady, proud. "When the agents came to me, I didn't realize what they had planned for me, not until it was too late."

Until the first binding mark appeared.

"Three marks," she whispered and he heard her, even with the wailing alarm. "Three and I'm completely helpless. With two"—she swallowed—"my powers became so weak, I wasn't able to fight back against the bastards."

Shit. "I'm getting you out of here."

But she shook her head. "There are others here. I won't leave them."

"Others?"

"A wolf shifter . . . and a vampire. I won't leave them."

A woman's scream ripped through the air. *Jana.* He lunged forward. Catalina grabbed his arm. "They want you. They've seen what you can do. If they can keep you here, if they can use you—"

"No one's gonna fucking use me."

"They were going to kill me two days ago," she told him, her lips trembling. "Then they realized I knew you. I'm alive just because—"

Another scream. *Jana.* He broke Catalina's hold. "Cat, get out of here! Run, and I'll find you!" But first, he was getting Jana.

"I'm alive because I told them your weakness." Her whispered words floated behind him. "I'm sorry, Zane."

He spun back to face her. "Cat?"

Her shoulders were slumped. Her head down. "They were going to put on the third bind. I didn't have a choice. They know about—"

The drugs. Shit.

She looked up at him. A tear tracked down her cheek. "I'm sorry."

The screams had stopped. He could smell smoke drifting in the air. Coming closer. "Fire's coming." *Catalina's weakness.* "Get out. Just run!"

Fear had her eyes flaring wide, but she shook her head. "Not without the others." She stumbled down the hallway, lifting her hand toward him. "Come with me, Zane. Don't go back, they're waiting for you! It's all a trap."

He knew it, but . . . "They've got someone I—" Someone, what? Someone he needed? Someone he sure as shit wouldn't leave behind? *She didn't leave me.* "I'm not leaving her," was all he said.

Catalina's lips parted, and her eyes seemed to lose a bit of focus. The shift in her glance always happened when she used her magic. "No." A bit sad. "You can't leave her."

There wasn't time to waste. Zane ran down the hall, bellowing Jana's name.

A mass of swirling and crackling flames shot down the hallway. He shoved the fire to the side even as water poured down from the sprinklers above him. *What the hell?*

The door to the holding room was open. He rushed inside, and the smoke shoved its way down his throat. *"Jana! Jana, pull back the fire!"*

But Jana was lying in the middle of the room with her hair a black curtain around her face. Flames ate at the walls and the ceiling.

Beth stood near those flames, her body swaying.

Hell. He poured his power out as he fought the flames. The heat scorched his flesh.

The fire retreated from him, and he leapt to Jana's side. She was slowly pushing herself up.

"Pull it back," he growled, locking his fingers around her arms as he drew her close. "It's okay, baby, I'm here now, you can ease up on the f—"

She blinked at him. Her eyes were tired, weak, and dark blue.

He heard the laughter then. Wild, wicked laughter. He turned his head and found Beth staring at him—with eyes gone dark red.

"N-not me . . ." Jana whispered as her hands twisted to hold tight to him. Her nails sank into his skin. "Not a-anymore."

Another ball of flames shot straight at him. He threw his body over Jana's even as he sent the fire slamming into the south-side wall with a psychic surge of energy. Jana coughed beneath him and shuddered.

"You're going to die, demon!" Beth yelled, her voice rising above the flames. "You're both going to burn!"

Zane glanced up and saw the flames rolling over the ceiling. Looked like clouds of fire. Not. Good.

"You should have joined us when you had the chance." More laughter from Beth. "Now I'll just burn you until there's nothing left."

The hell she would.

Zane threw up his hands, pushing a powerful wave of energy at her just as Beth's flames came for him again. The flames froze in mid-air, caught between them, and Beth screamed.

"She won't be able to . . . handle it. . . ." Jana coughed again and pushed against him. "Not the first time . . . not . . ."

The flames swelled. They shoved against his hold. Burned so hot.

"The ceiling's gonna fall. . . ." Jana jerked from beneath

him. "We've got to get out of here!" Her hands grabbed at his arms. "*Come on!*"

Beth screamed again, a loud, desperate cry as she fell to her knees. The flames erupted, shooting across the room, and chunks of the ceiling fell down, crashing onto the floor.

He ran with Jana, holding back the fire and charging for the door. The smoke, heavy and gray, blocked their path, but they barreled straight through it and, with his help, through the flames.

Beth's yells followed them, blending with the piercing alarm, and the crackle of the fire.

He and Jana thundered down the hallway. Guards were running, hell-bent on getting away from the flames so they didn't even toss him or Jana a second glance. The guards sure didn't try to stop them. *Too busy running.*

Zane risked a glance behind him. The fire was destroying everything, burning so bright. Sending screams of terror into the air. As he watched, two men appeared near the back wall. Chameleons being forced out of their camouflage because of the fire's heat. One of the bastards was the one who'd attacked Jana.

He was burning, screaming as he fell to the ground. The flames flared higher around him and the other chameleon. Trapping them, killing them.

Zane's legs pumped as he searched for a way out of the nightmare. *Not Jana's fire.* What the hell had happened? And why hadn't Jana mentioned that Beth was an Ignitor?

Fuck. Just when he'd thought he could trust her . . .

They burst through some double doors and out into the night. Jana sucked in deep gulps of air and fell to her knees.

The clean air almost seemed to burn his lungs. "Jana . . ." His voice sounded like gravel.

Her head turned toward him. Her eyes were wet with tears. From the smoke? Or something more?

"Why didn't you tell me?" He lifted her up and carried her farther away from that burning building and the screams that echoed inside. "Why didn't you tell me what Beth could do?"

She just shook her head.

"*Fuck.*" He sat her down near the edge of the swamp. "Stay here."

She grabbed his arms. "Where . . . are you going?" she rasped.

"I've got a friend in there. I'm not leaving her for the flames." He wouldn't leave Catalina to her worst nightmare.

"Friend?" Her brow wrinkled. Ash stained her cheeks. "With . . . Perseus?"

Yeah, okay, that sounded screwed. "Just stay here, okay?" But even as he said the words, he knew she'd be gone when he came back. It was her perfect chance to run. "They've got supernaturals caged in there." His voice grew stronger with every word, just as those flames were growing stronger with every second that passed. "I'm not letting them burn."

Perseus was dying tonight, burning to the ground, but they weren't taking the paranormals out with them.

He whirled away from Jana and ran right back into the fire.

Jana shook her head, stunned, as Zane disappeared into the smoke again. What was he thinking? Didn't he realize those flames weren't going to stop? They were blazing out of control. Even a level ten couldn't fight them—not with an Ignitor constantly charging them up. *The first fire is always the hottest. Too strong. Can't stop it.*

She lifted a shaking hand to her head. Oh, God, how had this happened? One minute, that girl had been running toward her, and Jana had been getting her charge strong enough to blast, then—

Then Beth had been in control of the flames.

And I'd had nothing.

Jana had been surrounded by fire but, for the first time, completely at its mercy. If Zane hadn't come in there, she would have died.

Her eyes squeezed shut. *I've got a friend in there. I'm not leaving her for the flames.* Beth had taunted him about a friend. *We've got a friend of yours waiting to meet you.*

What friend?

She stumbled to her feet. A guard ran out of the smoke. He didn't glance her way. He just raced for the truck parked near the line of twisted trees.

Trying to get away?

She sucked in another breath and went after him. "Hey, hey, wait!"

He grabbed the door handle and wrenched open the door. "Look, buddy—"

He swung around to face her. Jana slammed her fist into his face. She might not have her fire right then, but she wasn't helpless.

The guy sank to the ground. She went with him, patting his pockets, finding his keys, a cell phone, and—*yes!*—a gun. Jana tucked the gun into the waistband of her jeans and glanced back at the fire. Zane was in there. Other paranormals were trapped inside. She looked down at her hands. Cell phone. Keys. The perfect time to escape. There were no more ties to her past. Perseus wouldn't come after her. She could get away clean.

But Zane was in the fire.

Zane.

She punched in a quick series of numbers on the cell phone. Numbers she'd memorized earlier, when she'd seen Zane make one of his calls. The phone rang once, twice—

"Who the hell is this?" a snarling voice demanded.

Jana's fingers tightened around the phone. "I'm calling about Zane Wynter." She didn't have a whole lot of time to waste.

"Zane?" The voice quieted. "Is he okay?"

"Kinda hard to say." She bit her lip and rose, stepping away from the fallen guard and keeping his keys. She had to strain to make her voice louder and clearer when she said, "He's in the fire right now."

"*What?*"

"I don't know where we are," she said. "Some damn swamp."

Other voices murmured in the background, then he told her, "Just keep the phone on. We can find you."

"Send some fire trucks, would you?" She watched those flames blaze. They'd burned through the roof and were reaching so high. With a fire like this, there was only one way to stop the flames. Just one . . . "People are still inside. They need help."

A pause. Then he asked, "Is it your fire, Jana?"

It should have been. "I'll keep the phone on," she said. "You just get help out here, got it? Perseus is burning, but I'm not letting them destroy Zane."

Then she put the phone on the hood of the truck and made the stupidest move of her life. She went back into the fire.

"Help me . . ." The voice drew Zane in closer. It was weak, rough, desperate.

Not Catalina.

He found himself in the same conference room he'd been in when he'd first seen Catalina. The fire had already come inside, the flames surging against the walls. The guards were gone. They'd cleared out fast, but then, his psychic blast wouldn't have kept them knocked out for long.

He'd never seen a fire like this one. Even with his power, it was hard to push the flames back. And if he hadn't been so high on the demon scale then he never would have been able to clear a path back inside. The fire was too wild.

The flames weren't just sticking to the walls. They were surging forward, actually tracking people—as if they were intent on killing. Hell, they *were* intent. An Ignitor aimed the fire where she wanted it. Beth wanted the fire to kill, and it was. Only, it wasn't just killing Beth's enemies. It was killing everyone.

"Help . . . me . . ." The voice came again and Zane hurried forward, even as he shoved back those greedy flames. He rushed down the hallway and turned right. Another room, this one with chains on the walls.

He found Davey on the floor. His legs were pinned by a

heavy metal cage that had fallen onto him. Hell, this must be some kind of damn containment room. Fire circled around Davey, but the demon held the flames back from him, keeping a protective circle around his body. A circle that barely seemed to be holding. Blood dripped from his temple. "*Don't leave me here.*"

Zane stared down at the kid. "You chose the wrong side."

Tears leaked from his eyes. "I chose the—the only side that I had! I was trying—trying to save l-lives!" The fire inched closer. Young Davey wasn't a strong demon, that much was obvious, or he would have freed himself by now.

A weak demon. A kid. One who'd been pulled in and used by humans gone crazy with their own power.

"Tell me where you keep the paranormal prisoners."

The flames inched closer to Davey's legs. That circle was failing. The demon screamed.

"*Tell me.*"

Davey broke. His face crumpled and he cried out, "End of the hall, go right!" He pointed with a trembling hand. "Third door! They weren't hurt, they weren't—"

"They were." Disgust had his voice thickening, but Zane waved his own hand and the metal flew off Davey's legs.

The guy gasped, staring up at him with wide eyes.

"We're not all evil, kid. You need to start realizing that."

Davey pushed to his feet. Almost fell right back down. A broken leg wouldn't stop a demon. The guy could still manage to get out of there.

Zane turned away from him. He tore down the hall. "*Catalina!*" With two binding marks, she'd never be able to control the fire. If it came after her the way it had come after the others . . .

Burn, witch.

Her worst fear.

His feet pounded on the hard floor as he searched for her, running down that snaking hallway and following the desperate directions Davey had given him. If the kid had been lying . . .

Zane turned a hard right, then slammed his foot into the third door he saw. The door shattered and flew forward and he saw Catalina on the floor. Her hands were jerking at the chains that bound two men to the wall.

She whirled toward him with a gasp, but the fear left her eyes when she saw him. *"Zane! Help me!"*

The fire hadn't gotten to them yet. Smoke seeped inside the windowless room from the vents, but otherwise, they were okay. He hurried forward and grabbed the manacle on the first guy's hand. The man, blond, young, with glinting blue eyes—*shit, the guy I saw when I went into Jana's mind*—just shook his head. "You can't break 'em. They're reinforced, even I can't—"

Zane shattered the manacle. "You can't because they're made of silver." *They know your weakness.* The old story about werewolves and their silver weakness was based on some fact. He broke the other manacle. The shifter stepped forward, then staggered. Long cuts and incisions covered his chest and legs. Fuck.

Catalina jumped to her feet and put her arms around him, trying to help him to balance.

The other guy hadn't moved. His skin was gray, his dark head hung low, and the scent of blood was heavy around him.

"Be careful, Zane," Catalina said, "they've bled him for days, and he hasn't—"

The guy's head snapped up when Zane got close, and wickedly sharp fangs came at his throat. Zane caught the guy's chin in one hand and held tight. *"Easy."* Black eyes stared back at him. Not demon eyes. The sclera was still white, but the iris had faded to pitch black. A vamp in hunting mode. No, a vamp who was starving. "I'm not on the menu."

The vamp snarled. Zane fired a fast glance at Catalina. "We leave this one. He's too far gone. Vamps attack anyway and he's—"

"Please." A desperate whisper from the vampire. *"Won't . . . bite. . . . Don't . . . leave. . . ."*

"He comes with us." Catalina stared at him with a raised chin. "They drained his blood for the last four days. He's starving."

"All the more fucking reason to leave him here." Zane didn't ease his grip. *Wasting time. Was Jana still outside? Had she already left him?* "A hungry vamp is a dangerous vamp." No, *any* vamp was a dangerous vamp. "We don't have a lot of time. The fire's coming—"

"I-I know, but we can't leave him!"

He glanced back at the vamp. At those dark eyes.

"*Won't . . . bite . . . you. . . .*" the vamp said again. His fangs were still out, his eyes still so dark. "*Begging . . .*"

His jaw clenched. "If you do, you're dead, Drac." Simple fact. He eyed the chains holding the guy. Looked like the same kind of metal he used for his cuffs. "Cat, is there a little something extra on these . . . ?"

He glanced back and saw her trembling nod.

"Do you have enough magic to break it?"

She sucked in a sharp breath. "I'll use everything I've got."

Too dangerous, she shouldn't—

She began to chant, low but fast, breaking the spell that had been weaved on the cuffs.

"*My* spell," she whispered as her shoulders sagged and her face paled and more shame flared in her eyes.

Shit. They'd forced her to help keep the vamp trapped. Bastards. If this place weren't already burning to hell and back . . . Growling, he broke the manacles, snapping the locks and freeing the vamp.

The vampire fell forward and slammed into Zane. Zane caught him, grunting at the impact. That vamp's teeth were way too close to his throat. There was only one vamp in the world he'd bleed for, and Dee wasn't anywhere near them. "Watch it," he ordered, but the vamp just slumped harder against him.

He looked down. The vamp's eyes were closed. The guy was dead to the world—well, again.

Zane hefted him up and draped the vamp over his shoulder. "We've got to get out of here, we've got to—"

"*You're not going anywhere.*"

Shit. He *knew* that they'd taken too long. He turned around and found Beth in the doorway. Flames flickered behind her, bright orange and red flames.

Beth's red stare—the stare of an Ignitor charged up and burning hot—tracked across the room, landing briefly on them all, as if marking them. Maybe she was. *Aim and fire.* "None of you are leaving." A brief smile. "Not alive, anyway."

Zane dropped the vamp to the floor and stalked forward. The guy's groan rumbled in his ears, blending with the crackle of the flames. "Cat, get 'em all out." He'd take the Perseus agent on.

"*How?*" Catalina's scream. "There's only one door, and she's—"

Blocking it with a wall of flames. Yeah, he saw that.

"The walls are reinforced with steel. Your witch is too weak to break out." Beth came closer. Those flames danced right along with her. "They're all too weak to do anything but die."

They might be. He wasn't. Zane sucked in a deep breath, letting his own power swell. Then, spinning away from Beth, he blasted a long, hard wave of energy at the far wall. The wall exploded, shooting outward with a scream of metal. "Go!"

The fire caught him then. A hot lick that raced up his legs and back. Instantly, he pushed down the flames but, dammit, that had *hurt.*

Beth's laughter filled his ears. "Bad mistake. You just traded your life for theirs."

Because he'd given the bitch the perfect moment to strike. *Shit.* And he still had to focus his power, use his energy to protect the others, because she'd let the fire loose and it was racing for Catalina. And Catalina—she stood frozen, staring at the flames with eyes too wide, terrified, as—

Jana jumped through the hole he'd knocked into the wall. "*Zane!*"

No, shit, no! "Get out!"

More laughter. "Oh, no, she's just the one I was hoping to burn. Payback's coming," Beth said.

Jana's gaze widened. The flames were spreading too fast. Eating the floor, the walls . . .

And burning like a bitch at his back.

Hold it . . . control it . . . He couldn't focus his attack on Beth. Not with the fire so close to the others. He pushed against the fire, but the flames kept flaring higher. *Her fire's stronger than—*

Jana ran for Catalina. She grabbed the witch's arm and yanked her. "*Move!*"

Catalina shook her head and finally seemed to snap back to reality. She turned and hauled ass, dragging her shifter with her.

Yes . . .

"The man on the floor—get him!" Catalina screamed to Jana.

Um, not a man, not really—

Jana dove over the flames and grabbed the vamp's hand. "I've got him. Zane—stop Beth! Save yourself!"

She *did* have the vamp. She grabbed both his wrists and she started pulling him toward their new escape hole.

So Zane turned his attention back to the woman who was trying to burn him.

"*No!*" Beth screamed, and the fire flared higher, hotter. "She's not getting away!"

"Yeah, she is." *But you're not.* He could concentrate just on her now. And he knew how to stop an Ignitor.

The flames circled them, caging him and Beth together. Her eyes were so red he couldn't even see her pupils anymore. Red as fire. Her body trembled and drops of blood splattered from her nose.

"You started the fire at Night Watch, didn't you?" he asked. Another Ignitor, it made sense now, it—

"Yeah, yeah, I paid the assholes to torch the place." Her voice rasped out. More blood flew from her nostrils, and she began to shake. "My plan, my call—and it would've worked fucking perfectly! The FBI was going to grab Jana, more of the paranormal assholes were going to burn—killing two fucking birds!"

His hands clenched. Before he ended this, he had to know . . . "Who is your boss? Who set this whole nightmare up?" Who was behind Perseus?

She laughed at him. Laughed with madness and power echoing in the wild sound. "I *am* Perseus. A human killing the monsters."

He didn't want a lesson in Greek myth. "Who's your boss?" he roared over the flames. Who'd begun the chain of death? He had to know, he had to—

"My game," she told him with a sick smile. "What? Don't you think a human could do it? Don't you think a human could take down demons? Could send them to hell?"

"I think . . ." Shit, it was hot. Sweat trickled down his face and back. "Humans can be damn dangerous."

Another laugh. The fire leapt higher. "Yes . . . we can."

"Your fire is getting out of control." *Wait . . . just wait.* He had to give Jana time to clear out with the others before he struck. Perseus was about to explode.

Implode.

Her eyes widened. "Scared, demon? Because you know I'm stronger than you? You can't stop my fire!"

That circle of flames closed tighter.

"No, I'm not scared." He shook his head. He didn't hear Jana's footsteps anymore. Couldn't, not over the crackle and roar of the flames. "But you should be." *Only one way to stop an Ignitor's fire.* He sent his own fire and power plunging right at her. The blast hit Beth in the chest, and she stumbled back, screaming.

The fire went wild. Uncontrolled, for that brief moment, the circle broke and the flames licked back toward Beth, turning on her. Delicate human flesh.

Beth didn't get up.

But a scream rose above the flames. Pain filled. Afraid. Female. Not coming from inside—*outside*.

Jana.

She'd gotten out, but what—who—had been waiting for her? *Fuck, fuck!*

Another scream broke the air. Then, "No, dammit, *stop!*"

Zane lunged for that hole in the wall, shouting her name. The smoke and flames chased him as he burst outside.

He flew forward, sucking the fresh air into his lungs. "Jana!"

There. Jana was near the swamp. On the ground . . . with that asshole vampire over her. His teeth *in* her neck. She was pounding his back, kicking, shoving, while her right hand struggled to reach a gun that was just a few feet away.

But where was her fire? Why hadn't she just burned the asshole to ash?

"Get the fuck away from her!" He roared.

The vamp didn't stop. Snarling, Zane lunged forward and closed the distance between them in seconds. He grabbed the vamp by his neck and hauled the bastard back.

Jana cried out, and he saw the blood dripping down her neck. *Her blood.*

He threw the vamp into the muddy swamp water. "Baby, fuck, baby, are you okay?" Her face was stark white, and she was shaking.

And crying. Jana—*crying?*

He'd kill that bastard, and he'd make sure the vamp stayed dead. His fingers trembled when he touched her neck. Her blood stained his fingers.

The world went red.

Zane surged to his feet and locked his stare on the vamp. The bastard was rising from the water, his eyes open, his fangs bared.

Jana's scream. Her blood. Fucking bastard!

Chapter 13

"No!" Catalina flew in front of him. Zane shoved her to the side. Now wasn't the time for the witch to—

She grabbed his arm and held tight. "He didn't know what he was doing, Zane! They bled him nearly dry! It was instinct. He needed to survive, he needed—"

"He *attacked* her." And where the fuck had Catalina been while the vamp shoved his teeth in Jana? Water dripped down the vamp's body as he sloshed toward the shore. His stare was still black and his fangs glinted.

Rip. Him. Apart.

Catalina's nails dug into him. "Please, Zane, he-he didn't mean—"

"Screw what he meant." Jana's voice. Strong. Angry. She ran up beside Zane. "I'm not on the damn menu." She shot the vampire, blasted him right in the chest with a bullet from the gun she held in her trembling hands.

"*No!*" Catalina screamed.

Too late.

Blood blossomed on the vamp's chest. He stared at Jana a moment, his eyes flickering between blue and black, and he whispered, "S-sorry . . ." right before he toppled back into the water.

Catalina ran after him, chanting, whispering her spells—they wouldn't do much good. Not with her being so weak. And if that vamp rose again . . .

He's mine.

Jana's hand was shaking so much. *Damn blood loss.* Zane caught her hand and took the gun.

An explosion rocked the ground. Jana slipped, tumbling to her knees. Zane glanced over his shoulder. The Perseus buildings had just blown to hell and back. Guards were running, screaming, and that fire was blasting out of control as—

Fuck me. Beth was running out of the building. The flames were chasing after her, and she was headed right for him.

He grabbed Jana, pulling her to her feet. He'd protect her, make sure that—

Those flames raced toward them. Beth shrieked, "I can't stop it! Help! Make it stop! Make it—"

This time, Zane was the one who fired. His finger squeezed the trigger and the bullet thudded into Beth's heart. She gasped, shuddered, then pitched back on the ground.

The flames sputtered, then began to die, burning down slowly.

"I made it stop," he said quietly, staring at her prone body. He'd made it stop, the only way he could. His left arm wrapped around Jana and held her tight.

"Z-Zane . . ."

His head tilted down toward hers.

"This wasn't supposed to happen," she whispered, and she blinked away the tears in her eyes. "It wasn't . . ."

He kissed her. Because right then, he damn well had to. *Vamp attacked her. Could have lost her.* In the end, despite their powers, Ignitors were only human. Unlike the vamp asshole, an Ignitor couldn't take a bullet and rise again.

So easy to kill. Too easy.

His lips brushed against hers. Light at first because shit, she was delicate. So fragile. But her hands rose and sank into his hair and she arched up against him, kissing him harder, pressing her mouth tightly to his.

Zane's tongue thrust into her mouth. His hold was too hard. He knew it, but he couldn't manage to ease his grip. *Can't let her go.*

The world fell down around them, but he held her close and wondered how in the hell she'd come to mean so much to him. So much that he was ready to kill for her.

"*Zane!*" The shout broke through the chaos, but he didn't let Jana go. Not yet.

"*Zane, fuck!*" Footsteps thudded toward him. "I come to save your ass and find you gettin' ass!"

Jude. Perfect timing, as always. Slowly, Zane lifted his head. His gaze craned to the right and met the shifter's. "Arriving late to the party?"

Jude whistled as he took in the scene before him. "What the hell did you do?" The question wasn't for Zane, though. No, when he asked, his stare locked on Jana.

Tony ran up behind them. "Fire trucks are coming but—shit, *Catalina*? What are you doing here?"

"Like I said," Zane murmured, "a party." A death party.

Jana stiffened against him. "The cop?" Her whisper. She shoved against Zane, and he let her go, only because he knew there was a hell of a lot to work out. Sirens blasted in the distance. The fire trucks. Probably police cars, too.

Zane exhaled heavily. "You sure took your sweet time tracking me." Jude was usually a much better tracker. He'd thought his friend would arrive sooner. Before the fire and screams.

Tony rushed toward Catalina. She had one arm around the vamp, and she was struggling to pull him out of the water.

"What the hell happened to him?" Tony demanded.

Catalina's green eyes darted to Jana.

"I did," Jana said, squaring her shoulders and stepping even farther away from Zane. What was up with that?

Zane's eyes slit when Tony offered a hand to the vamp. "Watch it, Tony." The cop would need the warning. "The asshole with Cat bites."

"*Shit.*" From Jude. Yeah, the shifter understood—he would have caught the vamp's scent.

Instead of reaching for the vamp, Tony drew his weapon and leveled it at the guy. "My bullets are laced with holy water. Make one move at me, come at me with those teeth, and the first bullet goes between your eyes."

Tony always believed in being prepared. Smart guy.

Jana slipped back a few more steps.

Fire trucks and police cruisers flew onto the scene. The low flames flickered, and the smoke billowed. Then the uniforms burst out of their cars. Hell. Showtime.

Her neck burned. It ached and throbbed and *burned.* What the hell? You try to do something nice for someone, like oh, drag a guy's butt out of the fire, and as payment, he bites you. Did she look like a freaking buffet?

As the cops swarmed the scene, Jana eased deeper into the darkness. The firefighters were blasting the remaining flames with hoses from their trucks. Not that there was much point in fighting the fire now. Those flames were dying on their own. Without the Ignitor to fuel the fire, they would sputter out.

The Ignitor.

Jana cast a fast glance at Beth's body. Beth had lost control at the end. The fire had been too new to her. She hadn't been able to control the flames.

Because those flames were mine. The power was mine.

But Beth had taken the flames from her. And now—now she was just . . . human.

A human with a lot of blood on her hands and too many cops close by.

The butt of the gun pressed against her lower back. She'd taken it from Zane, stolen it right out of his hand while he'd kissed her.

I can still taste him. I still want him.

But Zane was about twenty feet away now and talking to that woman. The one with the pale blond hair. The one who touched him too much. The chick who'd saved the vamp. Zane hadn't attacked the vampire. He'd frozen, because of the blonde. Catalina. *The witch.* She'd heard the woman chanting when they came outside, and she'd felt the wind ripple around her in response to those words. Yeah, the blonde was a witch, though she seemed to be pretty weak in terms of power.

Beth had been right after all. There had been someone in the Perseus compound that Zane cared for. His weakness.

But Perseus was dead. Gutted. The guards and agents who'd survived the flames had fled into the swamp. The cops would search for them. If they didn't find them, Night Watch would. She didn't know what kind of bullshit explanation Zane was giving to the cops then, but it was obvious from their expressions that he had the guys eating out of his hands. The fact that he had a cop at his side—that Tony guy from Baton Rouge—probably just made his story all the more believable.

Yeah, the cops were on Zane's side, but when the smoke cleared, they wouldn't be on her side. No, she was still a wanted woman. They'd come after her, and she didn't particularly like the thought of spending any more years locked away from the world.

She stared at Zane. Watched him gesture to Beth's body. Jana swallowed. Time was running out. She needed to leave but . . .

Zane.

His gaze cut to hers. His eyes glinted, reflecting the fire. His face was hard, tight, and her breath shuddered out as she stared at him.

She'd gone back into the fire for him. Did he know that? Did he—

Zane turned away and started walking toward the back of an ambulance. Catalina was with him. . . . so was the vamp.

He turned away.

Jana kept her shoulders up. She blinked. Once. Twice. Swallowed. They'd had a deal. She'd given Zane what he wanted—Perseus. Justice for the hunters who'd died in the fire.

Now the deal was over.

"Miss?" A cop approached her with his brows drawn low. "Miss, we're gonna need to ask you a few questions."

Questions that she couldn't answer. *Hi. I'm Jana Carter. If you check, you'll see that I'm wanted in connection with a series of arsons. What? Oh, yeah, the fire tonight was arson, too. It looks like my M.O.? Really . . . um, look, why don't you just shove me in jail forever?*

She stared at the cop and shook her head. "I can't talk to you."

He blinked. "Miss?" He was a harmless looking fellow. Big, brown eyes. Pale cheeks. A bit of a receding hairline. Well, he appeared harmless . . . except for the badge and the gun he carried.

How could she get away from him? Without, of course, assaulting him. *Don't want to add assaulting an officer to my rap sheet.*

But then he gasped and those puppy dog eyes widened.

"Uh, are you okay?" she asked.

He fell to the ground.

Jana jumped back. Her heart slammed into her chest. "What the—" She found herself staring into eyes that she'd never forgotten. Bright blue eyes that seemed to shine. No, that *did* shine—with the light of the beast. *Shifter.* The wolf she'd been ordered to kill.

"You planning to stand there all night?" he demanded, and she saw that he was sweating. In the chilled air, he was sweating. And shaking. "Or do you have a plan to get out of here?"

Once more, she looked at Zane and only saw his back.

The wolf closed in on her, and Jana knew what choice she had to make.

Survival. That's what life was all about, right?

Good-bye, Zane.

The EMT was a demon. Low level. Zane took one look at the guy and saw right through the glamour. "We got a vamp here," he murmured to the EMT as he steered the guy and

Catalina toward the ambulance. Catalina wasn't releasing her hold on the vampire—probably because she knew just how much Zane wanted to rip the bastard apart.

Can't. Not with all the humans there . . .

"Get him out of here," Zane told the EMT. "Before he starts gnawing on the humans or before I have to cut his damn head off."

The EMT's eyes bulged, but he nodded quickly.

Zane glared down at Catalina. "You don't know what you're doing with him."

The vamp was weaving on his feet. He slumped forward and fell into the ambulance. The demon EMT grabbed him and shoved him onto a gurney. Then he strapped the vamp down, nice and tight.

"He didn't meant to hurt her," Catalina said. Finally, she wasn't touching the vamp. "He was starving, desperate. . . ."

No fucking excuse. Zane leaned into the ambulance. "Hey, asshole . . ."

The vamp's eyelids flickered.

"You and me are gonna be meeting up again." Once this mess with Perseus was cleaned up. "I'll find you," he promised the vamp. "Count on it." Because he wasn't getting away with attacking Jana.

The sirens screamed on. Catalina jumped into the ambulance. She bit her lip and stared down at him. "Zane . . ."

He grabbed the door and slammed it shut. He didn't trust himself to talk to her then. Not with the scent of Jana's blood still on that vamp.

He spun away and marched back toward Tony. Covering up an *Other* event with a dozen humans wasn't easy. He'd been forced to break his normal rule about not slipping into a human's mind without permission. Because, yeah, some of the cops and firefighters had seen things they shouldn't have. He'd needed to blur their memories.

Behind Tony, a team tagged and bagged Beth's body. "Where's the gun?" Tony whispered.

Zane blinked. Hell, he'd forgotten all about that. He'd

kissed Jana and—"Jana took it." Not that he blamed her. Not one bit. After the vamp's attack, she'd want to protect herself.

"We're gonna need it." Tony sighed and ran a hand through his hair. "This shit is gonna hit the fan, and we'll need—"

"You won't need anything, son." A man walked up to them. He strolled right through the smoke. He had on brown pants, a loose white shirt, and a badge. He inclined his head toward them, and when he flashed a smile, his white teeth looked a little too sharp. "I'm Chief Jeremiah Daniels." He paused. "And I understand you took down some of the bastards who've been targeting us." The South rolled, nice and heavy, in his drawl.

Us.

The chief's dark skin was unlined. Daniels could have been fifty or thirty. One thing for sure, he wasn't human. Behind him, more cops piled out of new vehicles. "*My* men," Jeremiah said with a nod. "My . . . uh, special unit." A grim nod. "They'll know how to handle the agents still alive." And the human cops began to be pushed back by the new arrivals.

Zane studied the chief. "If you knew about Perseus, why the hell didn't you take 'em down?"

That wide smile flashed again. "Because you beat me to the punch, son."

Right.

"Pak called me. Told me you boys would need some help cleaning up." He shrugged. "I got this scene."

Good.

"But I'm going to need the Ignitor," Daniels said, and Zane stiffened.

"The hell you are. Jana didn't do this! It was the other one—"

Daniels watched him with narrowed eyes. "Other one?"

Zane jerked his thumb toward the body bag. "That's the Ignitor who started the blaze."

"*Two* Ignitors?" Tony whistled. "Man, talk about playing with fire."

But the chief didn't look at Beth's body. "I knew Beth Parker. She was a low-level psychic, but she was no Ignitor."

"Then why were her eyes burning red as the flames ripped through the place?" Zane asked, voice tight. "I know what I saw, and I'm telling you—"

"The only Ignitor is Jana Carter," Jeremiah said flatly. "I got my own psychics on the team, and when an Ignitor is in the area, *I* know."

No, the guy was wrong.

"I need to talk to Ms. Carter. And I need to have that little chat with her before the suits from the FBI get here."

The extermination list.

Daniels nodded. "Now you're understanding, demon. We don't have much time. Where is she?"

Zane glanced back at the trees. Jana had been there moments before, watching him. He'd been leading that vamp bastard to the ambulance, determined to keep the guy away from Jana. But now . . .

Now the spot was empty. No, not empty. A cop was on the ground. On his knees, rising slowly.

"Shit." The curse was Tony's, but they both took off running at the same time. Zane reached the cop first. He caught the guy's arm and hauled him the rest of the way off the ground.

"Where is she?"

The cop blinked. "Wh-who?" He rubbed the back of his head. "Wh-what hit me?"

Not what. Who.

Tony huffed out a breath. "Wasn't there a pickup truck parked over there"—he pointed to an empty space near some twisting pines—"a few minutes ago?"

Zane's hold on the cop tightened. "You were talking to a woman."

"I was?"

Hell.

The cop's eyes widened. "*I was.* Y-yeah . . . I-I wanted to ask her some questions." He shook his head and winced. "*Where is she?*"

That was the question Zane wanted answered. He caught the whiff of blood and knew that someone had hit the cop.

"Uh . . . Zane?" Tony tapped him on the arm.

Jaw clenched, he let the cop go. The guy scrambled back but eyed him with a frightened stare.

"Hollis, get over here!" the chief called out. Officer Hollis rushed to obey, even as he still rubbed the back of his head.

Tony leaned in close. "Where's the shifter?"

With his strong nose, Jude was helping the cops search for the dead. "Jude's with the—"

"Not him."

He glanced at Tony.

"The bastard I saw running away from Catalina when I got here. It looked like he was coming to help her and the vamp, but when he saw me and Jude, the guy turned tail and ran."

Turned tail? Nice.

"I saw his fangs and his claws. I *know* he was a shifter."

He was. Now they were missing a shifter—a shifter who just might have a score to settle with Jana.

"We found the truck," Chief Daniels told him an hour later as he crossed his arms over his wide chest. They were back in the city, at the police department, and Zane's whole body tightened with tension.

"Where is she?"

"Hold on, son." Daniels shook his head. "I said we found the truck. Not her." He paused. "Something you need to know . . . there was blood in the truck."

The world seemed to narrow then.

"The girl was gone, but one of my cops—" Daniels leaned in close. "Officer Wiley . . . he's got a good nose on him." Right. Because he was probably a shifter. "And he said he smelled wolf all over that damn pickup."

Zane's back teeth clenched. "Get an APB out. The wolf is

about six-foot-one, maybe one-eighty, blond hair, blue eyes."
Sharp teeth.

"I already got an APB out on your girl," Daniels said. "I'll make sure the uniforms know to look for him, too."

But they'd already ditched the pickup. Hell, now they could grab any vehicle, any time.

"I figured she'd just run." Daniels sighed. "Until I found out about the blood. Now I'm not so sure she went willingly."

They were alone in the chief's office. A small office, and one with a really crappy view. Zane forced his hands to unclench. "The vamp bit her back at the swamp. The blood could have come from that bite." *Could* have. But if that shifter had gotten her . . .

Should have left his ass chained to the wall.

A knock rapped at the door.

"Come in," Daniels barked.

The door opened, and Tony poked his head in. "We've got company." Company that had made his whole face harden.

"Tell 'em to take a fuckin' number!" Daniels bellowed. "I've got a missing—"

"A missing what?" A female voice asked.

The chief froze, then grunted out, "Shit."

Daniels might be surprised, but Zane had caught the woman's scent, so when the door swung open fully and Special Agent Kelly Thomas appeared next to Tony, he wasn't surprised.

But he was annoyed.

"Where is she, demon?" Agent Thomas asked, staring at him. "I heard the call on the police scanner. I know about the fire out in the swamp." She walked into the room, her heels clicking. Tony, his mouth tight, shut the door behind her. "And I *know* an Ignitor set that fire."

Zane rolled his shoulders. *Jana, where are you?* "You're right. An Ignitor did set the fire."

Her eyes widened. "You admit she—"

"Beth Parker started the fire. I can testify to that. So can two other witnesses." He'd make sure Catalina didn't disappear before backing up his story, and he'd also be sure not to kill the vamp until that guy could back up his claim, too.

The special agent's teeth snapped together and she gritted out, "Another one?"

"I can dig up other witnesses who will testify that Beth Parker started numerous fires in the area." He was bullshitting now, but screw that. Jana wasn't being exterminated. "Parker was the Ignitor, not Jana Carter."

The silence in the room was so thick he could feel it weighing on him.

Kelly's cheeks flushed a dark, violent red. "Jana Carter is a killer."

Maybe, but they weren't killing her. "I've already talked to Pak. He's calling his contacts at the FBI and clearing this mess up. You've been after the wrong woman, Special Agent."

If looks could kill . . . "The hell I have been."

He shrugged his shoulders. "Jana Carter isn't your prey anymore." The chief wasn't saying anything. Surprising, but good. The guy was going along with his story.

"Yes, she is." And her stare touched on the chief. "You backing him?"

Jeremiah's bushy brows climbed. "The evidence indicates that Beth Parker was the one who started—"

"*Give me Jana Carter.*"

Zane leaned forward and quietly said, "Not going to happen."

Her eyes widened as she stared at him. "You're in the middle of a federal investigation. I could have you arrested for obstruction, and don't think you're just walking away after that crap you pulled in Baton Rouge—"

"You pulled a gun on me, lady. I was just defending myself." And he'd do it again. Real soon, if she didn't back off.

Tony stepped between him and the agent. "Jana Carter isn't here." Ah, a calm voice. "We have no idea where she is."

That was the absolute truth.

"She was with him." Kelly pointed her finger at Zane. "They traveled down here together. My sources say they stole a Ford and—"

"What sources?" Zane asked, curious. *She knew the make of the car they'd used.* Sonofabitch. Perseus hadn't come after them—she had. "Would those sources be the assholes you sent to run our car off the road?"

Kelly didn't answer.

Tony swore.

Her back straightened. "Jana Carter is a fugitive, she's—"

"Gonna be cleared by the FBI any damn minute," Zane promised. Pak had pull. Zane would be covered for his ... incident in Baton Rouge.

And Jana had better be cleared, too. He sauntered around Tony. "I'm afraid your job's over here, Ms. Thomas. Pack it in. You're not after Jana anymore."

But she wasn't backing down and he could see the calculation in her gaze. "You really don't know where she is." A hard laugh filled the tight room. "Did she fuck you over, too? She screwed you, left you, and you're still idiot enough to try and protect her?"

He glared back at her. "Stay away from Jana."

She shook her head. "I'm doing my job. My job is to find her, to stop her—by any means necessary." Her gaze could have singed him. "Don't you remember? That *was* your job, too. Before you decided to have sex with a killer."

Kelly spun away and stormed for the door. "I'm finding her, and I'm doing my job." Her fingers curled over the door-knob.

"He was your stepbrother," Tony said.

Zane blinked. Uh, what?

"Brent Martin, one of the two doctors killed in that fire a few months back. The fire you *think* Jana started in that lab."

Her spine was flagpole straight. "I don't think it. I *know* she started that fire. I *know* she killed him."

Tony whistled. "This thing has been personal for you from the beginning. It's not about doing your job. It's about getting some kind of revenge."

She threw a fuming gaze back at them. "Jana Carter killed two innocent men."

"Innocent my ass," Zane muttered. "Lady, you don't know what the hell has been going on down here."

"Brent was researching paranormals—"

"He was slicing them into little pieces to see what made them tick," Zane told her bluntly. "And guess what? Some of those paranormals didn't like getting cut up. Some of them fought back."

"Like your Jana?"

He wasn't touching that. So he said, "He was working for Project Perseus, a bunch of bastards that couldn't be trusted. You're FBI. Start digging. Check 'em out."

"She already knows about them," Tony said quietly. "From my intel, the FBI had been trying to get someone inside Perseus for months." A pause. "Was your stepbrother an agent? Was he working both sides?"

"No," she snapped. "He didn't know what was happening. He was just trying to help—"

"Bullshit." Jana's memories burned through Zane's mind. "He knew what he was doing. He knew he was hurting them, and he didn't care."

"You don't know what the hell you're talking about, you don't—"

"Investigate him," Zane said. Simple. "Find out for yourself." But he could tell by the expression on her face that Agent Kelly Thomas had already made up her mind.

The only thing she planned to do was hunt. And, as the door slammed shut behind her, he realized he had to find Jana before she did because the FBI agent didn't seem to care about orders.

Just revenge.

"I don't think your girl is the cold-blooded killer Agent Thomas believes she is," Tony said.

Zane forced his teeth to unclench. "She's not." Dead certainty.

"Um . . . tell me . . . have you wondered how Jude and I came to find you? How the cavalry"—he inclined his head toward Daniels—"knew where we all were?"

He'd just figured that Tony and Jude had tracked him. When it came to tracking, Jude was the best.

"We found you because Jana called Pak. She told him where you were, and she told him to haul ass and get help out there."

Then she'd come back into the fire and tried to pull him out herself.

Where are you? The question was burning him alive. "We have to find her." Before Agent Thomas did.

Two nights later, Zane stood on the doorstep of his house, the night air crisp around him and worry a cold, hard weight in his chest.

The New Orleans cops hadn't been able to find Jana. Jude hadn't been able to track her. *He* hadn't been able to find her.

The woman had vanished, and he was scared as all hell.

What if Daniels was right and she hadn't disappeared willingly? What if that shifter had taken her? Agent Thomas might not be the only one jonesing for revenge.

The cops had rounded up over twenty guards and agents from Perseus. Davey had gotten away. Maybe, just maybe that kid would be smart enough to start fresh somewhere—and to choose fucking sides better next time.

Perseus was dead. Jana *should* have been safe from them. *So where the hell are you, baby?*

He shoved the key into the lock. Tomorrow, he'd use every resource Night Watch had to break apart the *Other* world. He'd already been up nearly forty-eight hours straight, only catching a few hours' worth of sleep, as he searched for Jana. It had taken the cops a day to realize she'd left the city. A whole wasted day. Should have known that right away.

He kicked the door shut behind him and shoved the dead bolt home. He had to find Jana before the FBI did.

Pak had told them to call off the dogs, but he knew the order wasn't going to stop Thomas. That woman was gunning for Jana's blood.

Jana.

The last time he'd seen her, she'd been standing under that willow tree. Blood had trickled down her throat. She'd been too pale. Her eyes too wide. He'd wanted to run to her, but he'd needed to get rid of that dick vampire.

He dropped his bag. His eyes were grainy, and he was in serious need of a shower. Zane couldn't remember the last meal he'd eaten and—

Not alone.

The awareness seeped into his pores. He hadn't bothered to turn on the lights. No need. His vision was almost as good as a shifter's in the dark. His sense of smell was almost human, but his vision was far superior. He let his gaze sweep to the left. To the right.

Then up, to the second story. His bedroom. The faintest of creaks reached his ears. Someone was up there.

Someone had picked the wrong demon to screw with.

He took the steps three at a time. Moving fast, but not making a sound. The bedroom door was open, just as he'd left it days before. The bedcovers were wrecked. He could see the mess through the door. *Not* the way he'd left the place. He caught the movement of a shadow. His uninvited guest.

Mouth tight, he launched through the door and attacked.

Their bodies collided and the intruder stumbled back. He followed, going in for the kill and—

And her breath feathered over his cheek. Her scent—wild, sexy—filled his nostrils and he knew, he *knew* even before he saw the wild curtain of black hair that his intruder was Jana.

He caught her before she could hit the floor. He yanked her up close, held her tight, then they fell together onto the bed.

His mouth took hers. Had to. His tongue thrust past her

lips and drove deep into that sweetness that he'd missed. Her body was soft beneath his, but her fingers were strong on his shoulders. Her legs had spread, and he thrust against her, shoving his jeans-clad legs between her thighs.

She tore her mouth from his. "You'd better know who the hell I am." Anger there.

And he realized that, to her, it was pitch black in the room. "Baby, trust me, there's no forgetting you." The anger was there, boiling just beneath the surface for him because she'd scared him. "*Where the hell have you been?*"

Her fingers dug into his shoulders. Growling, he grabbed her hands and pinned them against the mattress. "Jana . . . *why did you run? Where did you go?*" Why did you leave me?

"I came here." Her breath feathered against him. "To you. I thought . . . I thought I'd be safe here."

The rage left him at those simple words.

"You were safe with me in New Orleans." He kissed her again. His tongue swiped over her lips. Into her mouth. "You shouldn't have left," he whispered. "Do you know how fucking crazy I was?"

"The cops were there." Her voice was just as soft as his had been. Hushed in the darkness. "I couldn't let them take me in. I-I *couldn't.*"

"You're not going to jail." He wouldn't let it happen.

"Zane, I—"

"You're not." He kissed her once more even as his hands went to the snap of her jeans. They'd talk more. He'd tell her about Beth and the cops and the plan he'd already set into motion but for now—now if he didn't have her soon, his control would shatter.

He unsnapped the jeans and jerked down her zipper. Why couldn't he get enough of her? Why was he so desperate for her?

Jana's hands were on him now, moving just as greedily as his own. She shoved up his shirt, and her nails scored his flesh.

He heard the thud of her shoes as they hit the floor. His followed right behind 'em. She lifted her hips, and he yanked the jeans down her legs. The scrap of lace—sexy panties—disappeared with them.

His fingers pushed between her folds. Found her warm. So warm. He eased his finger inside her and she was fucking tight. Her cream began to coat him as he stroked her, getting her ready, because she *had* to want him as much as he wanted her.

Her hands pushed between them. Then she was the one yanking at the button of his jeans and pulling down the zipper.

When she tried to touch his cock, Zane stopped her. "Can't . . . baby . . . too close." Because he was about to explode. He shoved off the bed. Zane grabbed the condoms out of his nightstand and went back to her.

She stripped off her shirt, but kept on a black bra that cupped her breasts so well. Her dark hair spread out on the pillow behind her. His fallen angel.

He sheathed his cock, rolling the condom quickly into place. He caught her ankle and pulled her toward the edge of the bed. Zane leaned over her, and took another taste. His mouth pressed against her sex, his tongue licked over the tight button of her need, and he tasted that rich cream and that sweet flesh.

She shuddered against him, a ripple that he felt right at his mouth. His tongue pushed into her.

"*Zane* . . ."

His fingers worked her even as his mouth took and *took*. Not enough. Not even close. Not—

She jerked against him, coming on a long rush as she gasped his name.

Fucking perfect.

He pulled back and positioned his cock at the wet entrance of her sex, then he drove deep in one long, hard thrust.

Her eyes were wide open. On him. The contractions from her climax squeezed his cock. *So damn good.*

He withdrew, then plunged back into her. Jana locked her legs around him and held tight.

Not soft. Not easy. Not this time.

Too desperate. Too much fear and worry inside, too much lust.

His thrusts were fast and frantic as he pounded into her, and she met him, arching and driving right back at him. Her breath panted. His heartbeat thundered in his ears. Faster. Faster.

When she tensed beneath him, he knew another climax was close. He kissed her, thrusting his tongue into her mouth just as her orgasm hit.

Holy fuck.

His spine tightened. He plunged into her. Again. Again. His fingers bit into her hips. The bed squeaked. Sweat slickened his body.

So wet and tight and so—

Jana.

He erupted into her, coming on a blast of pleasure that burned through him, singeing his flesh and leaving him hollowed out, weak . . . and wanting more. Of her—always more.

Special Agent Kelly Thomas stared up at the darkened house on Louis Avenue. She'd known that Zane Wynter would be coming home sooner or later, so she'd just waited for him. No need to follow the man around the state, not when she knew where he was heading.

Home.

Zane was her key. She knew it. The man was a fine hunter, one of the best. All the Night Watch hunters had solid—and dangerous—reputations when it came to tracking and apprehending their prey. Hell, that was why the FBI contracted out with them so much. Why should the agents get their hands dirty when Night Watch could handle the blood so much easier? She'd thought this case would be handled fast by Night Watch, by Zane. *Guess I thought wrong.*

Zane knew how to take down Ignitors. He didn't let their humanity stop him. He killed them, end of story.

Or, that had been the end, until Jana Carter came along.

Back in New Orleans, she'd seen the way Zane's face hardened when he talked about her. Seen the slight widening of his nostrils, the lock of his fists. He'd been worried about the woman. Worried about a cold-blooded killer.

Men always let their dicks confuse them. Give 'em a good ride, and they'd forget every moral they'd ever had.

Looked like the hunter had fallen for his prey. Pity. Would he wise up in time? Would he realize she was just using him? Probably not. Most men were too stupid to see what was right in front of them.

Brent hadn't been like that. He'd been a nice guy, sweet, always ready to lend a hand, and always happy to make room for a stepsister who hadn't felt like she ever really belonged anywhere.

He'd been there for her, the first person in her whole life who cared, and now, she'd be there for him in death. She wasn't letting his killer walk away. No way did she buy that bullshit story about Beth Parker being an Ignitor. The FBI had a file on Parker. The woman was a psychic, one who'd worked with Perseus for too many years, but she *wasn't* an Ignitor.

Hell, she'd even gotten that info backed up by a demon who'd escaped the fires at Perseus. The guy had found Kelly at her cheap hotel room. He'd been trembling, scared, and he'd told her that she needed to keep watching Jana.

Jana. That woman was the killer. Jana was the one who would pay for her crime. And Jana was the one she would catch.

Her eyes never left that darkened house. Zane was the key. He wasn't just going to let Jana walk away; she'd seen that in his eyes, too. He wouldn't stop until he'd found his little firestarter.

No sense racing against him and trying to find Jana first. No sense in that at all.

She just needed to step back and watch him. Sooner or later—and Kelly was betting on the sooner part—Zane would lead her right to Jana.

Her gun was a solid weight in her holster. When she found the Ignitor, she wouldn't shoot tranquilizers at her anymore. Time for this hunt to end.

Time for Brent's justice.

Jana's heartbeat shook her chest. Her body still trembled with aftershocks of pleasure and Zane—he was all over her. Covering her, still *in* her.

She never wanted him to move.

Biting her lip, Jana let her hands curl over his shoulders. She'd been afraid to come to his place. Not sure if he'd want to see her, but also sure that she couldn't just walk away from him. She'd walked away from everything and everyone else in her life, but she hadn't been able to turn away from him.

Zane's dark head lifted and she wished that she could see him as well in the dark as he seemed to see her.

"You're crying," he told her and, shocked, she realized he was right.

His fingers smoothed over her cheeks and he brushed the tear drops away.

She swallowed. "I don't want to . . ." *Run anymore. Spend my days looking over my shoulder, always wondering when the cops will come.* "I know I'm on the extermination list, and I shouldn't be here—"

"I'm getting your name off the list."

A shocked laugh broke from her lips. "Sure you are." His fingers were warm and a little rough on her skin. But then, her demon was a little rough. "Even you don't have that kind of power, Zane." That meant she wouldn't have much time with him, but she'd take what she could get.

"Is that why you left me in that swamp? You were afraid of being taken in?"

She smiled and knew that it would be twisted with sadness. "I'm a wanted woman." A woman who'd finally found something *she* wanted. "Me and the cops don't mix so well." Never had.

He stared down at her, saying nothing. Then, he pulled away from her. His flesh slid slowly out of her body, and she ached at the loss.

He rose and disappeared into the bathroom. A few moments later, he came back. He stood next to the bed, staring down at her. Jana gazed back at him, seeing a dark, looming shadow and feeling . . . vulnerable with her jeans gone, just clad in the bra. She reached for the covers and yanked them over her body.

"Why did you come to me?" he demanded in a voice gravel rough.

Ah, the million-dollar question. *Because I wanted you. Because I knew you'd keep me safe. Because you're the most dangerous badass demon I know and I need you. Because . . .*

No, no, she wouldn't even go there in her own thoughts. She sat up and tugged the covers with her. "You and I had an agreement."

He waited, a dark shadow.

"Something . . . something happened to me in that swamp." Said in a rush.

His fingers brushed her cheek and, slowly, his hand slipped down to her neck, to the skin that still ached. In the light, she had a lovely yellow-and-black bruise. She wasn't sure how strong his vision was, and she hoped he couldn't see it, or the tremble that slipped over her at his touch.

"I should have staked that bastard."

She swallowed and remembered the raw flash of fear that had pierced her when the vamp had locked his teeth on her. She hadn't been helpless in so long, but in that moment . . .

"I didn't expect him to attack." That had been her mistake. Any vamp was a dangerous vamp—she *knew* that. But in the flames and the fury and her fear for Zane, she'd forgotten.

"*Catalina.*"

Jana blinked.

"The witch told me to save him . . . and that shifter."

Jana stiffened a bit. "She's the friend you had inside Perseus." That made her worried. Very, very worried.

"She wasn't there by choice. They were binding her."

Her breath left in a rush. She'd heard of witches being bound before. Their powers were slowly stolen from them. Three binding marks . . . then a witch was helpless. Almost . . . human.

Join the club.

"You seemed close." Okay, crap, she couldn't keep the jealousy out of her voice.

"We were."

Were was nice and past tense, but it also sure implied that a whole lot *could* have gone on between him and the witch. "You went back in to save her." That point had stuck with her. He'd braved the fire for the witch.

"Catalina almost burned once before."

Something clicked then. "The other Ignitor . . ." The one he'd killed. "Did she . . . ?"

"She started the fire that went after Cat, yeah."

He'd killed to protect the witch. Then he'd been willing to fight the flames for her again in that swamp. Jealousy tasted like acid on her tongue.

"I went back for her." He paused. "And you came back for *me.*"

Jana licked her lips, and her fingers curled tighter around the covers. "I-I had to make certain you were okay." Sure, the big bad demon could probably handle anything, but she hadn't planned to walk away and leave him in the fire.

"Why didn't you tell me that Beth was an Ignitor?"

Her heart slammed into her ribs. "She wasn't—"

"The cops are pinning the other arsons on her." His words cut through her soft whisper. "Beth was spotted at the scenes of the other fires. She's the one who's going down for them, not you."

She shook her head and tried real hard to suck in air. "But she wasn't—"

"Pak has some *Other* friends in Louisiana. When Catalina and I told them that Beth was an Ignitor—we saw her eyes and that fire—they put the pieces together. You're clear, Jana. You don't have to run from the cops anymore."

Perseus wasn't after her. The cops—were they really going to let her go?

"You should have told me about her sooner," he said, an edge creeping into his voice.

Enough. She needed to see his eyes when she talked to him. Jana jumped from the bed and hurried toward the far wall. She flipped the switch and light flooded into the room. "There was nothing to tell!" she snapped. "Beth was an average-level psychic until that night. But she—" Ah, hell, this was the part she'd dreaded. "She took something from me." *My fire.*

He hadn't bothered dressing. His arms were at his sides, his cock still up, and he just . . . waited.

"She had someone else with her. A new Perseus recruit." She could still see the woman coming toward her. "After you left, Beth offered me a deal."

The faint lines near his eyes deepened. "What kind of deal?"

Her breath blew out on a hard sigh. This was the part she'd dreaded. "She offered me a chance at a normal life. All I had to do was leave you behind and take it."

You'll lose the fire, but get your life back. Leave the demon. Walk away and the life you always wanted can be yours.

Beth had sounded so tempting. So very tempting.

When the lights in the upstairs room flashed on, Kelly froze. Then she saw the shadows. *Two* shadows. But Zane had gone in alone.

"Jana." Her whisper. She smiled. Talk about an easy mark. Now, she just had to get her girl, without that demon interfering.

Luckily, she knew the perfect way to take out a demon.

Every demon she'd ever met had the same weakness, regardless of their power level.

She'd done her homework on Zane. Since that bastard had stopped her from taking Jana, she'd had the Bureau dig into his past. She knew all about his family. His father.

Like father, like son.

Yes, she knew the demon's weakness, and if she played her game just right, she'd use that weakness to her advantage.

And maybe, just maybe, she wouldn't even have to get her hands dirty on this one. She could let the demon do the dirty work for her.

He could kill Jana Carter.

No, before she was finished, he *would* kill Jana.

Chapter 14

"Did you take the deal?" His voice was expressionless.

Jana shook her head. "I wasn't going to leave you there. I'd already seen what they did to paranormals." Seen, and never been able to forget. "But Beth wasn't the type to take no for an answer."

The pealing of a bell echoed through the house. Jana's eyes widened. *His doorbell? Someone was downstairs?*

Zane didn't look away from her. "What happened?"

"She—the other psychic came at me. She was human. I-I didn't want to hurt her—"

The doorbell rang again. "Zane . . ." she whispered, glancing toward the door, "What if . . . ?"

"Whoever it is can go the fuck away."

A furious pounding carried through the house. Their guest was slamming a fist into the door. "The wolf shifter, Marcus, I told him I was coming to you." They hadn't spoken much during their drive because, hell, what was there to say? They'd both just wanted to get away from that swamp, as fast as they could.

He knew she'd been the one sent to kill him. He also knew she hadn't carried through with her orders. Then they'd both become prisoners.

Until that night . . .

Freedom.

"So you did go with him." An edge sharpened in Zane's words.

She nodded and crept toward the door. "He was the one I told you about. The one Perseus wanted me to kill."

The pounding stopped.

"Zane, what if it's him or—" Or any of the other assholes who could be after her?

His gaze hardened. "Stay here."

Sounded like a great plan to her.

He yanked on his jeans and hurried out of the bedroom. His footsteps thudded down the stairs. Her breath caught. Zane could probably handle anyone down there, but—

"What the hell are you doing here, Tony?" Zane demanded, and his voice carried easily to her.

Shit. *The cop.* Jana scrambled for her clothes. She pulled on her jeans—no time to search for the underwear—and shoved her arms into her shirt as she tugged it over her head.

Tony. He didn't know she was here. Zane would cover for her, it would be fine. She'd be able to leave after—

"Jana!" Zane's booming voice exploded up the stairs.

Horror filled her. No, no, he wouldn't just sell her out like that. Not after—*after what? The sex? Like a man couldn't turn his back on a woman just because they'd screwed.*

Jana rocked back on her heels. What if it had been a trap? What if Tony had been watching the whole time, and Zane was just going to turn her over to him?

"Jana . . ." Softer.

Zane stood in the doorway now. She hadn't even heard him approach. Tony loomed behind him.

Her shoulders straightened. So be it. "Let me get my shoes, Captain, and I'll come with you." She'd survived being locked up once before. She'd survive again. Right?

Damn cages.

Her gaze darted to Zane. What the hell had she really thought would happen? *Good guys don't fall for the bad girls.* Zane was firmly aligned on the side of the "good" guys.

She knew that. Why had she even tried to pretend? Why had she come back to him?

Because he got to me. He'd slid right past the surface and worked his way under her skin. He was her weakness now, one that she'd have to watch.

Jana shoved her feet into her shoes.

"How long have you been here?" Tony asked quietly.

She turned to face him and deliberately kept her hands loose at her sides. "Since yesterday." Zane's stare bored into her.

"What happened to the wolf shifter who was in that swamp?" the cop asked.

Jana shrugged. "We split up once we got to Baton Rouge." Why did it matter?

"So you . . . *were* with him."

Was this an interrogation? "Yeah. Yeah, I just said I was."

"Did he try to hurt you?" The question was Zane's.

Jana blinked. "Ah . . . no." Okay, and now her stomach was knotting.

"I need to talk to that wolf," Tony said.

Good luck with that. She bit the words back.

"Jana . . ." Zane stepped closer to her. "There's been a killing."

Her stomach twisted again. "In this city"—she kept her voice low and calm—"there are often killings."

"Not like this." Tony shook his head. "Not when a woman's throat is cut from ear to ear, and I find freaking dog hairs all over the scene."

Hell, now the questions about Marcus made sense. "No, he's not—"

"Lindsey Meadows, a college student, was killed right outside of her dorm room. Several hundred kids were in that dorm, and no one heard a damn thing." Tony's voice vibrated with tension. "She was last seen having dinner with a blond male."

"Sound familiar?" Zane asked.

She licked her lips. "I-I don't . . . he *didn't* kill those girls in New Orleans."

"Maybe not. But I need to find that wolf," Tony told her, "and I need to find him now."

Tony wasn't after her. The knowledge finally sank in. He wasn't there to haul her to jail. He was after the shifter because he thought Marcus was a killer.

She remembered pain-filled blue eyes. Hands that trembled. "He didn't attack those girls. He wasn't the killer." No matter what the news stories had implied, Marcus hadn't been guilty.

"Maybe he wasn't a killer before," Tony said, "but I need to see for myself what he is *now*. If Perseus had him all these months, if they've been screwing with his head, there's no telling what he is."

Her fault. She hadn't realized that Perseus had him—or that vamp who'd taken his bite out of her. But she *should* have known. When she'd escaped the other lab, there had been paranormals there, too. They'd gotten out when she escaped. Her fire had let them all run free.

But, of course, Perseus had another facility. Another backup plan.

Was there another pit still out there? If they'd had one backup location before, wouldn't they have another now?

Zane turned away from her. "I want to see the crime scene."

Tony frowned. "My men have—"

"I can find things they might have overlooked."

Demon senses.

"Let me at that scene. Let me see what I can find before you start this hunt."

Because Zane had seen Marcus and the marks on his body. Trapped. Tortured. She swallowed.

Tony nodded, his face grim.

"What . . ." She took a deep breath. "What about me?" Usually a cop would have tried to cuff her by now. But Tony . . .

He shook his head. "Didn't Zane tell you? You're clear." His voice was bland. "The arsonist who started the fires in New Orleans was killed in that blaze at the Perseus headquarters."

That deep breath burned in her lungs.

"As far as I'm concerned, you're clear, Ms. Carter."

Zane had been telling the truth. He'd done it. He'd gotten her life back.

"But I *need* that shifter."

Her life was back, but what about the wolf's?

She strode forward and grabbed Zane's hand. "I'm coming with you."

He stared down at her and a frown pulled his brows together. "You don't need to—"

"Maybe it's time I started doing something for somebody other than myself." The words came out too fast. She lifted her chin. "Marcus was hurting so much when I first found him. He didn't ask for any of this."

Zane's gaze held hers. "We never do."

No, they didn't. But fate just came calling. When she called, you had to answer, even if you'd rather slam down the phone.

"Let's get Jude and Erin out there," he told the cop. "If a wolf killed at that scene, they'll know."

"Ahead of you, Zane. I already gave 'em a call," Tony said.

Zane brushed his fingers over her cheek. "Stay with me, every second. The PD has cleared you, but the FBI . . ."

No, she knew she'd still be high on their extermination list. They'd want their pound of flesh, and so would all the paranormals out there she'd pissed off before. Once they found out about her new weakness, hell, it'd be like sharks who'd sensed blood in the water. They'd come at her in a feeding frenzy.

"Pak's working on them," he continued. "But Special Agent Thomas has you in her sights, and she's not going to back down easily. For her, it's personal."

Jana blinked. "Personal? I've never done anything to that woman."

Zane and Tony shared a long look.

"What? What am I missing?" she demanded.

"It's personal for her," Zane said slowly. "Because one of the men who died in that fire in New Orleans was her stepbrother. Brent Martin. The scientist who—"

You'll be awake when I do this and, trust me, it'll hurt like a bitch.

"I remember him." Another guy who'd gotten off on giving pain.

"She's not gonna back down." Zane's gaze was steady. "You have to watch your ass with her."

Now, more than ever. Because if—*when*—Agent Thomas came gunning for her, Jana wouldn't have the flames to aid her. Not anymore.

Good thing she still had the gun she'd stolen from the Perseus agents. A girl could never be too careful.

Personal. Hell. But these days, weren't all the hunts personal? Always personal and always deadly.

It was dark outside, the sky pitch black—no moon, no stars. The kind of night that Jana normally loved because it gave perfect cover.

Tonight that covering darkness had a tingle of shivery awareness skating down her spine.

They were outside a college dorm room, in the alley that ran just behind the building. The flickering, fluorescent lights trickled a pale glow onto the scene. Tony was ahead of them and already bending under the yellow line of police tape. She could just make out the bloodstains on the ground. Jana's lips pressed together. Jeez, couldn't someone have cleaned that up?

"So you think we've got a wolf hunting again?" The voice was feminine, soft, and tinged with a hint of the South.

She hadn't heard the woman approach. Careful now, Jana

slipped deeper into the shadows and watched her. Tall, slim, elegant, the lady seemed perfectly poised in the alley.

The woman's small nostrils flared as she drew in the scents. If she hadn't been watching her so closely, Jana would have missed that telling movement. *Shifter.* Because no human would be making the effort to *inhale* in an alley.

Jude was behind her, and his hand pressed against the small of her back. His nostrils widened as his gaze swept the alley. She knew he—*both* of them—would be able to see a whole lot more than she could.

"I don't know what we've got," Tony said, running a hand through his hair. "You tell me, ADA."

ADA? As in assistant district attorney. Crap. Jana hunched back into that darkness a bit more.

"I don't smell a wolf, not anywhere around here." The ADA's head cocked. "But you know some shifters can disguise their scents."

"Like that bastard who was after you," Zane muttered.

Uh, someone had been after the ADA?

"Yeah." The growl was Jude's. There was still rage there. "Like him."

"If you let me see the body," the ADA offered, "I can tell if the marks were made from claws." A faint smile lifted her lips. "You could say I've got a lot of experience with wolf marks."

Tony edged away from the yellow tape. "Jones has the body at the morgue. I already told him you'd be coming." He sighed. "He said she didn't struggle. One swipe—one fast attack to the neck—and she was dead."

Just like the victims back in New Orleans.

"A human killed those girls." Jana's voice sounded way too loud.

The ADA looked her way. Not with surprise. The woman had known she was lurking there the whole time.

"There was no record of a suspect being apprehended for those attacks," Tony said.

"Because Marcus Malone killed him," Jana said. "The

shifter's girlfriend was one of the vics. The *only* time he killed was when he was putting that murdering bastard out of his misery. Marcus might be a wolf, but he—wouldn't do this."

She felt the weight of the ADA's stare. Hell. What was her name? What had Tony said? Erica? *Erin.*

"Haven't you heard?" Erin asked. "Most folks know that wolves are psychotic."

Jude inched closer to the ADA.

Jana walked out of those shadows. "Marcus had plenty of chances to hurt and kill." *If that had been what he wanted to do, I never would have made it out of that truck.* "He tracked his prey, and he put a sick, sadistic man out of his misery. That's all."

"Seems like you know a lot about Marcus," Zane noted blandly. "Talk a lot on that ride up, did you?"

"When you *fled* the scene of a crime?" Tony tagged on.

She ignored them both.

Erin's gaze stayed on her. "I understand," the ADA said slowly, "that this particular wolf was held captive and tortured for the last few months. Something like that could make any man break. And a wolf . . ." She shrugged.

"It's not easier for a wolf to break," Jana said, fighting to keep her voice even. "It's harder. Yeah, I know wolves have the rep for being crazy, but they're also smart and incredibly strong. Strong enough to live through hell and survive." Just like Marcus had. They hadn't needed to talk. She'd seen the truth in his eyes.

They'd walked out of hell together.

Erin's head inclined toward her, and it seemed like the tension in Jude's shoulders eased, just a bit.

"If the shifter didn't kill Lindsey Meadows," Jana told them, "then we've got a real big problem here." She had to point it out, though surely everyone had realized that.

Zane's arm brushed against Jana's. Okay. She hadn't meant to walk to his side. Not really. Her gaze darted to those bloodstains and then back to the ADA's eyes. *Humans were so weak.*

It sucked to be weak, and she sure wasn't about to show weakness now. She hadn't been given the chance to finish her confession with Zane. He didn't know the truth. None of the others knew. As far as they were concerned, as far as the rest of the world was concerned, she was the big, bad fire queen. Get in her way, and she'd burn you to ash.

"This crime . . ." Even the locations were identical. The freak in New Orleans had always picked alleys just behind the vics' dorms or apartments. "The kill—" No defensive wounds. No sign of a struggle. "—and the victim type are all the same. It fits the serial's M.O." What was up with the timing of this kill? So close to Marcus's arrival in town. Too close. "Someone knows about what happened with the serial killer in New Orleans. About Marcus. And I think that person's trying to set him up."

"Why?" came from Jude.

"Because he was the only actual named suspect in New Orleans. He made the papers. Someone wants the spotlight on him again. Someone wants the cops after him." *Hunted.* "Someone is turning him into prey again." *The supernaturals who cross the line have to be eliminated.* The old spiel from Perseus.

Perseus. Her breath heaved out. "They know."

"Uh, who knows?" Erin asked.

"Project Perseus. They knew all about Marcus. They could be—"

But Zane caught her hand. "Perseus is dead, Jana. The organization is finished. The guards who survived were rounded up. Beth was the leader of that group . . . the guards confirmed it. She'd started Perseus after a vamp killed her father."

She knew about the vampire. *I found my father on the ground. The bastard had torn his throat open.* Beth's shaking voice whispered through her mind. Because at the beginning, when she'd first approached Jana, they'd talked. Almost been . . . friends.

No, no, they'd never been friends. Beth's psychic talent

had just made her real good at reading people. And she'd known how to get to Jana.

She offered me a family. A place to fit in. Things had been fine until Jana turned away from the system. Then the claws had come out.

"Beth wanted vengeance," Jana spoke slowly. "And I gave it to her." The first vamp she'd killed for Perseus had been the one who'd drained Beth's father.

Thank you. The only words Beth had spoken after that fire. But Beth's eyes had been blazing.

That death hadn't been enough for Beth. Nothing had ever been enough.

So *she'd* been the one to start Perseus? Jana had always thought Beth took orders from someone else.

"She's dead," Zane said. "The Perseus group is finished."

"Nothing ever dies easily in this world," Jana whispered. The instinct to survive was too strong.

Marcus Malone knew when he was being hunted. He'd spent too much time being prey not to know that feeling.

He glanced back over his shoulder, his nostrils flaring. He didn't see anyone, didn't smell anyone, but he *knew* some bastard was out there. Hunting.

I need to get out of this city.

Perseus had burned. Those flames had lit the night, and he'd escaped that hellhole, but he couldn't shake the feeling that someone—something—had risen from the flames.

Coming after me.

There was only one person in this town he trusted. One woman who'd been through the fire.

Maybe he should have been afraid of her. After all, Jana had been the one to hunt him before. She'd also been the one to hold back the fire because she'd realized he wasn't the sadistic killer Perseus had made him out to be.

And she'd come back for me. He'd caught her scent over the fire and looked up . . . and Jana had been there. She'd pulled him from those flames in the swamp. Saved his ass.

So he'd returned the favor. He'd gotten her away from the cops. Gotten them both to safety.

But this town wasn't safe. He swiped a hand over his brow. Not nearly fucking safe enough. Jana thought her demon could protect her.

Her eyes had been so dark. "If you need me, I'll be with Zane."

"You really think you can trust him?"

A faint smile had lifted her lips. "He's one of the good guys."

Marcus didn't have a lot of experience with good guys. He didn't trust the demon, but he did trust Jana. She'd studied him, looked beneath the surface. His hands were stained with blood, but that kill—he'd just been avenging his Rita.

Rita.

A blinding pain shot through his head. Those fucking headaches. Every time he thought of Rita, his head seemed to rip open.

He pushed through the bushes and stumbled toward the house on Louis Avenue. Jana would help him. He'd tell her about the eyes on him . . . because those eyes could be turning to her. He and Jana were linked. Whoever was after him, well, the asshole could come after her, too.

Together, they'd be stronger. Those bastards at Perseus had made him so weak. That bitch had come and touched him, while Beth had stood back and laughed. She'd touched him then—

Weak.

He was still weak. Too weak. Almost like a human. And the headaches . . . *Sonofabitch.*

He stumbled and nearly fell onto the porch. The house was dark, but it was late. The demon had to be there, with Jana. They had to—

"Wondered how long it would take for you to crawl out of those shadows." The voice whispered from the darkness.

It was a voice Marcus knew. He froze. No, *no.* But he

turned his head and fucking sure enough, the asshole was there. Smiling at him.

"Did you really think going to the fire whore would save you?" The insidious whisper slipped right under his skin. Marcus kept his eyes on his stalker, aware of the sweat that had burst from his skin, even on the chilly night.

"Jana's been here, hasn't she?" the bastard asked.

But she wasn't there now. Marcus heard nothing from the house. *Jana.* He needed her, but she was gone. Hell.

The asshole looked up at the house. "Been in bed with her demon?" Laughter. "Who would have thought . . . he was supposed to *kill* her, not screw her."

Marcus's claws should have been out. They should have been out and his teeth should be razor sharp. But he wasn't changing. Because that little bitch had touched him.

You'll be normal, Marcus. Isn't that what you want? To be normal? To have a life? No more pain, no more monster. Just a man.

She'd let the girl touch him. . . . Then . . .

More laughter and the stalker's hand lifted. Claws had burst from the jerk's fingertips. *My claws.*

They'd taken too much from him in that prison. Not his life, but his beast.

A shifter who couldn't shift. How was he supposed to survive?

"I thought about letting you live." The wooden porch creaked. Nowhere to run, not with that devil in front of him. "I thought about it. . . ."

Those claws were up and so close.

A snarl lifted Marcus's lips. "I never thought about letting *you* live." No, he'd planned to go after this guy, as soon as his strength was back. He'd *felt* the beast trying to return. The transfer wasn't permanent, he was sure of it. Once the wolf had been strong again, he'd planned to hunt.

But he'd already been prey.

A ghost of a smile appeared on his stalker's lips. "Guess one of us is dying tonight."

Marcus's head pounded. His heart raced. He lunged forward with his fist raised. The beast inside was screaming, but trapped, trapped—

Claws slashed across Marcus's throat. The pain was hellfire hot, and the blood splashed down his shirt as he tried to breathe, tried to gasp, tried to say . . . *Rita.*

He fell to his knees.

"Two down . . ." The whisper filled his ears. The last fucking words he heard were . . . "Three to go."

Rita. He could see her now, could see—

The shifter and the ADA searched the scene. Their eyes—and their noses—probably didn't miss a thing. But, well, there wasn't anything to miss.

"You found dog hairs on the body?" Jana asked. "Just the body, nowhere else?" Odd. Those wolves sure were hairy beasts.

But if they weren't dealing with a wolf . . .

"Just the body," Tony agreed.

Setup. Didn't the guy see it? Marcus wasn't the one they wanted for this. No way would a wolf's fur—*so* not dog hair—have been left in one spot.

"There's nothing here. Take me to the body," Erin said flatly.

Tony nodded. "Let's go. You and Jude can follow me in."

But Erin hesitated beside Jana. "You don't really look like a killer."

Jana smiled at her. "I know. That's why I was so good at my job." *Was,* shit. She needed to be more careful.

Erin's gaze dropped to her throat. "What got ahold of you?"

Oh, yeah, that. "A vamp."

"Did you burn him? I mean, that's what you do."

"I didn't burn him."

The lady waited. Her dark hair blended with the night.

"She shot him," Zane said.

"And *you* didn't rip him apart?" Erin shook her head. "Zane, I'm surprised at your restraint."

Tony hurried to his car. "Come on, we need to get to the station. If this killer's hunting, we don't have time to waste."

Erin inclined her head. "You're right, you know," she told Jana.

About what?

"Not all wolves are psychotic." Her teeth flashed in a white grin. Hmmm . . . those teeth looked a little *too* sharp. "And surviving hell is easy for us."

Then she was gone. The ADA disappeared into the night with Jude and Tony.

"Come on," Zane said. "We need to go to the station and—"

Okay. A woman had to draw the line somewhere. "I'm not going to the cop house." Willingly step into the PD? Hell, no. She sucked in a deep gulp of night air. "She was a wolf? *A wolf?* Jeez, thanks for the head's up."

They walked out of the alley. A few college kids were milling around. Two guys. One girl with long, braided hair.

"She's wolf." A small hesitation. "And she's human. Erin's a hybrid."

Hybrid. She turned toward him, stopping under a street light. At least this one wasn't flickering. "A hybrid. Like you."

He nodded.

Jana licked her lips. "Back at Perseus, everything you told them . . . was it true?"

"Yes." His eyes darkened.

The night air grew colder. Another girl came out of the dorm, her shoulders hunched, her hair down. She was moving fast, and her blond hair flew behind her. After what had happened there, Jana didn't blame the girl. She'd be running fast, too. *Don't want to be caught out alone.*

"My dad was a sick, sadistic bastard," Zane said. "One who just happened to be a demon."

Okay. Not exactly a sweet walk down memory lane. She inched closer to him and felt the warmth of his body seep into hers. "My stepfather was a perverted freak who got off on hurting people, and he happened to be human." She forced a shrug. "Guess you just can't ever tell about folks, hmmm?"

His gaze bored into hers. Black now, she could see that. "You don't care that I'm a demon, do you?"

Um, no. Hadn't she proven that by all the wild, hot sex she'd had with him?

"Have you ever been afraid of me?" he asked her.

Sometimes. Because he made her feel too much. But she didn't say that. Instead, she asked him, "You been afraid of me?"

She expected him to grin. Expected some smart-ass answer. His lips tightened. "Yes."

So not the answer she'd wanted to hear.

His hold on her tightened. "You scare me . . . because you make me weak."

"I don't—"

"You push me to the edge. With you, I'm always afraid I'll go over."

"And if you do?" So what?

He shook his head. "Come on." The others had already left. Gone to the PD.

He opened the passenger door for her. Jana climbed in. Her legs slid over the leather. Zane stared down at her, then leaned forward. "You trust me." He seemed surprised.

But, hell, not as surprised as she was because, yeah, she did.

He shook his head. "You shouldn't." Zane started to pull away.

Jana grabbed his hand. "I think you're the only one I *should* trust." He'd never betrayed her. Hadn't lied to her. Hadn't—

"You don't know what I can do."

She had a pretty good idea. She'd been with him in the fire.

His eyes were level with hers. "I killed him," he said, whispering the words. "My own father, and I didn't even hesitate."

Her fingers squeezed his. "You didn't—"

"I could still smell her blood on him. The bastard was high on his fucking drugs. Always the damn drugs. He killed her, gutted her, all because she tried to take away his drugs. She just wanted him to get clean."

Jana swallowed. "Get in the car, Zane." She didn't like him being in the open. "Let's go back home." She wanted to be alone with him. To hold him. Weird. She'd never wanted to just hold a man before, but Zane wasn't any man.

His jaw clenched. He pulled back, slammed her door, and hurried around to the driver's side. When he jumped in, he revved the engine.

Jana touched the masculine fingers that gripped the wheel so tightly. "You did what you had to do." She could understand that more than any other.

Slowly, his head turned to face her. His gaze was blacker than the night.

"I've got a lot of power inside me," he told her, his voice quiet in the stillness of the car. "Maybe too much. I can do things . . ." He shook his head. "Killing him was easy for me."

He'd never told her his demon power scale. She understood why. Most people feared the demons who tipped the scales. He didn't want to be feared, just accepted. "You've got power, but you've got control of it." The control was what mattered. Control separated the demons from the monsters.

"My control broke that night. I was just a kid." His fingers whitened around the steering wheel. "But I killed him in an instant." His lids lowered a bit. "What do you think would happen now if I lost my control?"

"I don't think you would." After everything they'd been through . . . no, the man had always been strong. Even when he faced death.

He laughed at that and shifted to reverse with a hard yank of his hand. "Baby, you don't even know how close I've been." The car slid back. He shifted again. "And you'd better hope you never see me that way. Because when my control shatters, hell comes calling."

If he was as high on the scale as she believed, yeah, that could happen.

He drove fast. His eyes stayed locked on the road, and not on her anymore.

"Don't go to the police station," she told him and kept her fingers against him. "Take us back to your place." Because she wasn't afraid of him—or the hell he promised.

The car raced forward. Faster, faster, into the dark.

Fury coiled tight in Zane's belly. Jana didn't understand. She didn't see him, not the real man. If she knew what hid under his skin, if they all knew . . .

They'd fucking run.

But she sat beside him, and she kept *touching* him. The woman should be pulling away. He'd tried to warn her while there was still time.

Because time was running out for Jana Carter. He'd realized that when he'd found her in his bedroom. She wasn't just a fast screw. Someone to hold in the dark. A body to give him pleasure. No, she'd started to mean more.

Hell, he wasn't even sure when the change had happened, but she mattered to him. Mattered more than anything or anyone else. And that was very dangerous.

No one got too close to him. He didn't let himself care. He even kept the other Night Watch hunters at a distance. Because when he cared too much, if he let someone slip past his guard . . .

Dangerous.

But already, the demon wanted her. Jana had a darkness inside of her that the demon in Zane liked. She knew the horrors in the world. Wasn't afraid of them. Wasn't afraid of *him.*

When she should have been.

He risked a glance at her from the corner of his eye. Fucking beautiful. Deceptively delicate. And . . .

Mine.

Maybe time had already run out for her.

He spun the car into his horseshoe drive and eased up on the gas. She'd called his place "home." Did she even realize that? Did it matter to her? It sure as shit mattered to him.

His headlights flashed across the front of the house . . . and illuminated the body on the porch.

What the fuck?

Zane slammed on the brakes.

"Zane?"

Jana hadn't seen the man. He killed the lights. "Stay here," he growled, already jerking free of his seat belt and shoving open the car door.

"Wait!" The buckle clicked as she unhooked her belt. "What's happening, I—"

"*Stay. Here.*" He wasn't about to risk her. Not until he found out what was happening.

The blood hit him. The thick, coppery scent hung in the air. Strong and fresh.

Hell.

His gaze raked the yard. He didn't see anyone else, but that didn't mean someone wasn't there, watching him.

Zane crept up the front steps, his eyes on the body. Worn boots, old, faded jeans, a too big, bloody blue shirt. When he saw the vic's face, the breath expelled from Zane's lungs in a rush.

He *knew* that face. Knew that dirty blond hair and those pale, haggard features. He'd seen the man just days before— when the wolf shifter had fled the fire.

Now, Marcus Malone lay on Zane's porch, his right arm stretched toward the door, like he was trying to get help. The poor bastard's throat had been ripped wide open. *Ear to ear.*

Zane's eyes closed. This kid hadn't been the killer.

Victim.

The car door groaned behind him. "Zane?"

He didn't want her to see this. She'd tried to save the wolf.

"What's happening?"

His enhanced vision showed him every detail of the scene. No defensive wounds on the shifter's body. And . . . his clothes weren't torn. The poor bastard hadn't even been given a chance to shift. The killer had come on him too quickly.

And how the hell did someone sneak up on a wolf shifter?

His head snapped up. *The same way a killer can—will— sneak up on a demon.* When you were dealing with supernaturals, all bets were off.

His gaze flew back to his vehicle. Jana stood half in, half out of the car.

He jumped off the porch and rushed to her side. "We've got a big damn problem." He pushed her inside and slammed the door. His eyes searched the night. *Can't see anyone. Can't hear anyone.*

But Marcus hadn't gotten much warning, either.

He hurried back to the driver's side. He'd have to call Pak and Tony. A cleanup crew was needed ASAP. They had to get the body out of there before dawn, before any neighbors could see what had happened. And Night Watch had to figure out—fucking fast—what they were dealing with here.

Perseus? Was the group still active? *How?* The agents were locked up, courtesy of Chief Daniels. Their leader was dead.

"Zane . . ."

He spun out of the drive.

"Zane, tell me what's happening."

He didn't want to. This world was full of things he didn't want to do. "Marcus isn't our killer."

She exhaled. "Well, I've been telling you—"

"He's dead." He yanked out his phone and called Pak even as his eyes snapped to the rearview mirror. No one followed them. Not yet.

"Wh-what?"

"His body was on my porch. The poor bastard's throat

had been ripped out." Someone had just killed a wolf shifter like it was fucking *nothing*. Wolf shifters were hard bastards to kill.

No time for defensive wounds. No time to attack. There'd been no blood under Marcus's nails. No torn clothing. Just like the other scene.

Who the hell had killed the guy and why?

The only links he had to Marcus were Jana and . . . Perseus.

Chapter 15

The morgue was cold and quiet, just like the fucking grave that it was. Antonio shifted his right foot and wondered how in the hell the ADA could just stand there peering at the gaping wound that *had* been the vic's throat. And Erin was *close*. Right down at the throat, staring with narrowed eyes. The scent alone should have been enough to choke her but—

"These aren't wolf claw marks. They're close, but they're . . . off. Just a little different."

Antonio's brows snapped up. "Ah, you sure?"

Her gaze met his. "I know wolf claw marks when I see them."

"So do I," Jude added, his voice rumbling. "And I know a shifter's scent when I smell it—there's not a drop of shifter odor on her." He shook his head. "The girl wasn't killed by a wolf."

Then *what* had attacked her?

Jude's phone rang. He hurriedly pulled it out of his pocket and turned away from them. "Donovan."

Silence.

"What the fuck? Are you serious?" Jude threw a glance back at them. "Yeah, well, we'd already figured it wasn't him."

Antonio knew the call wasn't bringing good news.

"We're still at the morgue. No, man, I don't know what the hell got ahold of her. The marks are *like* a wolf shifter's but . . . no, Erin and I both say they don't match." A brief pause. "Yeah, the scent's wrong." His eyes narrowed as he listened and paced. "Where are you? Do I need to come—"

He broke off. Erin edged closer to Jude. Her hand lifted to rub against his back. "Yeah, yeah, we'll wait for you," he said into the phone. "Hurry in."

Jude ended the call and huffed out a hard breath. His gaze met Antonio's. "I've got one guy you can mark off your suspect list."

His gut twisted.

"Marcus Malone didn't kill that girl."

"You sure?"

"Zane is." A long sigh. "Because the bastard who murdered the co-ed killed Marcus. Zane just found the wolf shifter's body. Malone's throat was clawed open. The poor bastard bled out on Zane's porch."

Well, damn. Just like Lindsey Meadows. Antonio's gaze lingered on her pale form. Someone was hunting in his city. Not being quiet about it either. Fast, brutal kills.

"They're linked." Obviously. He just didn't know how. A wolf shifter . . . a college kid . . . *why? What had made those two into targets?*

The door to the morgue opened with a squeak. His head turned, and his hand went to his holster. *Too much damn stress lately.* But at this time of night, no one else should be there—

And he sure as shit shouldn't be seeing Catalina.

But the witch stood in the doorway. Her eyes, wide and green, met his. Her white-blond hair tumbled down her shoulders, and her lips, normally dark red, but now light pink, were pressed into a tight line.

"Catalina?" Jude called, his voice gruff. "What are you doing here?"

"They're hunting me," she whispered as she came slowly into the room, her feet shuffling over the floor. "I could feel the darkness coming. I-I scryed. I had to see what was going to happen."

Scryed. A cold wind seemed to blow against Antonio's

neck. He didn't like it when Catalina pulled out her dark mirror and tried to glimpse the future. As far as he was concerned, peering into that mirror was just asking for trouble.

And the last time she'd gone looking to see what the future held, she'd seen death for her friends.

Luckily, she'd been wrong about that vision. Well, kind of wrong.

"You shouldn't have done that," Jude admonished. "You're already weak from the two binding marks. Your powers aren't strong enough—"

"No." She shook her head. "They're not. They're not strong enough for me to see who is coming after me, but they *were* strong enough to show that if I don't do something, I'll be burning."

Shit. What was the surefire way to destroy a witch? The fire. The old bastards during the Burning Times had been right about that move. Bind a witch, burn her, and you get her powers.

Catalina straightened her shoulders. "Someone is coming after the survivors."

Oh, he wasn't going to like where this was going. Antonio hurried to Catalina's side. The skin under her eyes looked bruised. Hell, *she* looked bruised. Too pale. Too fragile. He almost reached for her, but he stopped and clenched his hands into fists. "Where's the vamp?" The last thing he needed was that vampire popping up in the morgue.

"He's . . ." She swallowed. "Feeding."

Right.

Jude growled.

Catalina's eyes flashed. "He's not killing anyone! He's just drinking—"

"The way the bastard drank from Jana?" Yeah, he'd gotten all the details from Zane.

Catalina flinched. "He's being hunted, too. He has to be at full strength."

Survivors. Antonio rubbed the back of his neck. The knots were building beneath the skin. "Let's start at the beginning, and let's go real slow."

Erin and Jude closed in.

"First up, how the hell did you know we were down here?"

A ghost of a smile lifted her pale lips. "Pak told me."

Figured. Pak knew just about everything, and he'd certainly be keeping tabs on his hunter.

Antonio huffed out a breath. "Look, Catalina, I've got a dead co-ed and—"

"Lindsey Meadows."

Right. The media didn't know the victim's identity yet, but Catalina did.

She told him, "If you check your records, you'll see that Lindsey's half-sister disappeared about six months ago. Lindsey filed a missing person's report, but then she came back and said she'd talked to Laura, that everything was fine."

He'd already checked the records. He knew this. Tony also knew— "I'm guessing the sister isn't fine."

Catalina tensed. Her eyes widened an instant before the door pushed open again. Zane loomed in the doorway, and his little Ignitor was right at his side.

"I don't know if the sister is fine," Catalina said. "*She* knows." There was some anger there. Fear.

It made sense that a witch would fear the Ignitor. Any smart person *would* fear her. Catalina had always struck him as the smart type.

Everyone turned to look at Zane and Jana—and they waited.

Kelly Thomas edged onto Zane's porch, her gun drawn. She'd kept her eyes on the demon and tailed him back to his place—and she'd seen the way the guy high-tailed out of there. *Like the devil was chasing him.*

She could smell the blood, so she knew—

Kelly sucked in a sharp breath when she saw the body. The poor guy—his throat had been sliced right open, a sick smile that stretched far too wide.

The stench clogged her nose, and she stumbled off the porch. Wrenching out her phone, she dialed her contact with a press of her fingers. "Start a search for Zane Wynter and Jana Carter. What? No, I don't care what Miller said. They just killed someone. *Killed him.* Send some agents and the cops out to 133 Louis Avenue."

Her fault. Her fault that poor kid was dead. She should have struck faster.

But there'd be more innocent blood lost. She was putting an end to this hell.

Time to eliminate the Ignitor and the demon that Jana had brought to her side.

Okay, having everyone stare at her was . . . weird. Not like she was super comfortable being down there with the dead bodies, anyway.

The cop eyed Jana with a narrowed gaze. Seriously suspicious eyes. *What else was new?*

"Where's Laura?" Catalina asked.

Jana blinked. "Who?"

"Laura." The witch repeated. "Where is she?"

"I don't know any Laura." Jeez. Didn't they realize what was happening? Zane had called and told them about Marcus. They should have been—

"She's about five-foot-seven, and she's got long, straight brown hair. She wears glasses that are so thick—too thick. And her nose is crooked," Catalina spoke with her eyes still locked on Jana, "like it's been broken before, and she's got a small black mole near the corner of her chin."

The description had Jana's heart racing.

Catalina said, "Tell us where she is."

Jana took a deep breath. Then one more.

Zane's arm brushed her side. "What the hell are you talking about, Cat? Look, the shifter is dead. He was sliced open on my doorstep. Pak is sending a cleanup crew over, but we've got a damn serious problem on our hands."

"Yes," the cop said. "You do."

Jana realized her palms were starting to sweat.

"The survivors are being eliminated. One by one." Okay, that witch's voice was just eerie. So blank. So . . . dead.

It took a minute for the words to sink in. *Survivors.* Oh, shit. "You mean Marcus—"

"Someone's not happy that the supernaturals got out of Perseus alive," Catalina said. "I scryed. I saw . . . *I'm going to die.*" The witch sprang forward in a sudden burst of motion and grabbed Jana's shirt, yanking her forward. "*Where the hell is Laura?*"

"Catalina!" Zane lunged for the witch.

Yeah, she didn't need his help. The day she let a witch get the best of her in a fight . . . *That day ain't comin'.* The other woman was just embarrassing her now. Jana slammed her forehead into Catalina's. The witch howled and those nails—more like claws—stopped digging into Jana's shirt as Catalina stumbled back.

Jana fisted her right hand and got ready to punch the chick.

Zane's fingers curled around her fist. "Easy." His black stare glittered at her.

"I'm not the one who went crazy." And it stung, dammit, *hurt*, that he was telling her to back off. Crazy witch woman was the one who needed to be controlled.

We have a friend of yours.

Oh, right, but he cared about the witch. While she . . . hell, *what* was she to him? Did she matter?

Zane turned his head and focused on Catalina. "What the hell are you doing?"

Jana pulled her hand away from his.

Tears trickled down Catalina's cheeks. Oh, great, tears. Now Zane would probably crumble because the witch was pretty and crying and—

"*Why the hell did you attack her?*" Zane demanded.

"Because she was the last person to see Laura alive! I know she was!"

Okay. Catalina was right about that. Now all the eyes were back on Jana. She cleared her throat.

"Why is this Laura important?" Zane asked.

Catalina pointed toward the body on the gurney. A body Jana had been trying to ignore. "She's important because her sister is the one who had her throat torn out last night. Laura is psychic. She was working with Perseus. I saw her there. She was—"

"She was there the night the flames went wild." Jana tried to keep her voice emotionless. She licked her lips and met Zane's stare. "She didn't . . . survive the fire." Flat words. Quiet.

But she'd never forget the sight of Laura dying. A touch . . . the woman had touched her, stolen her fire, then transferred it to Beth. *All with a touch.*

But Laura hadn't understood the flames. The fire had been too much for her, and by the time she'd tried to give the power to Beth . . .

The fire had consumed Laura. She'd burned, from the inside out, even as Beth screamed and ordered that Laura touch her and transfer the power.

Before she'd died, Laura had managed to transfer some of that power. And even that bit had proven too much for Beth in the end.

Catalina's shoulders sagged. "Lindsey must have known about Perseus."

"That's why she canceled the missing person's search." Tony slowly shook his head.

Missing person's search?

"She knew where her sister was," he muttered, running a hand through his hair. "Laura must've called her. She must've—"

"She told her sister too much about Perseus." Catalina's voice held a hint of sadness. "So much that someone thought Lindsey had to die."

Now there were two dead in the city: Lindsey and Marcus.

Erin cleared her throat. "Um, sorry if I seem dense here, but I thought you guys had taken down Perseus? Isn't the group dead?"

Catalina shook her head. "Someone is still alive. Someone with a lot of power."

Someone who wasn't afraid to kill.

"We're all on the list. Everyone who was there while the place burned." Catalina's eyes darted to Tony, Jude, then Zane.

"Fuck the list," Jude said instantly.

Catalina looked at Jana. "Bet you're at the top of the list, Ignitor."

Jana forced a reckless smile. "Bring it."

"Still so brave?" Catalina asked, narrowing her eyes. "Even after what happened to you?"

Oh, shit, she *knew.* Jana kept her chin up. "What do you want me to do? Run away into the shadows? Hide while someone else dies?" Who did the witch think she was talking to? "I'm not going anywhere. If some asshole is out there hunting survivors, I'll be ready to face him." With or without her power.

"No, you won't be," Catalina said, drawing back. "Not when death has you in his sights."

"Thanks for that happy little update." Didn't sound like a fuzzy Christmas card, but when had life *ever* been a fuzzy Christmas card?

"You scryed." Zane stepped back from the witch and came closer to Jana. *Finally.* "What did you see?"

"I saw me getting torched." Her gaze came back to Jana. "Some people like to watch those flames burn."

Okay, now she was pushing too far. "I've never burned a witch. *Never* killed someone who didn't deserve my fire. You think I killed for shits and giggles, is that it?" She closed the distance between her and the witch. "My stepfather was a perverted freak. Those demons and vampires—they tortured and *murdered* humans. They came after me, so I stopped them. I didn't—"

"It's okay, baby." Zane was there, wrapping his arms around her and pulling her back against the warm, strong lines of his chest. "You don't have to explain a damn thing to them."

Her gaze flew around the room. Jude stared unblinkingly back at her. Erin . . . there was understanding in her gaze. Tony scowled. The witch—ah, screw her.

"What else did you see, Catalina?" Zane demanded.

Her lips firmed. "Logan got staked. I mean, he-he *will* get staked."

The vamp who'd tried to make her into his buffet? Was she supposed to care about what would happen to him?

"We don't have much time," Catalina whispered. "The killer is closing in."

Zane's arms were strong and steady. His scent surrounded her. "Did you see who was coming?" His words seemed to vibrate around her.

Catalina shook her head. "I'm too weak." A brief hesitation. "We all are." Those words weren't directed at Zane. *Catalina knew too much.* "They weakened us, and now we're just prey to them. That's what they wanted. For us to be the ones who were hunted."

"You're not going to be hunted," Jude said. "I'm not weak. Zane's not. We're—"

"Isn't he weak?" Catalina asked as her eyes bored into Jana. "I saw what happened when Logan bit you. His dark side almost took over. Do you know what happens when Zane loses control?"

"Fuck. Enough of this," Zane blasted. His hold was unbreakable, but a hard knot had formed in Jana's chest. "I'm not losing control and no one else is dying. *No one.*"

His words were a vow.

Catalina pushed past them. "I hope you're right. But I'm afraid that you're dead wrong." Then she ran out the door, her shoes slapping against the floor.

"Follow her," Zane ordered.

Jude nodded quickly.

"She's not running again, and she's not dying," he added.

Jude's fingers skated down Erin's cheek. "Be safe," Jana heard the ADA whisper softly.

Jude kissed Erin, a light, tender press of the lips. Then he was gone as he trailed after the witch.

Zane's breath feathered over Jana's ear. "There's a dead body on my porch."

Jana took a slow breath. It seemed to burn her lungs. *Marcus hadn't deserved to die like that. He should have finally been free.*

"Tony, you're gonna want to get some of your men out there to work the scene with Night Watch. Send those who know the score."

Tony nodded and eased past them as he headed out the door.

"I'll call the DA," Erin said, brushing back her hair. "I'll make sure he understands Night Watch has point on this one."

"Thanks, Erin." Again, his voice vibrated behind Jana.

Erin stopped next to them. "It doesn't matter what others think about you," she told Jana. "It doesn't matter if they think you're a freak or a monster . . ."

What if I am?

"They don't know you." A wisp of a smile lifted Erin's lips. "They don't know *us*."

Then she was gone.

"Let's get out of here." She didn't like the smell. Didn't like the bodies. Didn't—

Zane kept a tight hold on her as he led her from the morgue. They hurried down the hallway, raced up the stairs and—

He pushed her back against the hard, stone wall of the stairwell. His eyes glittered down at her. "You're holding back on me."

Jana swallowed. His eyes were so dark. Really, a demon's eyes shouldn't have been sexy. Scary maybe, sure. Not sexy.

But his were. So sexy her knees shook and her panties were getting wet.

He slapped his hands on either side of her head. "What aren't you telling me? Fuck, don't you know by now, you can trust me? I'm not going to turn on you."

Her breath caught. "I do trust you." A painful admission. She'd never trusted anyone fully. Certainly not those assholes at Perseus—and her wariness had sure paid off. But she'd never trusted her handful of lovers or her so-called friends.

"No, you keep waiting. Keep watching me. You think I'm going to screw you over." He shook his head, and she saw the muscle flex in his jaw. "What do I have to do? How do I prove to you—"

He didn't have to do anything. "Beth offered me a deal in that shithole." She'd told him that part already. But now it was time for the full confession. "If I walked away and left you on your own, I could get my life back."

"How were you supposed to—"

"She said she could take away the fire. The witch was right. Laura was psychic. She just had to touch me, and she could get my fire." *Do it, tell him.* "She could get the fire . . ." *Do it, tell him.* "And transfer the power to someone else."

His whole face hardened. "*Beth.*" He shoved away from the wall.

"I-I told you she wasn't an Ignitor." And she hadn't been. "But that night, she got my power. Beth got it, and she used it to attack you and everyone else in that place." She'd burned Perseus to the ground. Even though she hadn't gotten the full rush of fire—not like poor Laura—Beth still hadn't been able to control the flames. Only Jana could control the fire.

Beth should have realized that as soon as the psychic burned.

He turned away. His shoulders were ramrod straight, and the fury rolled off him in waves. "Was it worth it?"

What? She stood frozen against the wall.

"I knew there was something different about you. I couldn't figure out . . ." A harsh laugh. "And you shot the vamp. You didn't incinerate the asshole. You *shot* him."

Her lips were too dry. Jana swiped her tongue over them and forced herself to step forward. "I tried to call up the fire when he attacked me, but nothing happened."

"Because you'd fucking traded your fire and *me* for your freedom." His voice echoed up the stairwell. "And here I thought you . . ."

He thought she—what? Her heart slammed into her chest. "Zane, it's not like that!" Her hand reached out to him.

He glanced back at her, his face a hard mask. "I pulled you out of that fire at Perseus. I went back for you before I helped anyone else." Disgust had his lips tightening. "And you'd already screwed me over."

Then he walked away. Zane marched up those stairs. Walked. Away.

No. "I went back for you, too!" He kept walking. "Zane! I went back into the fire, when I didn't have any power, *for you*. I wasn't leaving you, dammit! I wasn't going to let you burn!"

But he was still leaving her and her heart seemed to burn in her chest. *Don't leave me.* She ran up the stairs after him. He was close to the exit, the one that led to the back parking lot. She grabbed his arm and forced him to stop. She yanked him around—and made him look at her. "Where's your trust?" she whispered.

His eyes were as cold as black ice.

Damn him. "You think I sold you out so easily? You think I tossed you over to be damn *normal?*" Her nails dug into his arms. "My fire is the only thing that has saved me over the years. First from that bastard who tried to break me. He came into my room, every freaking night and watched me. I knew what was coming, *I knew*, and I prayed for some way to stop him."

The mask began to crack. Screw him. She wasn't done talking.

"My mother didn't believe me. No one would help me. *No one.* He started hitting me, and it got worse, and worse, and I knew he had so much more planned. I knew—" She broke off as emotion clogged her throat. "I prayed, and I got my fire. *I stopped him.*" Over the years, the fire had kept her safe. Always. "When the assholes in the dark come after me, *they're* the ones who run away scared because I control the flames. *They're* the ones who beg for mercy. Not me."

She felt the wet trickle of his blood on her fingertips. Her nails had dug in too deep. Her hands lifted, and her fingers balled into fists. "I stopped wanting to be normal a long time ago."

His nostrils flared. "But you still sold me out."

Her laugh was brittle. "Would it have killed you"—she asked him, stepping toward the exit now because it was her turn to leave him—"to have trusted *me*, just a little bit?"

Good sex. No, great sex. Maybe that was all they'd ever had. Why had she expected more? "A human was coming at me." She didn't look in his eyes as she spoke now. She couldn't. "Beth was shouting some crazy shit about me being normal, saying all I had to do was walk away." Laura . . . the girl's eyes had been wide. Sad. Tears had glittered behind her glasses. "I didn't want to hurt Laura. She didn't seem like a threat to me."

He shifted and edged closer to her.

"I thought . . . I thought Perseus was using her, just like they'd used me. I didn't want to hurt her," she said again as the memory surged through her. "Then she lunged at me. She touched me and barely let her fingers skim down my side."

And it had felt like the woman sliced her open with a hot knife.

Jana tossed back her head. "If you don't believe me, *look*." Her eyes held his. *"Look."*

She felt the hard psychic push against her mind.

Laura stood before her, the woman's thin body trembling. Hell, where was Zane? "Don't take another step."

Laura froze.

"What happens when she takes the fire away? Where does it go?" Jana asked.

Beth didn't answer and the girl wasn't speaking. Her eyes looked so big behind the glasses, and her skin was stark white.

An alarm sounded then. A high-pitched, whining alarm. Beth jerked and swore. "Dumb bitch. She should've just done her damn part."

What?

Footsteps thundered outside.

Beth's face hardened. Her hand lifted and she stabbed a finger in the air toward Jana. "The demon is going to die. If he won't help us, then we'll rip him apart.

"But first . . ." And the guards spilled into the room. "First we're taking that fire from you. We're taking it, and we're going to make sure you're nothing but a corpse when we leave this room."

Now, this was the Beth she knew and hated. "Bring it, bitch." Jana let the charge shoot through her. "If you think you're strong enough, come on." A line of fire split the floor between them. Charge more. Charge. "Let's see if you still like my fire."

"Shoot her!" Beth screamed at the guards. "Not the head or the heart, but shoot her! Take her down!"

The bullets flew through the air just as the flames blazed higher.

Laura stumbled forward, careening dangerously close to the fire. Jana lunged toward her. Laura's fingers brushed her arm.

Pain. It sliced through her. Agony that burned and burned and burned.

Jana screamed and fell to the floor.

Beth's laughter echoed around her. "Give it to me! Give it to me!"

Something was ripping out of Jana. Clawing its way out of her body. Burning claws, hacking their way to the surface. Tears streamed down her face. "Z-Zane . . ."

"He can't help you. He won't."

Her palms slapped against the floor. She forced her head up. Those flames . . .

Laura stared back at her with eyes too wide. Beth was holding the girl's hand, squeezing tight. "Give it to me."

Smoke began to drift from Laura's nostrils. From her mouth. Her eyes.

"Give it to me!"

Jana tried to speak, but blood trickled from her lips and splattered onto the floor.

Laura's pale skin reddened. Beth laughed. Laughed and took the power.

Beth's hand fell away from Laura just as the fire erupted. Laura screamed.

So did Jana. She screamed for Zane because she knew Beth was going after him, and she couldn't do a damn thing to stop the bitch.

"Get out!" The snarl broke from her lips as Jana's temples throbbed. He'd seen e-damn-nough. *He hadn't believed her.*

Zane's breath heaved out, and the bastard reached for her. *Reached for her.* Right, like she wanted him touching her then. "I'm not the one with the trust issues. I didn't turn on you, haven't *ever.* Hell, I came back to you. I could have run. You wouldn't have ever seen me again, but I came to your house."

"Why?" Seemed torn from him.

"Because I'm a damn idiot." She grabbed for the door.

"Jana—"

Her fingers curled tight around the doorknob. "You got to me, demon." She was ashamed to admit it. She'd fallen so easily. Started falling that first day, when he'd come through the fire for her on Francis Street. She'd thought she could count on him.

A good guy, her ass. Just another wolf inside. No, a demon inside.

She wrenched open the door and hurried outside. The cold night air bit into her face and arms and cut right through her clothes. Her teeth chattered before she was even halfway across the parking lot.

"I'm not letting you go, Jana!" His words carried easily on the wind. Loud, angry. Desperate? No, not desperate. Zane was never desperate for anything.

But those *were* just the words she needed to hear, the words that *pissed her off*. Jana spun back to face him. "You don't *let* me do anything. I do what I want, always have, always will. And right now, I'm leaving you."

He didn't rush toward her. Didn't run. Just . . . stalked her. Slowly. Like she was prey and he had her cornered. *He doesn't*.

His eyes blazed with emotion that she couldn't read. So much emotion swirling in those deep eyes. "Is leaving me really what you want?" he asked.

Not answering that. She couldn't have what she wanted. That was obvious. *He didn't trust me. Had to look in my mind to see the truth.* "There's a killer in this town, apparently coming after *me*." Talk about kicking a girl when she was down. "According to your witch girlfriend, I'm dead center on the target list and—"

His eyebrows shot up, but he kept coming at her. "Catalina isn't my girlfriend."

"Screw that. You've slept together." Why was she bringing this up now? Like this mattered with all the other crap that was happening. *I don't care what he does with the witch. I'm leaving. Not my business anymore.* The back lot was deserted. Frost had settled over the handful of cars parked there, and a small pool of light spilled from the building.

"We have slept together," he confirmed and Jana wished, *wished*, she had her fire back then.

Zane stopped in front of her, bracing his legs, and throwing back his shoulders. "But we've been over a long time. Catalina knew she wasn't the one for me."

"What? Did she scry that, too?" she tossed out as her breath formed a cloud in front of her face.

"Yes, she did."

He caught her arm and pulled her close. "Don't leave me." Not an order this time. Probably as close to a plea as the man had ever gotten. "Everything is so screwed up, but shit . . . *I need you, Jana*. More than I've ever needed anything."

She needed him. She wanted to punch him right then, and dammit, she needed—

His mouth crashed onto hers. Hot. Hard. Desperate. *Wild.* Just what she wanted. His tongue pushed into her mouth, drove inside and claimed her, and her heart thundered against her chest. It would be so easy, so easy to give in. But . . .

But Jana pulled her mouth away from his lips. *Hurt.* The wound was too fresh for her to give in to the rush of lust. "Why?" she whispered, letting more emotion out than she should. "You want me for sex?" That wasn't enough for her anymore.

"Fuck, yeah, for sex, but *more.*" There was *more* glittering in his eyes. "Give me a chance, baby. I know I can be a dumb bastard, but *give me a chance.*"

"You don't trust me." Couldn't he see? Without trust, they didn't have anything.

"No, I don't trust myself. Not with you." Stark. "I want you so much, need you, that I don't trust myself." He huffed out a hard breath. "You're *in* me, Jana. Beneath skin and bones, and even if you had traded your fire for me . . . shit, I'd still need you just as much."

What? Oh, damn . . . the man was making her weaken.

"I don't care what powers you have. I don't care if the fire is gone."

But she thought it was coming back. She'd almost felt the charge a few times. Maybe—maybe the transfer had only been temporary. Knowing Beth, she'd probably killed the other paranormals who'd lost their power. *Hit 'em while they're weak . . .* Yeah, that was Beth's M.O. So the woman might not have even realized . . .

My fire can come back. Well, she hoped it could. If not . . .

"Stay with me," Zane said, "we'll finish this asshole out there hunting and then we'll—"

"You'll both die." The words were as cold as the night, and *too damn close.*

Jana broke from Zane's hold and whirled around. Special Agent Kelly Thomas was there, pointing a gun right at them, and *smiling.*

Chapter 16

Aw, hell, but she had bad luck. "I don't need this now," Jana said. Zane's hands were steel tight around her. "I don't need—"

"Do you think I give a shit what you need?" Kelly snapped at her.

"You can't take her in." Zane's voice vibrated with fury. "She's clear on those arsons. Your boss knows that. Miller isn't after her. You're supposed to be standing the fuck down."

"I was." The woman's smile looked like a shark's. "Then you and the Ignitor had to go and start killing again." She shook her head but her gun didn't waver. A long, black silencer covered the end of the weapon. Not a good sign. "I found that poor man's body on your porch tonight. What was his crime, hmm?"

"We didn't kill Marcus," Jana said, aware that her breath came too fast. *A silencer?* The agent had really gone over the edge.

"Marcus." Kelly repeated the name sadly. "On a first-name basis with your victim? So you knew him, and you killed him."

"We didn't—"

"He was dead when I found him." Zane's thundering voice cut across Jana's words. He edged forward, placing his body between hers and the special agent's. "Jana didn't hurt him, and neither did I."

"Right. I'm supposed to believe that."

Guess everyone was having trouble with trust tonight.

"You're not taking her in." Zane shook his head. "She's off the list. Agent Miller doesn't want her. You're not—"

"Screw what Miller wants. I'm taking you both in." That gun still didn't waver, and Jana was real tired of it being pointed at them.

"I'd like to see you try," she threw at the agent. "You really think you can take us both down?" Kelly didn't know about her power loss. The agent would think she was as fire strong as always. And Zane, well, he *was* strong. Far stronger than the agent. "You're out of your league, Special Agent."

"The hell I am."

"You know what I can do," Zane said softly. "Don't make me show you again."

"I'm a *federal* agent. You can't threaten me."

Um, he could and had.

Kelly's voice pitched higher as she said, "I'm taking you both into custody until this mess is sorted out."

"No," Zane told her quietly. "You're not. You don't understand what's happening here. You don't realize—"

"I realize some poor guy is dead on *your* doorstep. I know Jana's a killer, and her lover—well, it looks like he is, too." She drew in a deep, shuddering breath. "Cuff her."

Jana blinked. "Um, what?"

"Screw this," Zane snarled. He was fully in front of her now, shielding her with his body. Jana felt the hot rush of his power in the air. A hard buzzing filled her ears, like a thousand bees. Her knees began to sag, and her vision blurred.

"I'm not going out easily this time, demon," Kelly said. "You won't get to me so fast. You'll just take *her* out."

Zane's head jerked back around, and he stared at Jana with wide eyes. Demon eyes. Eyes so dark. Eyes that had seen into her.

"I wasn't prepared for you before," Kelly said. "I am now.

My stepbrother believed in sharing his findings with me. He studied the monsters, and he told me how to fight 'em.'"

Bitch. "Not monsters," Jana managed.

"Yeah, you are. Now *cuff her* or I'll shoot you both." Jana couldn't see the agent, but Kelly sure sounded close. "The bullet will blast right through you, Wynter. Through you, and *into her.* You'll survive. Odds are good she won't."

Silence hummed for a moment. Then Zane was there, catching her wrist, his fingers warm around the flesh. She felt the cold bite of metal and heard the soft click of the cuff locking.

"We've been here before," she whispered as the buzzing slowly faded from her ears. His magic cuffs. Unbreakable. Whatever happened, they'd be together. The Feds wouldn't hurt him. They might want her head on a platter, but the Bureau wouldn't take out a hunter. Pak wouldn't let them.

"This is going to hurt you," he whispered, and the words feathered against her ear as he leaned in close, almost as if he were kissing her. "But I'm not letting her take us out of this lot. I'm taking *her* out."

Sounded like one fine plan to her. "Guess I'll see . . . how strong you are," she breathed the words back at him. Jana pressed her face into his neck and inhaled his scent.

You don't really want to see this.

The words drifted through her mind. His words.

Jana frowned. "What—"

His fingers slid over her cheek. "I'm sorry." Then he spun around. "Now what? We're—"

"Step to the side, demon. I want to see her face."

But Zane shook his head. "No. Put down the fucking gun. If you don't"—he exhaled on a heavy breath—"you'll wish you had."

Thunder echoed in Jana's ears. No, not thunder. *Gunshot.* The agent had shot Zane! "No!"

But he laughed. *Laughed.* And the bees were back in her head. Buzzing like crazy. The earth seemed to roll and tilt, shaking beneath her. Jana fell to the ground, and the cuffs jerked on her hand.

"That the best you got?" Zane taunted. "Cause it's not even close to being good enough."

Rising to her knees, Jana caught a glimpse of the agent's face—right before Kelly was lifted into the air by unseen hands and tossed back five feet. She crashed into the bumper of a patrol car.

"I *told* you to put the gun down." He took a step forward. "I'm done with warnings."

The ground was bucking and rolling again. Lightning streaked across the sky, and Jana grabbed tight to Zane's hand. "Hold on, Zane, just—" His blood was on the ground. Around her. Her back teeth locked. "We can—"

"*Zane!*" The cop's voice. Tony barreled out of the building with his gun drawn. He took in the scene with a quick glance. *Blood. Cuffs. Woman sprawled over the back of the squad car.*

Kelly started laughing then. What the hell was up with the laughter?

But then Zane stumbled. His body shuddered and Jana's heart seemed to stop.

Kelly had shot him, but with *what?* The agent's gun lay on the ground, dropped, forgotten.

Zane lifted his right hand toward Kelly, and her laughter cut off. Her face drained of color, and she started gasping for breath. Desperate, she clawed at her throat.

"Let her go," Tony said flatly. "I'm here, man. I've got her. She's not going to hurt you or your lady again."

But Zane didn't let her go. Kelly's body started bucking on the car. Long, thin, bloody scratches appeared on her arms.

"Zane, let her go," Jana whispered, worried, really worried, for *him.* Because this wasn't Zane. He didn't attack this way. He took his opponent down, he didn't . . . torture. She grabbed his chin, and jerked his face toward her. "Let her go!"

His eyes. They flickered wildly from green to black. Again. *Again.* "Zane?" Fear threaded through his name.

His eyes squeezed shut. Kelly sucked in a deep, hard breath. "Knew . . . i-it . . ." she gasped.

Screw her. Jana pressed a fast kiss to his cold lips. *Zane.* "We'll get the bullet out, and you'll be fine. You hear me? Everything's—"

"*Get away from me.*"

She blinked at him.

"*Get. Away.*" His hands came between them. He tried to shove her back.

But the cuffs weren't letting her go anywhere.

"Where's the key?" she whispered, but the only answer she got was the roar that burst from his lips. A roar that shook her and shattered the night.

Then the green bled totally from his eyes, leaving only the black, and Jana knew she was in trouble.

"What did you shoot him with?" The shouted words came from Tony. "What did you *use?*"

Jana couldn't look away from Zane. Not from that darkness.

"M-my brother . . . he made something sp-special for the demons." Kelly's voice was ragged, so strained, but satisfied. "It'll rip his mind apart."

Drugs. Zane's father had been lost to the drugs. He'd killed Zane's mother because of his addiction. Zane hated the drugs. He'd hate this.

Her left hand—the uncuffed hand—lifted and feathered over his cheek. "I'm sorry. Just hold on." They'd weathered a storm like this before. They could get through it again.

A trickle of blood slipped from his nose. He smiled at her. Not Zane's smile. Too . . . cold. Too cruel.

Not like Zane.

"Where's the key?" she whispered again.

"Not . . . *leaving* . . ."

"He doesn't h-have the k-key!" Kelly yelled. Jana forced

her stare to find the bleeding agent. Tony had a death-grip on Kelly's arm, and he was trying to cuff *her*. "I stole it from his car while you were in-inside. H-hid it—*you'll never find it!*"

Okay, the agent was getting on her last nerve. Feeling sorry for a woman could only last so long.

Kelly smiled at her. No, more of a baring of her teeth. "He's going to . . . k-kill . . . you."

Zane's breath blew over Jana's neck. A shiver skated down her spine. Then his mouth pressed against her skin, and the edge of his teeth bit into her neck.

"*Tear her f-fucking throat open!*" Kelly screamed.

"Shut the fuck up!" Tony roared back at her.

The bite became painful. Not a lover's nip. More. Her hands flattened on his chest. "You're going to be okay—"

"*Rip her—*" Kelly's words ended in a gurgle. Jana was still staring at her, and she saw the agent's eyes roll back into her head. Kelly slammed forward, breaking free of Tony's grasp and ramming her head into the cement. She didn't get up.

Zane.

He licked her neck. His head lifted, and he stared at her. Then he ripped her shirt open. *With just a thought.*

"Shit!" Tony's feet pounded toward them. "Man, what are you doing? You can't—"

Tony jolted to a stop, then he flew forward, his body slamming into the thick concrete wall. *Like a puppet on a string.*

Not Zane. Not her Zane. This wasn't him. "*No!*" Her scream echoed in that cold night. "Zane, *stop!*"

This time, he was the one to laugh, and that laughter chilled her to the bone. The good guy was totally gone. The demon was in charge, and he was staring at her with blood-lust in his eyes.

He's going to k-kill you.

Oh, damn, it sure looked like he just might.

Jude Donovan caught the scent of blood in the air. It was a scent that called to him, that tempted him, and one that made the beast inside salivate. Catalina was in sight, and even though the witch was all but flying down the street, she wouldn't be able to get away from him. *He* was faster.

But that blood . . . He turned his head a bit. The scent came from behind him. His nostrils flared. *Back to the left.*

Where he'd left Zane and his Ignitor.

Hell.

He cast one final glance at Catalina. She was running as if wolves were after her. Or maybe as if a tiger shifter were on her tail. Smart woman.

The blood.

The tiger inside roared, and so did the man. He spun away and thundered back down the road, running after that sweet smell, sucking it deep inside, and pounding across the pavement as he raced back to Zane and Jana.

Blood.

He cut through an alley. Jude came up in the back of the squat, cement building, and he saw Tony ram into the wall.

Jude's fangs burned in his mouth and his claws burst out. Tony might be an ass sometimes, but nobody hurt his friend, not even—

Zane. Shit.

Jude snapped his teeth together. No, no, this wasn't right.

"Fight it," he heard Jana say, her hands tight on the demon. Were they handcuffed together? Again? "I know the drugs are strong, but you can do this, you *can.*"

Drugs. No, no, Zane and drugs did *not* mix. The guy never even touched a cigarette because he was too afraid of the addiction, and of the darkness that the addiction brought.

"Zane!" he barked out his name, hoping to get his friend's attention.

Zane's body stiffened. Jude felt a rush of hot wind against his body, and he clenched his muscles. Zane's head turned toward him, a slow, gliding move, almost like a snake's. Those eyes . . .

Oh, dammit. Jude stepped forward. *If I ever turn like my old man, kill me.* Zane's quiet voice from so long ago. A late night at Delaney's bar when secrets had come out. Secrets about drugs, demons, and death. *Promise me, you'll hunt me.*

"*No!*" Jana screamed just as that hot wind rushed against Jude again. This time, that wind picked Jude up like he was a rag doll, and he hurtled through the air. *Fuck, fuck, fuck.* He lifted his arms and protected his head right before his body thudded into the concrete wall at the back of the building.

"No, Zane! Stop, he's your friend!"

But Zane wasn't gonna be stopping. Didn't she realize? Zane wasn't in control right then.

I-I never want to be like him. Him. Zane's father. The murdering bastard who had slaughtered Zane's mother.

The tiger snarled inside as the shift pressed ever closer. It would be so easy to change. To let that burning fire of the tiger consume him. *Attack. Kill. Protect.*

But if he shifted . . . he and Zane . . . dammit, one of them wouldn't survive.

The hot rush of air came at him again.

One of them *might* not survive now. Jude's claws scraped across the cement as he shoved back to his feet. His gaze darted to the left. To the long, thick metal pole that secured the side of that trash bin.

"Zane! Don't hurt him! Listen to me, *listen* . . ."

The demon wouldn't listen. The demon would destroy. Trapped to him, bound by those cuffs, the woman was helpless. Unless she used her fire.

Why the hell *hadn't* she used her fire?

The same reason I haven't used my tiger.

Because this was Zane.

His fingers wrapped around that bar. Zane was kissing the woman, holding her tight, caging her body against his even as his power filled the air. He'd never seen the demon let loose so much energy. Lightning crackled across the sky and streaked far too close to earth. Too close to Zane.

The metal screamed as Jude ripped it free. He saw Zane

tense at the sound, saw him try to jerk up, but Jana grabbed him and held tight. *"Don't let me go!"* She held the demon's head in her hands. "Don't!"

She was all the distraction he needed. Jude lunged forward and slammed the bar into the back of Zane's head.

When Zane fell, he took her to the ground with him. Gasping, shuddering, Jana hit hard and her body shrieked a protest back at her.

Zane's eyes were closed, and his black lashes cast shadows on his cheeks. "Zane?"

"He won't be out long." The hunter. Jude. He'd gotten up fast. He grabbed for the handcuffs and tried to yank them apart.

"It's not going to work," she whispered, feathering her fingers over Zane's face. "You know they're enchanted. The agent took the key. Without it . . ." She let the sentence trail off. He knew what would happen. There'd be no separating her from Zane.

Not that she planned to leave him. Not now.

He'd tried to tell her to leave, before the drugs swept through him. Tried to warn her away.

Why? So he could face the darkness alone?

Jude dropped her hand and ran for Kelly. He pulled the agent up. Jana saw her head dip and sag. Jude drove his hands in the pockets of her jeans.

Jana shook her head. The agent was too smart to have just pocketed the keys. She'd planned this too well.

He'll k-kill you.

The agent had planned, all right. She probably thought it was the perfect ending for Jana. Killed by her lover.

Jana's fingers curled around Zane's arms. "Help me."

The shifter kept struggling with the agent's limp body. Thanks to that header into the concrete, Kelly would be out for a long time. Too long.

But Zane . . . he healed fast. She licked her lips. *"Help me."*

Jude's head snapped toward her. She caught a glimpse of his fangs. His claws. Jana could clearly see the indecision on his face. He thought she wanted him to attack Zane.

Jude shook his head. "I *can't*—"

"We have to secure him." Her fingers were light on Zane's flesh. "He's going to wake up soon." A few minutes. If she knew her demons, and she did know them pretty well, he'd probably be out no more than five minutes, tops. While he was out, the drug would finish pumping through his body. When he woke up . . . She swallowed. "We need a room he can't escape. He can't be near anyone. He'll . . . hurt them." *Kill.*

She rose and struggled to pull Zane with her. "*Help me,*" she said again, and this time, the shifter was there. He grabbed Zane and hoisted him up.

Tony groaned as he began to rouse. *Still alive.* Good. For a minute there, she hadn't been so sure.

The shifter tossed Zane over his shoulder and carried him easily. Jana stumbled right behind them, the handcuffs pulling her in their wake. They went back inside. Down to the basement.

"A normal room isn't going to work. He'll be able to get out, he'll—"

"This used to be a psych hospital, before the city took the building." Jude entered a room to the right.

No windows. Thick walls.

"The door is reinforced steel. It only locks from the outside."

He lowered Zane to the floor. Jana slid down to his side.

"I'm not leaving you in here with him." Jude's eyes were too bright, glittering. *I can see the beast he carries so clearly now.*

"You are." Her words sounded confident, almost cocky. With those shifter senses, though, she bet the guy could hear how fast her heart was racing. Could he even smell her fear? "Lock us in. Then go find the witch. She can break the cuffs." Not that Jana planned to leave him, even then.

Jude eyed the door, and then looked back at her. "No damn way that lock will hold him. Zane is strong. He'll blast right through it."

Her fingers intertwined with his. *Still out.* "Then send Tony after the witch. You stand guard on the other side of the door. But you don't come at him, you hear me? Not unless . . ."

Unless, what? Unless Zane attacked him? Like he'd done just minutes before.

"I don't want to hurt him," Jude said. Might as well be her own thoughts.

"And I don't want him to hurt you." She didn't want Zane to attack anyone, especially not his friends. *Stronger than I'd thought.* And, yes, it sure seemed like her demon had a very dark side. No wonder he kept that side leashed.

"Your fire . . ."

"It's no good." Like she'd ever use the flames on Zane. The bastard might have pissed her off before because he didn't know how to trust, but he was still . . . Zane.

And his eyelids began to flutter. If he saw the shifter, he'd go into instant attack mode. "Get out!"

"I can't leave you with him, I can't—"

She laughed at him and made her voice drip ice as she said, "Do you really think I need protecting?"

But he didn't take the bait. His lips tightened. "Yeah, I do."

Almost sweet. But they didn't have time for sweet. "If he sees you, he'll try to rip you apart." Her heart slammed into her ribs. "I'll keep him calm, I'll—" A groan broke from Zane's lips. "*Just go!*"

Jude eased back a step. One. Another. "I'll be on the other side of that door." Making sure no one entered—no one who could get hurt, she knew. And making sure, also, that Zane wouldn't get out. "But I'll be able to hear everything. If he attacks you, I'm coming in."

She nodded, the movement jerky and hard. Fair enough. If Zane started psychically tossing her around the room—*like he'd tossed the others outside*—she'd want the shifter's backup.

But Zane wasn't going to hurt her. *I trust you, even if you can't trust me.*

Jude hurried out and shut the door. The bolt slammed into place with a clang.

Jana crawled on top of Zane and straddled him. What drug had Kelly given him? *Something my brother made . . .* Hell, that could be anything! In those few days that Brent had held her in his lab, she'd learned he'd liked to play God, stirring and mixing and creating torments for his "experiments."

The last time Zane had been hit with a drug, he'd wanted her. Sex and fury could be a potent combination. *Sex and fury.* He'd pulled back. The man had fought the demon's pull. Because of his hybrid blood? Had he been able to fight the drug because his body chemistry was so different? Or had he just been strong enough, because, shit, *he* was strong?

No more time to think—his eyelids flashed open. Pitch-black eyes stared up at her. He bucked beneath her and nearly sent her right onto the floor.

"It's okay!" She leaned down close. "Everything's fine." *Liar, liar.* She sealed her mouth to his.

His tongue thrust past her lips, and his hand clamped over her hip. His erection rose, long and thick, against her.

Zane. She called his name in her mind and wondered if he would hear her on the link they'd used before. Would the drug amp up his psychic power? Would it let him in—

An image flashed in her mind. Her. Him. On this same dirty floor. She was on top of him, and he was thrusting his thick cock into her.

She gasped into his mouth right at the moment she felt his hand yank open the snap of her jeans.

"*Jana!*" Jude's bellow.

Her head shot up. Zane stared at her, nostrils flaring, cheeks flushed. "It's okay!" she yelled back. "I'm fine!"

But Zane was growling. His hands were on her jeans. Shoving them down and the damn cuffs were in the way and—

"I'm coming in!" Jude told her.

Zane's head whipped toward the door. The bees buzzed in her head again, and the sexy image faded. A red haze seemed to cloak her vision. *Her vision, or Zane's?*

"No, stay back!"

She grabbed Zane's chin. "Stay with me," she whispered to him and kissed him again. *Stay with me.* That psychic link between them was there, and Zane was using it. She just wasn't sure the demon knew it.

Jana kicked out of her shoes and ditched her jeans. He ripped her panties, shredding them. His hand bit into her hip. Too hard. Too strong.

"Zane . . ."

He yanked down his zipper. His cock sprang free. As wide as her wrist, head bulging, moisture already beading from that tip.

His cock pushed into her, drove inside, and she shuddered against him.

No. Jana shook her head. Hadn't happened yet. Just another vision, one coming from him, hadn't—

He rolled her beneath him. The hard floor pressed into her back. He pushed her legs apart and positioned that cock right at the entrance to her body. No foreplay. No caresses, no—

Flesh to flesh. She only had a second to process that fact, then Zane thrust into her, a long hard drive that had her crying out.

He blinked, and his eyes narrowed. "J-Jana . . ." His voice was hoarse, confused. A flash of green appeared near the edges of his irises. "What the fuck . . . am I do—"

Her legs locked around him. "Fucking me." Now that the shock had worn off, her body was adjusting, fast. Her inner muscles clamped around him.

"S-sorry . . ." Sweat beaded his brows. "C-can't . . . stop . . ."

"I don't want you to." She arched her hips against him. "I want you to *move.*"

The green bled away. Only black again. Such darkness in her lover's eyes. Such hot darkness.

His cock pulled out of her, a rough slide of flesh. The cuffs banged against the floor as he held her arms. Then he drove into her, again, again. Hard, plunging thrusts that had her moaning, gasping, and shoving up against him because the pleasure was so intense.

He bit her, right where her neck curved into her shoulder. A bite that didn't break the flesh, but made her arch beneath him. *More.* His hips rocked against her, and he thrust into her, slamming all the way to her core.

His tongue licked the light wound he'd made. A moan rumbled in his throat. Hell, maybe in hers. Her flesh was so sensitive that every fierce stroke had her tensing. And wanting more.

His cock swelled within her, thickening even more, and she started to come. Jana choked out his name as her climax hit and the flames burned through her.

Zane pumped into her. Her sex was slick and eager now. *Withdraw. Thrust.* The slap of their bodies filled the room, and the scent of sex surrounded her.

More.

She could have sworn he whispered the word, but his mouth was still on her neck. Licking, sucking.

His hips pistoned against her. Her sex squeezed him as the after-shocks of pleasure trembled inside her.

His hand jerked down, yanking those cuffs. Her shirt still gaped open. He yanked her bra up and his mouth closed around her right nipple.

Zane!

Her sex clamped around him.

His tongue traced the nipple, and then he started to suck. And to fuck.

Her eyes squeezed shut.

See me. See us. His voice.

And she saw them. With her eyes closed, she saw the fast thrust of his cock into her sex. The withdrawal. The thrust.

He sent the images into her mind, and the pleasure seemed to intensify. *More. More.*

From him? Her?

More. She'd take it. Take everything.

Take him.

The second climax had her breath catching and her heart racing. She held on to him as tightly as she could. Hard enough to bruise.

He drove into her once more, then stiffened. The hot splash of his release filled her and she heard him gasp her name.

Jana's eyes opened. In pleasure, his face was so beautiful. So perfect. A lump rose in her throat.

And they'd done it. *We beat you, Agent Thomas.* Zane hadn't turned on her. Hadn't attacked. A smile began to curl her lips.

Then his hand rose and wrapped around her neck.

Chapter 17

Catalina threw another fast glance over her shoulder. No one was back there. She'd ditched Jude. *How the hell did I do that?* Her stomach clenched. You didn't lose a tiger shifter unless he *let* you lose him.

"Where are you going, Catalina?" At the sound of that soft, feminine voice, Catalina's blood froze. She'd known when she came back to Baton Rouge with Logan in tow that this meeting would be coming, only a matter of time.

Slowly, carefully, she turned to face the woman she'd once considered a friend.

Sandra "Dee" Daniels stood in the shadows, her small body almost completely hidden. There was a slight shuffle of footsteps, then Dee stepped forward. Her blond hair was cut haphazardly around her face.

Normally, Dee would have flashed her a wide smile. They would have gone out for drinks. Talked smack about men. Maybe exchanged some secrets. But that was all in the past.

"Jude sent you after me," Catalina said with certainty.

But Dee shook her head. "No, Tony did."

Ah, Tony. Figured. He and Dee had a . . . pretty intimate past. Of course, that was back in the days before Dee had changed.

Dee smiled now. Only it wasn't the one Catalina had wanted to see. It was a new, harder smile, one that revealed Dee's fangs.

From vampire hunter to vampire all in a few short days . . . yes, Dee's life had changed. That change had been one of the things that sent Catalina running from the city.

Dee offered her hand, palm up. "I'm going to need you to come with me."

Catalina shook her head. No, no, she had to go and see about Logan. He was weak, and he'd need her help to get out of Baton Rouge. Especially with someone from Perseus still hunting them.

"I can see the bite marks on your neck," Dee told her. "And I can almost feel the guy in the air around you."

Dee wasn't your average vampire. She hadn't been Taken, the term for the humans who were transformed by a blood exchange with a vampire. No, Dee was so much more. Born, not made. A vampire who hadn't even realized her true power until death came calling.

And she sent the asshole packing.

"W-we're being hunted, Dee," Catalina said. "We have to get out!"

"Running?" *Again?* The unspoken word hung between them.

Catalina kept her chin up. Dee didn't understand. She didn't know what it was like to be weak. To see the fire and know it was going to burn your skin away while you screamed.

Catalina spun away—and slammed into Dee. She'd never seen the woman move. Wouldn't have, not with Dee's power. "You're coming with me," Dee told her and grabbed her wrist.

Catalina blinked back tears. "I don't—"

"One spell is all I need, Cat. One spell, then you . . . and your vampire . . . can get out of town."

She licked her lips. "Y-you'll . . . let him go?"

Dee held her gaze. "Unless he goes after humans, he's off my radar."

But he'd gone after the Ignitor. He'd been desperate, starving. Did Dee know what he'd done? Catalina would need to keep Logan away from Zane so the demon wouldn't come for his revenge.

Only a matter of time.

Catalina forced herself to nod. "Okay." It was the only deal she'd be getting. Better take it, grab it with both hands, and hold as tight as she could. "I don't have much power." Painful to admit, but her binding marks weren't fading yet. And why not? They should have vanished when Beth died. Beth had been the one in charge at Perseus. The one to trap her and to use her. *Why haven't they faded?*

"It'll have to be enough." Dee pushed her toward a car idling near the curb. Catalina sucked in a breath when she saw the driver. *Simon.* Dee's vampire lover.

The two were a perfect killing team.

"Who needs my spell?" she asked, suddenly very worried as she climbed inside the vehicle.

Dee jumped in behind her and the car door slammed. "Zane."

The last thing she'd expected. "Zane? Why?"

Simon floored the gas.

"Because someone pumped the poor bastard full of drugs." Dee sighed. "And we both know what can happen to him when the drugs get into his system."

Goose bumps rose on Catalina's arms. Yes, she knew. And, once, long ago, she'd seen. Scrying. He'd always asked her not to do it. But the future teased and taunted, and she'd had to know.

Zane . . . eyes black as the night. Face bloody. The earth bucking beneath him. Death . . . a shroud he carried. One look, one touch, the prey fell before him.

"Hurry," she whispered to Simon and, when he looked up into the rearview mirror, she saw his jaw clench. "*Hurry.*"

Jana's breath caught as she stared up at Zane. His face could have been carved from fire and fury. Such hard, fierce lines. And his hand, as it wrapped around her neck . . .

"*I . . . hurt . . . you.*" Gravel rough. Like the man was struggling to speak. Maybe he was.

She realized his fingers were feathering over the bite mark on her neck. He was worried about that? Jana couldn't help it. She laughed. A quick, light gurgle of sound.

He blinked at her.

"Zane, trust me, you've got worse marks on you." Because she hadn't been gentle at the end. Her nails had dug into him and held tight.

"*Should . . . have . . . run.*"

"Maybe." She curled her fingers around the steely muscles of his arms. "But you know I don't ever do what I should do."

The bees began to buzz in the back of her mind. "*Go . . .*"

She glanced down at the cuffs. "Can't, remember?"

His gaze followed hers. Those bees got louder. Louder . . . The cuffs broke apart. "*Go.*"

Those all-powerful, unbreakable cuffs fell to the floor.

He pushed against her, his cock still thick and swollen, and the move seemed almost helpless.

More, please.

But then he pulled away, sliding out of her, and jumping to his feet. "*Leave . . .*" Still that gravel-rough voice. "*While you . . . can.*" He yanked up his jeans.

Jana licked her lips. Tasted him. She swallowed and wondered what the hell she should do. What did a woman have to say to make a man understand she wasn't the kind to wilt when things got tough?

Slowly, she rose to her feet. She took a few fast moments to dress, to adjust her clothes, and felt the aches and tingles in her body as she moved. Then she faced him with her legs braced apart and her chin up. "You're not going to hurt me."

But he shook his head. "*Will . . .*"

"No." She was certain. "You're stronger than whatever that agent pumped into you. You're the strongest man I've ever met." *True.*

"*Not . . . man . . .*"

He was right. So much more than just a man. "You're not like your father."

His teeth snapped together and the floor seemed to roll. Good thing she'd locked her knees. She'd figured that was coming. "You're not your father, and I'm not your mother."

"*Weak . . . human.*"

Yeah, he just had to throw that in her face, right?

"Zane, trust me. We can do this, together."

He hesitated, his powerful body shaking, and in that instant, she really thought that she might be getting through to him. Breaking past the darkness and getting to the man.

Then she smelled the smoke.

Her eyes widened. "Zane . . ."

She saw his nostrils flare as he caught the scent and then he was running for the door. Just as he reached out to grab it, the door swung open. Jude was there, filling the doorway. His claws were out.

"No!" *Don't attack, don't!*

Zane's fingers wrapped around the shifter's throat. Jude's claws pressed against Zane's stomach. "Demon," Jude growled, "you in control?"

Zane gave the barest of nods.

The claws dropped. "Good. Cause we need to get the fuck out of here."

Zane didn't free the shifter. Jana saw his fingers whiten as he tightened his hold. She sprang forward and caught Zane's shoulder. "*Let him go.*"

Zane's fingers fell away. Her breath heaved out. "What's happening? What's—"

"Fire." Jude bit out the word even as he whirled away. "Coming fast. We need to get up a level and get *out.*"

She gave a quick nod, but he didn't see it. The shifter was already racing away. No, he was *shifting.* Out in the hallway. She heard the crackle and hiss of the flames, but she also heard a roar. Like . . . a tiger's roar.

She ran to the doorway. Jude was on all fours, with his

head down. As she watched, fur exploded along his body. Bones snapped, popped. Elongated and reshaped. The man disappeared and a tiger—*holy hell, one big white tiger*—appeared in his place.

Another roar seemed to shake the building, then the tiger launched forward as its giant body soared through the air.

Jana sucked in a deep breath. Then one more. *White tiger.* She'd never seen a shift like that before. Sure, she'd heard about them, but she hadn't actually *seen* someone transform. Oh, damn. Oh, shit.

"*Fire's . . . stronger. . . .*" Zane's voice muttered in her ear. "*Go . . .*"

She didn't need to be told twice. Jana ran after the tiger, with Zane at her side. They thundered up the stairs. Smoke billowed in the air, choking her, and stinging her eyes.

The stairwell exit door was broken and hung drunkenly open. Thanks, no doubt, to the tiger. They went through the doorway and seemed to step into hell. Fire—everywhere. Burning so bright and hot.

There was no way to get out. The flames were too strong. The exits were blocked. The windows covered by the flames. *How?* How had the blaze gotten so strong? Not a normal fire. No way. This one was definitely—

Zane shoved his hands forward, as if he were pushing against something. The flames rolled back, rolled, then sputtered, dying low before the windows. The tiger crouched, then leapt forward, easily breaking through the glass.

Jana ran after him, only to be pulled back by Zane. "Wait, what are you—"

He picked her up, tucked her head against his chest, and flew through the window. The glass had to cut him, but the guy didn't even grunt, and he landed on his feet—*on his feet.* His knees barely buckled as they touched down outside. Then he was running away from the burning building with her held tight in his arms.

Her hands dug into him. "Zane . . . is . . . is anyone else inside?"

He froze.

Humans worked there. Sure, it was nearing three a.m., but someone should have been inside. Guards. Attendants. Someone.

And that fire was burning so hot now.

He put her on her feet. Spun back around. The tiger was pacing, growling.

"Where's Tony?" she asked, coughing a bit to clear her lungs as she looked to the left, then the right. The lot was deserted. "And the agent, where is she?"

Were they in the building?

Zane sprinted forward. The tiger attacked. Its paws slammed into Zane's chest, and he knocked Zane back.

Snarling, Zane leapt, his eyes on the building. Once more, that tiger came at him, swiping this time with his claws. A long, hard swipe that drew blood across Zane's chest.

A hot wind blew against her face. The bees . . .

"*No!*" She grabbed Zane. "He's a shifter. He'd *smell* people if they were inside." But Jude was doing everything he could to keep Zane *out* of that building. Because no one was inside? Because if Zane went back in, he wouldn't be coming out?

Zane shook her off and lunged forward once more. He caught the tiger's front paws, holding them tight, and didn't even flinch under the cat's great weight.

"*What the hell?*" A woman's startled cry. "Zane, Jude, get away from there!"

Because they had gotten too close to the flames. The flames that had shot even higher, even brighter.

In the distance, a siren began to wail. *Hell.*

The woman rushed toward Zane and Jude. Wait, was she crazy? Was she really going to try and get between a demon and a tiger? The lady was small. Freaking tiny, with really bad hair. Blond, but cut oh-so-badly. And she was cursing. Swearing constantly under her breath.

"Dee!" a man bellowed. But that call came too late. "Dee"

had already gotten to the two fighters. She punched the tiger in the side. Hard.

He roared and turned toward her.

"Don't even think of biting me," she yelled at him, snapping her teeth together. Her incredibly sharp teeth. "I'll bite back." *Vampire.*

So was the dark, dangerous man who ran after her. Jana caught sight of his fangs glinting in the dark.

No, not more vampires.

Jana's hand rose to her neck, and her fingers pressed lightly against the still tender skin. A shiver skated over her body. Her heart already raced too fast, and the desperate beat began to shake her chest.

Vampires. Near Zane. Closing in . . .

Her hands clenched into fists.

"Take care of him!" Dee ordered her vamp friend. The male grabbed Zane's arms and held them behind the demon's back.

Zane immediately head-butted the guy. Blood poured from the vamp's nose.

"Shit! It's me, Zane, it's—"

"Would you *shift back* already?" Dee shouted at Jude as Jana stared at them, rage and fear twisting inside her.

Can't just stand here. Can't let them hurt Zane.

"She's charging up." What? Another freaking voice?

Jana turned her head, just a bit, and saw the witch walk into the back lot. *Catalina.*

"She's charging up," Catalina said again, "and she's going to attack."

Can't charge up. That wasn't fire spiking her blood. It was plain old fury. But the vamps didn't know that. "Get away from Zane!" She wanted her fire back!

At her words, Zane twisted and drove his fist into the male vamp's bloody face. The vamp flew back ten feet.

"Uh, oh." Dee shook her head and turned her back on the shifter. "Guessing this is why you're still in tiger form."

Because Zane was amped up, almost wild? Unstoppable.

The blonde's gaze returned to Jana. Black irises—a vampire in hunting mode. Jana's vision began to narrow.

Dee held up her hands. "I'm here to help him, not hurt him."

Right. Like any vamp was there to *help*. She'd tried to help that other vamp in the swamp, and he'd literally bitten the hand that reached to help.

Zane launched at the tiger. They fell to the ground, rolling. *Oh, damn.* The tiger's teeth were so close to Zane's throat. Then Zane twisted and threw the tiger against a car.

"*Help me.*" The vampire—Dee—her voice was so deep and compelling. It seemed to slip right under Jana's skin. To slip inside . . .

No. Jana's body tensed. "He just wants to get inside, to make sure no one else is—"

"No one else is in the building. Jude would've smelled 'em. That death trap was for you and Zane." Dee marched closer to her. "Call him off."

She blinked. "What? I can't—"

"I think she can," came from Catalina and the witch began to close in on her, too.

"Call. Him. Off," Dee repeated. "Because I don't want to have to hurt him."

Jana's eyes narrowed. "You think you can?" Right then, she didn't think anyone could stop him. The tiger's claws didn't even come close to his flesh now. He moved too fast, and he seemed far too strong.

But the male vamp was on his feet and heading forward with his hands up.

"No, Zane!"

Zane spun toward her, and Dee grabbed her. For a small chick, she was damn strong. *Too strong.*

"Come away from the building, Zane." Dee's soft order.

More sirens. The cops and firefighters would be there any minute.

"We have to get the hell out of here, and I need you to

focus, got me, demon?" The woman's claws were at her throat. That rage and fear spiked again in Jana's blood.

"Dee . . ." Catalina's shaking voice. "You, um, need to be very care—"

The vampire screamed and dropped her hold. Jana spun around and saw that Dee was clutching her hand. A hand that was smoking. *Yes, oh, yes. The fire's back!* She was back!

Jana's lips began to curve. Then the male vamp tackled her. Jana's head thudded into the ground and the world disappeared in a curtain of black.

Jana was on the ground. Not moving. A man had her in his arms. He said, "Oh, fuck—" just as Zane launched at him.

"No!" The blond female was there again. Glaring up at him with her vampire eyes. "Zane, she's okay, but we have to get out of here! Do you hear me?"

He grabbed her arms. Everything was too loud. Too dark. The fire seemed to call him, and Jana—*Jana* was the only constant in his world.

Eyes closed. Unmoving. Vamp holding her.

This had happened before. He wasn't going to let her be hurt again.

He shoved the blonde aside.

"Shit, Zane!" And she was back, grabbing him. Shaking him. Strong for someone so small. "*It's me.*"

Her voice seemed distorted, echoing almost. He frowned and studied that face. He . . . knew her.

"Dee. It's Dee." Her head turned to the left. "Dammit, shift already, Jude! Don't you hear those sirens? We've got like five seconds to scram."

He blinked. Dee. The name clicked in his mind. She was . . .

"Tell me you remember me." She stared up at him. "I've only been working with you at Night Watch forever. *It's me.*"

Dee. Sandra Dee.

Vampire.

He broke free of her hold. The male vamp lifted his hands,

but didn't attack. Jana's head lay cradled in his lap. "She hit her head. I didn't mean—" The vamp broke off, swallowing. "I just didn't want her to hurt Dee."

The fury was easing inside Zane. No, not easing. He felt like he was about to crash. His heartbeat slowed, and his breathing roughened. He took Jana, hoisted her into his arms, and held tight.

Get away. They had to leave because of the—

Sirens. For some reason, a reason he couldn't remember right then, Jana didn't like sirens. She didn't want to be around cops.

He held her tighter. Zane inhaled her scent and started running away. No, not running. Barely walking. His legs didn't want to move. Holding Jana seemed so hard.

"It's going to be okay." He looked up when he heard the woman's soft voice. An angel stood before him, her long, blond hair feathering around her pale face. "You're safe, Zane."

Those were the last words he heard before his knees buckled and he fell onto the ground, pulling Jana down with him.

"We're being hunted." The voice drifted through the fog that surrounded him.

Zane tensed at that voice. One so important to him. *She's okay.* If Jana was talking, then that meant she was all right.

He tried to open his eyes. Couldn't.

She was all right, but what the hell was wrong with him?

"Who's after you?" Another feminine voice, but sharper, harder.

"Someone from Perseus." A pause, then Jana said, "At least, that's what the witch said. I-I'm worried . . . have we heard from the cop, from Tony?"

Silence.

"He was outside that building. He would have seen whoever set the fire." Jude's voice now. "I saw him, *before* . . . He came to find me inside. I told him to—"

"To send me after Catalina," Dee said. Yes, *Dee*. That sharp voice was hers.

Jude's snarl hung in the air. "Tony wouldn't have just left us to burn."

Zane tried to open his eyes again. Nothing. He tried to lift his hands, but couldn't move. *What the fuck?* What had the drug done to him?

"Pak's got a search on for him," Dee said. "For him and Agent Thomas."

A soft sigh drifted in the air. "Tony was there the night Perseus went up in flames." Jana's words came slowly as if she hated to say, "Catalina said we were all marked for death. What if he's been taken by Perseus?"

No. His hand jerked, hard, and Zane felt something snap.

"Okay," Jude drawled the word. A long whistle filled the air. "Our demon just broke a steel restraint. I'd say he's coming back to us."

Soft fingers wrapped around his. "Zane?" Jana whispered. "You coming back?"

Open damn eyes, open. Because he needed to see her.
Jana.

Light filled his vision. Too bright. Then she was there, leaning over him, that dark curtain of hair surrounding her face, a blue-and-black bruise high on her forehead.

The other restraint broke as he shoved upright.

"Yeah, he noticed the bruise," Dee murmured. "See, told you it was a good idea to station Simon outside."

Simon. Dee's lover. The vamp he remembered tackling Jana. His teeth snapped together.

"Are you really back this time?" she asked softly as her brows pulled together.

This time? Just what the hell had been going on?

He reached for her and skimmed the back of his hand down her cheek. "I'm back." His voice grated, but she didn't wince. Didn't so much as look away from him.

"Good." Her lips tried to curl, that dimple peeking at him,

and she blinked quickly. For an instant, Zane could have sworn that he saw the glint of tears in Jana's eyes.

She'd stayed with him. He remembered that. The blood-lust had burned inside, and she'd stayed. She'd let him—

Zane sucked in a sharp breath. "Baby . . ."

She leaned forward and kissed him. A soft, fast press of her lips. "You didn't hurt me."

"Hell, no," Dee grumbled. "You didn't hurt *her*. You weren't even close to hurting her. It was anyone dumb enough to get between the two of you that you decided to *hurt*."

That was damn good news. No, it was fucking fabulous news.

Jana tried to ease away. He caught the back of her head and pulled her close, and he kissed her the way he needed to. Deep and long, tasting and taking, and promising so much more to come.

"Aw, hell." The frustrated sigh was pure Dee. "Can't you get a room once we're done figuring out who is trying to destroy you? You know, we've got the little matter of someone setting a fire to kill you, and your girlfriend."

Slowly, Zane lifted his head. He could taste Jana on his lips now. Just what he wanted. "No one was trying to kill us with the fire." He turned his head and saw Dee's face tense.

"Then why—"

"Someone trapped us so Tony would be easy prey." The knowledge pissed him off. "This guy is doing up-close and personal kills. Slicing throats, not burning prey."

"Well, maybe he changed his M.O." Jude crossed his arms over his chest. "Because that fire was damn wild. If you hadn't calmed it down . . ."

He'd always had a way with the fire. Jana twined her fingers with his.

"We have to find Tony," Dee said, voice fierce. "The guy's pretty much freaking helpless. He's just—"

"Human?" Jana finished quietly. Then she shook her head. "Just because we're human, it doesn't mean we're helpless."

"Oh, don't worry, I wasn't making that mistake about

you." Dee's blond brows rose. "Not making that mistake at all."

Zane frowned, struggling to shove the last of the fog from his mind. His temples throbbed as he demanded, "How much time has passed?"

Jude exhaled. "Too damn much."

Fuck.

"You were out an hour. I tried to pick up Tony's scent from the scene, but—" His shoulders lifted, then fell in a hard shrug. "It was like the guy had never been there."

Someone strong was jerking them around. "The claw marks were *like* a wolf's." He spoke quietly as he pushed his way through all the evidence.

"But Marcus didn't kill anyone!" Jana was adamant.

"No." He kept his gaze on her. "And Beth wasn't an Ignitor, not until the girl touched you."

Her eyes widened, and he knew she understood where he was going.

"The person killing, he's from Perseus," Zane said.

"Or *she* is," Dee added. Dee knew very well that women could be as dangerous—or more dangerous—than men.

"If Beth was using a psychic to transfer power from one person to another, hell, it stands to reason she would have done this switch more than once." He pushed up from the table, and for an instant, darkness swirled around him. The echoes of fear and fury pumped in his blood.

Not. Again.

Jana's hair brushed against his cheek as she steadied him. "It's okay," she whispered.

With her there, it was. Because she hadn't turned from him. She'd stayed with him through hell.

She'd held the demon and loved him. His teeth clenched. He hoped the woman understood, she wasn't getting away from him now. Not unless she really wanted to break him.

Weakness. The need for drugs that so many of his kind possessed. But the drugs didn't call to him. Jana called. Only her. Yeah, he was addicted—to her.

She was his weakness.

Don't let them know your weakness. The voice drifted through his mind, and Zane tensed at the memory.

"Beth would have made sure she tested the psychic's power before trying to take my fire." A furrow appeared between Jana's brows. "She would have planned everything, been sure there were no mistakes." A hard laugh escaped her. "But she didn't realize how hot that fire would be." Her laughter died. "Neither did her psychic." She swallowed and her eyes grew sad.

He ran the back of his hand down her arm.

"So . . . wait, you're saying those bastards at Perseus found a way to transfer powers?" Jude whistled. "Someone took your fire?"

She nodded jerkily.

"Shit." He rocked back. "And you think—you think somebody took a shifter's gift, too?"

"Gift, curse, all the same damn thing." Jana heaved out a hard breath. "If they could take my fire, they could take someone's beast. They could take anything."

Jude paled a bit. *He didn't want to lose his beast.* "You sure that psychic is dead?"

She nodded.

Dee strode forward. "But you *burned* me."

"The transfer doesn't seem to be permanent."

Dee's gaze measured her. "Do you believe there might be another psychic out there who can steal powers, too?"

"I think there probably is, somewhere," Jana said, her eyes narrowing. "For a while, I thought I was the only one who could start the fires. Then I found out there were more like me. Why not have more like Laura?"

"Hell. Just what we don't need." Jude seemed to be sweating. Zane didn't blame him. The last thing a shifter would want to hear is that his beast could be taken from him.

"Did Marcus shift?" Zane asked Jana, pulling her attention back to him. "When you were with him, did Marcus's claws grow, did his teeth—"

"He was too weak to shift." Said with sadness. "Just like he was too weak to fight off the bastard who came for him."

The bastard that he suspected had Tony. The light overhead shattered and sent down a hail of sparks.

"Easy," Dee said.

Fuck easy. *Where was Tony?* "I'm not standing here with my thumb up my a—"

The door flew open. Catalina stood in the doorway, sweating, chest heaving, and with what looked like tear tracks of blood on her cheeks. "I found him!" A broken mirror, the glass gone black, was gripped tightly in her blood-soaked hands. Simon loomed behind her, but Zane knew the blood hadn't come from a vampire's bite. No, this time, it had come from something far worse.

"Dee, tell me you didn't ask her to—"

Dee brushed by him and headed for Catalina. "We needed to find him. She had to scry."

Dee had never understood about scrying. She didn't realize . . . Cat looked into the spirit world every time she tried to see the future. And the spirit world . . . it looked back at her. When Death looked at you, it was never a good thing.

He marks you. She'd told Zane that once. Told him that she'd felt Death's claws in her flesh. He'd seen the scars on her back to prove the claim.

"What did you see?" Jude asked, circling close to her.

Her chest heaving, she said, "Demons—demons were all around him. Closing in."

"A den?" The question came from Simon. He was right at Catalina's back. Good thing. The woman would be collapsing soon.

Catalina nodded. "It was black. Covered in darkness. Like a fire had scorched—"

"I know the place," Jana cut in, a thread of excitement in her voice. "If you're talking about demons in a den and fire, then you're talking about Dusk."

Because she'd lit up that place. Scorched the walls and ceiling.

Catalina swallowed. "Th-there's not much time." Her gaze met Zane's. "Death's already there." She turned her body a bit, and he caught sight of her shoulder, and the long, bloody claw marks that ravaged the back of her arm.

He heard Jana's gasp and knew she'd seen the marks, too.

"Who has Tony?" He had to understand just what he was walking into at that den.

A trickle of blood slipped from her mouth. "A demon. I saw—saw his eyes. So dark. So black."

Her own eyes began to close. He lunged forward.

But Simon had her. He caught the witch and lifted her up high against his chest. Shit. With all that blood, he'd better not be—

Simon shoved Catalina into Jude's arms. A muscle jerked in his jaw, and Simon stepped back, fast.

"Didn't . . . let you down this time." Catalina's voice was a whisper. "This time . . . did my part. T-tell Tony . . . didn't . . . leave him alone."

"We'll tell him." Because they *were* finding him alive. "Just rest, Cat. We'll get him."

And he'd make the bastard who took him pay. Perseus had picked the wrong demon to screw, and the wrong human to take.

Hold on, Tony.

Zane wrapped his fingers around Jana's. Help was coming—and help would be in the form of that Perseus bastard's worst nightmare.

Chapter 18

"How are we going to do this?" Jana asked. Her gut tightened as they approached the darkened shell that was Dusk.

Dusk. Well, dawn was actually breaking as they headed for the hollowed-out demon's den, and dawn wasn't a real good time when your backup consisted of a pair of vamps. Vamps were weaker during the day. Pretty much at human level. Since they were about to go up against some amped-up demons . . .

Yeah, stronger backup, or maybe *actual* dusk would have been better.

"We're going in, and we're kicking ass until we get our man back," Dee said, not looking real fazed by the fact that the sun had started to rise.

The male vamp, Simon, was at her side. Figured. From what Jana could tell, he always stayed pretty close to her. Tall, dark, scary . . . the guy had done a major freak-out when the blonde was hurt. A freak-out that still had her head throbbing.

Her eyes narrowed. She'd owe him for that. And she always paid her debts.

"We don't know how many are waiting inside." Tension had tightened Zane's muscles. They were three blocks away from the den. "So you two will be our distraction."

The vamps nodded, but didn't look particularly happy.

"You go in the front, loud and strong, and we'll take the back." Zane pointed at Jude. "You go with us."

The big shifter's face was etched into tight lines of fury. "I can smell his blood from here."

Oh, that couldn't be good. *Death's already there.* That was what the witch had said. The last thing Jana wanted to do was walk in there and find the cop's dead body. For a cop, Tony hadn't been a bad guy. Not really bad at all.

The bees began to buzz in Jana's head. She reached for Zane. "It . . . hurts when you do that."

He blinked, then glanced quickly at Dee and Jude. They both shrugged, each with No-I-Don't-Know-What-the-Hell-She-Means expressions.

"They're not human," she muttered. "I am. When you amp up the power, I can feel it."

His eyes widened. "Then you stay here. Because if we go in there, and I find Tony and he's—" He shook his head. "You need to be far enough away that the blast doesn't hit you."

The blast? She shook her head. "No, you need me."

"He's got two vamps," Simon said. "And a shifter. I think we've got this covered."

The vamp really wanted payback from her. She didn't look away from Zane. "You need me."

"I told you already," he said. "I need you more than I've ever needed anyone." He almost looked sad for an instant. No, not sad. Like he was—

"So I hope you understand when you wake up," he continued, "I only did this to keep you safe."

Then those bees swarmed in her mind. The green bled from Zane's eyes, and the darkness she saw in his gaze seemed to reach out to her. She felt his arms catch her as she fell, and then . . . nothing.

"She's going to be so pissed with you." Dee shook her head and frowned down at Jana's body. "And when that woman gets angry"—she shook her right hand—"she burns."

He grunted. "I'd rather have her pissed than hurt."

"So what . . . you're just going to leave her here?" Dee asked, lips pulling down. "What if some of the other assholes out here find her?"

Good fucking point. He grunted and looked at Jude. "Keep her safe."

"But you need me in there! You don't know what's—"

"I *need* you to stay with Jana." The shifter would understand. He might not like it, but he'd understand. Jude had his own lady that he'd die to protect. "I can track Tony. He's human. I can send out a psychic wave and feel him once I'm inside." He just had to get closer to make contact. *"Jude, keep her safe."*

When had she come to mean so much? Come to mean . . . everything? When she'd gone after the demons who'd attacked him? When she'd braved the fires at Perseus for him? When they'd made love and she whispered his name?

Hell, it didn't matter when. She was under his skin, locked in what was left of his heart, and he wasn't risking her.

Don't let them know your weakness.

The killer already knew, and Zane would be damned if he put Jana at risk. He would have left her back at Night Watch, but the drugs had dulled his powers and he hadn't been able to put her out then.

Now his strength had returned. Real good thing.

"Be back soon, baby," he whispered and brushed a kiss over her still lips. He looked up at Jude.

The shifter nodded his head in agreement. "Watch your ass, demon."

"Always." He squared his shoulders, ignored the throbbing in his head, and walked away from the woman who could break him. The demons were waiting for him. Holding the human he called his friend.

"Distract them," he ordered Dee and knew that she would. With her new vampire skills, she'd tear a path right through any demons who were waiting inside. She and Simon would be more than a match for at least a dozen demons. Well, they'd be a match while the sun stayed low. Since time was against them, they all needed to haul ass.

But how many were inside? Catalina hadn't told them for sure. Just that Tony was surrounded by Zane's brethren.

He split from the vampires and kept to the waning shadows. The stench of burnt wood and ash hung in the air. He slipped down the alley, moving as soundlessly as he could. He sure didn't want to tip off his prey. Not now.

The back door was boarded up. Boarded from the outside, as if someone had tried to keep the demons *in.*

He stared at those boards and let his power flare. The nails began to ease out of the wood. Slowly, so slowly, and carefully. The nails dropped to the ground with a soft clink. He caught the boards before they could fall.

Then he heard a roar. A loud, guttural cry of female fury.

Dee. Timing her distraction perfectly. More shouts filled the air as the demons inside attacked or *were* attacked.

He eased open the door and went into the hollowed-out hell. The scents were stronger. The ash stained his fingers when his hand brushed against the wall. The odor of blood was stronger. Thicker. His heart slammed into his chest. *Too much blood.*

Zane's breath rasped out. If Tony was dead . . .

A floorboard squeaked and he whirled around. A demon stared back at him. A demon with the face of innocence and eyes blacker than the ash. Screams echoed from the front of the den. Curses filled the air.

The demon smiled at him. "I was wondering how long it would take for you to get here," Davey said, and he shook his blond head. "I mean, it's not like the human had that long to keep living. We were running out of time."

Zane lunged for him and grabbed the kid by his shirt. He jerked Davey close. "You fucking bastard." *Davey.* The kid. The barely legal asshole.

My damn fault. I let him live.

Davey must have read the thoughts on Zane's face because

he laughed. "Guess you're wishing you'd just let me burn, huh? But don't feel too bad. I would've gotten out anyway."

But the little bastard had been all but begging for help then. As powerful as he seemed now, why would he have—

He'd taken the shifter's powers. And his weaknesses. That cage—Zane would fucking bet it had been made of silver. *Couldn't move it, could you, asshole?*

Zane shoved his fist into Davey's face. The demon's nose shattered, and blood sprayed in the air. "Where. Is. He?"

Davey wrenched away from him. That perfect smile was bloody now. "I got 'em both, you know."

More screams. "*Vampire bitch!*"

Something heavy thudded, shaking the den. Probably a demon hitting a wall.

"I've got the cop." Davey swiped the back of his right hand over his mouth and smeared the blood. "And the agent."

His back teeth clenched. *Attack.* "I'll find them both after I kill you."

"No." Davey shook his head. "You'll find their bodies. I sprayed the blood all around the place. Without a shifter, you won't be able to find 'em. Not until it's too late."

Fuck that. He'd send out his blast and he'd *find them*.

"Tell you what . . ." Davey nodded, as if he'd just reached some kind of big, damn decision. "I'll let you hunt 'em. I'll give you two minutes—because hey, you're supposed to be the big, super demon, right? The badass hybrid."

Zane didn't speak, but his nostrils flared. He sent out his power, searching for Tony. Searching . . .

And he hit a damn brick wall of darkness.

Davey laughed and jumped back. "Really, did you think I'd make it that easy? I can't let you just probe and find them."

The fucker had blocked the humans. Shielded them somehow.

"Two minutes," Davey said again. "And this whole place will be going down. Think you can save one of them in that time?"

Flames began to flicker near Davey's feet.

Zane sent out a hard burst of his power. The flames didn't die. They didn't flicker. They surged higher. Hotter.

"I learn from my mistakes." Davey bared his teeth. Teeth that were too sharp for a demon. "This time, I'm using all of *my* power, too."

And the little bastard was strong.

The lines of fire raced across the room, then the fire split in two, one branch of flames snaking toward the right, one to the left.

"Better hurry," Davey murmured. "If the fire gets there first . . ."

Shit. Zane ran to the left.

"Choose well, demon. Because one of them is already dead. No point in saving the dead."

Death is already there.

"'Course, vampires don't like the fire too much, either, do they?"

Zane didn't look back at the taunt, but he felt the rush of heat and knew that Davey had sent another blast of flame out into the den. How was the demon so strong? Because he'd stolen power from the shifter? Or from a hell of a lot more paranormals?

"*Dee! Simon! Get the hell out of here!*" Zane shouted, and he kicked down the door on the left, ignoring the flames that burned his legs and his arms. That blood . . . he raced down the hallway, getting a few desperate inches in front of the fire. *Hurry, hurry.* Another door. Another—

His foot slammed into the door. Wood shattered. The thick stench of death hit him then. "No! Fuck, no, Tony!" He shoved his way past the broken wood.

But Tony wasn't the one on the floor. Kelly lay there, her eyes wide open, and her throat ripped out. The flames raced toward her, as if homing in on her.

"Tony!" He spun around, but the flames were walling him in. Zane pushed his power at them, but that fucking kid was stronger than he was. Stronger than any demon he'd ever seen.

Playing with me before. Just jerking me around.

More screams rose over the flames. Dee. Simon. They needed him.

Zane stopped pushing his power at the flames. He just ran forward and jumped right through the fire.

Something tapped her on the cheek. "Hey, pyro, come on, wake up." Another tap, harder this time. "Zane's not even around now. You've *got* to wake up soon."

Zane. Her eyelids flew open, and she found Jude staring down at her, his nose less than an inch from hers.

"About time." He grabbed her arms and hefted her up. Because she'd been on the ground. *What?* Why had she been lying on the ground? "I'm smelling *fire*, and I'm not leaving my team in there alone with the flames."

Fire? His team? She stood on shaky legs and turned—then caught sight of Dusk. Jana sucked in a sharp breath. "That ass left me."

"No, he tried to protect you."

Same thing.

"But now they *need* us."

Yeah, she could see that. "Then let's get the hell in there."

Zane raced after the second snake of fire, even knowing that he was too late. The den fell around him. The beaten walls couldn't hold up against the flames again.

"Zane!" Dee's desperate voice called through the fire and the smoke.

"Get out!" Vamps had a tendency to burn way too fast, and he didn't want Dee burning because she was trying to save his ass. "*Go!*"

Everything was falling around him. He lunged forward, no longer even feeling the blazing bite of the fire on his flesh. The door had burned, and he rushed inside. Zane flew down a corridor, following the flames and—

Tony's desperate eyes met his. The cop had a gag in his mouth, and he was handcuffed to a chair—and flames were eating at his legs.

Zane leapt across the room and knocked Tony back. They hit the floor, hard, and he started slapping at Tony's legs. But those flames—those flames flared brighter.

They homed in on Kelly. They're fucking doing the same with him. Zane had to get Tony out of there. He grabbed the cuffs, jerked, and they broke apart.

Tony started slapping at the flames.

"Run," Zane shouted.

Tony coughed. Choked. "Wh-where?"

Because there was no way out. The flames had circled them. The flames had—

Zane blew out the back wall. He hoisted Tony over his shoulder and hauled ass, running right for the streams of sunlight he could see flickering through the smoke.

He hit the cement, and felt the bite on his knees. Zane glanced back. The flames were higher, surging and twisting, but not coming past the edge of Dusk.

Maybe there were some fucking limits to Davey's power after all.

Tony coughed and heaved against him. Zane lowered him carefully.

"You got him!" Dee ran up to him, her face stained by soot. Simon was at her back. Sweat sliding down his face. "I knew you would!"

He hadn't been so sure.

Tony was crouched on the ground now, almost hacking his lungs up.

"Those demons are burning in there." Simon's voice was cold, hollow. "They were pumped up so high that they ran toward the flames, not from them."

The roof collapsed on Dusk. Far, far away—sirens called out. The human cavalry. Coming, at long last.

He slapped his hand on Tony's shoulder. "You're gonna be okay."

Tony turned toward him, his eyes stained red, and the skin on his hands blistering. He wouldn't be healing so easily from those wounds. No, as a human, he'd carry the scars. "F-fucking k-kid . . ."

Zane tensed. He could see the claw marks on Tony's neck now. Not deep enough to kill. Just deep enough for Davey to play.

"D-demon's eyes . . . sh-shifter's . . . claws . . ."

Dee hurried to Tony's side. "Easy." She pushed him back onto the ground. Her hands were so gentle on him. She brushed back his hair. "Just take it easy." There were tears swimming in her eyes because she'd seen the full damage to Tony's legs. "Simon, get a damn ambulance!"

Simon took off running.

"Who did this to him?" Dee whispered.

"I did." Because he'd been soft. He'd shown his weakness, and Davey had seen it.

She looked back at him with a furrow of confusion between her eyes. "What?"

"Stay on guard, Dee." Because he knew Davey hadn't died in the flames. He knew and—

And a tiger's roar shook the streets. Oh, shit. *No.*

But Davey was going after everyone who'd brought down Perseus, and Jude had been there that night.

"Kill anyone who comes close—and if it's some eighteen-year-old kid with demon's eyes and blond hair, don't fucking hesitate." Because he'd hesitated.

She nodded.

An ambulance sped up, following close behind Simon as he rushed back to Dee. A fire truck raced behind it.

Zane followed the roar as fear tightened his heart. If Davey had found Jude, the bastard had also found Jana.

Jana. He didn't realize he'd screamed her name.

Zane rounded the corner, running fast to the spot he'd left Jana. She was supposed to be safe. She was supposed to be—

She was locked against Davey. The bastard's claws were at her throat. Jude stood less than five feet away from them, his own claws out, and his fangs bared. *"Let her go!"* Jude snarled.

But Davey just jerked her closer against him, and blood leaked down her throat. "Stay back!" Davey ordered and his eyes flew from Jude to Zane. "Both of you, stay the fuck back, or I'll rip her throat out!"

"Then you'll die," Jude told him, edging closer. "Because your shield will be gone. I'll be on you, and *you'll* be dead."

But Davey, smart, slick Davey, just smiled his still-bloody smile. *"She'll* be dead."

Jana's gaze met Zane's.

"He'll be crazy." Davey stared right at Zane as he tossed that out. "And you, shifter"—now his eyes darted back to Jude—"you'll get your ass kicked five seconds later. Because I'm the strongest damn thing you've ever seen."

Jude growled in response, but his body had frozen.

"I knew you'd come for her," Davey said, and he wrenched Jana back a step. "When I left the fire and I caught her scent . . ." His head lowered toward her hair, and he inhaled deeply. "I could have walked away, could have just got in my car and left, coming back to hunt another day. But with such great prey close by, how could I leave?"

Sick fuck. "She isn't prey."

More blood trickled down Jana's neck, but she didn't make a sound. "She's the prey I've been after for a very long time."

"Y-you . . ." The word seemed to break from Jana's mouth then. "Not B-Beth, was it? You were Perseus."

What? This damn kid? No fucking way.

Davey's smile flashed again. "I was wondering if you knew. Beth liked to take credit for every damn thing, but Perseus—that was my baby."

"What the hell?" Jude shook his head. "You're *Other.* Why would you hunt your own?"

Davey's gaze again tracked to Zane. "Why would he? Why would you?" He licked away some of the blood on his lips.

Zane saw Jude's hands clench into fists. "We go after the

bastards who have crossed the line. We don't hurt innocents. We stop the *Other* who can't stop themselves."

"So do I." Davey blinked a bit, as if surprised they'd even doubt him. "Perseus goes after those who hurt humans, we—they—"

"That's a damn lie!" Jana's eyes were bright. "Marcus didn't hurt any humans. He—"

Davey's left hand wrapped in her hair, and he yanked her head back. "He sliced open the throat of Clayton Ridgeway."

"Because Ridgeway *killed* Marcus's girlfriend! And a dozen other women!" Jana didn't sound scared. Didn't look it either. Her eyes were so bright . . . and starting to become streaked with the faintest of red lines.

Zane sucked in a sharp breath. *Charging up.* Could Davey tell?

"Doesn't matter what Ridgeway did." No smile lifted Davey's lips now. "Paranormals *can't* kill humans. The two worlds aren't meant to cross. When they do, hell comes."

Hell comes. "The two worlds cross all the time." Zane risked a few steps closer. The claws didn't dig any deeper into Jana's throat. "That crossing . . . that's how you and I got to be here, right? Hybrids, both of us. For me, because my mother loved a demon, and for you, because your dad—"

"*Don't talk about him!*" The scream echoed through the night.

Yeah, okay, obviously he'd just found Davey's weakness.

"My dad did the damn best he could. He couldn't help that a demon tricked him, got into his mind and—"

"Is that what he told you?" Zane asked quietly, keeping the emotion out of his voice. *Her throat was still bleeding. If those claws dug in a bit more . . .* "That your mother used her power to work into his mind and steal his will?"

"*She was a demon.* She tricked him. Made him think she was human." Sweat slid down Davey's temples. "He didn't even know, not until she had me, not until he saw her eyes change."

Well, shit. "The delivery, right?" Because when you were having a baby, you probably weren't real focused on holding the glamour.

"He saw her for what she was then."

Jana slammed her elbow into his stomach. "Demons are fucking people, too!"

"*Jana!*"

Davey snarled and held her tighter, harder. "The bitch deserved what she got!"

"What?" Jana taunted him. Always taunting, always pushing . . . and giving Zane the chance to slip ever closer. "What did she deserve? You for a son? The woman must have really screwed some people over to get—"

He whirled her around and drove his fist into her jaw. Jana went down, and Zane lunged forward as the fury burned through him. Davey was reaching for her again, death in his eyes, when Zane slammed into the bastard. "*Don't fucking touch her!*"

They crashed into the ground. The air thickened around them. So hot. Heavy with power and rage.

But Davey wasn't attacking. He just stared up at Zane. "You understand. I know you do. You killed your father. You know what a sick bastard he was."

And I'm not like him. He'd been afraid, for so long, but . . .

Demons are fucking people, too. Jana's words rang in his ears. His strong, fierce Jana. "He was a bastard all right, but not because he was a demon. Just because he was one twisted addict who got off on his drugs and on giving pain to others."

Davey blinked. "No, no, you understand—"

"What do I understand?" He kept his arms loose at his sides. The attack would come again. He knew it. Jude circled behind the other demon. Jana rose slowly to her feet. He caught sight of blood dripping from her lips. *Fuck.* "I'm a demon, Davey. You are, too. And you're a twisted asshole, that I know."

"But you're not, Zane." Jana's voice. Still strong. "You're not like your father or like Davey."

He stared into Davey's black eyes. Demon eyes, but eyes filled with hate and fury. "No, but I think our Davey might be one hell of a lot like *his* old man. He taught you to hate, didn't he, Davey? Taught you to destroy the things that were different in this world. To destroy the things he didn't understand."

Davey charged him with his claws out. "The bitch deserved to die! She would have made me evil, made me—"

Zane sidestepped the attack and drove a fist into Davey's back. "You *are* evil. You don't even realize it."

Davey hit the ground.

"*You* killed a human, Davey. That girl at the college—Lindsey was human."

Davey jumped back to his feet. The wind began to roar around them. "The bitch would have told what she knew about Laura and Perseus. I wasn't gonna let that happen."

"Why? Because then the big lie about Perseus defending the humans would fall apart? Because the truth is that you were just using the psychic to steal power, power that you took, that Beth took, hell, that others at Perseus probably took, too? Because deep down, you all just wanted to be the badasses that people feared in the night?" Zane shook his head. "Give me a break—"

The wind slammed into him with the force of a bus. Zane flew back and rammed into the brick wall. He heard Jude's hard grunt and turned just in time to see the shifter slam face first into the side of a garbage dumpster. The shifter's body slid to the ground, and a large dent hollowed the side of the dumpster.

Zane pushed to his feet. "That the best you've got?" His shoulder had been dislocated. No big deal. He was also pretty sure that the back of his head was bleeding. Still, he was walking, and he was ready for his turn to attack.

Davey stared back at him. "You can't beat me."

He was pretty sure he could. "I'd say I have a fifty-fifty shot." More, because Jude was starting to push to his knees. *Can't keep a good shifter down.*

"Marcus wasn't the first." Davey spit on the ground. "And Laura wasn't the first transference psychic we found, either. Our first psychic didn't last as long, though, but Donna did manage to steal a Born Master's youth for me."

Zane kept his face blank. Born Masters were the vampires who were born with the immortal power already locked within them. Then they hit their late teens or early twenties and stopped aging. If that little bastard had really managed to steal a Born Master's youth . . . "How the hell old are you really, Davey?"

"Forty-eight." Davey licked his lips. "I look real good, don't I? 'Course, Donna didn't look as good. The psychics can be weak sometimes, you know. They take the full hit of the power—that blast can be hell on a human."

Jana stood behind Davey. Zane saw that the red in her eyes had darkened even more. *Charging.* Beth hadn't permanently stolen her power. Those odds of kicking Davey's ass were looking better and better.

"What happened to Donna?" Zane asked, trying to keep Davey focused on him.

A little shrug. "Let's just say she got a little *too* young. Her body couldn't handle things. I stole what I could from her before she . . . well . . . before the end came for her."

Shit. "So after Donna, you lucked out and found Laura."

"Luck had nothing do with it." His gaze darted to Jude. The shifter was still on his knees, with his head down. "It took us *months* to find her and—"

Zane attacked. He shoved his psychic energy right at Davey, blasting as hard as he could. This time, Davey was the one to fly through the air. He flew into the window on the side of the building, smashing glass and disappearing inside.

Zane ran forward and grabbed Jana's arm. "Get the hell out of here," he told her. "Run. Go to Dusk. Find Dee. You've got to get out—"

Shards of glass flew into his arms and back. Swearing, he shielded Jana as the glass flew. The sharp edges embedded in his skin and dug deep.

"She's not getting away." Davey's voice was darker. Harder. He climbed from the broken window, knocking glass off his shoulders. "She betrayed Perseus, and that bitch is dying tonight."

"Zane . . ." Jana breathed his name and her fingertips pressed against him. Even through the clothing, he could feel the heat of her skin. *Come on, baby, burn.*

"Why does she matter?" he yelled at the asshole. "You took her power away. She's not a threat to you."

"No." A fast agreement. "She's not . . . now she's just easy prey."

"I thought you didn't hurt humans!" Sick freak. Zane concentrated and the glass shards slipped from his body—and then they flew right at Davey. They hit the demon in the face. Davey howled.

"Run, Jana!" Zane launched forward. He heard the snap and crunch of bones. Jude was transforming. When Jude shifted, he'd be a white tiger, and they'd tear the demon apart. This fight was ending.

He reached out, his hands ready to rip into Davey. The demon disappeared. Zane grabbed only air. *What?* Laughter teased his ears and a chill skated down his spine.

"The second *Other* I drained was a djinn. Those djinns . . . they can move fast. So fast."

So fast it seemed they vanished into thin air. Turning slowly, Zane locked eyes on Davey. The bastard had Jana again.

"Just so you know"—Davey's eyes narrowed—"she wasn't running away. She was running *after you.* Kind of sweet, hmmm?" He held up his claws. "You know I got these from my last transfer. One slice . . . that's all it will take, and everyone will know that you don't *fuck with Perseus.*"

"*Don't.*" The word was bit out, and it was directed at the

poised tiger, not at Davey. Because Jude had shifted completely now, and if he attacked . . . *Jana's dead.*

"Doesn't matter," Davey said, his grin coming back. "She's still dead."

His gaze jerked to Jana's. The whites of her eyes were blood-red now. But Davey hadn't looked at her. He didn't even realize . . . "I should have told you sooner. I should have trusted you sooner," Zane told her, needing to say these words. Needing her to understand. Everything she was—"*I love you.*"

"Oh, that's so fucking sweet," Davey sneered. "My old man told me that my mother said the same crap before he slit her throat." Davey's claws came up to Jana's throat. "Wanna tell him the same thing? Wanna tell him—"

Jana smiled at Zane.

Burn him. The whisper floated through his mind. He swallowed and pushed his power forward, wanting to be ready to attack with her.

Jana tossed back her hair and she said, "Fuck you." Not words for Zane. The snarl was for Davey as she spun toward him. The demon's claws slashed over her skin. Blood poured. "*Go to hell!*" Then the fire erupted. *Her* fire.

And Zane pushed all of his energy, all of his fire, at the demon, too.

Davey screamed—it was the last sound he ever made as the demon erupted in flames.

Chapter 19

There wasn't much left of Davey. Zane stood in the alley and stared at the flickering flames. No matter how much power the demon had stolen, he hadn't been able to heal from an Ignitor's blast, not delivered at point-blank range with a full charge.

That fire had burned so high. So wild.

Cops were coming. Firefighters, too. The EMTs would be there, but there wasn't anything they could do to help Davey.

"Where is she?" Jude asked him, his voice gruff.

Zane glanced back. Jude had on a pair of jeans, nothing else. At least he was back in human form. "Gone," he said, and the word felt hollow.

Jude's eyes widened. "Aw, shit, man, the fire—"

He laughed at that. "No, no, that fire didn't touch her." She'd been safely away from the flames. He'd run forward, and pushed her back even more as he tried to make sure the bastard was gone.

No coming back from that. Davey had been strong, but not strong enough.

He'd turned back to face Jana just as he'd heard the shout of approaching cops, but she'd been gone.

"What do we tell the cops?" Jude asked him softly.

His gaze raked the night. He could still smell Jana. Her blood. Her scent. Rising over the smoke and ash. "We tell them that a killer confessed to us, then he torched himself."

"There'll be questions."

"There always are."

Cops hurried toward them. "Hands up!" one shouted.

He put his hands up, and then he looked past the uniforms and into the shadows. Her scent lingered so strongly in the air.

Don't leave me. The psychic order left him before he could stop it, because, hell, yeah, he was desperate.

"We're hunters," Jude said. "With Night Watch. We were tracking a killer." He kept his hands up as he talked fast.

The cop who'd barked the order, an older, balding man, sniffed hard, and his face tightened. "What the hell is that smell? What's burning?"

"That'd be our killer," Zane said, keeping his own hands up as his gaze swept from the cops to that darkened alley. "Or what's left of him."

The cops began to gag.

Softly, so softly, he heard the sound of retreating footsteps. *Jana.*

He stepped forward, but the older cop had his gun ready and Zane knew he wasn't *supposed* to hurt humans. He couldn't chase after her.

Not yet.

Run then, baby. He hit their mental link easily. Touched her mind and felt her fear and her worry. *I'll find you.*

Because he'd meant what he'd told her before—and he wasn't about to just let her disappear into the night forever.

Coward. Jana put a hand to her throat and felt the wet warmth of her blood. Damn that demon, he'd slashed her good and deep.

The cops were there now, demanding to know what was going on. Wanting to know what had happened to the killer.

She sucked in a deep breath and could still taste the flames. *He felt the fire.*

Her fire, and Zane's.

She stumbled away. She'd have to get to a hospital. She'd need stitches and explaining the wounds would be a bitch.

She needed the hospital and she needed—

Don't leave me.

Zane's voice seemed to echo in her mind. She froze. For an instant, she could feel him. His strong arms around her, his breath on her face. *Zane.*

A tear leaked down her cheek. She forced herself to keep going. One step. Another. So many damn cops. She'd have to watch herself.

Run then, baby. Again, his voice seemed to drift right through her. *I'll find you.*

Such a dark promise. But what would happen when he found her? They weren't going to get a happily ever after. That wasn't what waited for her. The fire was back. Whatever Laura had done to her, it hadn't been a permanent deal. *Thank God.*

She was back.

She slunk deeper into the shadows, aware that her blood was dripping onto the ground. She'd spent so much time hiding in the shadows. Hiding and running. And now she was running away from the one man who'd actually looked at her and said . . .

I love you.

"What the hell am I doing?" she whispered. *Fear.* She tried to pretend that she was never afraid, but at the first sign of those boys in blue, she'd turned tail and left Zane.

No, they might not have a happy ending, but maybe it was time she started facing up to her past. And to her choices.

She broke from the shadows and immediately saw a female cop with a curly mass of brown hair. The cop's eyes widened when she got a good look at Jana.

"Miss! Miss, are you okay?"

What the hell? Did it *look* like she was okay? "Get me . . . to a hospital." Okay, so she was a selfish bitch. She needed treatment, but she did manage to say, "And by the way . . ."

Surprisingly strong arms closed around her.

Jana licked her lips. "I . . . killed a man tonight."

The cop's eyes flashed demon black. "No, honey, what you did was put down a rabid dog." Those black eyes burned down at her.

They were the last sight Jana saw.

He'd answered a million damn questions, and he was done. "Handle it," Zane ordered Jude and turned away. The scent of Jana's blood was driving him crazy. She shouldn't have left when she was hurt. She should have let him take care of her.

He rushed down the alley, following that scent. The farther he went, the more blood he smelled. A fist squeezed his gut. How badly had she been hurt? *Jana?*

No answer. He couldn't feel her at all anymore.

Fear whispered through him.

"She's gone."

His head turned to the right when he heard the soft voice. A cop stepped forward, her hair tumbling over her shoulders.

"Where is she?" Obviously, they were talking about the same she.

"Hospital. She passed out, and I loaded her into an ambulance." The cop's brows rose. "'Course, that was after she confessed to killing a man."

Hell. He didn't blink. He knew the cop. Had known Paula Channing for years. After all, he'd made a point of knowing all the demons on the force. But was Paula a demon first and a cop second? Or was she . . . ?

He cleared his throat. "Obviously, she was confused. I just told Officer Hill that the suspect poured gasoline on himself and ignited—"

"I'm guessing a container with trace amounts of gasoline will magically appear in the evidence room later, huh?"

He shrugged.

"Good. That will make things easier." She gave him a

smile. A smile that died too fast. "I saw what happened to Tony. That bastard needed to be put down."

He had been.

"Your girl's at Mercy General, with Tony." Paula turned away and headed back into the shadows. "And don't worry," she tossed over her shoulder, "I've already forgotten what Jana said to me."

When Jana opened her eyes, her throat hurt. Her jaw ached. And a man with midnight-black hair, a too fancy suit, and dark eyes stared down at her.

"Hello, Ms. Carter." His voice was Southern, rolling slightly and soft. "My name is Jason Pak. I'm one of the . . . managers . . . of Night Watch."

She lifted her hand and touched her neck. No, not her neck, bandages.

"You needed some stitches. Nothing too major," he murmured, easing a bit away from the bed. *A hospital bed.* "But the doctors didn't want to take any chances."

Great. She looked down and found herself in one of those really annoying paper hospital gowns. Jana tugged the IV out of her arm and shoved up to a sitting position. Then she swung her legs over the side of the bed. Lucky for her, when her feet touched the floor, her knees didn't buckle.

But, she was pretty sure Pak got a glimpse of her ass.

"You don't need to run," he told her. "The cops aren't looking for you."

Oh, right. She glanced over her shoulder at him. "Since I confessed to killing Davey, they probably are."

He smiled. "Self-defense."

True. She had the claw marks to prove it.

"But they aren't after you for Davey's death . . . or for any of the other arsons that were linked to you. Ah, or to your aliases."

She blinked at him. "Want to run that by me again?"

"Actually, I have a job I'd like to offer you, Ms. Carter."

He crossed his arms over his chest and gave her what really looked like an alligator's grin. "So why don't you get back in bed? I think you might like what I have to say."

She didn't move. "I'm not going to be your assassin." *Been there, done that.*

"Is that what you think Zane is? My assassin?"

Jana swallowed. She wasn't touching that, and right then, thinking about Zane hurt. *I love you.* She blinked, real fast. "Look, I've heard this sales pitch before."

"Night Watch isn't like Perseus."

No.

"We won't destroy your life." He paused. "But with us, you can finally have a life."

Tempting bastard.

"And wouldn't you like that? Wouldn't you like a chance to put down some roots? To stop looking over your shoulder and just settle down?"

The hospital door flew open. Zane stood in the doorway. His face was stained with soot, and his chest heaved.

Zane.

"I thought so," Pak murmured and eased toward the door. "We'll talk again soon, my dear. Very, very soon. Your talents would be such an asset to our organization."

"Beat it, Pak." Zane stalked toward her.

Pak smiled that gator grin and exited the room, closing the door softly behind himself.

"You ran from me." Zane seemed to bite off the words.

She nodded. *Scared.* She was still scared right then. Nothing, no one, had ever mattered to her as much as he did. *I love you.*

He couldn't love her. Not really. "You shouldn't," she whispered, the words slipping out.

Zane frowned at her. "Shouldn't what?" Then his eyes fell to her throat. "Oh, fuck, baby . . ." His fingers reached for her.

She stepped back, ramming into the bed. "When you

touch me," she told him starkly, truthfully, "I can't think of anything but you."

His face softened. "That's okay. No, that's real good."

But it wasn't. "I'm not . . ." She cleared her throat and tried again. Talking was so hard when his lips were close and she could all but taste him. "I'm not the kind of woman you should love."

He touched her. His fingers slid down her cheek. Feathered over the bandages on her throat. "You're the *only* woman I should love."

He didn't understand. "Zane, I *like* the fire." That should be wrong. Liking the flames. The fury. The power. She'd used that fire, so many times. Would use it again. "I'm not some sweet, confused girl. I've attacked people. I've hurt them, I've—"

"You ever hurt an innocent man or woman?"

Jana shook her head.

"I think you're too hard on yourself, baby."

He wasn't seeing who she was. "And I think you're too easy on me. Inside, you're good, so you think that everyone else is like that—"

He laughed at her, then he leaned in, and let his lips press lightly over hers. "How many times," he whispered against her mouth, "do I have to tell you *I'm not good?*"

Her heart slammed into her ribs. "You saw what I did to Davey."

"No, I saw what *we* did." His eyes were on hers, slowly fading to black. "Together, we're pretty damn unstoppable."

Together. That word sounded so perfect.

His hand curled around her chin. He held her so softly, and she knew he'd seen the bruises there. "I don't like seeing you hurt."

A fast laugh escaped her. "I don't exactly like being hurt."

"You're so damn beautiful."

That dried up the laughter.

"When you smile, your whole face just lights up." His lips

pressed against hers again, and she wanted to sigh into his mouth. Wanted to wrap her arms around him and hold on tight but . . .

But I've got blood and death on my hands. I've spent my life running. What will I do when he looks at me and sees what I really am?

"What the fuck?" His head lifted and his eyes were narrowed. Hard. "I *know* what you really are. You're a woman. *My* woman. A woman who's strong. A woman who isn't afraid to fight for those she cares about and, yeah, baby, I *know* you care. You're a woman who's had a real shit-hand dealt to her, but you kept fighting. Kept living. You're the most beautiful thing I've ever seen. The strongest woman I've ever met, and you're *mine*."

Could he hear her heart racing? Her hands were clenched into fists, and her nails dug into her palms because she wanted to touch him so badly. "You shouldn't . . . go into someone's mind unless she lets you."

"You let me. You finally dropped the wall you had between us when Perseus burned to hell. You let me in." He tilted her chin back. "Don't shut me out now. Hell, baby, don't you get it? You try to say that I'm good . . . but only you see that. To the rest of the world—to me—I'm a screwed-up demon asshole. You're the best thing that's ever happened to me."

She didn't know what to say. What to do.

"I know I've fucked things up a few times with us. I should have trusted you sooner. When I found out about the deal Beth offered, hell, I just—*it was your chance for a normal life.* I thought you'd take it."

"Normal isn't me."

One side of his mouth hitched up. "It's not me, either." His gaze searched hers. "I don't want you to run from me. I want you to give us a chance."

Oh, damn. She wanted that chance. Wanted it so badly her whole body shook. "I left . . ." She sounded like a croaking frog, so Jana tried again, saying, "I left you in the alley because the cops were there. My instincts with cops . . . hell, they tell me to run."

"But you *stopped* running." Those black eyes saw everything. Saw into her so deeply. "You found a cop, and you confessed."

"Maybe the blood loss made me temporarily insane."

He waited.

Hell. Okay, she *could* do this. "Or maybe I didn't want to run. Maybe I wanted to stay here." *With you.* No matter what the consequences were.

"I already told you, baby, the cops aren't after you anymore."

"Others will be." He should have fair warning on that. "I've pissed off a lot of people in my time." And she'd keep doing it in the years to come. It was just her way. Playing it safe really wasn't her game.

"I piss folks off every day." He shrugged. "I'm not worried about what might come our way."

Our way. Oh, but that sounded good.

"I meant what I said in that alley," he told her. "I love you. And whether you're here in Baton Rouge or tearing through the South, I want to be with you. I'll stay by your side." His gaze held hers. "You can count on me."

She knew that. She'd known it from the beginning. When a guy raced inside a burning building to save you . . . you knew that guy was something special.

He wasn't afraid of her fire. Wasn't worried about her past. He just . . . wanted her.

Jana threw her arms around his neck and pulled Zane close. He grunted, but then his arms were around her, holding her just as tight. Tighter.

"I love you, demon," she whispered in his ear, taking the biggest risk of her life. Loving someone else.

A slight shudder shook his body and then his mouth was on hers. He kissed her hard, deep. With passion and fury. With love.

He could take her fire. Take her fury.

Their tongues met.

He could take everything because she knew he'd give her everything he had in return.

Her demon lover. The man who'd walked through the fire.

His head lifted. His black eyes saw into her. Saw past the mask that fooled so many others.

She smiled at him, and knew she'd met her match. Finally, the perfect man to light her fire.

Catalina Delaney eased away from hospital room 309. Jana was fine. She was with her demon. They were together, holding each other so tight. Just like in the vision Cat had seen so long ago. The vision that told her Zane hadn't been the man for her.

Her shoes squeaked a bit as she headed down the hallway. She slipped inside the elevator and rode up to the burn unit.

Her fingers shook, and she clenched her hands into fists. When the elevator doors opened, she hurried outside. So many cops were standing and sitting in the waiting area, hoping to see Tony. They wouldn't be getting in yet.

They didn't have her connections.

Pak nodded to her and pointed to the door on the far right. She hurried inside and paced down another corridor.

Then she saw him. Tony's face was still just as perfect as always. But his hands . . . his legs . . . she swallowed and crept toward the bed.

"You'll be fine," she whispered to him, and began to chant. Her binding marks were gone. Her power was finally back—*fully* back. Pak thought she could help heal Tony, and she'd prove the charmer right. She'd pay back her debt to him, and her debt to the cop.

Did Tony even remember the debt she owed him? Probably not. It had been so long ago. He'd just been a rookie on his first beat. She'd been a lost kid.

So long ago.

His lashes stirred as she pushed the past from her mind and chanted. The air shifted around her as her power pulsed.

Tony would be all right. Better than before, with time.

"Cat . . ." His whisper, when he shouldn't have known she was there.

Unable to stop herself, she leaned forward and pressed her lips against his cheek.

She'd had visions of him over the years, too, and she knew that someday . . . *someday* . . .

Pak smiled as he pushed the hospital door closed. He turned around to face the crowd of cops, crossing his arms over his chest. He'd make sure Catalina wasn't disturbed. No one needed to see the magic that his newest recruit was working.

Catalina would make a fine addition to his team, and so would Zane's Ignitor. So much power there, just waiting.

Two more on the side of the hunters. The Daveys of the world had better gear up. Hell *was* coming for them. Because his team was always watching. Always waiting.

He nodded to one of the demon cops.

Yes, Pak was ready and so was Night Watch.

Come and get us, assholes. His team was the best in the business, and even the devil couldn't take them out.

But he'd sure like to see the bastard try.

Take your pick of the
LORDS OF PASSION,
a steamy anthology featuring
Virginia Henley, Kate Pearce, and Maggie Robinson . . .

The Hague, Holland
November 28, 1719

"Damnation, Cadogan, you've the devil's own luck. You've won every hand we've played for the last sennight." Charles Lennox, Duke of Richmond, pushed his chair back from the games table and wiped his brow. "Stap me! I'm wiped out—you've had the lot!"

General William Cadogan glanced at his darkly handsome opponent. He was the illegitimate son of the late King Charles, who in his old age had impregnated his mistress, Louise de Kerouaille. "Would you like me to tally up, your grace?"

Richmond waved a negligent hand. "By all means, let me know the damage."

The dashing Irish general didn't take long. He had a damn good idea of what the duke had wagered and lost in their endless games of *écarté*. The duke was a heavy drinker, which was the main reason for his losses. The general set the seven scorecards down on the table, one for each night they had played. "I tot it up to a little over ten thousand guineas."

"*What?*" Richmond howled. "Are you jesting?" By the benign look on Cadogan's face, Charles Lennox knew he was serious. He downed the glass of gin sitting before him. "I don't have it. You'll have to accept my marker."

The men sitting at the table, who had been observing their deep play, began to murmur. Richmond flushed darkly. A gentleman always paid his gambling debts. His shrewd mind quickly inventoried his assets. Land was out of the question—the aristocracy accumulated property; it never relinquished it. Besides, the Earl of Cadogan already owned the hundred-acre Caversham estate on the outskirts of Reading.

Horses were the next things Richmond thought of. His family seat, Goodwood, at the foot of the South Downs, had a racing stable of Thoroughbreds. The thought of parting with his horses made him feel physically ill.

He looked across at General Cadogan. "You have a daughter, I believe."

"I do, your grace. Her name is Sarah."

"How would you like to make Sarah a countess? My son, the Earl of March, is without a wife." Lennox believed no man could resist such a magnanimous offer.

But the Earl of Cadogan, who was Marlborough's top general, and largely responsible for Britain's victories in the wars of Spanish Succession, was a shrewd negotiator. That was the reason he had been given the diplomatic duties concerned with resettlements among Great Britain, France, Holland, and Spain.

"My daughter, Lady Sarah, has a dowry of ten thousand pounds. If I gave you my daughter and her marriage settlement, I would have to pay you ten thousand instead of *you* paying *me* ten thousand." He raised his hands in appeal. "It doesn't fly, your grace."

"Charles is heir to my dukedom of Richmond and all the estates that encompasses," Lennox pointed out. "Lady Sarah could become a duchess." *Surely it's not necessary to remind you that we have royal blood?*

"A marriage between my daughter and your son, and heir, could be the solution."

Cadogan paused for emphasis. "Without the marriage settlement, of course."

"Curse you, general. You're not negotiating with the enemy here!"

"Since we are civilized gentlemen, I propose a compromise, your grace."

"Let's split the difference," Richmond suggested. "Your daughter's hand in marriage along with a dowry of *five thousand*."

The other men at the table leaned forward in anticipation of Cadogan's answer.

"Done!" The general's reply was heartfelt. He raised his hand to a servant. "Drinks all around. We must toast this historic union."

The Duke of Richmond raised his glass. "Here's to you and here's to me, and if someday we disagree, fuck you, here's to me!"

All the gentlemen roared with laughter and drained their glasses.

"I shall send for my daughter immediately."

"And I shall summon my heir," the duke declared.

"The *Green Lion* is a lovely name for a ship," Sarah exclaimed as they boarded at the Port of London.

"I only hope our cabin is warm. This is a dreadful season to be crossing to the Netherlands," Lady Cadogan said with a shiver.

"I'm glad I'm wearing my woolen dress and cloak. This is so exciting!"

The pair was shown below to their cabin, and when their trunk arrived, it took up most of the space between the two bunks.

"Such cramped quarters," the countess complained. "It's a good thing we will be arriving before dark tomorrow. But at least the cabin is warm."

"Oh, I think we are under way." Sarah grabbed hold of the bunk rail as the vessel swayed. She was bursting with excitement. "May I please go up on deck and watch as the *Green Lion* navigates through the Thames?"

"If you must, Sarah. But when the ship approaches Graves-end, you must come below decks immediately. Daylight will soon be gone, and the wind will be so fierce, it could easily blow you overboard," her mother cautioned.

The grave warning did not deter Sarah; it made her more eager to go up on deck.

"Thank you, Mother. I'll be careful."

Sarah climbed the stairs that led onto the deck and pulled her cloak tightly about her. She watched the docks recede slowly, but soon lost interest in looking back. She much preferred to look ahead and made her way to the very front of the vessel. She stood in wonder as the banks of the river widened. She breathed deeply, filling her lungs with sea air, as if the smell of tide wrack were the elixir of life.

She lifted her face to the cold breeze as she heard the gulls and terns screaming overhead. *What an exciting life to be a sailor!* Sarah stood enraptured as the ship reached the estuary and headed out to sea. She became aware that the light was fast fading from the day, and the moment the ship sailed into the North Sea, the wind whipped her cloak about and she remembered that she must go below.

The fierce wind was against her as she lowered her head and began to run. Suddenly she collided with someone, and the impact knocked the breath out of her.

"You clumsy, idiot girl! Watch what you're about, for Christ's sake."

Sarah paled as she stared up into the furious face of a young man. "I'm . . . I'm sorry, sir," she gasped.

"Sorry, be damned!" He blocked her way. "You haven't the brains of a bloody baboon, barreling down the deck like a loose cannon."

"I have to get below—I promised Mother."

"We all want to get belowdecks to a warm cabin, damn your eyes."

"You are frightening the girl, Charles. Let her pass," Henry Grey said quietly.

Charles Lennox grudgingly stepped aside. "The witless girl needed a lesson. I hope you remembered to bring that bottle of rum. It's colder than a whore's heart tonight."

When the Countess of Cadogan and Sarah stepped from their carriage at the Court of Holland, a liveried attendant ushered them inside. Margaret's father had been Chancellor of the Court before he retired, and the servants showed her great deference.

When they arrived at the suite of rooms that had been assigned to General Cadogan, he flung open the door and welcomed them warmly.

"Margaret, my dear, I hope your voyage wasn't a rough one."

"It was tolerable. December is no month to be at sea."

"It was an absolute necessity, my dear. We couldn't let an opportunity like this slip away." He looked at his young daughter and gave her a hug. "Were you seasick?"

"No, Father," she said breathlessly.

"That's my girl. Take off your cloak and let's have a look at you."

Sarah removed her cloak and bonnet. She smoothed her hands over her flattened hair. "I must look a fright."

"Nay, child. The wind has put roses in your cheeks."

Sarah blushed with pleasure at the compliment.

William raised his eyes to his wife. His daughter's figure was slight and her face extremely pale. "I hope you've brought her a decent dress to wear tomorrow."

"You gave me such short notice, there was no time to have a new gown made. In any case, it's cold. A woolen dress will suffice."

"Have you told her?" William asked.

"I thought it best to wait until we arrived. You may have that pleasure, my lord."

Told me what? Sarah went very still. She had an ominous feeling that her mother was being sarcastic. She doubted that *pleasure* would be involved. She couldn't find the words to ask, but the apprehensive look in her eyes questioned her father.

"We'll wait until after dinner," he said heartily. "Sarah looks like she could use some food. There's nothing like a thick broth to warm the cockles of your heart. After dinner, Sarah and I will have a private chat."

"I'll go and unpack." She sensed that her parents had something to discuss that concerned her. Something was in the air, and she took refuge in the short reprieve.

When she lifted the lid of the trunk that had been delivered to the bedchamber, she stroked her hand over the rich material of her mother's gowns. One was purple velvet, embroidered with gold, and another was black, quilted brocade decorated with crystals.

Sarah carefully lifted them from the trunk and hung them in the wardrobe, along with two other day dresses and the lovely whalebone panniers that went beneath. Her own clothes had been packed on the bottom, and as a result were slightly creased. As well as flannel petticoats and knitted stockings, she had brought only two dresses. One was oyster-colored wool with a cream frill around the high neck, and the other was gray with fitted sleeves that ended in white ruffles around the wrists. She wished that she had panniers to hold out her skirts. They would help disguise how thin she was, but her mother had decreed that she was still too young for grown-up fashions.

Sarah hung her dresses next to her mother's and sighed with resignation at the contrast between the rich, fashionable gowns and her own plain attire.

Since the hour was late and the ladies had been traveling for the past two days, the trio ate dinner in Cadogan's suite. Tonight for some reason Sarah's appetite was nonexistent.

Her mother gave her a critical glance. "You must eat more. You will never fill out if all you do with food is push it about your plate."

Her father changed the subject. "What are you learning at school?"

"Latin," she said softly.

"Latin? What the devil good will Latin do you? Surely French would be better for a young lady of fashion."

I don't feel like a young lady of fashion. "We say our prayers in Latin."

"I wager you have some uncharitable names for the nuns."

Sarah's eyes sparkled with mischief. "We call them the 'Sisters of the Black Plague.'"

Cadogan threw back his head and laughed. It tickled his Irish sense of humor. "By God, I warrant they teach you not to spit in church, and very little else." He bent close.

"I think a change of schools is in order. What d'you say, Sarah?"

"Oh, I would love it above all things."

When they finished eating, the earl gave a speaking nod to his wife and she excused herself so that her husband could have privacy for the chat with his daughter.

Cadogan led his daughter to a chair before the fire and sat down opposite her. "The time has come when we must think about your future, Sarah."

She nodded but made no reply, knowing there was more to come.

"I have no son, so I want the very best for my daughter." He paused to let his words sink in. "For some time now I have been searching for a suitable match for you. I would never consider any noble of a lower rank than my own."

Sarah's blue eyes widened. *You are talking about finding a future husband for me.*

"Not only must he be titled, he must be heir to wealth and property."

You married a lady from the Netherlands. I hope you don't look for a match for me here. She clasped her hands together tightly. *I want to live in England.*

"I have been offered a match for you that surpasses all my expectations. It is an undreamed-of opportunity that will raise you to the pinnacle of the aristocracy. A premier duke of the realm has asked for your hand in marriage for his son and heir."

Sarah sat silently as questions chased each other through her mind. *Who? Where? When?* But most puzzling was *why?*

William Cadogan's face was beaming. "The Duke of Richmond is offering marriage with his son, Charles Lennox, the Earl of March." He leaned forward and patted her hand. "Sarah, my dear, you will be the Countess of March, and the future Duchess of Richmond."

"I . . . I can't believe it," she murmured. "Are we to be betrothed?"

Her father waved a dismissive hand. "You are to be *wed*, not betrothed!" He loosened his neckcloth. "Fortunately, Richmond and his son are here at The Hague."

"So we will be able to meet each other and see if we suit?" she asked shyly.

"Of course you will suit! The marriage contracts have already been drawn up. You will meet each other at your wedding . . . tomorrow."

Sarah was stunned as a sparrow flown into a wall. *"Tomorrow?"*

Don't miss Elizabeth Essex's Brava debut,
THE PURSUIT OF PLEASURE,

out now from Brava

"I couldn't help overhearing your conversation." He wanted to steer their chat to his purpose, but the back of her neck was white and long. He'd never noticed that long slide of skin before, so pale against the vivid color of her locks. He'd gone away before she'd been old enough to put up her hair. And nowadays the fashion seemed to be for masses of loose ringlets covering the neck. Trust Lizzie to still sail against the tide.

"Yes, you could." Her breezy voice broke into his thoughts.

"I beg your pardon?"

"Help it. You *could* have helped it, as any polite gentleman *should*, but you obviously chose not to." She didn't even bother to look back at him as she spoke and walked on, but he heard the teasing in her voice. Such intriguing confidence. He could use it to his purpose. She had always been up for a lark.

He caught her elbow and steered her into an unused parlor. She let him guide her easily, without resisting the intimacy or the presumption of the brief contact of his hand against the soft, vulnerable skin of her inner arm, but once through the door she just seemed to dissolve away, out of his grasp. His empty fingers prickled from the sudden loss. He let her move away and closed the door.

No lamp or candle branch illuminated the room, only the

moonlight streaming through the tall casement windows. Lizzie looked like a pale ghost, weightless and hovering in the strange light. He took a step nearer. He needed her to be real, not an illusion. Over the years she'd become a distant but recurring dream, a combination of memory and boyish lust, haunting his sleep.

He had thought of her, or at least the idea of her, almost constantly over the years. She had always been there, in his mind, swimming just below the surface. And he had come tonight in search of her. To banish his ghosts.

She took a sliding step back to lean nonchalantly against the arm of a chair, her pose one of sinuous, bored indifference.

"So what are you doing in Dartmouth? Aren't you meant to be messing about with your boats?"

"Ships," he corrected automatically and then smiled at his foolishness for trying to tell Lizzie anything. "The big ones are ships."

"And they let *you* have one of the *big* ones? Aren't you a bit young for that?" She tucked her chin down to subdue her smile and looked up at him from under her gingery brows. Very mischievous. She was warming to him.

If it was worldliness she wanted, he could readily supply it. He mirrored her smile.

"Hard to imagine, isn't it, Lizzie?" He opened his arms wide, presenting himself for her inspection.

Only she didn't inspect him. Her eyes slid away to inventory the scant furniture in the darkened room. "No one else calls me that anymore."

"Lizzie? Well, I do. I can't imagine you as anything else. And I like it. I like saying it. Lizzie." The name hummed through his mouth like a honeybee dusted with nectar. Like a kiss. He moved closer so he could see the emerald color of her eyes, dimmed by the half light, but still brilliant against the white of her skin. He leaned a fraction too close and whispered, "Lizzie. It always sounds somehow . . . naughty."

She turned quickly. Wariness flickered across her mobile

face, as if she were suddenly unsure of both herself and him, before it was just as quickly masked.

And yet, she continued to study him surreptitiously, so he held himself still for her perusal. To see if she would finally notice him as a man. He met her eyes and he felt a kick low in his gut. In that moment plans and strategies became unimportant. The only thing important was for Lizzie to see him. It was essential.

But she kept all expression from her face. He was jolted to realize she didn't want him to read her thoughts or mood. She was trying hard to keep *him* from seeing *her*.

It was an unexpected change. The Lizzie he had known as a child had been so wholly passionate about life, she had thrown herself body and soul into each and every moment, each action and adventure. She had not been covered with this veneer of poised nonchalance.

And yet it was only a veneer. He was sure of it. And he was equally sure he could make his way past it. He drew in a measured breath and sent her a slow, melting smile to show, in the course of the past few minutes, he'd most definitely noticed she was a woman.

She gave no outward reaction, and it took Marlowe a long moment to recognize her response: she looked *careful*. It was a quality he'd never seen in her before.

Finally, after what felt like an infinity, she broke the moment. "You didn't answer. Why are you here? After all these years?"

He chose the most convenient truth. "A funeral. Two weeks ago." A bleak, rain-soaked funeral that couldn't be forgotten.

"Oh. I am sorry." Her voice lost its languid bite.

He looked back and met her eyes. Such sincerity had never been one of Lizzie's strong suits. No, that was wrong. She'd always been sincere, or at least truthful—painfully so as he recalled—but she rarely let her true feelings show.

"Thank you, Lizzie. But I didn't lure you into a temptingly darkened room to bore you with dreary news."

"No, you came to proposition me." The mischievous little smile crept back. Lizzie was never the sort to be intimidated for long. She had always loved to be doing things she ought not.

A heated image of her sinuous white body entwined in another man's arms rose unbidden in his brain. Good God, what other things had Lizzie been doing over the past few years that she ought not? And with whom?

Marlowe quickly jettisoned the irrational spurt of jealousy. Her more recent past hardly mattered. In fact, some experience on her part might better suit his plans.

"Yes, my proposition. I can give you what you want. A marriage without the man."

For the longest moment she went unnaturally still, then she slid off the chair arm and glided closer to him. So close, he almost backed up. So close, her rose petal of a mouth came but a hairsbreadth from his own. Then she lifted her inquisitive nose and took a bold, suspicious whiff of his breath.

"You've been drinking."

"I have," he admitted without a qualm.

"How much?"

"More than enough for the purpose. And you?"

"Clearly not enough. Not that they'd let me." She turned and walked away. Sauntered really. She was very definitely a saunterer, all loose joints and limbs, as if she'd never paid the least attention to deportment. Very provocative, although he doubted she meant to be. An image of a bright, agile otter, frolicking unconcerned in the calm green of the river Dart, twisting and rolling in the sunlit water, came to mind.

"Drink or no, I meant what I said."

"Are you proposing? Marriage? To me?" She laughed as if it were a joke. She didn't believe him.

"I am."

She eyed him more closely, her gaze narrowing even as one marmalade eyebrow rose in assessment. "Do you have a fatal disease?"

"No."

"Are you engaged to fight a duel?"

"Again, no."

"Condemned to death?" She straightened with a fluid undulation, her spine lifting her head up in surprise as the thought entered her head, all worldliness temporarily obliterated. "Planning a suicide?"

"No and no." It was so hard not to smile. Such a charming combination of concern and cheek. The cheek won out: she gave him that feral, slightly suspicious smile.

"Then how do you plan to arrange it, the 'without the man' portion of the proceedings? I'll want some sort of guarantee. You can't imagine I'm gullible enough to leave your fate, or my own for that matter, to chance."

A low heat flared within him. By God, she really was considering it.

"And yet, Lizzie, I think you may. I am an officer of His Majesty's Royal Navy and am engaged to captain a convoy of prison ships to the Antipodes. I leave only days from now. The last time I was home, in England, was four and a half years ago and then only for a few months to recoup from a near fatal wound. This trip is slated to take at least eight . . . years."

Her face cleared of all traces of impudence. Oh yes, even Lizzie could be led.

"Storms, accidents, and disease provide most of the risk. Don't forget we're still at war with France and Spain. And the Americans don't think too highly of us either. One stray cannonball could do the job quite nicely."

"Is that what did it last time?"

"Last time? I've never been dead before."

The ends of her ripe mouth nipped up. The heat in his gut sailed higher.

"You said you had recovered from a near fatal wound."

"Ah, yes. Grapeshot, actually. In my chest. Didn't go deep enough to kill me, though afterward, the fever nearly did."

Her gaze skimmed over his coat, curious and maybe a little hungry. The heat spread lower, kindling into a flame.

"Do you want to see?" He was being rash, he knew, but he'd done this for her once before, taken off his shirt on a dare. And he wanted to remind her.

And keep an eye out for Donna Kauffman's latest,
OFF KILTER, coming next month!

Turn the page for a fun, flirty preview . . .

"**M**an up, for God's sake, and drop the damn thing."
He supposed he should be thankful she could only turn his heart to stone.

"We're not sending in nude shots," Roan replied through an even smile, even as the chants and taunts escalated. "So, I don't understand the need to take things to such an extreme—"

"The contest rules state, very clearly and deliberately, that they're looking for provocative," Tessa responded, sounding every bit like a person who'd also been forced into a task she'd rather not have taken on. Which she had been.

Sadly, that fact had not brought them closer.

She shifted to yet another camera she'd mounted on yet another tripod, he supposed so the angle of the sun was more to her liking. "Okay, lean back against the stone wall, prop one leg, rest that . . . sword thing of yours—"

"'Tis a claymore. Belonged to the McAuleys for four centuries. Victorious in battle, 'tis an icon of our clan." And heavy as all hell to foist about.

"Lovely. Prop your icon in front of you, then. I'm fairly certain it will hide what needs hiding."

His eyebrows lifted at that, but rather than take offense, he merely grinned. "I wouldnae be so certain of it, lassie. We're a clan known for the size of our . . . swords."

"Yippee," she shot back, clearly unimpressed. "So, drop the plaid, position your . . . sword, and let's get on with it. It's the illusion of baring it all we're going for here. I'll make sure to preserve your fragile modesty."

She was no fun. No fun 'tall.

"The other guys did it," she added, resting folded hands on the top of the camera. "In fact," she went on, without even the merest hint of a smile or dry amusement, "they seemed quite happy to accommodate me."

He couldn't imagine any man wanting to bare his privates for Miss Vandergriff's pleasure. Not if he wanted to keep them intact, at any rate.

He was a bit thrown off by his complete inability to charm her. He charmed everyone. It was what he did. He admittedly enjoyed, quite unabashedly, being one of the clan favorites because of his affable, jovial nature. As far as he was concerned, the world would be a much better place if folks could get in touch with their happy parts, and stay there.

He didn't know much about her, but from what little time they'd spent together this afternoon, he didn't think Tessa Vandergriff had any happy parts. However, the reason behind her being rather happiness-challenged wasn't going to be his mystery to solve. She'd been on the island for less than a week now, and her stay on Kinloch was as a guest, and therefore temporary. Thank the Lord.

The island faced its fair share of ongoing trials and tribulations, and had the constant challenge of sustaining a fragile economic resource. Despite that, he'd always considered both the McAuley and MacLeod clans as being cheerful, welcoming hosts. But they had enough to deal with without adopting a surly recalcitrant into their midst.

"Well," he said, smiling broadly the more her scowl deepened. "'Tis true, the single men of this island have little enough to choose from." The crowd took a collective breath at that, but his attention was fully on her now. Gripping the claymore in one fist, he leaned against the stacked stone wall, well aware of the tableau created by the twin peaks that framed the MacLeod fortress, each of them towering behind him. He braced his legs, folded his arms across his bare chest, sword blade aloft . . . and looked her straight in the eye as he let a slow, knowing grin slide across his face. "Me, I'm no' so desperate as all that."

That got a collective gasp from the crowd. But rather than elicit so much as a snarl from Miss Vandergriff, or perhaps goading her so far as to pack up and walk away—which he'd have admittedly deserved—she shocked him instead. By smiling. Fully. He hadn't thought her face capable of arranging itself in such a manner. And so broadly, too, with such stunning gleam. He was further damned to discover it did things to his own happy parts that she had no business affecting.

"No worries," she stated, further captivating him with the transformative brilliance of her now knowing smile. She gave him a sizzling once-over before easily meeting his eyes again. "You're not my type."

This was not how things usually went for him. He felt . . . frisked. "Then I'm certain you can be objective enough to find an angle that shows off all my best parts without requiring a more blatant, uninspired pose. I understand from Kira that you're considered to be quite good with that equipment."

The chants of the crowds shifted to a few whistles as the tension between photographer and subject grew to encompass even them.

"Given your reluctance to play show and tell, I'd hazard to guess I'm better with mine than you are with yours," she replied easily, but the spark remained in her eyes.

Goading him.

"Why don't you be the judge." Holding her gaze in exclusive focus, the crowd long since forgotten now, he pushed away from the wall and, with sword in one hand, slowly unwrapped his kilt with the other.

He took far more pleasure than was absolutely necessary from watching her throat work as he unashamedly revealed thighs and ass. He wasn't particularly vain or egotistical, but he was well aware that a lifetime spent climbing all over this island had done its duty where his physical shape was concerned, as it had for most of the islanders. They were a hardy lot.

There was a collective gasp from the crowd as he held a fistful of unwrapped plaid in front of him, dangling precariously from one hand, just on the verge of—

That's it! Tessa all but leapt behind the camera and an instant later, the shutter started whirring. Less than thirty seconds later, she straightened and pushed her wayward curls out of her face, her no-nonsense business face back on track. "Got it. Good! We're all done here." She started dismantling her equipment. "You can go ahead and get dressed," she said, dismissively, not even looking at him now.

He held on to the plaid—and his pride—and tried not to look as annoyed as he felt. The shoot was blessedly over. That was all that mattered. No point in being irritated that he'd just been played by a pro.

She glanced up, the smile gone as she dismantled her second tripod with the casual grace of someone so used to the routine and rhythm of it she didn't have to think about it. "I'll let you know when I get the shots developed."

He supposed he should be thankful she had saved him the humiliation of publicly rubbing her smooth manipulation of him in his face. Except he wasn't feeling particularly gracious at the moment.